BEHOLD

THE

STARS

The Signal Bend Series

Book Two

by Susan Fanetti

THE FREAK CIRCLE PRESS

Behold the Stars © Susan Fanetti 2013

All rights reserved

Susan Fanetti has asserted her right to be identified as the author of this book under the Copyright, Design and Patents Act 1988.

This is a work of fiction. Names, characters, places, and incidents are a product of the author's imagination. Any resemblance to actual persons, living or dead, events, or locales are entirely coincidental.

Cover design by Flintlock Covers

ISBN-10: 1503369854
ISBN-13: 978-1503369856

Dedicated with love to my Freaks.

With an extra helping of love for Shannon Flagg.

Sharing our stories is the best part.

The Guide and I into that hidden road

Now entered, to return to the bright world;

And without care of having any rest

We mounted up, he first and I the second,

Till I beheld through a round aperture

Some of the beauteous things that Heaven doth bear;

Thence we came forth to behold the stars again.

Dante, *Inferno*, Canto XXXIV

CHAPTER ONE

Isaac held the heavy bag while Lilli punched and kicked. She was doing well, her blows powerful and accurate. She was uncharacteristically leading with her left, since she was still wearing a brace on her right hand, having broken it a couple of months ago in a fight with an old nemesis—a fight that had almost cost her life. It had been just more than two weeks since she'd gotten the cast off, but Lilli worked hard to be strong and fit, and she'd hadn't been able to tolerate any more 'recuperation' time. Isaac had barely gotten her to agree to work out with him so he could be there if she hurt herself. In fact, that had been quite a battle, and he'd had to use his position as club President, setting terms. It hadn't gone over well, but they'd gotten past it, and she'd finally agreed.

The clubhouse of the Night Horde Motorcycle Club was the only place remotely resembling a gym within probably fifty miles of Signal Bend, Missouri. For a variety of reasons, Lilli had been hesitant to work out in the clubhouse, or even visit, for that matter, but things were different now. She was officially his old lady. She'd even moved in with him after she'd gotten out of the hospital. And she'd agreed to marry him. Someday. When they could get the town safe again.

Signal Bend was one of those dying rural towns that peppered the Midwest. Too remote to be served and protected by the traditional business and legal apparatus, not remote enough to survive the commercial siphoning from exurban middle class strip-mall sprawl. The town had been starving to death until some of the townspeople started to cook meth. Now the meth trade was keeping the rest of the town alive. Isaac didn't want that crap in his town, but there was no other way to keep the lights on. So the Horde worked with the cookers to get their product out of Signal Bend and into the cities to the northeast and southwest—St. Louis and Tulsa. The whole I-44 corridor was their turf.

Lawrence Ellis, a major player from Chicago, was trying to unseat the Horde and take over Signal Bend for his own production. He was setting up to make his move soon—any day now, probably. Until the Horde could deal with Ellis and the Northside Knights, the crew from St. Louis that was doing his bidding, Isaac and Lilli couldn't seriously contemplate settling their personal life.

Isaac would be forty in a few months, and he'd never thought he'd have or even want a family beyond the Horde. He'd grown up in a hard home. Not a home at all. An abusive father, a suicide mother, a runaway sister. Until he met Lilli, he'd expected to live his life alone in the old farmhouse he'd grown up in. Now, though, he wanted it all—wife and children, a home, warm and full. He *needed* it. He hated that Lilli wanted to wait. He understood it, but he hated it. But she was with him, and for now that was enough. The rest would come in time. He had to believe that was true.

She backed off the bag and put her hands on her hips, her chest heaving. "Want to spar?"

That surprised him. She was ex-Army and well trained in hand-to-hand combat and self-defense, but he had ten inches and more than 150 pounds on her, and he had experience of his own. They'd never sparred before. "Nah, Sport. I don't want to hurt you."

She laughed, a saucy light in her bright grey eyes. "Oh, dude. That's a challenge if ever I heard one. You think you can hurt me?"

"You think you're a hundred percent?" He turned a meaningful look to her braced hand.

"Close enough. Come on, biker man, you chicken?"

He didn't want to hurt her. Still vivid in his memory, and in his dreams, was the image of her lying pale and weak in a hospital bed, depleted of more than half her blood, comatose for days. It hadn't even been three months since then. But he couldn't deny her. She was standing there in her tiny little black spandex shorts and her tight little bright green top, showing a lot of beautiful, muscled belly and basically all of her sleek, strong legs. Her grin was wide, and tendrils of her long, dark hair clung to her damp neck. She was about as sexy as she could be without being totally naked and writhing under him.

Which presented its own set of problems, and Isaac looked over to the side wall, the top half of which was all windows. The weight room had been the scheduling office when the clubhouse had been Signal Bend Construction, run by the Night Horde, and the windows looked into the main room, what was now known as the Hall. At the moment, just about everyone in the Hall was taking in the show. There was something for everyone: Lilli in her tiny workout clothes, Isaac bare-chested, wearing only a pair of black sweats. The Horde were trying to be circumspect about it, trying not to ogle the boss's old lady so obviously as to be disrespectful. Not doing a great job of it, but at least trying. The girls, though, were standing right at the window, staring at him. A couple even had their hands on their hearts.

Lilli was the jealous type. Not crazy jealous, but territorial—quite a lot like he was, actually, though a bit slower to violence. She followed his glance to the window and saw their audience. With a smug, assertive grin, she walked up to him, reached up over his shoulder, grabbed his braid, and pulled his head to hers. He knew what she was up to, and as soon as she'd gotten close enough, he put his hands on her hips and pulled her against him.

When their lips met, and her tongue pushed into his mouth, Isaac felt the same electric bolt of desire he always felt, audience or not. He slid his hands over her ass, completely covering her shorts. Without thinking of anything more than her, her body so close to his, the perfect, hot scent of her sweat, he curled his fingers under the snug hems circling the tops of her thighs. He growled, deep in his chest.

She released her hold on his braid and pulled back from the kiss with a wicked grin. Isaac looked over to the window and saw that the women were moving on. The guys, though, were being more obvious—at least until they saw Isaac seeing them.

Isaac laughed. "Marking your territory, Sport?" He'd called her Sport since he first met her, when she wouldn't tell him her name. It had stuck. The first thing he'd seen of her was her '68 Camaro Super Sport.

"Call it serving notice. I figure you've banged all the women out there, right?"

He was more discerning than that. "Gimme some credit—not all of them. And none of them since I met you."

She nodded. "I know. Just making sure they know you're off the menu." She swept her hand down the length of his bare arm. "So, we gonna fight, or what?"

The boxing ring was out in what had been the loading bays. They'd definitely have an audience out there. He could think of ten good reasons right off the top of his head that the two of them sparring was a bad idea. But he could see the resolve in her eyes. "Lilli, you sure about this?"

She slid a hand into the waistbands of his sweats and boxer briefs. The feel of her fingers so temptingly low on his belly made his heart race. "Isaac, it's just a spar. We're not going to be trying to kill each other. Think of it as foreplay."

That was fair. Their sex got pretty rough. "Okay, baby. We're careful, though. Right?"

She just smirked and sauntered out of the weight room. He followed her to the ring. So did everybody else, once they understood what was afoot. Isaac heard them making bets. The Night Horde MC was a small club, and their outlaw streak was usually fairly low-key—their involvement in the meth trade notwithstanding—but they were a rowdy bunch, and any prospect of violence, recreational or otherwise, got their blood up. Isaac knew that the chance to openly watch Lilli in the ring was only adding to the enthusiasm. Len and Victor, the two loosest cannons in the club, were calling the bets, amping things up. Len, the club Sergeant at Arms, was calling odds in Lilli's favor, with a sardonic eyebrow raised to Isaac. When Lilli heard him, she turned and blew him a kiss. Len caught it and planted it on his cheek. Isaac rolled his eyes. Lilli was not remotely girly, but she knew how to use everything she had going for her, brains or body, whichever worked best. Both at the same time, most often.

Showdown, Isaac's VP, stayed back a bit, arms crossed. Isaac met his eyes. Show was the steadiest thinker. Isaac's chief advisor and confidant, he knew more than anyone else in the club what was in his President's head. So he knew Isaac's misgivings about getting in the ring with Lilli.

Lilli climbed between the ropes straightaway, but Isaac paused for a second, asking himself if he was really going to throw punches at his woman. The woman he'd thought would die, only a few weeks ago.

The one who was bouncing in the middle of the ring, the dare gleaming in her eyes.

Okay, Sport. Okay. He climbed in.

He knew if he really punched her, he'd really hurt her, but he needn't have worried. He started out pulling his punches, but within in a couple of minutes he was actually trying to make contact. He couldn't. They were fighting two different spars. She was lithe and quick, and he couldn't catch her. He was a brawler; his way was to overpower. She was doing some kind of martial arts dance he couldn't track. She dodged and feinted and ducked and dived, always bouncing, always moving. Mostly, she played defense, letting him swing and miss. Twice, she kicked him—or, rather, she came in with a kick and stopped at the last second, simply touching her foot to his chest or back and then pulling away before he could grab her.

"Are you trying, love?"

Their spectators hooted at that. Bart, the club Intelligence Officer and the youngest patch, called out, "Oh, snap!" Isaac spared an angry glance his way, and Bart took a step back. Good. Shithead.

Despite his worry about her, he was starting to get a little pissed. "Don't goad me, baby. I can make sure you pay." He saw her getting cocky, losing a sliver of that intense focus. When she dropped her guard, he was ready, and he came in with a jab to her midsection. He'd meant to pull, but by then he only had half an idea he'd connect, and he wasn't being as careful as he wanted to be. He connected, nearly full power, and sent her to the mat on her back, breathless.

"Shit! Sport, I'm sorry. You okay?"

She kipped up to her feet—impressing the hell out of him and everyone watching—and grinned. "That's what I'm talking about! Let's do this!"

The pace picked up a lot then. When she connected after that, there was some pop behind it, and Isaac was taking more of a beating than he wanted to let on. She never let her guard down again, and he never got another good swing in. Finally, she ended the fight by sweeping his feet out from under him after he'd missed with a hook. The crowd erupted when he landed on his back. He stayed down, not because he couldn't get up, but because the whole encounter had him about nuts, teetering wildly between concern and competition. She was strong and skilled and obviously could more than hold her own, but the mere thought of hurting her was more than he could deal with.

"Giving up, love?" She bounced over to him, keeping just out of reach of his hands and feet. Even now, even when he was on his back, she was vigilant. The woman had focus.

"What can I say? You bested me, Sport." He sat up and held out his hand to her. She gave him a distrusting look, and he turned his palm up. "No trick, baby. You won." She took his hand and he came to his feet. When he was up, he grabbed her and pulled her close. Dripping sweat now, she smelled even better to him, like sex incarnate. "That was foreplay, right?" Gripping her head in his hands, he bent down and kissed the sass out of her, not stopping until she relaxed completely against him. The crowd exploded in howls, whistles, and cheers. He released her head and grabbed her hand. "Okay, folks, show's over." Bending to Lilli's ear, he whispered. "We need to get to my office."

With a laugh and a toss of her long, chestnut ponytail, she slid between the ropes and jumped to the floor. Badger, one of the new Prospects, handed her a towel. When Isaac landed behind her, he took a towel, then grabbed Lilli's hand again and pulled her out of the bays and down the hall to his office, ignoring everybody else. His hand on the small of her back, he sent her into the dark, windowless room ahead of him, then locked the door behind them and flipped the switch that turned on the lamp on the bookcase. She was on him as soon as she turned around, and they kissed fiercely for several brilliant seconds, but then he held her off. They had some air to clear first.

"What was that about, Lilli?"

She looked honestly confused. "What do you mean? That was just some fun."

"Not for me, no. And there was more to it than that. What's up?" He'd been thinking about it the whole time they were dancing in the ring. She'd had a look about her—contentious, somehow. It had felt off to him. He brushed the damp strands of hair from her temples. God, she was beautiful. "What's goin' on, baby? Tell me."

She huffed and backed away, walking across the room to sit on the couch. "I don't know. I guess I need you to see that I can take care of myself again. I don't need a bodyguard, Isaac. You haven't been hearing me, so I wanted you to see it instead, I guess."

Ah. Isaac went over and sat next to her, laying his hand on her thigh. "Have I been hovering?" He knew the answer. He'd had a hard time leaving her since their confrontation with Ray Hobson. When he'd had no choice but to go, he'd left one of the other patches, or a Prospect, with her. She'd hated that. But she was recovering from serious injury. She'd almost died. And he needed to keep her safe. It was his fault she'd been hurt in the first place.

She had a point. He knew she did. He understood. But she needed to understand him, too. "Okay. Fair enough. You can take care of yourself. I get it. I'll back off some. But you have to understand me, Lilli. You don't know what it was like to sit next to that bed, with you so still and pale, not knowing if you'd ever be with me again. I can't lose you, Sport. Shit's about to get insane around here, and I have to keep you safe."

The look she gave him was frustrated, but indulgent. With a little laugh, she laid her hand on his. "You can't keep me safe, Isaac. Especially not when things get insane. You know what I can do. You know the skills I have. I can handle myself."

"Hobson got the better of you, Lilli. He almost killed you." As soon as he said it, he regretted it. Lilli was suddenly all cold fury. And he knew it was a shitty thing to say. She'd been racked with self-doubt when she'd come out of the coma and realized how close she'd come to failing at her mission to kill Hobson. It had been Isaac who'd killed him, who'd stopped him from torturing her while she bled out. She'd hated that she'd had to be rescued and that someone else—

13

even Isaac—had completed her job. He'd talked her down from that ledge. And now here he was dangling her off it himself. In the months they'd been together, Isaac thought that this was the first time he'd actively hurt her, said something aimed at a weakness. And he'd gone for a very tender spot. What an asshole.

She was rigid with anger now, her arms crossed and her hands curled into fists. But she hadn't gotten up from the couch yet. He squeezed her thigh and felt her muscles go hard at the touch. "I'm sorry, Lilli. That was a shitty thing to say. I didn't mean it."

"Yeah, you did. And fuck you." Now she got up. She grabbed her bag from the floor by the desk and turned around. "Is there someplace else I can change, or do I have to use the nasty bathroom?" She'd changed into her workout clothes right here in his office. He'd changed with her. If she wouldn't change in front of him now—that was bad. That was her looking for distance he didn't want her to have.

He stood and went to her. She didn't move away, but she wouldn't look at him, and the vibe she was giving off was almost toxic. "Don't, Lilli. Stay here. With me. I really am sorry. I'll back off. I will." He put his hands on her stiff upper arms, and she finally turned her eyes to his. They were shiny with almost-tears. Lilli wasn't quick to cry, so he knew how deeply his words had cut. Goddammit, he was such a dick.

"I need to be strong, Isaac. Don't try to take that away from me. I won't let you, and it'll ruin us."

"You are strong, Sport. Jesus, you're like a shield-maiden, or a Valkyrie or something. I don't want you to be anything less than you are." He swallowed down a lump that had begun to grow in his throat. "You make me stronger. I need you with me. It scares me to think of something happening to you."

She sighed. "You know all your Norse mythology and chess references make you a nerd, right? Deep down under all that muscle, ink, and leather, you're a huge nerd." She relaxed her arms and put her hands on his bare chest, curling her fingers into the hair there. "I'm afraid for you, too, you know. It's a two-way deal between us."

Relieved that the tension had broken between them, Isaac leaned down to kiss her forehead. "I know. We need to take care of each other."

"We need to trust each other, love. That's what we need." She pushed away and opened her bag. "Now, though, I want to change so we can talk to your guys." She had an idea for a way to deal with Ellis, and he was calling in the officers so she could explain it to them.

She pulled her clothes out of the duffel and stripped off her workout clothes. As she changed back into street clothes, so did he. So much for sparring being foreplay. He'd screwed that one up royally. He'd have to make it up to her later.

CHAPTER TWO

Lilli was still hurt and angry, but she set it aside. There was a growing pile of stuff she was setting aside, though, and it wouldn't keep forever. She and Isaac had some things they needed to work out. What was happening between them was new for both of them, and their love and desire for one another wasn't sufficient to help them figure out how to make it work. Not without talking.

She knew he was worried. What had happened with Hobson was bad. Because she'd almost died, yes. But more than that, because she'd been made weak. It had rocked her and given her a fierce determination never to be weak again. It had rocked Isaac, too, though, and he was just as determined to protect her. These were not compatible goals, at least not the way they were approaching them now.

Lilli was finding it difficult, too, to live with someone else, a partner. She'd never done it before. It had been a decade since she'd been in a serious relationship. Hell, it had been a decade since she'd had anything resembling a real home, and that one had been her father's. It didn't help matters any that she'd moved in with Isaac right after she'd left the hospital. It had set up a paradigm where he took care of things, including her. On top of that, she'd moved into his family home, in which generations of his family had lived and raised their children. She wouldn't think of asking him to live elsewhere, but it was his house, through and through—the walls, the floor, the furniture steeped in decades and decades of his family history. She hadn't yet figured out how to make it her place as well.

Isaac wanted to share it with her; she knew that. He wasn't possessive about it at all; that wasn't the problem. He would do anything to help her settle. He'd given her a room of her own, his childhood bedroom, which served as her office and private space. She loved it, and she was decorating it to her taste as she figured that out, but it was still his old bedroom, even though he had no nostalgic connection to it and always knocked and waited to be welcomed in.

He wanted marriage and kids, too, and soon. He wore his need for a family like an emblem on his chest. Lilli had never even considered having kids. She wasn't actively opposed, but she had no idea how to be a mother. Her own mentally unstable mother, who'd killed herself when Lilli was ten, was no model. She knew better how to be a father. For that she'd had a wonderful model.

Isaac wasn't pushing, not really. Despite his clear desire for a settled family life, he was obviously trying very hard not to push. He loved her and knew that she needed time to adjust. There were too many changes going on in her life, and she hadn't gotten her feet steady yet.

Sometimes Lilli felt like he almost made it worse by trying so hard. She had nothing to fight against but her own discomfort.

Until now. Isaac had finally said what he was really thinking, unvarnished. He thought she was weak. He thought she couldn't take care of herself.

That, she could fight against.

Now, though, she needed to focus on a different fight, so she set her hurt and anger aside and let Isaac lead her into the Horde meeting room, which they called the Keep. She'd never been in that inner sanctum before. She hadn't spent much time in the clubhouse yet, though that was changing. Before, when she wasn't sure she'd be able to stay in town, she was reluctant to move too deeply into Isaac's life. Now, she knew she could stay, so she was getting to know his brothers. On the whole, she really liked them. They were her kind of people, the kind who lived lives so close to the edge that they had no time for petty bullshit. They were loud, violent, raunchy, and uncouth as fuck. They were also honest and, in their outlaw way, honorable. In Lilli's opinion, most had a lot more honor than the average law-abiding citizen, because they were so often face-to-face with real consequences.

Isaac's officers were already sitting around the big table when he led her in. Showdown, his Vice President; Len, his Sergeant at Arms; Bart, Intelligence Officer; and Dan, Secretary. They all stood when she came in, and Show wheeled a chair around between his seat and Isaac's, so she could sit next to her man. Honor and chivalry; sometimes it was best found under leather kuttes and unruly beards.

Lilli sat and put her hands on the burnished ebony table. She knew Isaac had made it. He was a brilliant woodworker, making everything from furniture to art to wee tchotchkes with his own hands. This piece—huge and heavy, of gorgeous wood, with an intricate braid making a rim near the center—was masterful. She was proud, and she turned to him. He was watching her, his own pride clear in his green eyes. She smiled but said nothing. She didn't need to.

He cleared his throat. "Okay. We need to talk about Ellis. We need to work a better strategy than the eight of us, three Prospects, and a handful of townspeople standing across Main Street waiting for Ellis and the Northsiders to run us down. We've got guns, but not enough. We have an offer for some men from The Scorpions, but not enough, and they'll bring heat from law with them, because they are much bigger players than we are. I know it's unusual to bring an old lady in on a meeting like this, but you know Lilli has special skills. She knows people with other special skills, and she has an idea that might work. Might at least give us some room. Because right now, we're bowling pins, waiting to be knocked down."

He put his hand on Lilli's shoulder and gave it a squeeze. She knew it was for support and encouragement, meant with love, but it irritated her nonetheless. They needed to talk—tonight, when they got back home. If she didn't clear the air, she wasn't going to be able to deal. The conversation they'd started in his office wasn't finished. It needed to be.

"Lilli's going to explain her perspective on what's going on and how she thinks she can help. Then we'll decide if we should take her idea to the club." He turned to her and gave her shoulder another squeeze. "Go ahead, Sport."

With an effort not to seem like she was shrugging him off, Lilli leaned forward and got clear of his hand. "Okay. Isaac is right that you don't have enough man or fire power to take this guy head on. The forays he's made—starting with Mac Evans and real estate, harassing Will Keller, now kids and women getting followed home from school and town by unfamiliar SUVs—all of it shows a guy with lots of patience. Which means he has the resources to be patient. Isaac says that he's a heavy duty dealer, an empire guy. You don't fight a guy like that face to face."

Show, Len, and Bart, who'd already had some serious conversations with Lilli, sat quietly and waited for her to continue, but Dan sat forward. "Hold on. Lilli, I mean no disrespect. I know you were in the Army, in the war, and I know you have that experience. Shit, I just saw you hand Isaac his ass in the ring. So I don't mean to offend when I say what the fuck do you know about running meth? Or fighting dealers? This is turf shit, plain and simple." He turned to Isaac. "Boss, I know you got yourself a fine woman, but I do *not* understand why she's sitting at this table. This table is no place for a woman. It's just wrong." He sat back, arms crossed. His stance was defiant and strong, but Lilli could see, like a shadow behind his eyes, that he knew he'd just spit over a line. She turned her gaze to Isaac and saw his fists clenched, his knuckles whitening. His temper was going to kill the discussion. His eyes burning, he opened his mouth. But before he could speak, Lilli put her hand on his rigid fist. He closed his mouth and looked down at her hand, momentarily distracted.

She started to speak up and respond to Dan herself, but now she felt a big hand on her other arm—Show was holding *her* back. She almost shook him off, but then she recognized that Dan wouldn't hear her now. More important than her need to establish herself was their collective need to get Dan on board. He wouldn't hear her, no matter what she said; he needed to hear from a brother. So she sat back and gave Show the floor.

He stood. He was big, almost as big as Isaac, and he towered over the table. His voice was deep, but he was surprisingly soft spoken. Lilli had never heard him shout. He was always measured, and when he spoke, the words came steadily, as if each one had been weighed and considered before it was uttered. "You're right, Dan. This is the first time a woman has ever sat in one of these chairs. And I think you're right that this is a turf war. But you're dead wrong that what Lilli knows can't help us. All war is turf, brother. In the desert, on Main Street, it's all turf. And this is a new day. We're not fighting another crew for our little acre. We're fighting a guy with ties to people in Washington D-damn-C. He's out of our reach. Lilli says

20

she has a way to bring him down some, or at least get him distracted. We need to give her our ear. We're not talking about putting a patch on her back, Dan. We're only in this room because it's convenient. It's not a club meeting." He sat down as if the matter were settled. Lilli looked at Dan, who did indeed seem somewhat mollified.

Isaac did not, however, and now he leaned forward. "Show's right, and his head is cooler than mine, but I tell you this, Dan. When I bring someone in who could help us, I don't fucking care who it is or where they sit, you keep your trap shut and fucking listen. You don't like the way I run things, then fucking challenge me." Tension in the room crackled like static as everyone reacted to that.

Now Dan stood. "Don't threaten me, Isaac. I'm your brother. I got a right to say my bit. I was right there with you that day in the woods. It was my hand on her throat, keeping pressure so she wouldn't bleed out. She's sitting in Wyatt's damn chair. I voted with everybody else to send him to his Maker for the way he went against the club and sold her out to Ray. Wyatt and I patched in together, but I voted aye, and I knew it was the right thing. So don't threaten me or make me out disloyal because I got a problem with a woman at our table."

He was talking about her like she wasn't there. It shook Lilli hard to hear *again* about how weak and helpless she'd been that day, completely at Hobson's mercy. She remembered every second until Isaac killed Hobson and took her in his arms. She'd passed out then and come to days later. That was how these guys saw her—that limp, bloody body. It was how they still saw her. She hated it with a force too big to fit in her head. She was not weak. She was not.

She realized that she'd put her hand over the scar on her neck, and she jerked it away.

And now Isaac was standing, looking fit for murder. This was getting out of hand. Lilli was over it; she wanted this done. She spoke up. "Fuck, guys. I'm sure everybody's dick is equally enormous, okay? I promise I'm not staking a claim on the damn chair. I'll say what I came to say and leave you to your circle jerk."

Probably not the most prudent thing to say in a room full of angry, aggressive men, but she didn't care. She cast a defiant glance around the table, though, and saw that Len, Bart, and Show were smiling— trying not to, but smiling. Dan still looked pissed. So did Isaac, but she stared him down until the corners of his mouth lifted a little. Then he made a "go ahead" gesture, a short wave of his hand, palm upturned. But he didn't sit until after Dan did.

When she could see again through the haze of testosterone, she cleared her throat. "It's simple, really—or, no, it's not simple, but it doesn't take much to explain. Bart's the hero here. I can put him with a really top-shelf hacker, one with deep experience, and they can work together to get Ellis where he lives. Literally. Get intel on his closest associates, find the weak links among them. Players like this, the weak spots are always closest. You don't get at the big bads from a distance. You get them walking their dog or getting a coffee. To get that close these days, you need a hacker."

Dan laughed, contempt and anger blazing out of the sound. "We're gonna use a computer to take down the guy who's got men chasing our kids down in the street? That's bullshit. Isaac, come on, man!"

Lilli answered. "No. You still need your guns. You'll still get your bullets and bloodshed. But he'll be weaker. You'll know things about him and how he works that he couldn't imagine anyone would know. And maybe you'll have a chance to hold him off. Your only chance."

She pushed back from the table and stood. "My friend is the best of the best, and he's already keen to help. He won't work for free, but he'll work on a friend rate. What he mostly needs is an exit plan for his current situation—maybe a chance to prospect for a position as an Intelligence Officer with a friendly club. You want him to help, I can put him together with Bart." Smiling at Bart, she added, "You're good, bud, but this guy has hacked stuff you've had no need to bother with. The *most* elite systems. He can show you some magic tricks that'll knock you back." Bart grinned at that. He had a sweet, crooked smile.

Finally, she scanned the room. The faces were mostly friendly, but the tension was thick. "Okay, that's what I've got. You boys can get back to measuring." She looked down at Isaac. "I'm going to ask a Prospect to ride me back."

She was still angry from before, and even angrier now after this stupid meeting, so she was gratified to see the surprise register in his eyes. All he said, though, was, "Not gonna wait?"

"Nope. Had about enough of this shit for today." She walked around him, to the door.

As she pulled it open and headed through, Isaac called out, "The van, not a bike!"

She froze. He was seriously getting pissy at the idea of her riding on someone else's bike. Right now, after all that. Being with a biker was not always what one might call an empowering experience for a woman. Certainly not on this day. "Whatever," she called back, understanding even as she said it that she sounded like a petulant teenager. She felt like one, too. Also not especially empowering.

As the door closed, she heard him yell, "Lilli!" She ignored him.

When she found Erik, and he happily agreed to take her, she was sorely tempted to insist they go on his bike. But she knew she'd be getting him into real trouble, probably of the painful variety, so she rode back with him in the van. To Isaac's home. Which was supposed to be her home, too.

She wondered if it ever would be.

~oOo~

When she got back, she did some work, finishing and submitting a decoding project from her secure satellite internet connection. The internet was a fairly rare commodity in Signal Bend, as was television. There was no cable, and most of the residents couldn't afford a dish. The Horde had a powerful dish at the clubhouse. Tuck had one at No Place, the town bar. Isaac had one at the house. For most everybody else, television was a special event. In many ways, the town was trapped in a kind of time warp.

Lilli had come into town with a laptop and satellite phone for her highly classified government contract work as a translator and decryption specialist. She used her own connection when she worked. When she finished for the day, she shut everything down and locked it up in her new desk. She trusted Isaac completely, but what she worked with was sometimes so sensitive, translating messages in Arabic and Farsi that had been snagged and tagged as possible terrorist communiqués, that she kept to protocols as much as she could. She'd let Isaac know too much, simply by telling him what her work was.

She was still agitated and angry from the confrontations at the Horde clubhouse, so she went out to work on the yard. Isaac had neglected almost everything outside, doing no more than keeping the yard around the house mowed. Lilli wanted a garden. She wanted a lot of gardens—flowers and herbs and vegetables. It was autumn, so not the right season to do much, but she'd found catharsis in coming into the yard to clean out the old beds and prepare new ones. Show's wife, Holly, thinning her own beds, had given Lilli bulbs for gladiolas, daylilies, tulips, and irises—which Holly had called "flags"—and Lilli had been working on a big bed along the wide front porch.

Holly was the first—the only, really—woman in town Lilli thought might be something of a friend. They didn't have a lot in common; Holly was a stay-at-home mom with three girls, and, since she'd married Show, she never went farther from Signal Bend than the occasional trip to Springfield. But she was kind and had a decent, dry sense of humor. She'd been a Horde old lady for something like fifteen years, and, though she was obviously not a fan of the club, she seemed happy to help Lilli understand the culture. A day like today was a clear reminder how much help Lilli needed in that regard.

She dug in the porch bed energetically this afternoon, setting in bulbs for spring blooming. Usually physical exertion kept Lilli centered, or got her there in those rare instances when she was losing her cool. Well, those instances had once been rare. Not so much anymore. She felt less level these days than she could remember feeling ever before. Even when her dad died, she'd maintained.

She'd done what needed to be done and moved forward. Now, she felt edgy most of the time.

When there was nothing more she could do outside, she went in and washed up. She fed the kittens—one of Isaac's mousers had dropped a litter several weeks ago, and they'd just been weaned. She had to feed them on the side porch, because they rarely wanted to be in the house for long, but she'd installed a pet door in the kitchen so they could come and go at will. She'd never had any kind of a pet before, and she loved those furry little mischief-makers. Everything they did was adorable. Isaac? Well, he was coming to terms with the idea of cats in his house. He wasn't much of a pet guy, but he seemed to like her interest in the cats.

He'd never even named the mousers. She'd named everybody, the kittens—two black and white boys, a solid black boy, and two calico girls—and the mousers, after Dickens characters. The kittens were Pip, Tim, Dodger, Biddy, and Estella. Mom, a little ginger tabby, was Miss Havisham. Not that the snoot cared in the slightest whether she had a name. The other mouser, a huge black tom and very likely the baby daddy, was Fagin. He steered clear of people. There was another cat roaming around, Isaac said, but Lilli had never seen him or her.

When she filled the bowls and freshened the water, all of the kittens came rolling onto the porch, mewing at her and crawling over her feet, so she sat cross-legged on the floor and got in some quality time. Havi, the mama, came up the short steps and sat at the edge, watching, occasionally licking a paw and sweeping it over her whiskers. Sitting on the floor with kittens crawling on her, feeling the pinpricks of tiny claws kneading her arms, Lilli finally began to feel a little calmer. The kittens got to a part of her she didn't really recognize. She hadn't figured that out yet, but she loved having a lap full of them.

She sat for awhile, looking out over the yard. The summer had been hotter than normal, and the fall warmer, so the leaves turned late, and the yard was burnished with autumn color. The big sugar maple was on fire with brilliantly red leaves, the late afternoon sun streaming through. It was pretty here. And quiet—the only sounds natural, animals and rustling foliage. She liked it. It was getting late, though, so she lifted sleeping Stella and Dodger from her legs and went back into the kitchen. She figured she should probably make some dinner. She didn't know when Isaac would be home, but he was rarely very late without calling.

~oOo~

She was deep into chopping vegetables for stir fry, her mind turning the day at the clubhouse over and over. She didn't have the guys' respect. All they saw was a woman lying limp, her clothes in tatters, at the feet of a predator. Even Isaac now saw her as someone to protect, someone who'd stand behind him, not beside him. God, she hated that. The more she replayed the day, the more agitated she got. The knife was flying through carrots and peppers and onions.

And sweet Jesus, here she was cooking fucking dinner, waiting for her man to get home. God, she was even barefoot! All she needed was to get knocked up—which Isaac was dying for—and she'd be living the cliché. What the fuck had happened to her life?

She wasn't paying enough attention, and finally the big knife went right through her forefinger, slicing off a sliver from the tip. *Motherfuck!* It hurt like hell, and she dropped the knife and stuck her finger in her mouth. Her chaotic, angry thoughts already had her tense; now, her finger stinging and bleeding freely, she just snapped. She hacked at the big wooden cutting board with the knife, then just threw it all, knife and board, with its piles of chopped vegetables, across the room. Still not satisfied, she cleared everything off the worn old prep table. Two of the kittens had stumbled inside through the pet door; now they beat it back out to the porch.

Lilli stood in the mess, panting. Well. That was new. She was clearly losing her mind. Her hand felt wet, and she looked down to see that her finger was bleeding quite a lot. She was leaving a little puddle on the floor, and there were a couple of thin stripes of splattered blood on the walls, apparently from when she'd thrown shit. What a mess. And she was still shaking.

Fuck it. Fuck it all. She left the mess, went to the bathroom to bandage her finger, then got dressed and went for a run. Just fuck it all.

CHAPTER THREE

It had taken Isaac longer than he'd expected to get out of the clubhouse and head home. The meeting had been long and tense, and afterwards, he, Show, and Bart had sequestered in his office for a couple of hours, working through some plans. The Horde was going to work with Lilli and her team to try to work Ellis from his flank. The vote was split, with C.J. and Dan protesting vehemently the idea of an old lady so deep in club business. Even though he, too, had voted to send Wyatt to his maker, C.J., who'd been Wyatt's sponsor and close with both Ray and Wyatt Hobson, harbored a stewing kind of ill will toward Lilli, Isaac suspected. He'd have to keep an eye on that.

And Dan had just about blown a gasket at some of Lilli's parting shots. Isaac had talked him down, he thought, but he was going to need to talk to her about watching her mouth. A woman just did not throw around terms like "circle jerk" at MC members sitting around their table. Not even Lilli would get away with that more than once.

Lilli's black Camaro was parked outside the garage; Isaac pulled his Dyna up to the house and dismounted. It looked like she'd done a lot of work in the yard. The thought of her shaping things up and making her mark on the place made him smile. He stepped carefully over the herd of kittens doing acrobatics around the porch and went inside.

"Hey, Sport!" he called. He hoped she wasn't working. They needed to talk. Things between them had really been off today—more than just today, in fact—and he didn't like it. Something was up with her. She was tense and restless a lot of the time.

A kitten—one of the black ones, so…Tim? Dodger? Whatever—ran into the front hall, the leafy green end of a carrot dragging along from between his teeth. Isaac bent down and picked up the little shit, pulling the greens away. The kitten batted at it, and Isaac laughed and set him back on the ground. Lilli must be making supper, and since she didn't answer, she must still be pissed. Great. Isaac walked through the living room and into the kitchen.

Where he stopped dead.

Jesus. Oh, Jesus.

The kitchen had been ransacked. There was food everywhere, the big knife was on the floor, the cutting board was by the door, two chairs were turned over. And, oh *GOD*, there was blood. A pool of it on the floor, and stripes of it on the walls, the floor, the cabinets.

Oh, Lilli. Oh, no.

He pulled out his burner and dialed. As soon as Show answered, Isaac jumped in. "Show, they got Lilli. Jesus fucking Christ, they got Lilli!"

Show was calm, but his voice was sharp. "What do you need?"

"I gotta find her. Sweep—who's in?"

"Everybody but Ceej. You want me to send 'em out?"

He pushed panic back as hard as he could and tried to think. "Yeah—fuck, we're thin. You, me, Len east on 44. Dan, Havoc, and

Vic west. Bart, Badger and Erik in town." Wait—Badge didn't have a bike yet. "Badger in the van. Dom stays in the Hall."

"Got it. I'll send 'em out. Len and I'll be ready to ride when you get here." Isaac put the burner back in his pocket and ran out to his bike. If Ellis had her—he shook off the thought and rode back into town, keeping his eyes peeled all the way.

~oOo~

Riding down I-44, no sign of Lilli or any vehicle that might have her, panic pounding in his temples, Isaac almost didn't realize his phone was buzzing against his chest. Not bothering to slow down, he pulled it out of his kutte and looked. Bart. He pulled to the shoulder; Len and Show followed suit. "Yeah!"

"Got her, boss. She's good. She was running. Got her in the Hall now. She's pissed, but she's here."

Relief came over him so fast, Isaac thought he might actually puke. Then rage came up right behind it. "Thanks, brother." He gritted it out through clenched teeth and ended the call. He wound up and almost threw his phone into the weeds, but he pulled back at the last second. "Motherfuck! Son of a bitch! Goddamn motherfucking son of a bitch!"

"Isaac, what? What's up?" Show was on him, grabbing his shoulder. When Isaac faced him, he saw real worry, and he realized that he hadn't said yet that she was okay.

31

"She's fine. Bart has her at the clubhouse. She was running. Jesus! There was blood all over the kitchen! What the hell?"

Len and Show were laughing, but Isaac found no humor in the situation at all. He should probably tell Bart to have a Prospect take her home, because he didn't trust himself to be around her right now. But no. He wanted her where people were keeping track of her. He wanted her to stay the fuck where she was. He'd just have to keep his hands to himself until he'd figured out how to calm down. "Both of you shut the fuck up and let's go."

They mounted their bikes and headed back to Signal Bend.

~oOo~

Isaac was in the lead when they walked into the clubhouse. Lilli was at the bar, a bottle of Bud in her hand, laughing with Dom and Bart. Apparently she was over being pissed. Good for her. He sure the fuck wasn't. She turned when he came up—no, she was still pissed, just saving it for him. He didn't say anything at first. He stared at her, and she at him. He wanted to grab her and drag her back to his office, but he knew that would cause an explosive scene, and he had recovered enough equanimity to want to avoid that. So he just said, "Office?"—making sure to make it a question, lest she kick up a fuss about him giving orders. She waved her hand in an "after you" gesture, and he walked through the Hall without another glance at her. She'd better be following him.

She was, and he closed and locked the door behind her. He spun back to her, ready to yell, but she was standing there, alive and unhurt—wait, the blood. He grabbed her arms, looking for a wound, and found it on her finger. All this shit over a cut finger? He pulled her into his arms and held her tight. She held off at first, but then put her arms around his neck. "Fuck, Lilli, you scared the shit out of me. I thought you were hurt or dead or—I didn't know what to think. I thought I was gonna stroke out."

"I was running, Isaac. Just running. It's a thing I do. You know that."

He pushed her away a little. "Not anymore you don't. No."

"What?" She pushed away a lot, shoving at his chest until he let her go. "Who the fuck do you think you are?"

"Who do I think I am? I'm your old man. I'm the President of this MC, I run this town, and it's *my fucking job* to keep you safe!"

"You are completely deluded. You're arrogant. And you're an asshole. It's not your job to do anything about me. I take care of *myself*. I do what I want. Go where I want. When I want."

Oh, he was not in the mood for her warrior woman bullshit. "Are you stupid? Did you forget there's a fucking army of assholes about to come down on our heads—already doing drive-bys past our families? And you're out running? After dark? You *must* be stupid."

He knew that would kick her anger up a notch or two, and she didn't disappoint. She took a swing at him—and not some pussy slap, but a roundhouse punch. It was the roundhouse that saved him. Too much swing; he saw it coming and caught her fist in his hand. She spun, trying to get his arm behind him and tip the power balance, but he was ready for that, too, and dragged her back against his chest. "I'm bigger and stronger than you, Sport. Give it up. You need to calm down, and we need to talk."

For that, he got an elbow in the solar plexus. Hard. Winded, he loosened his hold, and she broke free. "You are a cocky piece of shit, Isaac Lunden. And you don't know me at all if you think you can make me do *anything*." She went for the door.

With two big strides, he got there at the same time and blocked her. "You're staying put, Lilli. You are not leaving this clubhouse without me." This time she jabbed, and got him in almost the same place as her elbow had. Ow. "Fuck, Sport. I am trying very hard to keep my cool. You're not making it easy."

"Yeah? Well, fuck your cool. Come at me. You pulled all your punches in the ring today. You think I didn't know what you were doing? Asshole. Come at me. Let's *go*. You're so big and strong. Show me how you can protect me better than I can myself." She swung *again*, but he deflected it. The woman was out of her head.

He was 6'7", 280. She was 5'9", maybe 130. Only thing giving her an advantage over him was speed. He was not going to swing at her. He wanted to—fuck, he didn't think he'd ever wanted to hit a woman as much as he wanted to hit her right now. But he was not going to. The memory of knocking her down in the ring was still painfully sharp in his head.

He had to get out of this room. He reached behind him and opened the door. "I'm gonna take five, so we can both calm down. You stay put. Do *not* leave this room. You do, and I will have you hog-tied right in the middle of the Hall and dragged back here, I swear to

God." He meant it. He walked out and closed the door on her screamed "FUCK YOU!"

Where had his levelheaded woman gone? This was the kind of drama he'd been assiduously avoiding most of his adult life. He went out into the Hall, and came face to face with his club and its attachments, all trying awkwardly to pretend like they hadn't heard at least ninety percent of the fight. Fan-fucking-tastic.

Show walked up and handed him a beer and a shot. Isaac nodded and tossed back the shot, then took a long, calming draw from the beer.

"I talk to you a minute, boss?"

Isaac sighed. What kind of trouble couldn't wait until he had Lilli sorted out? He was tired. So fucking tired. "Yeah. The Keep." He turned, and Show followed. Before they got to the door, he went back to the bar and put his hand on Len's shoulder. Speaking at his ear, he said, "Do *not* let her leave that room. Understand?"

Len grinned, and Isaac wanted to shove that look right down his throat. "You got it, boss." With a pat to Len's back—rather harder than what might be considered friendly—Isaac went back through the Hall and into the Keep. Show was already sitting in his chair; Isaac joined him, taking his seat at the head of the table.

"What's the trouble?"

Show cleared his throat and sat forward, arms on the ebony table. "Not club business. Not directly, at any rate. This is more brother to brother. I know you'll say if I'm out of turn. But I've been married a long time, Isaac. Maybe I know something about women, the way they think. Much as any man can know the mystery that is the female brain. I see something going on with you and your lady, and I want to give you my view. Might help."

Isaac's sense of offense was so extreme that it looped over on itself and landed back at amusement. He laughed. What an epically shit day. Now he was sitting at the Horde table, literally the seat of his power, whatever that was, getting relationship advice from a guy who hadn't fucked his wife in eight years. Shit, Show hadn't fucked anybody in eight years—just the random clubhouse blowjob. The worst part was Isaac *needed* the advice. He was completely baffled by what was going on with Lilli.

"Say your bit. I reserve the right to kick your ass when you piss me off."

Show nodded. "Noted." He paused for a moment, and Isaac knew he was collecting his thoughts. Show thought first, always. "Things are intense around here. More intense than I can remember in a good long while. There's danger in town like never before. You know I know that—Daisy, Rose, and Iris getting followed home twice, needing an escort to and from the school bus now. That's hard to swallow. It's hard to leave them, and Holly, every day, wondering if this is the day the Northsiders aren't going to be content only scaring our women. Holly's ready to homeschool the girls, but that won't even help. So I get it, Isaac. I've got a beast in my belly, gnawing away every second I'm away from my family. I understand."

Isaac nodded. He knew that Show had even more to lose than he did. He couldn't imagine being afraid for his children. No, that was wrong. He could imagine it. He imagined Lilli pregnant and in danger, he imagined Lilli and their baby in danger, he imagined all of it. But for him it was imagination. For Show, it was reality.

"But my girls *are* helpless, for the most part. Holly hates guns. We fought tooth and nail when I insisted I have my guns in the house. They're locked up so tight they might as well be somewhere else. She refused to learn to shoot. You know she tries to ignore most things about the club. She likes to think of me as a feed store manager, nothing more. When I'm on club business, she says I'm off at 'my club,' like I'm on the fuckin' golf course. She won't even let us have a dog for protection, because she's afraid it would turn on the girls. Somebody comes into my house when I'm away, my family will die. Or worse."

He was quiet again. Isaac had nothing he could say, so he sat and waited to see if Show had more. He did. "Lilli's not like Holly. She's an actual soldier, Isaac. Shit, she was a combat pilot. She's trained with more weapons than we've ever seen, and with hand-to-hand fighting—not just brawling, but actual technique. She could kick half our asses in a straight-up fight. Maybe more'n half of us." He looked pointedly at Isaac. "Even if we weren't pulling punches."

"Was it that obvious?"

Laughing, Show shook his head. "Not to everybody, probably not. To me, to Lilli, probably Len? Definitely."

"Well, what was I supposed to do? Bloody my woman's nose? Break her ribs? I'm twice her size! Not to mention that I love her and don't want to see her hurt!" He was yelling, because Show was pissing him off. He was fucking tired of being told he was wrong because he was *trying to take care of his woman*.

"You're assuming that you could hurt her—and yeah, if you make contact, you're gonna. But even pulling punches, you barely could touch her. She had you, brother. She saw how you fought, and she

37

used it against you. She'd've won that spar straight up. With her brain, not her fists."

Isaac was weary, and he was angry. He took a breath and held his temper. "Yeah, she's smarter than me. Great. Get to the point, brother. What's your big advice?"

"Just this—think of what happened in the ring as a metaphor. While you were pulling punches, she was learning the fight. And she saw you pulling. She knows what she can do, and she knows you don't believe it. Now, women, far as I can tell, they need their self-concept. You know what I mean? They can't just be in the world and do their thing. I think we do that better, not care so much what people think. Women, though, they need to be able to define themselves by what they do and how they're known. I'm not saying I understand it all, because Holly confuses the fuck out of me half the time, and don't even get me started on daughters. But I wouldn't be surprised if it hurts Lilli that you think she's weak—that you don't trust that she can take care of herself."

"That's such a load of crap! Jesus, Show! I never said she was weak. I tell her she's strong all the time. I know what the fuck she can do. I'm the one that brought her into the Keep and stirred up all that shit, because I know she can help!"

Show laughed. "You *tell* her she's strong? Are you brain damaged?"

Enough of this shit. "Fuck you, Show. Advice time is over. You and Holly don't have what I want with Lilli. I don't know what kind of marriage you have, but it's not what I want. So, yeah. I'm done." He stood.

Show slammed his hand down on the table and stood up. It was far out of character, and Isaac was actually startled. "Don't talk about my marriage, brother. You don't know how to keep something going. You've done nothing but wet your wick since you were twenty-four. I was there for what happened with Tasha, remember. You were an asshole to her. Don't be an asshole to Lilli. She's a one-of-a-kind chance. And you shut her up in your office like a badly behaved dog." He walked around the table. "Fuck it. I hope she kicks you to the curb." He threw open the door and stormed back into the Hall.

Isaac stood there, suddenly seeing the fight with Lilli through Show's eyes. Through Lilli's, too.

What a shit day. He left the Keep and headed back to his office. Who the hell knew what he was going to find in there.

CHAPTER FOUR

Lilli could not believe she was still sitting in Isaac's office. What a fucking asshole. Telling her to stay put. Fuck him. And everybody out there knew it, too. They knew she was sitting in here like a docile old lady, doing what she was told. She stormed to the door.

She turned the knob, but then she stopped. He would do it—she absolutely believed he'd set the whole club on her and tie her up. Just to make his point. He'd turned into a fucking caveman, and it was working. She couldn't stand the thought of the whole club coming down on her like that. Especially not after today.

Fuck!

She turned and went across the room to sit on the couch. Sitting here waiting for her man. No. Not her man. Fuck this. This was not the life she wanted. She would not become Holly, hanging her wash, sewing curtains, and baking bread all day. No fucking way. Not worth it. She'd rather be alone.

She sat there and worked out what she would say when Isaac found his way back to his office. How she would end it.

~oOo~

He was gone a lot longer than five minutes. When the door opened slowly, as if he thought maybe she'd fly at him—which, sure, had been a consideration—she'd had plenty of time to calm down and prepare what she would say. She hadn't lost so much of her anger that the enormity of what she was about to do had really sunk in, and that was good. She could be sad later. Now, she just had to figure out how to get herself free. From all of it.

Assured that the coast was clear of flying women, Isaac stepped in and closed the door. "Baby, we have to talk." He smiled. Apparently, he'd found the calm he'd gone looking for.

Lilli was sitting in a corner of the couch. "Yeah, we do. I want out."

He walked toward her and sat down in the middle of the couch, not quite on top of her, but closer than she really wanted. "I'm sorry for making you stay in here. I—I was being an asshole."

"Yeah. But it's not what I meant. I want out of this." She waved her hand between them. "Whatever the fuck it is."

The shock on his face was absolute. He hadn't seen it coming at all. Lilli didn't know what to think about that. Did he think it was going well between them? "Lilli! Baby, no. No! We just need to sort through some shit."

"There's too much shit, Isaac. Too much. You need a woman who's something I'm not. You're trying to make me into something I'm not."

He grabbed for her hand, but she pulled away. It hurt him that she did; she saw it in his eyes. She saw deep hurt and something like fear. "No, Lilli. You're wrong. I'm fucking up, I get that, but you're wrong. I don't need something you're not. I need you. You. Who you are."

"No. You need someone who'll hide behind you, who'll do what you say because you say it. You need someone who doesn't need to be your equal." She stood up and headed for the door. When she got there, she turned back to him. He was still sitting on the couch, looking stunned. "I'm going back to the rental. The rent's paid for another few weeks. I'll be gone well before then. Just…give me like an hour to get my shit out of your house."

Now he stood. "Lilli, fuck! Wait—we need to talk this through. You're just—you're wrong!"

She didn't answer. She put her hand on the knob, and he said, "How do you think you're gonna get to the house?"

Shit. She dropped her hand and took a couple of steps back into the center of the room.

Bart had picked her up on her run and brought her to the clubhouse. Isaac's house was ten miles outside of town, in the opposite direction, so more like fifteen miles from the clubhouse. Fifteen miles was a run she could do, and she was dressed for it, but it was late. It was dark. She was stuck. "Will you let a Prospect take me?" She knew the answer.

"No. We need to talk."

Running in the dark it was. "Fuck this, Isaac. I'm done being forced." She headed back for the door.

This time, he moved, and again he put himself between her and the door. She thought about hitting him again, but, frankly, she was

42

exhausted, and sad was starting to overtake angry. He grabbed her upper arms, and she didn't fight him off.

"Do you love me, Lilli?" His green eyes bored into hers. He looked really upset, and guilt crept into the sadness that was starting to overwhelm her.

"Isaac, don't."

He shook her a little. "Do you love me? Tell me. Be true."

"Isaac…" She didn't understand what good it would do to keep this conversation going. She needed to get out—of this room, this town, this relationship. If that was what it was.

"*Do you love me?*"

"Yes! You know I do. It's not enough."

He shook her again. "How do you know it's not?"

"Because of this! What's happening right now!"

"This is a *glitch*, baby. Just a glitch. You and me, we don't know what the hell we're doing. We're fumbling, that's all. You want to throw it away because you're scared. Please, Lilli. Sit down and talk with me. Don't give up yet."

No. He was wrong. It wasn't a glitch. It was a failure. Lilli understood now that she was better off on her own. "Please. Just let a Prospect take me back to get my stuff."

His grip on her arms tightened painfully, and his eyes flashed. God, were they wet? He blinked and released her. "Okay. Come on. I'll

43

have Badger take you in the van." With a sigh, he opened the door and ushered her back to the Hall.

~oOo~

Badger dropped her off. He tried to stay with her, but she scared him off. Isaac hadn't told him he had to stay, so he wasn't that hard to scare. She'd made it pretty evident that she wasn't in a good mood.

She just wanted to get her stuff and get the hell away. She had an hour. She went upstairs and grabbed her duffels out of the closet in her office. No, not her office. Isaac's room.

Damn, this hurt. Damn. She always lost everything. Damn.

When she came down to get her clothes, the kittens were at the foot of the stairs, churning around in a big knot, making a ruckus. When she stepped off the staircase, they started climbing up her running pants. She spared a couple of seconds to sit on the floor with them. She hoped Isaac wouldn't force them all to stay outside now. It was starting to get cold, especially at night. Now, they all slept, with their mom, in the kitchen.

Lilli sat with them longer than she'd expected, and she was still on the floor, cuddling kittens, when she heard Isaac's bike. Fuck! Had it been an hour? No way it had been an hour. She set Biddy and Tim down and pushed the others gently off her legs and got up, hurrying back to the bedroom. She didn't know why she was hurrying; there was no way she'd be out of the house before he was in it, but she did *not* want another confrontation. She just wanted to get away.

44

He came in while she was pulling clothes out of the closet. She didn't have much. A bit more than she had when she'd gotten to town, but Lilli wasn't much of a shopper, and there wasn't really anywhere to shop, anyway, except online. Reluctant to turn around and face him, she made a production out of straightening the hangers.

"Lilli." He must have stopped in the doorway.

She didn't answer, just kept straightening hangers, telling herself to soldier up and face him. She couldn't. With her head still in the closet, she said, "You were supposed to give me an hour."

Then he was on her, his hands on her hips. She tensed, but he didn't try to turn her. "Lilli." He put his head on her shoulder. "Don't go. At least talk with me first. Not fight—talk. Please, baby." His voice sounded thick.

Something about the way he was holding her—gently, but there was something else in it, something she couldn't name—shook her resolve. She was confused again. What had seemed clear seconds ago was now, again, a jumble. She dropped the clothes in her hands. "Isaac, I don't know what to do."

He pulled her back against him, his head still on her shoulder. "Talk with me." He turned his head and pressed his lips to her neck. "Talk with me." His hands slid forward and spread over her belly. "Talk with me."

Her body was responding the way it always did to his touch, his scent, his sound. She didn't want to talk. She turned in his hold, and he pulled back just enough to look down into her eyes. He didn't want to talk, either. "Lilli. Please."

For a charged heartbeat, they simply stared at each other. Isaac's eyes seemed deeper and more intense than she'd ever seen them. Then she reached over his shoulder and grabbed his braid. As soon as she did, his mouth was on hers, fierce and emphatic, and he pushed her against the frame of the closet door. The edge of the jamb dug into her back, but she didn't care. She yanked on his braid, pulling him even closer, and opened her mouth, sucking his tongue deep and making him groan. He grabbed her thighs and pulled her up, hooking her legs around his hips. She hung on.

She was overwhelmed, riding the wave of his need, and hers. His hands were everywhere, moving frantically—pulling her ponytail loose and combing through her hair, caressing her sides and her ass, pushing between them to hold her breasts. His whole body was huge and hot on hers, his cock a granite swell against her core, his panting breath on her face. He tore his mouth from hers but didn't move back. His forehead on hers, he grunted, "Fuck, Lilli. I love you. I love you. Stay, baby. Stay with me."

Lilli pulled back. This was nuts. They couldn't fuck their problems away. She needed to go. But, God, she didn't want to. Part of her, a small part, but one that got loud when he was so close, wanted to do anything to stay. Her head was too full; she needed to think. Releasing her legs from around his hips, she pushed him off and stood. "Okay. Okay, let's talk. Not this. Talk."

He stepped back, nodding. She could see and hear him mustering control of himself. "Yeah. Good. Talk. Good." He brushed her hair back from her face. "Thank you."

"Yeah. Living room." She left the room and headed down the hallway. He was right behind her.

She sat on the sofa, and he sat next to her. With the exception of the big bookcases and entertainment unit that Isaac had built onto one wall, the furniture in this room was old—from the 1940s, maybe, with wood trim and fraying cream damask with faded red roses. At least three generations of Isaac's family had used this furniture. Even more than that had used this room. Lilli found it disorienting to live in a house so deeply saturated with someone else's history. It wasn't just living in an old house. She was living in a house that was, and could only be, uniquely Isaac's. She felt like an interloper. She'd never told him that, because there was nothing he could do, and she didn't want him to feel torn. She would never ask him to give up a home like this—his commitment to his town was founded on that kind of loyalty to place—but she just didn't know how to live here and not be a guest.

He took her hand and laced their fingers. "I'm sorry, Lilli. I went nuts. I got scared—really scared—and I just went nuts. I'm an asshole. You're right. But I can't lose you. Don't let me being stupid ruin what we have."

It stretched her fingers wide to be laced with his, so she changed the grip and folded her hand around his fingers, squeezing. "What do we have, Isaac?"

He'd been looking down at their linked hands; at her question, he jerked his eyes to hers. "You really don't know? Lilli."

She kept her eyes steady on his. "I'm asking."

For whatever reason, he didn't answer her, not right away. He turned and looked out the window, into the midnight dark. It was going to be a cold night, maybe the first frost. Isaac had spent time over several days last week chopping firewood, anticipating the coming cold. He'd told her he hated winter, when his bike spent too much time garaged, and he was stuck caged in his big pickup. Still looking out the window, he said, "No."

She was confused. "What?"

"No. I'm not gonna tell you what we have. You know. You tell me what's missing. Seems like that's the important thing right now—what makes you want to leave. What we don't have. What's not right?"

"Isaac, it's not that simple."

"Maybe it is. Or maybe it's not. Maybe we can't fix it. But I don't even know what's wrong. Will you give me a chance?"

"After today, you have to know what's wrong. You're not stupid."

"Yeah. I know. I was an ass. Show called me on it, too. You're both right. I'm not giving you enough credit. But Lilli—" He paused, his eyes shifting as if he were tracing a thought as it moved through his head. "I *know* how capable you are. Shit, Sport, I'm in awe of you. I know I was coming off like I think you're weak, but it's not true."

"Then why all the orders? Why are you trying to force me behind you?"

"Not what I was—look." He stood, still holding her hand, and gently pulled. "Come with me for a second." She let him pull her to her feet, and he led her into the kitchen and turned on the light.

Everything was just as she'd left it—chopped vegetables on the floor, chairs overturned, big knife on the floor, and blood, streaked on the walls and cabinets, and a small puddle in the middle of the

48

room, now smeared, with tiny reddish-brown pawprints all over the kitchen. She hadn't really seen all this when she was in the thick of it. She hadn't seen how it looked.

"I came home to this, and you were gone. No call, no note. Ellis and the Northsiders are out there, Sport. I saw all this and you gone, your car here, and *Nah, she's just on a run* is not a sentence that went through my head. I don't know what happened here, and now I don't even care. But when I came in here earlier, I thought I'd lost you." Turning to face her, he framed her face with his hands. She loved the rough and gentle feel of his palms on her skin. His touch felt like love to her.

"I wish I could explain how bad it felt to think I'd lost you. And it's not the first time. I know you hate to talk about it, but seeing you in that deer blind—"

"Don't, Isaac. No." She hated more than anything else the memory of lying there, first at Hobson's feet and then in Isaac's arms, her life draining away, barely able to move at all, subject to the will of others. Nothing left to her but her silence. She tried to pull away, but he held on, sliding his palms down her arms to take her hands in his.

"I know. It's just—you made everything different for me, Lilli. I see everything different. What I want in my life is different. The thought of losing you undoes me. I'm not used to feeling like this. I don't know what I'm supposed to do. I don't know how to deal with the kind of fear I felt today, and that other day, and all the days in the hospital before you woke up. I know you're not weak. I know you hate weakness. But Lilli, *I'm* weaker without you. Part of me wants to keep you in a little box where nothing bad can get to you, but I know that's not you. That's not the woman I love. I just—I want to do right by you. I want you safe."

49

Faced with the disaster in the kitchen, everything that had happened earlier in the night made a great deal more sense. A lot of this was her fault. What else should Isaac have thought? The kitchen looked very much like a fight had occurred. And one had—but it was Lilli versus her own head.

"I'm sorry, Isaac. I didn't realize how this looked. I'm sorry I scared you. And you're right. It wasn't smart to run in the dark and not tell anyone where I was. You're right. You were a caveman tonight, but I was thoughtless and reckless. Let's call it even?"

Smiling, he lifted her hand and kissed it. "Absolutely. But there's something else going on, Sport. You've been different, and it feels like it's been gettin' bigger. I think that's why we had this derailment today. I think it's why you want to go."

She didn't really have anything to lose, did she? She was already half-packed. "Okay. Can we sit again?" He nodded and, still holding hands, they went back to the faded damask sofa.

Not knowing how to start, she stared at a large cabbage rose on the back of the sofa. Isaac sat quietly next to her, waiting. She loved him for that, for giving her time to think what to say. "Remember when I told you that I didn't know what to make of myself, or my life now? How staying in town made that harder, because I couldn't even have my own name?" The sensitive nature of her contract work required a secure identity. She was here in town as Lilli Carson, though her true name was Accardo. Staying in Signal Bend meant giving up her name permanently.

Isaac nodded. "I remember."

"Your solution was to ask me to marry you. To take your name."

He nodded again. "That's not why I want to marry you, though."

"I know. But Isaac, everything in my life here is yours. I don't have anything."

His eyes went wide. She knew he'd been trying, but she was surprised by his surprise. She wondered what he thought about their life these past few months, and she realized that he had everything he wanted, except getting her pregnant. Maybe he hadn't seen what she didn't have.

"Lilli, what?"

"Your great-great-whatever grandfather built this house. The walls, the floorboards, the furniture is all Lunden. How many Lunden asses have sat on this sofa? How many Lunden women have cooked in that kitchen? When I'm cleaning out the planting beds in the yard, I'm wondering whether I'm pulling up the remains of a plant your grandmother seeded. The town is yours. People in town know me as yours. People introduce themselves to me with 'You're Ike's woman, right?' or 'Hey—you're Ike's old lady.' Isaac, I don't know where *I* am in all this. *I'm* what's missing."

They'd been holding hands the whole time she'd been speaking, and his hand had tightened steadily around hers until, now, it was hurting a little. Plus, he had hold of the hand with the cut finger, and she was pretty sure that was bleeding again. But she said nothing.

"Baby, I will burn this house down tonight. I don't care. I don't. You know growing up was shit for me. I don't have many good memories in this house. My home is with you. We can build a new one. We can move to another house—plenty of empty ones available. If you don't want to take my name, we'll figure out a way to get yours back. I want to marry you, but I don't care if you're a Lunden, if you don't want it. None of it matters. *You* matter. Tell me what you want, and I will make it happen—no. No. I'll get out of your way while you make it happen."

"And if I don't know what I want?"

"Then I'll get out of your way while you figure it out. Just—stay with me. Let me be part of it. If you love me."

She felt tears coming, and she closed her eyes to hold them off. She had expected him to feel guilty, or conflicted, or even to fight her. But he was all in. It humbled her. "Nothing in my life is like I thought it would be." She met his eyes. "I'm scared."

He laughed, a tired, ironic huff. "Oh, Sport. So am I." Bending toward her to brush a gentle kiss across her lips, he asked, "We okay?"

"Yeah. I'm sorry."

"Me too." He smiled. "Wanna make it up to each other?"

CHAPTER FIVE

He was exhausted, mentally and physically. Just exhausted. As soon as the danger had passed, at the sound of Lilli's voice saying they were okay, relief pushed through Isaac's veins and brought fatigue in its wake. But it didn't matter. They were okay. She wasn't leaving. She was in his arms, he was in hers, and she was soft and pliant. The fight was over. And she was still here. He dropped his head to her shoulder. He wanted to take her to bed, but he needed a minute.

She nudged her head against his. "Hey, love. Can I have a raincheck on the making up? I'm *starving*."

Laughing, he lifted his head and looked into her beautiful grey eyes. They were bright, sparkling, and her smile was sweet and calm. The storm had passed. He'd come so close to losing her. He didn't think he'd ever been on the emotional ride he'd been on this whole damn day. "Yeah, Sport. We should eat." He checked the old clock on the mantel—fuck, it was late. "Nothing's open. You in the mood to cook?"

With a gentle push, Lilli slid out from his hold. "Nope. I have a better idea. Come with me." She held out her hand, and when he took it and stood, she led him into the kitchen.

"Fuck. I keep forgetting about this mess." She bent down and picked up a leafy carrot top.

Isaac put his hand around her arm and pulled her back up. "Leave it for tomorrow."

"But there's blood, and vegetables everywhere. It's gross."

"It'll still be gross tomorrow. It's been here for hours. Blood's dried. There's nothing to hurt the cats. And it's too damn late, Sport. Let's just find something quick to eat and deal with this tomorrow." He put his hand on her cheek. "That okay?"

She smiled. "Yeah. You pick up the chairs, and I'll make dinner." She skipped—she literally skipped—to the cabinets as Isaac went to the table and set the overturned chairs to rights. The butcher knife was on the floor—that *was* a possible danger, so he picked it up and put it in the sink. He saw that Lilli was collecting bowls and spoons. When she went to the far cabinet, he grinned and went to the fridge for the milk.

Standing before the biggest cabinet, both doors open, she asked, "You want Cookie Crisp, Peanut Butter Crunch, or Lucky Charms?"

"There enough Cookie Crisp for both of us?" Lilli was a sucker for sugary cereals. She acted like a giddy little kid about them. It was cute as fuck.

Now, she was giving him an contemplative eye. "I suppose I could share. With the right person." She brought the box to the table.

"What's it gonna take to make me the right person?"

With a saucy grin that did his heart inestimable good, she walked up to him. He put his hands on her hips, and she grabbed his shirt in her fists. "Kiss me like you mean it. Then we'll see."

"Oh, baby, I always mean it." He bent down and kissed her. Like he meant it. She gave over to him completely, melting against him. He lifted her and set her on the table; his heart raced when her legs immediately circled his hips. Her tongue moving against his, her passion matching his passion, her breath mixing with his—there was something more, something bigger, in this contact, like the fight had released something that had been trapped between them.

She had his shirt open—he hadn't even noticed her undoing his buttons, so intent he was on the feel of her tongue, her skin, her breath, his hands in her hair. But now her hands were on his bare chest, her fingers combing through the hair there, and he was going to fuck her right here. God, he was so hard. He was painfully bound up in his jeans and like to bust a seam.

He tore his mouth away, panting, his vision tunneled. "Thought you were hungry, baby."

Her eyes were unfocused and heavy-lidded, her skin flushed. She laughed. "I am. I really am. I haven't eaten since breakfast. I feel a little lightheaded, and not just 'cuz you're a sexy motherfucker."

Last thing he wanted was for her to pass out. "Okay. We need to back it down, then." He cleared his throat and stepped back to help her off the table. They sat, side by side at the big cherry table he'd made, and she poured them each a bowl of kid cereal. She had a system to maximize the number of little cereal cookies she could get in a bowl and still add milk. He watched her do her magic, feeling unsettled by the power of his love for her. He'd almost lost her. Jesus Christ. He couldn't let that happen.

For a minute or two, they just ate, the only sounds of the room the crunch of cereal, the vaguely metallic chime of spoons against stoneware bowls, and the mewling tussle of the kittens who'd stirred from their sleep when Isaac and Lilli had come in. Lilli bent down and picked up one of the kittens—a long-haired, calico one. Isaac figured he'd have to get their names straightened out eventually. This one was one of the girls, so Stella or Biddy. Apparently, they had housecats. He had a sneaking suspicion that some or all of these beasts would eventually be sleeping with them, an idea that didn't thrill him. But he watched Lilli with this little furry moppet batting at her fingers, and he smiled. Her face was open and happy, and he knew three things. One—Lilli loved the kittens, really loved them. Two—he'd happily share their bed with cats as long as he was sharing it with Lilli, too. Three—Lilli was learning that she was a nurturer. He wanted her to know that. He wanted her to feel that. Because he wanted her to have his babies.

Another kitten—one of the black ones, so a boy—was climbing up his jeans. Instead of swatting it—him—back to the floor, Isaac picked him up and held it—him—in front of his face. He had a little white mustache. His bottom half dangling from Isaac's hand, he seemed perfectly content. He yawned, making a little squeak. Yeah, they were cute. "Which one is this?"

Smiling, Lilli looked over. "That's Pip. He has the milk mustache and the white belly. Tim has the paint-pot paws and white hairs in his ears. Dodger's all black—and the biggest. This"—she touched noses with the bundle in her hands—"is Estella. She and Biddy have the same markings, but Stella has long hair." He must have been making a face, because she laughed when she looked at him again. "You'll figure it out. If you care to know."

He looked at Pip. "I do care. And I think I got it now." Something occurred to him, and he turned back to Lilli. "They're yours, you know. They're you. In this house."

56

Setting Stella in her lap, she stared at him, her smile fading slightly. "Huh. Yeah, I guess that's true. I hadn't thought of it like that."

The mom cat—Lilli had given her a Dickens name, too, but Isaac couldn't remember what it was—walked over and stood up next to Isaac's chair, putting her front paws on his leg and nosing at Pip. Oh, right—Miss Havisham. She was collecting her brood. Isaac and Lilli watched as she herded them all over to the sleeping pad Lilli had set up for them. The kittens didn't nurse any longer, but they still slept in a pile on and around their mom. Stella was the last in. She didn't come until mom meowed. Isaac had never paid any attention to all this before, and he found it hilarious. He laughed out loud, earning himself a baleful glare from momma cat.

Meanwhile, Lilli had collected the dishes from their meal of Cookie Crisp. She rinsed the bowls and set them in the sink. She was yawning hugely when she turned back around.

Isaac stood and pushed the chairs in. "Let's go to bed, Sport. It's been a hell of a day."

"I need a shower. Since my last one, I worked out, sparred with you, worked in the yard, had a temper tantrum, took a run, and had another tantrum. I must smell like the Rams locker room on Sunday night."

He grabbed her and pulled her close. She actually didn't stink—or she didn't smell bad, not to him. She smelled amazing, in fact. "You know I love the smell of you. Don't wash on my account. I like you like this."

She laughed. "Okay. You're weird."

They went to bed, but they didn't have sex. By unspoken, mutual agreement, they undressed and settled in to sleep, Lilli curled snugly inside the curve of his body, her hand linked with his at her belly. Isaac nestled into her hair and breathed deep of her, feeling the last of the day's tension ease away. He sensed it when Lilli's consciousness dropped off, and she slept. He hoped this night would be a night without bad dreams.

Isaac felt good. Happy. A few hours earlier, he'd been pretty sure he'd never be happy again.

~oOo~

It was light when Isaac woke, and as soon as he was awake, he rejoiced that he was not alone. He hadn't lost her. He and Lilli were still curled together in the same position in which they'd fallen asleep. Almost the same position—Isaac's humungous erection was a new player this morning.

She hadn't dreamt. That was good. Her nightmares had been no more frequent since she'd been hurt, but they had been more intense. At least once, at least three nights a week, Lilli woke in a violent agitation. He figured it must be PTSD, from her combat tours in Afghanistan, made worse by what had happened in that deer blind, but she wouldn't talk about it much. She had, once, told him that they were death dreams, that she dreamt she was being brutally, painfully murdered. It hurt his heart.

But she'd slept through. He checked the clock on the nightstand. Quarter to seven. Okay, well, they'd only slept a few hours. He should let her sleep, and go back to sleep himself. But his cock, thwarted last night, had other ideas this morning. He was severely turned on, so much that he was having trouble staying still. He shifted a little, like a spasm, and felt himself slide against the soft silk of her bare ass. Oh, fuck.

She must have felt him in her sleep, because she moaned prettily and shifted, drawing her top leg up. Oh, that only made her more enticing. Her sweet pussy was right there. He could slide his hand over her ass...reach between...and God, she was wet. She was so wet, and hot, and he couldn't help himself. He slid his cock against her core, feeling her wet slide on him. It was just short of heaven. It felt so good, he almost didn't feel guilty for disturbing her slumber.

"Baby, baby, wake up. I need—baby. Wake up, wake up."

She moaned again and shifted, making a little stretch and doing amazing things to his cock. She was awake, and she looked over her shoulder at him. "Hey." Her voice was sleepsexy. "What's up? Oh—you are." She smiled. "I love it when you wake me up to make me come."

"So do I, Sport. So do I." He positioned himself and pushed into her, bringing his hand around to her clit. She gasped and pushed against him, bringing him deeper. *God*, she felt good.

"Hey—condom."

He wanted to tell her no. He wanted her to let him fill her with his seed, with his son or daughter, with his family. He knew it was irrational. He knew this was the wrong time—and not only because

Lilli wasn't ready. They were facing real, life-or-death danger any day. And he'd never wanted a family until a few months ago. It was crazy to want one now. But he did. It was taking over this thoughts, always occupying at least a corner of his mind. But he said none of that. She wasn't ready. She was afraid she didn't know how. She didn't want to be like her mother. He knew she wouldn't be, but she had to know it herself. So he kept his need to himself and said, "Right. Hold up," and reached over her into the nightstand drawer.

He pulled a strip of condoms out and tore one off. Lilli turned to her back under him, and he shifted to kneel between her long legs, spread wide for him. She was long and lean, and he devoured her with his eyes as he rolled the latex over his cock. His eyes traveled up to her face and met hers, bright and full of heat and need. Still holding his cock in one hand, he leaned down, slid his arm under her back, and pulled her up onto his lap, and onto his cock, in a fluid, strong move. As he penetrated her fully and quickly, she gasped and bit her lip, her eyes flashing. Lilli was strong and wanted people to know it, but Isaac knew she liked him stronger. She liked a little manhandling; she liked to be moved around, and she wanted firm touch. She wanted intensity.

"Aw, yeah," he growled, taking a moment of stillness to savor the feeling of her tight heat wrapped around him. She hooked her arms around his neck, and he felt her fingers lacing into his long hair, her blunt nails scratching gently at his scalp. She flexed on him, and he grunted. He could fuck her forever.

She leaned down and brushed her lips against his. "I love you inside me." Her voice was rough and low, not much more than a hoarse breath tickling his mouth. Easing his hands down the firm, satiny skin of her back, he grabbed her tight hips and lifted off his knees, surging into her. She cried out, her fists clenching in his hair and her

60

eyes rolling up. It was so good, so good, she felt so good. God, he loved her.

"Isaac, please." He knew what she wanted. After the night they'd had, this was not the morning for slow, luxurious sex. At least not first. He came up on his knees and laid her back on the bed. Pushing her legs up high, he pressed his hands against the backs of her thighs and slammed into her, groaning violently, getting as deep as he could, moving as fast and hard as he could. He knew she could take it; he knew she wanted it. She was all the woman he could handle.

Every time he hit home, she cried out, almost a scream. Her hands were tangled in his hair and pulling painfully; he cared not at all. In fact, he loved it, her fierce abandon, the way her body overtook her head when they fucked.

She was clenched tight around his cock, like she didn't want to let him go. His emotional overload was seeking its due, and he felt the familiar electric tension building in his gut. "Come on, baby," he murmured, shifting his hands off her thighs so he could get closer to her. Leaning on his forearms, still moving with force and rhythm inside her, he took a breast into his mouth, sucking deep and thrilling at the feel of her skin tightening against his tongue.

"Oh, yes. Harder," she whispered, her back arched, lifting her breast like an offering. "Harder." He bit down on the tight nub in his mouth and sucked hard.

She screamed then, and he felt her orgasm rising as it milked his cock. She took over the rhythm of their thrusts, her hips keeping a staccato tempo. He tried to keep up with her and hold himself off while her release went on and on, but he couldn't catch her rhythm. So he rolled and gave her the lead.

For the barest second, she looked surprised at the change, then, still deep in her throes, she smiled and leaned down, her hands clutching at his chest, and drilled down on him. "Oh fuck, oh fuck, oh fuck," she chanted.

Christ, she undid him. Everything about her was sex—her skin glistening sweat, her long, dark hair wild and tousled from sleep and exertion, her fingers pulling in his chest hair, her eyes unfocused with need, and her scent, sweet and real. The hot coil in his belly was too much to hold off anymore. He grabbed her hips. "Baby, I gotta go."

"I'm there. Go. Go." He sat up, and the shift of his cock inside her did it for them both. He grabbed her head and kissed her, and they came grunting savagely into each other's mouths.

When it was over, they didn't move. They sat in the middle of the bed in a hot, damp, heaving knot of afterglow, simply holding each other, silently but for the sounds of their spent breathing.

Isaac was the first to stir, pushing Lilli's wet hair off her shoulders and kissing her neck. "You're everything, Sport. Everything." He meant it. When he was with her, when they were good, he didn't give a shit about anything else. Sometimes, he wished they could just go. Go away.

She pulled back and combed her fingers through his hair, pulling it away from his face. "Don't say that, love. It's too much, and it's not true. Love can't be everything. It'll devour itself."

He didn't believe that. He knew they couldn't—and wouldn't—just abandon their lives and the people who counted on them, but he needed her to know where she ranked. "You're all I want, Lilli. A life with you. It's all I want."

"Isaac." A cloud passed through her eyes. He didn't want that.

"Okay. I just love the fuck out of you, Lilli Accardo."

She smiled brightly. Her name was important to her, something she shared with the father she'd loved so much, and she didn't get to hear it often. "And I love you." She leaned her forehead on his.

CHAPTER SIX

"Now, I really, really, *really* need a shower." Lilli leaned back and grinned at her man. She felt worlds better about things than she had last night. She'd let things fester. All of this—this life she was making, this relationship—it was all new, untraveled territory for her, and she wasn't trusting herself the way she should. She wasn't trusting Isaac the way she should. Or she hadn't been.

It was him, too. He knew what he wanted; she was still fumbling. He was used to getting what he wanted, so as much as he was trying to stay out of her way, he was a willful man. She didn't think everything would be rosy because they'd talked once. But she felt understood, and that was a start.

"You want company in that shower?" He wiggled his dark brows at her, his green eyes glinting.

"Nope. I think I'm doing this one solo, thanks." It was a thing with them, this shower dance. She preferred to shower alone, unless the shower was intended to be strictly recreational. He preferred to be with her wherever she was naked. He gave her the space she wanted, but he always asked.

Now, he sighed. "Fine. Your loss. Hey—I have an idea for today. You want to go to Springfield, check out some furniture stores?"

That caught her off guard. "What?"

"You were saying last night that Lunden asses have been stinking up the furniture around here forever, and you're right. Some of that stuff is eighty or a hundred years old. It's not there because I like it, Sport. It's there because I'm fuckin' lazy. I'm sure we could sell it—hell, maybe I'll just donate it to the Main Street shops. In fact, that's what I'll do. But you and I should pick out shit *we* like. What do you say? Wanna go shopping with me today?"

Lilli grinned. That actually sounded like fun. She'd never really been furniture shopping, and apparently, neither had Isaac. But the timing was terrible, she thought. "Can you leave town? With all this shit going down with Ellis and the Northsiders?"

"We've got scheduled patrols, and the town's on alert. Springfield's not all *that* far, and there's some business I need to do there anyway. I was going to send Len, but I'll go instead. Show will be in charge, and even if trouble comes up, we can get back to deal with it."

"You sure? Isaac—"

He put his hands around her face. She loved the feel of them, big and rough, the hands of a man who used them. And he really knew how to use them. "Baby, we've been through hell. We'll go through more before this is through. Let's take a day."

Lilli put her hands over his. The last time they'd gone away, to a weekend art show in Tulsa, where Isaac sold his woodworking, they'd grown closer.

And the day after they'd gotten back, Lilli had almost died.

"Okay, love. Let's go shopping."

65

~oOo~

Before they left, Lilli got in contact with Rick, her best hacker friend, who'd been instrumental in her dealing with Ray Hobson. She hooked him up with Bart, and, when she was satisfied that they were set up to work together on the Ellis problem, and Isaac had made the arrangements he needed to make to be gone for the day, they set off to shop for furniture.

They took his big, aging black and silver pickup into Springfield. It always soured Isaac's mood to drive what he called a cage, and the ride was quieter than Lilli would have liked, considering that this was mainly supposed to be a day off for them. For about half an hour, the only voices in the car belonged to The Allman Brothers, wailing mournfully from the speakers. Lilli's musical taste tended toward punk, so her patience with the music was short.

She looked over at him. He was lost in thought, his right wrist resting on the top of the steering wheel, his left arm propped on the door, his left hand rubbing over his beard. She knew he had a lot weighing him down—the responsibility for an entire town lay on his shoulders. Lilli hated that the town was saving itself by cooking and selling crystal. Isaac hated it, too. It was a nasty thing, and it made Isaac and the Horde, and Signal Bend itself, vulnerable to nasty men like this Lawrence Ellis. She wanted to help them find another way. She *knew* there had to be another way. But first, they had to turn Ellis away.

As Lilli watched, Isaac, still far off in his own head, sighed heavily. She almost said something to break his reverie, but then she had another idea. The truck was old enough that it had a bench front seat.

She undid her seatbelt and slid closer to him, laying her hand on his thigh. Coming back to earth, he turned and smiled at her.

"Hey, Sport. What—did you miss me, all the way over on the other side of the cab?" Taking the wheel in his left hand, he hooked his right arm over her shoulder and pulled her close.

"Something like that. You look like a man in dire need of something to take his mind off it all." He wasn't wearing a seatbelt—he never did. She took hold of his belt buckle and popped it open. Then she unbuttoned his jeans and pulled his cock out. It was swelling before she'd gotten her hand on it, and it was full and huge and hard by the time she had it out and bent her head toward it.

He was surprised, but he didn't stop her. "What—baby…oh, fuck."

After pressing a gentle kiss to his tip, she took his cock into her mouth, relaxing her throat and getting him as deep as she could. She wrapped her hand around the base of his shaft, so that she was touching, stimulating, all of him at once. He groaned roughly and shifted in his seat, lengthening his lap and easing her access to him. She released her grip around his base and slid her hand into his jeans to caress and squeeze his balls.

"Holy Jesus fuck, baby. Oh, God." Over her head, she felt him move the steering wheel. He was changing lanes to the far right. He'd slowed down some, probably now within spitting distance of the speed limit—which Isaac considered a friendly suggestion more than a law.

Sucking firmly, she drew her mouth back up his full length; then, when he was out, she ran her tongue all over him, flicking over his glans with the point of her tongue, flattening it out and drawing it up and down his length. He groaned again, and the truck shimmied a little. Maybe it wouldn't be a great idea to draw this out much longer.

Changing her position on the seat, she pulled her left hand from between them and wrapped it around his cock. She sucked him into her mouth again, and now, with one hand around his base, the other massaging his balls, and her mouth and tongue drawing him in, she set her task to getting him off, hard and fast.

"Gah—fuck!! Baby, fuck!" he yelled, the sound bouncing off the glass surrounding them. His right hand clamped down around her neck. When she felt his body go taut, his hand curling tightly around her neck and throat, she sped up, sucking and licking, rubbing and squeezing, until he shouted unintelligibly and shot a stream of hot seed down her throat. She stayed on him, swallowing, until he was twitching spastically, and she felt him soften just barely.

Sitting back, she tucked him gently away and closed up his jeans and belt. When she looked up, he was staring at her with wonder. She grinned. "So…we there yet?"

"Jesus Christ, woman. I fuckin' love you."

~oOo~

With Isaac in a much more relaxed mood, the rest of the ride passed pleasantly. They talked about what kinds of furniture they might be looking for. Lilli suggested that they not look only for furniture, but smaller things, like curtains and linens. He was amenable. Lilli

68

smiled, feeling fairly certain that, just then, Isaac would be amenable to absolutely any suggestion she might have about anything.

When they got to Springfield, a community too big to be rightly called a town, but too small to be really considered a city, Isaac told her he wanted to deal with his business first. He didn't seem inclined to tell her what that business was, and Lilli didn't ask, both because she was naturally disinclined to pry and because she'd come to understand the way the MC world worked, and that she was not entitled to full disclosure. He dropped her off at a little bookshop in a strip mall, and Lilli went in to kill some time.

Wandering in bookstores, especially little used bookshops like this one, made Lilli feel close to her dad. As a student of languages, she was an avid reader. It was something she'd shared with him. She had a trove of wonderful memories about her dad and his books—knocking quietly on his study door, hearing his welcome, poring through his shelves to choose something new to read. Or the times when he'd find her, book in hand, and suggest she read it so they could talk about it. When she got older, sometimes it would be her doing the suggesting.

Her father could be a hard, uncompromising man. She knew it was true, and she saw it sometimes in the way he dealt with others. She saw it in the way he'd erased her mother from their memories after her suicide. But never with Lilli. With his daughter, he was gentle and loving, always. His expectations were high, and his rules firm, but even as strong-willed as Lilli was, she'd never felt a need to rebel against him. They were always a team. Losing him had left her unmoored.

In a storage locker in California, all of her father's books, and hers, were closed up in boxes stacked to the rafters. Their books and not much else. She hadn't wanted almost anything from that house after her father died. She had not seen the books in ten years, since she'd filled the boxes and taped them shut. It occurred to her that she might arrange to have them shipped to Signal Bend, to Isaac's—their—house. If she was settling in, she could have her father's books.

Isaac was going to have to build more bookcases.

She'd been in the shop for about two hours and was leafing through a decorating book from the 1950s when she heard Isaac come up behind her. He had a distinctive sound—the soft crinkle of his leather kutte, the vague metallic jingle of his wallet chain, the hefty chunk of his boots. She smiled as he put his hands on her waist and squeezed. His mouth at her ear, he whispered. "Hey, Sport."

"Hey yourself. Business handled?"

"You bet. Whatcha reading?" He looked over her shoulder at the vintage decorating book. "Baby, if that's your style, we can leave everything like it is."

She laughed. "No, I don't think it's my style. But the book is cool—historically speaking. I think I'm gonna buy it." She turned and added it to the stack she'd accrued. He eyed it skeptically.

"Damn, Sport. Good thing I didn't leave you alone longer." He picked up the double stack—only about twenty books—and they walked to the front counter.

~oOo~

"What about this? I like the leather, and the lines are clean. I don't like all the puffy crap." Lilli ran her hands along the back of a long, black leather sofa with squared-off angles.

Isaac eyed it critically. "The puffy crap is what makes a couch comfortable. You know, for sitting." He sat down. "I don't know, Sport. We'd need pillows or something on it if we wanted to lie down, and I hate those pussy little pillows."

Lilli sat next to him. The sofa seemed perfectly comfortable to her, and she liked the way it looked. She could imagine it in the room. "I can't believe that a man who's been sitting on a broken-down, wood-frame sofa for all this time is being so picky. Absolutely any sofa in here would be more comfortable than what's in the living room now."

He stood and waved her off the sofa, too. She knew what he was going to do; he'd been doing it with every piece of furniture they'd looked at, and then he'd put the kibosh on every piece of furniture they'd looked at. She rolled her eyes and stood back. The sofa in question was arranged with other pieces—a matching chair, a cocktail table, end tables with lamps—for display. Isaac pulled the cocktail table away and turned the sofa over, lifting it clean off the floor and setting it back down, to examine its underside. Damn, he was strong. Lilli felt a nice little tingle in her nethers.

"Jesus Christ. What a piece of shit. Lilli, the damn thing is *stapled together*. Staples! No way we're spending a thousand bucks on trash like this."

The salesman—Ron was his name—who'd accosted them as soon as they'd come into the store and who'd since been becoming increasingly agitated by Isaac's behavior, trotted over to them again. "Sir, please. Please. I have to ask you, again, to stop doing that."

Isaac stood to his full height, which was considerably higher than Ron could even reach. Ron stepped back, his retail indignation quelled by his fear of the huge biker looming over him. "Buddy, I know why you don't want me looking, because this shit is shit, but I'm not buying anything without knowing how it's made. We need furniture, so we have to shop. Go on now; I'll put it back the way I found it." Then he did exactly that, lifting the sofa and turning it over. Ron swallowed at the demonstration of strength and scurried off with a muttered, "Let me know if you need anything."

Isaac brushed his hands. "Good. Got rid of him."

"You enjoy that, did you?" He answered Lilli's question with a grin and a wink.

She stepped up to him and wrapped her arms around his waist. "Seriously, love. We're not going to find anything that's made as well as you could make it. You're an artisan. This is mass produced stuff."

"That's the problem then, isn't it? I should make it. What they charge for this crap is fuckin' offensive. I could make a couch like that, with good hardwood instead of this pine crap, and true joints, and premium leather, for half as much."

"In what spare time are you going to make all this furniture? You already have orders to fill."

72

"If you can live with the Lunden ass furniture for a while longer, I will find the time, Sport. I will build anything you want. But please let's not spend our money on this shit."

She loved the idea of the house being filled even more than it already was with Isaac's woodwork. For that, she thought she could be patient. "Okay. Let's shop for curtains and paint, though, okay? I have an idea for the kitchen."

~oOo~

They found a home and bath superstore, and Lilli loved that place. They filled two carts, with new curtains for the living room, the kitchen, and the dining room (a room that never got used, but had beautiful furniture in it already); new towels for the bathroom; and a lot of new cookware. Most of what was in the kitchen now, though interesting and quirky, was not very functional. Isaac, not being a cook, hadn't noticed. They also picked up some storage pieces so that Lilli could better organize cabinets and closets. Enjoying herself immensely, she realized that she felt like she was outfitting her own house. The thought made her feel light.

Their last stop was a paint store. Lilli wanted to redecorate the kitchen. She was surprised when Isaac started to resist. They were standing at the paint sample display, and Lilli was describing what she wanted to do. The kitchen was an old farmhouse kitchen, and she wasn't planning to gut it and start over, but she'd had some ideas about making it fresher.

Isaac listened, but Lilli could see he didn't like the idea. She continued describing it, though, and then, when she was done, he said, "I like the strawberries—my grandma..." Then, he shook his head a bit and said, "You know what? Forget that. Sounds beautiful. What do we need?"

God, he was trying so hard. He was talking about the strawberry-print fabric on the open-frame cabinet doors. Lilli thought it was quaint, but it was badly faded and frayed. She wanted to repaint the cabinets black and do a funky fabric in a bright color, like orange or grass green. She was finding her way, though, never having thought about decorating with any kind of focus before. She knew that Isaac's grandma was someone who'd been good to him, and that had been rare in his family. The fabric had to go—it was practically decomposing—but she had an idea.

"What if we paint the cabinets dark green and find a new fabric with strawberries. It could be like an homage to your grandma."

He grinned. "That's okay?"

"Sure. I don't want to make your house my house. I want to make it our house."

"That's what I want, Sport. Ours." He wrapped his hand around the back of her neck and pulled her in for a brief but intense kiss. Then they picked out new paint cards and went to have their colors mixed.

Not long later, they loaded the truck with the last of their purchases, and Isaac secured everything in the bed, while Lilli rolled the cart to the parking lot corral. They were headed to a late lunch, or early dinner, next, and then back home. As she approached the truck, Isaac's burner rang. He answered it as they climbed into the cab.

"Yeah, Show. S'up?" Within a few seconds, something about Isaac changed—he grew tense—and Lilli's attention to his call sharpened.

"Fuck! Is he...oh, fuck, Show. I'm there as fast as I can. Oh, fuck...yeah, just go. Get everybody. I'm comin'."

He turned to Lilli, his face livid with shock, rage, and grief. "Will's dead. His place was torched. It's a fuckin' inferno. We gotta get back, and now."

CHAPTER SEVEN

Isaac tore down Will's long gravel drive, kicking up rocks and dirt in a wild plume behind his Ford. Lilli was braced on the passenger side, one arm locked against the window, her other hand on the dash, as the truck bounced crazily, but he wasn't about to slow down. Black smoke rose up before them in several thick columns, and the air already shimmered. They came over the last rise, and he felt sick. He was too late. They were all too late. Jesus. Will.

Will Keller's property was of fair size, about half woods, most of the rest arable land, on which, this year, he'd cultivated soybeans. The harvest done and winter coming, the land was lying fallow now. Most of the property lay in a shallow valley, and his whole life, Isaac had loved clearing the rise he'd just cleared on the Keller drive, to see the vista of Will's white house and red outbuildings—all freshly painted every ten years, even in the hard times—the white gravel drive curving in, all of it surrounded by the vivid greens of the house lawn, the crops, the forest. Like a folk painting. He'd thought it the prettiest property in Signal Bend, and he wasn't the only one who did.

It was ablaze, all of it—the house, the outbuildings, Will's truck at the end of the drive, the white fence along the field line—an inferno of hellfire. The main engine for the Signal Bend Volunteer Fire Department was on the scene, but there was no way it held enough water to battle this blaze. In fact, since it wasn't pumping, Isaac knew it was dry already. He skidded to a stop and jumped out of the truck, not even looking at Lilli. He leapt into the bed and unlocked the truck box, yanking out his gear. All of the Horde, like most of the able-bodied men in town, were volunteer firefighters. Standing in the bed, he pulled his gear on as quickly as he could, then leapt back to the ground.

He found Show and Havoc near the engine. Other men in gear were trying to make a firebreak between the blaze and the woods, which they'd fucking need—and now—if they were waterless. Show was on a walkie; Isaac grabbed Havoc by the shoulder and yanked him around.

"Where's the other fucking tanker?"

Havoc's face was beet red, and soaked in sweat. Isaac could tell from the state of his gear that he'd been in the blaze. "They couldn't get it started! On its way now, and Show's putting assist calls in to Millview and Worden. But we're dry now, boss."

"What about the pond—we can siphon that!"

Havoc shook his head. "Tried. Not enough hose. We're just trying to keep it back from the woods now, until we get an assist."

"GOD DAMMIT!!" Isaac kicked the side of the engine over and over, until Havoc pulled him off.

Then he heard the screaming—a horrible, strenuous sound full of terror and pain—and he wheeled around. The livestock barn was well engaged.

"Jesus Christ, the horses! Nobody got to the horses?!" He grabbed a fire ax off the truck and ran full speed toward the barn.

"ISAAC! FUCK!" Isaac heard Show yelling, and he didn't care. He'd just had to leap over his friend's burned body. If he could save one life, even if it was only the life of one of Will's beloved horses, he was going to do it. This was all his fault. He'd pressured Will not to sell to Ellis. He'd leaned hard—so hard that Will, his friend since grade school, barely spoke to him anymore. *Had* barely spoken to him. Ellis had threatened Will's family, and he'd had to move wife and kids to Florida to keep them safe. And Isaac knew, no question, that this fire, this murder was Ellis. And that made it Isaac's fault.

Lawrence Ellis wanted Will Keller's property, and he wanted it now. Having decided to make a major move to take over all of the Midwest meth territory, he'd identified Signal Bend—remote from everything, including law—as a likely location for his mass-production plans. He wanted Will Keller's property specifically because of its unique physical features—particularly its situation in the valley and the high, dense canopy of its forested acres, perfect for obscuring a facility from air and satellite surveillance. Ellis wasn't advertising any of that, of course. In fact, as far as anyone knew, Ellis had never been within the state boundaries of Missouri and certainly not in Signal Bend. He worked everything through dummy companies and third and fourth party representatives. It had taken Bart a lot of concentrated hacking to connect all the seemingly random dots.

Ellis had started out working strictly legitimate channels to acquire Will's property. But Will wouldn't sell, even when the offer had gotten very significant. Though the town had lost a lot of its population and most of its small farmers to foreclosure or simple concession to reality, those who stayed did so for reasons far beyond money. The Kellers had farmed this land for generations. Will was every bit as proud of that history and his property as his father had been, and his grandfather, and his great-grandfather, and generations beyond that. He would not sell to anyone, ever. Certainly not to a random stranger from the city.

That truth had been iron-clad until Ellis set aside legitimate strategies and went for threats and extortion. First, he set a few of the weaker-spined townspeople on him, trying to flip meth cooks, like Jimmy and Meg Sullivan, to pressure him to sell. When Isaac put a stop to that, Ellis went for Will's family, starting with vague threats and elevating to dead pets and night prowlers before the Horde sent Liza and the kids to Florida.

Then things had gone quiet for several weeks, with the exception of the occasional unfamiliar, blacked-out SUV cruising the school bus routes, against which the Horde had set out patrols. They'd achieved a kind of uneasy stasis, waiting for Ellis's next move.

Which was now.

As he ran, Isaac pulled his mask over his face and hit the oxygen. He'd run at the front of the barn, which was not yet engaged. The door was padlocked. He did a heat check and then raised the axe and aimed a blow at the hasp. He got a spark, but no break. Still the horses were screaming, and even through the filter in his mask, he could smell cooking flesh. He raised the axe again and this time struck the wood behind the hasp. He broke the lock away in two more blows.

By then, he was no longer alone. Havoc, Len, and Bart were with him. Even Jimmy Sullivan was running up, setting his gear on as he came. The rest of the men were working the firebreak. Isaac and Len pulled the door open. The scene that met them made Isaac despair.

As soon as the door was open, Comet, Will's daughter's bay gelding, tore past them, streaming blood and fire. He'd broken open his stall, and his forelegs were all but destroyed, but fear kept him on them. He was completely on fire, tail to mane. Len, who bred horses—and whose best mare had foaled Comet—ran after him. Isaac watched as the horse, panicked and in agony, ran and halted, turned, reared, ran, and halted, over and over again, weakening but still seeking succor. Then Isaac saw Lilli walking steadily, calmly toward the poor beast, putting his rifle, the one he kept in his truck, to her shoulder. She stopped, took aim, and fired once. Comet dropped, his pain over. Another firefighter—Evan Lindel, just nineteen years old—ran up with a fire blanket. Len took it and threw it over the carcass, smothering the flames. Then he ran back to the barn.

All of it had gone down in a matter of seconds. Behind him, horses were still screaming and men were shouting. Isaac ran into the barn. The horse stalls were on the side of the barn that had not fully engaged. Isaac thought that Comet must have broken out of his stall before he'd caught fire, the panic driving him into greater danger. Sailor, Will's girl's old Welsh pony, was dead. Will's three remaining horses, though nearly feral with fear, seemed unharmed. Isaac, Len, and Bart grabbed the halters and leads from hooks outside their stalls and quickly, carefully led them to safety.

Sirens wailed from the road—finally, finally, the second tanker was on the scene, followed closely by the Worden VFD. Finally.

~oOo~

When it was over, Isaac walked to his truck and dropped to the ground, still in his gear, sitting up against the back tire. The destruction before him was apocalyptic. The house was a blackened husk, two walls standing, the charred interior of the big two-story clapboard house, the core of which had stood for nearly two hundred years, bared to the world, remnants of insulation and wiring dripping from the gaping ruin like blood from a wound. Every single outbuilding was destroyed, with all of Will's equipment. The livestock barn was nearly razed, only a few charred boards standing up like rotted teeth. The air was redolent with the stench of burnt goat flesh. Will had kept a smallish herd of Nubian goats, for their milk and for vegetation control. They'd been closed up in the far side of the barn, the side that had engaged first. They'd likely been dead before Isaac had even arrived on the scene.

Comet's body lay, still smoking faintly, in the yard. Will's body had been collected by the County Morgue. Sheriff Keith Tyler and a couple of his deputies were roaming around. It took a lot to gain the notice of the Sheriff's department in Signal Bend, but this conflagration had done it. Luckily, Tyler was a friend of the Horde, who took a cut of the meth profit in exchange for playing nice. But Isaac was not in the mood right now to schmooze with law. He closed his eyes and rested his head against his truck.

He heard footsteps approaching, but he didn't look. Expecting to hear Tyler's voice, he was surprised when Lilli sat right next to him, against him, and laid her head on his shoulder. He'd barely seen her since he'd jumped out of the truck, except when she'd put Comet down. He had no idea what she'd been doing.

"I love you. I'm sorry. I know you loved Will."

He turned and kissed her head. "Yeah. You okay?"

"I'm fine, love. I did what I could to help, but I was never anywhere near the fire." She held out a bottle of water. "You need this. Drink it now. And apparently part of the volunteer firefighting protocol is to cater the event, because like eight women came with food. That's weird, right?"

Despite his exhaustion, grief, and guilt, Isaac laughed. "Round these parts, Sport, that's how women help. They feed the men. I'm not hungry, though."

"No. Didn't think so. But drink that right now." He did as he was told. As soon as the cool wet hit his tongue, he was glad he did, and he finished the bottle in one go. Lilli took the empty. "You want another?"

"Nah, I'm good."

She was quiet for a minute, leaning on him. He felt a little better, like having her close to him let him siphon some strength or calm or something from her. He kissed her head again.

Wrapping her arms around his arm, she whispered, "You were really brave and stupid, running at the barn like that, not knowing if you had backup."

"That's me. Brave and stupid. Just what you want in the guy in charge, right?"

Lilli sat up and faced him. "Isaac. You're a great leader. I've worked with a lot of not-great leaders. I see how good you are every day. The way you're respected, the way you think, the way you know you need Show to remind you to slow down. The way you care. This town is lucky."

He huffed and shook his head. She was wrong. He opened his mouth to say so, but Tyler walked up then and stood in front of them. "Gotta talk to you, Ike." That goddamn nickname. His father's name. Isaac hated it. He wished he could eradicate it. Instead, he nodded, and he and Lilli stood.

"I'm going to go check on the horses—we need to find a place for them, Isaac. Is there somebody I should talk to about that?"

Without thinking about it, Isaac decided. "We'll take 'em." The horse barn hadn't been used in nearly twenty years, but it was solid. "Talk to Len about borrowing his rig. He's got a four-horse trailer. They'll need to be tranq'd after all this, though." He tossed Lilli his phone. "Can you call Delia Borden? She's the nearest vet. See if we can get her out here to check them out."

Lilli nodded and walked away, already scrolling through his contacts. Isaac turned back to Tyler.

"Don't know what I can tell you, Keith, but ask your questions."

Tyler was a typical law-enforcement type. Just under six feet, visibly strong, but with a burgeoning beer belly. His face was deeply lined, his skin permanently ruddy, his left arm darker than his right from too many hours stuck out the driver's side window in the sun. His crew cut was blond, getting duskier as grey began to creep in. He looked like the last guy who'd get in bed with an outlaw MC, but he'd always been sympathetic. "No questions, Ike. I already know I'm not gonna get answers. Nobody's telling me squat. But something big is going down around here. You and me, we got an arrangement, but Keller was murdered. There's not much I can do to keep things cool."

"I don't want law handling this problem, Keith. That's nothing but a mess—for everybody. But there will be justice. There's gotta be a way." Isaac looked out again over the desolation that had been his friend's home. He thought he knew what to do. He turned back to Tyler. "What if Will wasn't murdered?"

"Had a bullet through the back his head. Burned to a crisp. Entire property destroyed. How is that not murder-arson?"

"Any evidence of an accelerant?"

Tyler crossed his arms. "Ike. Bullet. Through the back of his head. Execution style."

"Only if it goes down in the record that way, right? Your M.E.—is he soft?"

"Ronconi? Yeah. For the right price. But shit, Ike. You understand what you're suggesting I do?"

Isaac stepped up close and looked down at Tyler. "You understand that you go down with us if we get Fed heat, right?"

Tyler stared up at Isaac for a long, hostile moment. Then he sighed and shook his head. "Covering up a fucking murder and arson. This shit is piled way too goddamn high."

"I agree. But we still got to shovel it."

~oOo~

Once Tyler and his crew were clear, the fire engines had headed back to their respective garages, and Dr. Borden had given the three remaining horses more or less clean bills of health and tranq'd them for transport, Len, Isaac, and Lilli loaded them into the trailer and brought them home.

Len had filled the fourth stall in the trailer with some supplies, including blankets, bales of sweet hay, and a bag of feed, so ultimately, Gertie, Flash, and Ebony had a nice place to bed down. It was dusty, but solid and comfy. They were all dopey and docile at first, and Len joined Lilli and Isaac for a beer before he left. When he left, he gave Lilli a long, hard hug. Isaac watched, not jealous, but interested. He knew Len liked Lilli, but he felt like he'd missed something that had deepened that vague affection into friendship. He thought about asking, but decided to table it for a quieter time. He and Lilli walked back to the stable to check again on the horses.

Gertie, Will's wife's aging dapple mare, was slamming into the stall wall, over and over, hitting with enough force each time that she made a hard grunt. Lilli went to her and started to open the stall. Just as Isaac was about to stop her—warn her never to get into a stall with a distressed horse—Gertie screamed and threw her head up, and Lilli left the latch closed and took several steps back. Gertie resumed her slamming.

"Hey, missy girl, I just want to help. Not gonna hurt you." Standing perfectly still, but looking right at the mare, Lilli hit exactly the right soothing pitch. She kept talking, uttering gentle nonsense. It had to be instinct. Lilli was a girl from the suburbs who'd never had a pet before the kittens who were probably wreaking havoc in their house now. But Gertie was responding, her slams slowing. When she stopped and dropped her head, Lilli took a step toward her. Gertie raised and turned her head, giving Lilli a decidedly suspicious consideration, but she didn't spook this time. Lilli took another step. Gertie tossed her head and then settled. Another step—almost to the stall door now.

Then Gertie took her own step and dropped her head over the door. Lilli eased her hand slowly up and held it out. Gertie nosed it and then nickered.

"You're in, Sport. You're in."

Lilli took the last step. Gertie pressed her head against Lilli's chest and gave her a shove. Lilli looked at Isaac, worried. Isaac winked. "That's good. She just hugged you."

Grinning, Lilli stepped back to the stall and loved on Gertie for a long time, rubbing her nose and neck, cooing in her ear. Isaac was stunned and impressed. His woman, the horse whisperer. Who'd never ridden a horse.

Flash and Ebony, both younger and, frankly, stupider than Gertie, seemed to have recovered completely from almost being burned to death. Both had their heads buried deeply in their feed buckets. Isaac checked on them both, blanketed them for the night, then sat down on a saddle rack and waited for Lilli and Gertie to say good night.

~oOo~

Isaac stood in the shower and let the water stream over his aching body. The nearly-scalding water soothed him. He braced his hands on the tile wall and let his head drop.

He heard the shower curtain rustle, the rings jingle, and then Lilli's body replaced the shower stream on his back. Her arms encircled his waist, and she took his balls and cock in her hands. He was soft at first, but the feel of her talented, beautiful hands on him turned him to steel, despite the pain and loss flowing through his veins. Not changing his position, he opened his eyes to watch her hands on him. She laid her head on his back and jacked him off expertly, milking and pulsing, squeezing and teasing, her fingers stroking the underside of his balls in exactly the way she knew he liked. He came fast, hard, and explosively, his semen painting spikes on the aqua tiles. When he was done, he rested his forehead on the wall. Lilli pressed a sweet, lingering kiss to his back and left the shower. Neither of them had said a word.

She was waiting for him in bed when he came into the room. She'd turned the covers down for him, and he dropped his towel to the floor and slid in, naked, next to her. She rolled to her side, and he pulled her close to his chest. She was also naked, but he made no move to start something, and neither did she. When he kissed her shoulder, she put her hand up and laid it on his head. Then he put his head on his pillow and closed his eyes.

CHAPTER EIGHT

Lilli woke with a start, sitting bolt upright, her heart pounding. The dream evaporated quickly, as it always did. She looked over, expecting to see Isaac watching her, as he always was when she woke like this. But she was alone in the bed. She sat still for a second and listened, trying to hear if he was in the bathroom or the kitchen. The house was silent. Even the kittens were quiet.

She got up and pulled a pair of sweats and a t-shirt out of her dresser. She went through the house and checked. Isaac wasn't inside. She opened the front door—oh, shit it was cold—and went back to slide into her sneakers and grab a jacket. When she went onto the porch, she saw the lights on in Isaac's woodshop. She stepped off the porch and crossed the yard.

She could hear that he was working with one of his power tools: the specific high scream of metal penetrating wood. But it was deep dark, hours before dawn. He almost never left her alone in bed, and he never worked in the middle of the night. She opened the door.

He was standing at his lathe, turning a piece of dark wood. Bare-chested, in jeans, goggles on his face. Lilli knew better than to come up on him unawares, so she walked to the corner of his worktable and waited for him to see her. She'd often watched him work since she'd moved in. Isaac enjoyed her company in his shop, but he tended to turn deeply inward as he worked. If she asked a question, he would answer it—or, more often, he would begin to answer, then fade out as his focus on his work overtook his attention to her question. So she still didn't know much about what he did, but she loved to watch nonetheless. It was fascinating, and she was in awe of the beauty those big, rough hands could create.

He saw her when he paused the lathe and looked up to select a different tool. He turned off the lathe and pulled off the goggles, setting them on the table. "Hey, Sport. What're you doing awake?" As she walked to him and he put his hands on her waist, he asked, "Did you dream?"

"Yeah, but I'm out here checking on you." She brushed wood shavings from the hair on his chest. "Kinda weird time to be working, isn't it?" When he only shrugged, she asked, "What ya makin'?"

He turned his head and regarded the wood in the lathe. It was a long piece, maybe four feet, about three inches in diameter at its widest point. Isaac had turned several distinct and seemingly unrelated shapes into it. "I have no idea. I'm just turning. No plan." Setting her away, he removed the wood from the lathe and held it in his hands, looking down at it like he didn't know what it was or where it had come from. Lilli was worried.

"You want to talk, love? Maybe go back to the house and start some coffee?" Still looking at the wood, he shook his head. Then, when she reached out to put her hand on his arm, he jerked from her touch. That surprised her—in fact, it scared her. "Isaac?"

"Go back inside." His voice was low, and still he had not looked up. Lilli saw the wooden dowel in his hands begin to shake, just slightly. She'd been around enough freaked out soldiers in her day to have a damn good idea what was going on. She squared her shoulders and cast a studied glance around the room, making sure she knew where things were. Things she might need.

She spoke steadily, keeping an even pitch. "If you don't want to talk, that's cool, love. I'll just sit and watch you. I love to watch you work. But I'm not leaving you, Isaac. I'm staying put."

His head came up then, fast. He glared at her, his eyes red and wet—and angry. He laughed, and the sound was fearsome. "You're not leaving me? You were leaving me *yesterday*, Sport. YESTERDAY. You were out the fuckin' door, remember?" He raised the heavy dowel in one hand and brandished it like a club. Lilli darted a quick glance to his rack of gouges and took a small step back. "Do you know what I came in here to do? To start making you furniture. The furniture you need so you'll stay. I was going to make you a couch." He stopped waving the dowel and took a long look at it. Then he laughed again, bitterly. "I don't know what part of any couch this piece of shit would be. Fucked that up, too."

Grasping the wood in both hands again, he turned and swung, his hair flying and his muscles rippling with the effort. He brought it down, full force, on the worktable, about two feet from where Lilli stood. She twitched, but stood her ground, tensed to defend herself if she had to. He slammed the piece—his club, now—down again, and again, until chunks of wood began to shave off. Then, the need that was clearly consuming him still unsatisfied, he roared and spun. Charging at the shelves on which he stored his art show inventory, and roaring incoherently, he bludgeoned the vases, boxes, animals, and flowers that were his meal ticket. Lilli did not intervene. He would soon regret this, but he needed to do it. When he had not slowed after more than a full minute of destruction, she leaned over to his tool rack and pulled out a long, straight blade with a sharp, beveled point. In case she needed to disable him. Otherwise, she stood and waited.

Finally he stopped and, his chest heaving, soaked in sweat, he turned to her again. "You *should* leave me. You should get out. Get away. Because this place is dead. It's not even dying. It's just fuckin' dead. People keep looking to me to save it, but I'm the one pulled the goddamn plug. I'm the one that decided to help the fuckin' cookers instead of running 'em out on a rail. That was *my* idea. Took forever to get everybody on board, too. I brought it to the table, I leaned on my brothers to get it to pass. Meth put us on Ellis's radar. Meth got Will killed. It's all on my head. And here I stand. None of it's fuckin' touched me." He dropped the splintered wood. "Jesus Christ, Sport, we were in a fucking *paint store* while somebody was putting a bullet in Will's head and setting his whole fucking history on fire! We were *shopping*." He slid to the floor against a tall metal shelving unit. It rattled at first, threatening to topple on him, but then settled. He drew up his knees and rested his head on his arms. Lilli put the blade down and went to him.

She kicked the club away and knelt in front of him, laying her hands on his arms. "Isaac." She said nothing but his name. When he didn't respond, she said it again. He looked up. She knew the look. Haunted.

"I love you. I'm not going anywhere. I'm in. I'm here. Because we talked. You talked to me, and we worked things through. I'm not going to say we need to do the same for you right now. You'll talk when you're ready. For now, you can listen. Because I am here. You're not on your own. Not in this house, not in this town, not in this fight." She brushed his hair back from his face; he was soaking wet. "You didn't bring crystal to town, Isaac. You just figured out a way to make it do some good, balance out all the bad it does. You kept the people in town, people working at Marie's and at the feed store, and the hardware store. You did something good with something bad."

His expression had eased some as she spoke, and she turned and sat at his side, hooking her arm around his. "What happened to Will is not your fault." He flinched and huffed, but she held onto him and pressed her point. "It's not. It's Ellis. It's the scum he hired to get it done. You were right to pressure Will not to sell—and he knew you were. Otherwise, he would have sold anyway."

They sat quietly side by side on the floor of Isaac's woodshop. Lilli looked around. He'd done a lot of damage in those few minutes. She thought the damage he was doing to himself, inside, was worse. But she knew he would be deaf to anything more she said. So she sat with him and waited.

The sky outside the windows was just beginning to lighten from deep black to smoky grey before he spoke. "I can't do it, Lilli. I can't. I'm not good enough. Not strong enough. Not smart enough. I'm nobody special. I can't fight this guy. I'm gonna get people killed. Already have."

She hadn't been sleeping, but she had been deep in thought, thinking about the fire, and Ellis, and Isaac. And her dad, strangely enough. Shooting Comet had called to mind the one and only time she'd killed a deer. That time, she had not shot cleanly with her first shot, and the buck, like Comet, had been screaming and struggling. Her second shot had been true, but the experience had upset her very much. She loved her father, and she'd loved the way he'd been patient with her, had trusted her to make it right, but she'd never wanted to hunt again after that. Her father had taught her well that a gun's only purpose was death. Lilli found no joy in pulling a trigger—ironic, then, that she'd chosen a career as a soldier.

She stirred and sat straight when Isaac spoke. Now, she swung around to face him. He was staring at the floor in front of him. "Isaac. Enough. Look at me." She grabbed his beard and lifted his head. "You keep saying *I*. You really are an arrogant bastard, you know that?" He jerked his head, but she kept hold of him. "What about Show, and Len, and all the other guys you call brother? What about them? They're lined up to fight with you. They all agreed to run the town with you. They agreed to the meth. They are there to fight Ellis with you. It's their town, too. You're not a monarch, Isaac. You're the guy at the head of the table, but the rest of the chairs are filled, too. You are not alone."

Isaac stared at her. Lilli stared back. She let go of his chin and traced the line of the scar running up his left cheek. That scar, from just below his nose all the way to his temple, was something she'd never asked about. She'd simply accepted it as a part of him. She loved it, in fact. "How'd you get this, love?"

Blinking at the change of subject, Isaac took her hand away from his cheek and kissed it. "Long story."

She wouldn't push. Not her style. "Okay. You think you're ready to go in now?" She started to stand, but Isaac kept hold of her hand.

"My dad."

Lilli sat back down. "What?"

"My dad did it. He was a big drinker. A drunk. And, you know—a nasty son of a bitch. I was…twenty-two. I'd gotten a lot bigger than him by then, and he hated it. I'd had my top rocker about a year, and I voted against him at the table. First time. Swung the vote against him. Didn't do it to piss him off. Did it because he was wrong. That pissed him off worse, I guess."

He cleared his throat and blew out a stilted laugh. Staring at his hands, he continued. "It's weird. I've never told this story. Anybody else who'd care was already there. I'm sitting at the bar, drinking with the guys, starting to think about grabbing a girl. My old man's at the other end of the bar, watching me. All of a sudden, he's off the stool, charging me, yelling *fucking pussy pretty boy!* and he's on me, yanking me off my stool onto the floor—catches me off guard and off balance, and I just fall right down—and he's got his switchblade. He just...slices me. Never manage to put up any kind of fight. Doesn't hurt at first—shock, I guess—but blood's gushing like somebody turned on a faucet in my face. The guys pull him away, and he shakes them off. He stands over me, says, *see how they like you now.*" Isaac laughed again. "Then he just went back to his Wild Turkey, left me lying there, holding my face together with my hands."

Lilli was speechless. She rose up on her knees and kissed the scar. But Isaac wasn't done. "Show took me to get stitched up. I was staying at the clubhouse then, and when I got back my old man was sitting at the bar reading the morning paper. He gave me a look, then went back to the sports page, like nothing. I grabbed his fucking bald head in my hands and slammed it into the bar until he was unconscious. Nobody stopped me. Fucker never touched me again."

Because there was simply nothing to say, Lilli didn't try. Instead, she pulled on Isaac's legs, straightening them along the floor, and she opened his arms. She climbed onto his lap and held him close. After a moment where he was completely passive, as though he were not entirely in his body, his arms came around her, and he laid his head on her shoulder. They sat like that until dawn broke. Finally, Lilli got him to come back into the house. She took him to bed and held him while he slept.

~oOo~

Exhaustion had finally really claimed him, and Isaac slept hard that morning. Lilli lay with him as long as she could, but when she heard one of the horses—she thought it might be Gertie—raising a fuss, she slid out of bed and got dressed. Leaving a note on her pillow to let him know where she'd gone, she pulled on her boots and jacket and hurried to the barn.

It was Gertie yelling, but as soon as Lilli opened the doors and came in, she settled and dropped her head over the door, making a series of chuffing noises. Lilli went to her and rubbed her neck. She knew nothing about horses. They didn't scare her, but she wasn't comfortable not knowing things. She would have preferred to be out here with Isaac, so she could ask questions about what to do. When and how much to feed them. When to put them outside. *Where* to put them outside. The back door of the barn opened to a small enclosure which itself opened to a larger grassy area. Isaac had called it a paddock. She assumed that was the horse yard. But she didn't like to make assumptions about thousand-pound animals.

She looked around. She understood the halter and lead. She'd helped Len yesterday, after they'd led the horses away from the fire. He'd shown her how to halter them properly, and she'd helped tie their leads off, then gotten them water. She was touched to see the way Len cared about the horses. He'd been devastated by what had happened to the horse who'd come running out of the barn—Comet. After the blaze was out, he'd knelt on the ground in his gear, next to the smoldering body, and when he'd stood and came toward her, she could see he'd been crying. She'd hugged him. She hadn't thought about it; she'd just done it. And he'd cried hard. This beefy biker with tattoos from his fingers all the way up to his jaw. Lilli, herself broken up about what she'd had to do, had been deeply moved by the tenderness of his grief.

She gave Gertie a pat and went to check out the other two—both black, one bigger, with a white stripe down his nose—Flash—the other entirely dark—Ebony. They were both friendly, if a little more energetic than her Gert. She laughed to herself when she realized that she'd just thought of the spotted grey mare as hers. She should be careful about that. The horses did not belong to them.

Lilli explored the barn and the enclosures beyond it, trying to decide whether she should let the horses out. The barn was empty of anything they hadn't brought in from Len's trailer. There were shelves and racks that looked purposeful, but had nothing stored on or in them. Once she did a lap around the paddock and ascertained that the fence was solid and the gates closed, she went in, picked up Gert's halter, and strapped it on.

As she was opening Gert's stall, Isaac spoke up behind her. "She should go out last, Sport."

Lilli turned. He looked better. He was leaning on the side of the open barn door, in his customary jeans, boots, black button shirt, and leather jacket. No kutte; he didn't wear it at home. His hair was braided. It looked wet—he must have jumped in the shower.

96

"What?"

"Flash and Ebbie are young. They get antsy, don't like to get left behind. You put Gertie out first, they'll think they're missing out, and they'll be harder to control. Gert's a patient old lady. She'll sit and wait her turn." He walked to her and kissed her cheek. "Morning."

"Morning. Do they need to be on the leads?"

"You want to be in control of a horse when you're in a tight space like this, so yeah. But take the halter off, not just the lead, when you release them. Want help?" He nodded toward Flash.

"Nope. I got it." She went over and haltered Flash. Isaac walked out into the corral and climbed the fence. As Lilli led Flash out, she saw that he was filling a big water tank just inside the corral. She released Flash, and he tore off, bucking as he did a circuit around the enclosure.

When all three horses were out, the youngsters racing around, Gertie wandering off to eat grass, Isaac and Lilli sat on the fence and watched.

"You okay this morning, love?" Lilli studied Isaac's profile as he watched the horses.

"Better. Not okay. I need to call Liza, and then I gotta get to town." He turned to her. "I'd like you to come. Breakfast—well, lunch, I guess—at Marie's, give everybody time to talk to me about what happened. Then the clubhouse, so we can figure out our move."

"Yeah. Okay, of course." She put her hand on his where it gripped the fence rail. "I'm with you, Isaac. You're not on your own. I love you."

Still looking out over the paddock, he hooked his fingers with hers.

CHAPTER NINE

Isaac didn't know how he was going to make this call. He knew Liza had already been officially informed; Tyler called to let him know they'd reached her early in the morning. That didn't make what he had to do any easier, though—in fact, it might make it harder. She would blame him, she *should* blame him, and he would be calling in the midst of her first fury.

But he couldn't put it off. He had to do it right. He owed it to Will, and to the family he'd left behind, to do it right.

He sat at the dining room table and stared at his phone. He didn't know why he'd come into this room. He rarely came into this room. It had been the living room when he'd been growing up and for all the generations before that, as far as he knew, but he'd switched the living and dining rooms when he'd taken the house over. He'd had no need for a big dining space, and it was just more convenient for the living room, where the TV was, to be next to the kitchen, where the beer was. Plus, the fireplace was in there, and he liked that better in the living room than the dining room.

The furniture in this room was heavy, ornate, and very antique. The sideboard had actually come over with his immigrant ancestors, and it was carved and turned, stained so dark it was all but black. The table and chairs, chunky and rough-hewn, were handmade and stained to match by a grandfather a few times removed. He'd been surprised when Lilli told him she didn't want to replace these pieces, but he'd been glad for it. He wasn't entirely sure why; it was ponderous furniture. But he felt like it would be some kind of sacrilege to remove a piece that had stood under this roof for as long as that roof had been standing.

Lilli came in from the kitchen and leaned on the newel post of the staircase that bisected the house. "Can I do anything, love?"

What could she do? She had never even met Liza. But he loved her for asking, nonetheless. "No. I got it. We need to get moving when I'm done, though. You gonna be ready?"

She walked in and kissed his cheek, her hand on his shoulder. "I'll jump in for a super-quick shower and be ready in ten. That good?"

"Perfect. Thanks, Sport." It would help to have some privacy for this. When Lilli headed down the hall toward the bathroom, Isaac took a deep breath and dialed Liza's cell.

She answered on the second ring, and she jumped right in. "What is it that you could possibly want now, Isaac?" Her voice was thick and raw. He tried to imagine what her morning had been like, and he found that he could—some semblance of it, at least. He'd imagined losing Lilli often enough.

"I'm so sorry. God, I'm sorry, Lize."

"Are you? Are you really? What is it you're sorry for, exactly? Leaning on Will not to sell? Using your friendship to guilt him into doing what was right for you instead of what was right for us? Making him think you'd have his back? Where were you, I wonder, when he was dying and our life was burned down? At his back?"

No. He'd been in Springfield with Lilli, picking out curtains. He couldn't tell her that. "Liza, you know how much I love Will. And

100

you know how much Will loves that place. I…I'm just sorry. I want to know how I can help you."

On the other side of the call, wherever Liza was in Florida, whatever she was doing, she was laughing, a bitter, angry shatter of sound. "You're gonna be sorry, yeah. Got a call from Mac Evans, not five minutes after I got off the phone with the Sheriff. That interested party who's been trying to get the place? Made a new offer. Upped it a hundred grand. Guess that's what Will was worth. Blood money. I'm taking it."

"Jesus, Liza, no. Let me try—"

She cut him off. "Try what? To get the rest of us killed? I'm not fighting that shit. Nothing for us there now. I'm having Will shipped down here, and Signal Bend can kiss my ass. And as for how you can help me, well, that's easy. You can die in a fire."

The line went dead.

Isaac dropped the phone and laid his head on the table. For long moments, he didn't even think; his head was white noise. When thoughts returned, they were bleak. So much of what she'd said was right. It *was* his fault. Fighting Ellis had put Will in danger. Continuing to fight him would put his family in danger.

But selling now? If she sold now, Will's death was for nothing. *Nothing.* And Signal Bend was lost.

Signal Bend was lost.

He was still sitting with his head on the table when Lilli came back from her shower. "Isaac? What's wrong?" He opened his eyes to see her squatting at his side, her damp hair pulled back into a ponytail.

101

He felt the light, loving weight of her hand on his back. Jesus, she was beautiful. And she was with him. He sat up and pulled himself together.

"Ellis upped the offer. Liza's selling. We gotta go."

~oOo~

The lot at Marie's was packed, as Isaac had known it would be. Most of the townspeople were there, as were Len and Show. Isaac and Lilli were late, but he knew no one would leave until he'd gotten there. It was the way of things here. When big shit went down, people met at Marie's. Before the Horde ran things, they'd met here to talk to the Mayor, whoever that had been. Before Marie's, the story was that they'd met at St. John's, across the street. But Isaac was sure that people had congregated somewhere in times of trouble for as long as there had been people to do so.

Details about his call with Liza had clicked in Isaac's head as they'd ridden to Marie's. He went into the diner in a scarlet rage. The room went quiet, all eyes turning to him, and he scanned the room until he lit upon Mac Evans. He stalked toward the smarmy, shithead realtor and dragged him out of his booth by his pink-and-gold necktie. Evans squawked, but Isaac paid him no heed. He turned and started back toward the front door. He was going to kill the asshole, but he wasn't going to do it within splatter range of Marie's pie case.

Showdown moved into Isaac's path. "What's up, boss?"

"Step aside, Show. Mac and I have business." The weasel at the other end of the silk noose whimpered and puled. Show stepped aside and then fell in behind them. He caught movement at his periphery; Len was joining their little caravan. That was fine. They could watch, long as they didn't get in his way.

Lilli was still standing just inside the door, blocking it. She gave him a meaningful look—she was asking if he knew what he was doing. He nodded, and she backed off, clearing his way. He knew exactly what he was doing. He was going to rip Evans' arm off and beat him to death with it.

He dragged Evans to the side of the building and threw him against the wall. Released from Isaac's twisting grip on his tie, Evans gasped and took great swallows of air, his color fading from vivid puce to a pastier, greying pink. When he had enough breath to speak, he rasped, "What the *fuck*, Ike? What the *fuck*?"

Isaac punched him in the mouth with a fist full of heavy silver rings. Evans squawked again, his hands coming up to cover his split lips. Isaac leaned in close and snarled, "What were you told about carrying offers on the Keller place? What was our deal?"

Mac Evans was a toad who thought of no one but himself, but he was town, born and bred, and that had kept him alive. Ellis had found himself a patsy in Evans, and had used him in his early, most straightforward attempts to buy the Keller property. The Horde had pressed Evans hard to get him to flip back. In the end, it had been Show's offer of friendship and protection from the club that had done the job. Isaac had a strong kind of hate for Evans, who'd profited from dozens of foreclosures in and around town; he'd preferred force. But force hadn't worked. Neither, apparently, had friendship, not well enough.

"Jesus, Ike! It's my damn job!" The words were barely intelligible over the swelling mush of his mouth and the hands that covered it. But Isaac heard, and cocked his fist again. As Evans drew back into the wall, Show grabbed Isaac's wrist.

"Boss! You want to bring us into the loop here?" At Show's interruption, Isaac wheeled on him. Evans took the opportunity of Isaac's divided attention to make a feeble break for it, but Len grabbed him by the collar and launched him back into the wall. Then he leaned his tattooed hand on Evan's shoulder, holding him in place.

When Evans started to try to say something, Len slapped him hard upside his head. "Mouth shut, asswipe."

Isaac wanted to beat Show's head in for getting in the middle here. Undermining him. But it was his job to be the cooler head. Searching his own hot head and racing heart for some kind of control, Isaac found it and settled. He took a couple of deep, calming breaths and explained about his call to Will's furious new widow.

Show nodded and turned to Evans. "That's bad, Mac. Breaking trust with us. That's the kind of bullshit gets you hurt." He looked back at Isaac. "What do you need from us, Isaac?"

Isaac straightened his kutte. Waving toward the restaurant, he said, "I gotta get in there and deal with that. He needs a lesson. And we need to stop that deal from going through. Take him to the Room." He turned to Len. "Get Havoc, tell him bring the van. It's time to play."

Len nodded. "End result?"

"A lesson. Make sure he learns it, but don't end him. Anybody does that, it'll be me." He socked Evans in the gut to emphasize his point, then left Len and Show to deal with him.

The quiet was thick and eerie in the overflowing restaurant. The only sounds were Marie, Dick, and the couple of girls they had working with them keeping the coffee flowing. Lilli was sitting at the counter, drinking her sweet, milky brew from one of the old-fashioned heavy stoneware cups, white with two thin blue stripes, that had been the tableware at Marie's for its entire existence. He put his hand on his old lady's back and nodded to Marie, who, like everybody else in the joint, had been watching him since he'd come back in. "I get a cup?"

Marie smiled. "Comin' right up, Ike. Get ya anything to eat?"

"Maybe in a minute, hon, thanks." He turned and put his back to the counter. This wasn't the first time he'd been in a position to face the town in this way, but it was, by an order of magnitude, the most serious. Even the fucking mayor was sitting there, looking at Isaac, waiting for—for what? Wisdom? Solace? Salvation? Well, he had none to offer.

He felt a hand patting his back and turned to take the coffee Marie held out to him. Her smile was warm and confident. Everybody thought he would have the answer. He smiled his thanks, took a long swallow of the hot, bitter, black liquid, and set the cup on its saucer. When he turned around, Lilli put her hand on his where it gripped the counter.

He cleared his throat and started, not sure what he would say. "I know you're all here because you heard what happened to the Keller place, and what happened to Will, rest his soul." Most everybody

105

bowed their heads at that. A few murmured prayers. These were a godly folk, even those who supported themselves by cooking crystal meth. Isaac didn't much go in for religion, but he could respect the good that common bond did for a community. "I expect you got questions. I don't know if I have answers, but I'll tell you what I can, and then I got some things of my own to say."

First, he reported what had happened, to get the record straight and clear of the warping ways of gossip. As if he were covering a news story, he spoke dispassionately and without extraneous detail, but he gave a full report.

It was the mayor, Martin Fosse, who spoke out first. Mayoring a town like Signal Bend wasn't a gig that paid a full-time salary. Fosse owned Fosse's Finds, one of the Main Street 'antique' shops. "This is bigger than us, Ike. How the hell are we supposed to fight off the kind of evil that does what it did to the Kellers?"

There was a undulating wave of approving sound at the question.

"First off, you're right. No mystery that what happened at Will's wasn't an accident. Outside these walls, though, that's not the story. You know why we don't need outside eyes on our town, and I know you know better. We keep to ourselves, right?" As one, the people listening nodded. "But in here, you know, and I'll be straight.

"You all know we've had this trouble moving in on us for a while now. We're moving fast as we can, doing all that we can to keep it at bay, and a lot of you have been helping with that, riding patrols and whatnot. Well, we've been doing a good job, and now our enemy is coming at us harder. But don't think of him as evil. He's not the Devil. He's just a man. An asshole with reach and pull, but just a man. We need to stand strong. Bad as it is to lose Will—and everybody here knows who Will Keller was—*is*—to me"—his voice cracked, and he took a breath and cleared his throat. This was not the time to give in to grief. "We can't let it shake us. That's what our enemy wants. Stand strong. Come to the Horde if you need help. We stand together. I know it's askin' a lot, but I'm askin'."

Jimmy Sullivan, the cooker who'd first flipped for Ellis, still wearing a brace on the wrist Isaac had broken the night he'd found out, stood and faced him now, his Adam's apple bobbing. "What's that mean, Ike? How do we stand together? Seems like you're just askin' us to make ourselfs a easier target. Maybe it's time we take a seat and let it play out." Another rumble, this one lower, and not as obviously in agreement. Isaac turned a hot glare on the little rat until he put his bony ass back in his seat.

Taking a beat to secure control over himself again, Isaac answered the challenge. "We stand together by watching out for each other. The Horde need to meet today and work out some details, but we need to beef up patrols, and we need to stick together. Nobody's alone. Until we get a handle on what we're facing, nobody's alone. Ever. You see a car or truck you don't recognize, you call me, Showdown, or Len. Don't send your kids to the bus without an escort. Watch out for each other, keep each other safe. And when we call, you come. You come, and you come armed."

The front door opened, and Show came in. Isaac met his look, and Show nodded. Evans was handled. Show took a step to the side and leaned back against the wall next to the door, his arms crossed over his broad chest.

"Years now, we've been keeping this town rolling by will power and devil's bargains. A good friend and a wise man told me that after times of trouble, you look around and see who's left. Those are the people you know will stand and fight. Well, we're who's left. Most of us sitting here live in the houses we were born in. Hell, some of you sleep in the *beds* you were born in. This is the only place we have that. It's only here, and we give a shit about keeping it. If we were going to fold, we'd have folded when everybody else did. I'm askin' you to remember that and to keep fighting for what's ours. Our birthright. Our legacy. And I'm tellin' you that the Horde will fight for this town to the last man."

~oOo~

It was almost an hour after he was done speechifying before he, Lilli, and Show were able to get out of there. Show grabbed his arm as they were walking to Isaac's bike. "I'm going to follow Holly home, boss. I'll meet you at the clubhouse."

Isaac turned. When he'd said nobody alone, he'd meant it. He wasn't leaving Show to ride back from his place on his own. "We'll ride with you."

"Nah, I'll be fine. Holly'll flip if she's got both of us on her tail."

Holly needed to get up over herself, and, in Isaac's opinion, Showdown needed to get his old lady in hand. Show was a tough son of a bitch, but he liked a quiet home, and he gave his wife, prone to histrionics and ill-suited to club life, wide leeway to keep her drama down. "We'll ride with you, Show. Statement, not a question. Holly will deal." Isaac pulled his burner out of his pocket. "And I'm callin'

108

Erik to meet us there, keep with her and the kids today. I'll have Dom ride with him, then he can follow us back."

Show and Isaac stared at each other for a couple of seconds, then Show nodded and turned to his bike. Isaac handed Lilli her helmet; she took it and then grabbed his hand. She'd been quiet all the time they were in Marie's. Every time he'd turned to her, he'd met her eyes. She'd seemed thoughtful, considering.

"Hey. You did great in there. I'm a little in awe of you right now."

He pulled her close and leaned down to kiss her. "I had no fucking clue what I was gonna say. Wouldn't be able to repeat it if I tried."

"Well, then, I'm a lot in awe of you, because I don't think you could have said anything better." She ran her fingers through his beard and then onto his cheek to trace his scar. It felt strange that she knew its story. Strange, but good. "Hey, can we talk before you go into the Keep? Is there a few minutes for that?"

He turned his head to kiss her palm, then stepped back and put his helmet on. "Sure, Sport. What's on your mind?"

Fastening her own helmet she said, "I'll tell you when we get there." He nodded, and they mounted up and followed Show and Holly.

~oOo~

Isaac took Lilli's hand and led her into the clubhouse, Show and Dom coming in behind them. Most of the Horde were in the Hall,

109

waiting. Isaac scanned the room and didn't see Len, Havoc, or Dan. He turned to Vic, sitting at the bar next to Bart, who was on his big laptop. "Len and Hav in the Room?"

Vic nodded. "Yeah, boss. Want me to get 'em?"

"Yeah. Tell 'em to put their friend on ice for awhile. We're in the Keep in ten. Where's Dan?"

Vic stood up, on his way to the Room. "Ain't seen him yet."

Bart looked up from his screen. "Want me to call him?"

Isaac nodded. "Yeah. Don't like strays right now. You find anything?"

"Some. You want it before the Keep?"

"Just bring it to the table." Isaac pulled gently on Lilli's hand and headed toward his office.

Once there, he led her to the couch and they sat down together. He was curious; Lilli had been quiet and thoughtful since they'd left the house. He thought he understood; this was his show, and she was learning that it would take her some time to earn the regard of the town. That she would earn it Isaac had no doubt, but until then, she was an outsider, and she knew to be careful where she laid down her two cents on town business.

He picked up her hand and pulled it onto his lap. "What's going on in that head, Lilli?"

"Do you know what the offer on Will's place is? How much, I mean?"

The question threw him completely. At first he just sat there dumbly, not sure what she even meant by asking and certainly not sure why it mattered so much it earned a detour from the real work of the day. Finally, he just answered. "I don't know. It's high—way over market. Last one was about $420,000. Liza said he upped a hundred, so $520,000, I guess. Way too rich for the Horde to match."

"I can match it. I can beat it, if necessary."

No, *now* Isaac was thrown completely. "What the fuck are you talking about, Sport?"

Lilli took her hand from his and got up from the couch. She walked the few feet to the bookcase and just stared down at it for a few seconds. She couldn't have found anything interesting in a bunch of binders and Harley guides. Still with her back to him, she said, "When my dad died, he left me a big life insurance policy. He didn't have many debts, and the house was free and clear. I couldn't stand dealing with almost any of it without him, so I sold the house and most of the contents. All the money—the insurance payout, the house sale, all of it, has been sitting for ten years. I haven't touched a cent. There's about a million and a half in it now."

"What?" Isaac stood. He didn't know what to think. Here was a chance to save the town, or at least to strengthen its position markedly, and his old lady was serving it up to him on a silver platter—no, on a fucking platinum platter. Diamond-encrusted. His stinkin' rich old lady. How had he not known this? Why had she not told him? It was a big secret to keep. Too big.

Lilli hadn't responded to his one-word question. She hadn't even turned around. Isaac was beginning to think that there was new trouble between them. He walked to her and put his hands on her shoulders. "Lilli, fuck. Why didn't you tell me? Why keep it from me? Do you not trust me?"

At that she turned, and he saw her eyes shimmering. When she blinked, a tear escaped each eye, and he brushed them away with his thumbs. She shook her head. "It's not that at all. I just…I never think about that money. I hate that money. I only have it because my dad died. It always felt like it would be exploiting his death to use it."

Isaac pulled her to his chest, and she hooked her arms around his waist and settled against him. As he held her, Isaac got his head around the information she'd laid on him, the offer she'd made. And what it had cost her to make it. That she was willing to use money that obviously caused her pain touched him deeply.

"Baby, no. I can't ask you to do something like that. It's too much."

She lifted her head from his chest and looked him in the eye. "Yes. It's the right thing. I think he'd be glad I used it for something like this. And anyway, you didn't ask. I offered."

"You know it makes you the next target. He's not gonna give up that easy."

"I know. Better me, with you at my side, than Liza and her kids. And definitely better than Ellis getting his hands on it."

He didn't know what else to say. She was right, and she was wonderful. He framed her face with his hands, running his thumb over her soft, lush lips. "I love you, Lilli. Jesus, I love you."

CHAPTER TEN

Isaac took Lilli's hand and led her out of the office and back into the Hall. The guys were already waiting for him in the Keep, so he kissed her cheek and went in, leaving her in the nearly empty Hall, only Dom and Badger, two Prospects, for company. There weren't even any girls around. Lilli thought that might indicate the depth of the danger more than anything else—things were so intense in Signal Bend right now that the danger whores who liked their men bad and rough were staying away.

The clubhouse seemed sad this empty, everything a little dark and worn out. Dom and Badger were sitting on one of the couches, playing a video game. Lilli walked up and stood next to the couch, and Dom paused the game immediately. "Get you anything, Lilli?"

"No, thanks, Dom. Mind if I sit and watch you guys?"

Badger, the youngest Prospect, the lingering traces of his adolescent acne giving his face a striped appearance and accounting for his nickname, said, "No, ma'am. Have a seat."

Lilli twitched a little at the "ma'am," but not because it made her feel old. Her military service made her tolerant of such forms of address, but she'd always preferred "sir" to "ma'am," as her squad had known. She didn't correct Badge, though; he wouldn't understand. She simply smiled and took a seat in a leather armchair nearby.

The guys were in the Keep for a long time. Lilli sat and watched Dom and Badge kill zombies, not really paying attention, but it gave her somewhere to focus her eyes while she thought. She'd been sure and steady with Isaac when she'd told him she wanted to buy the Keller property, and she knew it was the right call to do so. But her stomach clenched at the thought of using her dad's money. Not because it wasn't a good reason, but because she could see and feel a door between her and that money, a door she'd have to open. She was already preparing herself to have the contents of her California storage locker shipped to Signal Bend—her dad's books, his military medals and awards, her nonna's pottery, the rest of the few heirlooms and mementoes she'd kept. But the money…it seemed to Lilli that to use it would finally release her father from her life.

It was the right thing. No question. Lawrence Ellis getting hold of that property would end Isaac's town. Lilli would do whatever she could to stop him, and because her father had died too soon, Lilli had the power to stop him. She would use it. But it would break her heart.

Both doors to the Keep opened and slammed back against the wall. Dom and Badge leapt up, abandoning their game and coming around the couch to be ready for whatever the patches ordered them to do. Len was out first, looking ready to do violence. In fact, the whole club came out looking intense and intent. Len grabbed Dom by the shoulder of his kutte and, without saying a word, dragged him out of the clubhouse to the lot. The other guys followed. Badger stood there, looking at loose ends.

Show trailed the pack, with Isaac coming out behind him. Show made a turn and headed down the hallway. Isaac came up to Lilli. He put his finger through the belt loop on her jeans and pulled her close to kiss her cheek.

114

"Is Dom okay?" She knew better than to ask, especially standing in the middle of the Hall, but she was worried about how abruptly Len had pulled him away.

But Isaac didn't seem to mind the question. "What? Yeah. Len's giving him a job." Sliding his hand around her waist, he turned to Badger. "Badge, you're taking my old lady home, and you're staying with her until you hear from me or Show. Got it?"

"Yeah, boss. Sure thing."

"Good. You got a piece?"

"Yeah. In my room." Like all the Prospects, Badger lived in the clubhouse.

"You need to holster it. Get one from the closet back there if you need it." Badger nodded and headed off down the back hall, toward the dorm rooms.

Now that they were alone in the room, Lilli turned to Isaac. "I don't need skinny little Badger watching out for me, Isaac. I'm actually offended. I can break that kid in two."

He grinned. "I know, Sport. Think of it as the buddy system, not a bodyguard. Nobody's alone. Okay?"

It still felt like she was getting a minder, and she made a face, but she nodded. She'd think of it as keeping on eye on Badger instead of the other way around. "Where are you off to, then?"

His face got serious quickly. "We're heading into St. Louis to collect on what's owed for Will. Don't ask more, Sport."

They were heading into trouble, then. Lilli knew St. Louis was a dangerous place for the Horde, especially now. She had a million questions boiling in her gut, but she didn't ask. He'd tell her when he could. She turned in his embrace and wrapped her arms tight around his neck, tucking her head under his chin. "Okay. Be careful, love. Please."

"Always. I love you, baby."

"I love you." She pulled up and looked him in the eye. "Should I do anything about the money?"

He nodded. "Yeah. I called Liza while we were at the table. She'll sell to us, Sport. She wants five hundred—and that includes the horses. If you're sure about this, do what you need to do." He brought his hands to her face and held her gently. "Only if you're sure."

"I'm sure. I'll take care of it." Her stomach boiled harder. Isaac bent down and kissed her. Feeling the weight of the day, and what they had yet to face in it, she opened her mouth and drew his tongue in. He grunted and wrapped his arms around her, bending forward and clutching her close as he forced her to lie back in his arms. They kissed like that, fervently, almost violently, until Show cleared his throat.

"Sorry to break up the party, boss." Show was standing there, his huge hand wrapped around Mac Evan's scrawny neck. Evans looked like he'd had a very, very hard day so far. Lilli couldn't find much sympathy for him.

Isaac released her and turned to Evans. "So, Mac. What do we know now?"

116

Evans' voice was weak and raspy. "Clear any offers for Signal Bend properties through you."

Isaac nodded. "Good man. And I've got good news for you. While you were indisposed, we worked out a deal for Will's place. Lilli here is going to buy it. Deal's all worked, just needs ink on paper. You'll get yourself a nice, juicy commission, too. So it's all win-win. And you don't have to deal with any of Ellis's people. You hear from them, you tell me or Show, and we'll handle it from there. Good?"

"Yeah. Yeah, Ike. It's great. Really. I'm sorry I forgot." Evans smiled weakly.

Isaac grabbed Evans by his now-tattered silk tie, and Evans whined. "It would sure make me happy if you'd stop calling me that fucking name, Mac. Buddy."

"Sorry, I—Isaac. Yeah, no problem."

"Good. Good meeting. Badge and Lilli are gonna drop you home. She'll tell you the details of the deal on the way, and you can get the paperwork done. *Today*." He turned to Lilli. "Okay?"

She nodded. "Fine."

Badger was back, struggling to work out the holster. Lilli rolled her eyes. Some bodyguard. She walked over and helped him get it strapped on properly and get his handgun seated. She turned at the weight of Isaac's hand on her shoulder.

"Gotta go, Sport. I'll call when I can."

"Okay. Love you."

"I love you, Lilli." He kissed her cheek, and he and Show headed out to the lot.

They dropped a very subdued Mac Evans off at his office so he could get the paperwork done for the sale. He promised to call as soon as everything was ready, then tottered off into the little bungalow. When he'd gone in and closed the door, Badger pulled back onto Main Street and headed toward Isaac and Lilli's place.

Lilli tried to make conversation, but all she got were the shortest possible responses, even when she'd asked him what kind of Harley he was thinking about getting. He was nervous, tasked with keeping the President's old lady safe. Lilli wondered, too, if he was just shy around women. He wasn't the kind of kid who probably got much play in high school, and he wasn't all that far past that time. Not a looker. Skinny, bad skin, teeth that would have benefitted from braces. But those teeth were strong and white, and he had beautiful, pale green eyes and thick, lush, long auburn hair. When he grew out of the acne, and if he put some muscle on, and some good ink, he'd be okay. That kutte on his back, especially once it bore a top rocker, would work wonders—even the Prospect patch had probably gotten his cherry popped.

He pulled up to the garage, next to Lilli's Camaro and Isaac's truck, and they got out. Lilli had her leather messenger bag with her. She preferred not to carry a bag, but with the way things were these days, she kept her Sig with her, and holstering her piece was too conspicuous under her jacket. So she carried a bag.

"Hold up a sec, Lilli." Badger stepped around and popped the strap on his shoulder holster. He wanted to take the lead. She let him, for the simple reason that her antennae were twitching, and she didn't want to take the time to argue with him. She didn't know why, if she'd seen or heard something that hadn't yet reached her conscious awareness, but something felt off. She knew not to discount that feeling. She walked a step behind and a step to the side of Badger and pulled her Sig from her bag, releasing the safety and cocking the gun as quietly as possible. He heard her and looked over his shoulder, his eyes wide.

"Lilli, what—?"

But Lilli didn't answer. The drive ran alongside the house; pulling to the garage brought one past the front of the house. Walking from the Horde van, parked at the garage, they'd approached the house sidelong, and they were now coming round to the front. Lilli was looking at the thing that she must have seen when they pulled up, seen without knowing. Now she knew, and she fought down the tearful horror swelling in her chest. Hanging from the porch roof, dangling like macabre wind chimes over the whitewashed railing: Havi and four of her tiny kittens: Dodger, Stella, Biddy, and Tim. Hanging by their fragile little necks. Havi was still twitching.

Whoever had done this must still be nearby. But there was no car. They'd passed no car since they'd turned onto Isaac's road, two miles back. Lilli grabbed Badger's arm and yanked him against the side of the house. He grunted and looked at her, confused. He hadn't seen.

Lilli pulled her bag over her neck and off her shoulder and dropped it to the ground against the house. When Badge made a noise as if to speak, she shook her head emphatically and put her finger to her lips. Scanning her surroundings as far as she could see, listening intently, she waited. Finally, she heard the faint creak of a floorboard.

At least one person was inside the house.

They had to know Badger and Lilli were out here. They had to have heard them pulling up in the van. And it was afternoon, a clear, bright fall day. Lilli and Badge had no element of surprise at all. All she could hope was that whoever was in there couldn't see her exact movements now.

She gestured to Badger to follow her, keeping low and quiet, and she moved down the side of the house to the kitchen porch. She stopped Badge at the side of the porch, putting him in the best position she could to protect himself and be ready to come when she called. She knew where the porch boards squeaked; he didn't. She couldn't let him up. She motioned for him to stand. He shook his head vehemently, his eyes wide and intent. She knew what he was trying to tell her. Isaac had given him a job, and it wasn't to sit back while the President's old lady went in to confront an intruder on her own.

She grabbed his kutte and pushed him back against the house, staring at him until he finally, reluctantly, nodded. Then she crept up onto the porch and flattened herself against the house, next to the kitchen door. The heavy door was standing open; only the wooden screen door was closed. But that worked on an ancient spring and squeaked like crazy. Normally, Lilli loved these old wooden screen doors, the way the screech of the spring and the thwappy bounce of the wood in the jamb when the door closed reminded her of summer vacations spent at a tiny lake cabin resort with her dad and Nonnie. But now, it meant she was announcing her presence.

Fine, then. She'd go in bold.

Lilli took a deep breath and let it out silently. Then, catching Badger's terrified head shaking back and forth so hard he must have been scrambling his brains, she grabbed the handle and yanked the screen door open. It shrieked, as she'd known it would. With a quick look to either side of the door, she stepped in. Then she started across the room. Fuck hiding. She wanted this guy. These guys. Whatever. If she took the right path, they couldn't get behind her. So she went forward.

She was halfway across the kitchen when a man she'd never seen before—a tweaker, obviously, death-camp skinny and covered in oozing sores—came into the doorway from the living room, holding a sawed-off shotgun. He was ready for her; she could see in the way his eyes met hers. But he hadn't pumped the shotgun. He raised it to do so, and Lilli shot him, blowing his nose into his brainpan. And through. She shoved her Sig into her jeans and grabbed up his shotgun.

At the shot, Badge came barreling into the kitchen. That was fine; they could both clear the house. He stared, shocked, at the body in the doorway, but when Lilli snapped her fingers and got his attention, he looked up at her and nodded. They went through the house together. Then they covered the yard and outbuildings.

The tweaker with his brains leaking all over the living room floor had been alone. Their bedroom had been ransacked, but there was nothing of any kind of value in there, and nothing else seemed to have been touched. Once they were sure that there was no other pressing threat, Badger got his burner out, but Lilli stopped him. What was going down in St. Louis was big. She didn't want Isaac distracted.

Badger, though, knew his job, and pushed back. "I gotta tell him, Lilli. He'll have my skin."

"No, Badge. You'll get them killed. He can't be worrying about me right now. We're okay. We're handling it. And I'll cover for you. Okay?"

She could see that he wasn't entirely convinced, but she could also see that he was too intimidated by her to fight much more. They got to work with cleanup. They got a tarp from the garage, wrapped the body, and dragged it to the toolshed. Lilli didn't want to dispose of it until she'd talked to Isaac. Somebody might know the guy. Badger did not. Once the body was locked in the shed, Lilli put Badger to work cleaning up the house. She went to the porch to take care of her babies. When Badge asked if she wanted help, she declined. No. This was her.

Letting tears come as they would, she cut Havi, Dodger, Tim, Stella, and Biddy down. They'd been hung with the clothesline that had been looped and hung on a hook on the porch wall, simple slipknots that had tightened as they'd struggled. Jesus God, what a horrible, sick, unimaginably cruel thing to do. Lilli's head rebelled at the thought. Why? Why?

Once they were down and freed from the rope, Lilli went for a shovel. She had to go into the toolshed and step over the body of the hateful piece of shit who'd done it. It was all she could do not to take the edge of the shovel to the body. But he needed to be as

122

recognizable as he could be with a hole where his nose had been, so she contented herself with a kick and went out to bury her pets.

There was a pretty tree behind the barn, and she thought to dig the grave there. As she was approaching the barn, she thought, for the first time, of the horses, who'd been silent all this time. She dropped the shovel and ran to the barn door.

She sobbed openly when she heard Gertie nickering at her. And then Flash and Ebbie tossed their heads over their stall doors. They were okay. Oh, thank God, they were okay. And there was Fagin, the big tomcat, sitting on an empty saddle rack. When he saw her, he stood, stretched, and hopped off, stalking to the nearest stall, an empty one. As Lilli went to Gertie to hug her broad nose, Fagin shoved a tiny black ball out of the stall. Pip. She'd been so consumed by the shock of the deaths that she'd not thought beyond them. Pip mewed and coiled around her ankles, and Fagin stalked away, his onerous task complete. Lilli laughed through her nearly hysterical tears and dropped to the floor, holding Pip to her face.

Finally, forcing herself to find composure, she released the horses into the paddock, then carried Pip into the house and closed him in their ransacked bedroom, away from the bodies of his mother and siblings, and away from the blood and brains of the man who'd killed them. Then she went back out and dug a grave to bury them.

When the burying was done, and the house was clean, it was nearly evening. She released Pip from the confines of the bedroom, got a couple of beers from the fridge. She handed one to Badger and they stood silently in the middle of the kitchen and drank.

Lilli stared at the doorway into the living room, where there had been not long ago the body of a man who'd come into their home.

123

Who'd cruelly killed their pets, who'd rifled through their things, and who'd clearly intended to kill her—and Badger, too, no doubt. Lilli stared at the spot his body had lain and worked it through her head. It didn't make sense. What had happened to Will had made an awful kind of sense—Will, with his loyalty to his home, was standing in the way of what Ellis wanted. Kill Will and destroy the home, eliminate that obstacle. It was a calculated strike in the war Ellis was fighting.

But sending a tweaker here? Why? Ellis would have a reason, but he couldn't know yet about Lilli's plan to buy the Keller place. Were the Northsiders going rogue and just fucking with Isaac? That didn't make sense, either. Ellis had too much power; Lilli had to believe that he wouldn't work with a crew that didn't respect him enough to fall in line. Then this was Ellis. So why?

Had to be a message. What was the message, then? Sending a single tweaker, the day after he'd burned Will down. A single tweaker, in Isaac's home. Causing mischief—would have been worse, if Lilli hadn't been on her guard. This was Ellis exposing Isaac's vulnerability, showing up his weakness. Isaac had a family of sorts now; that made him vulnerable.

Lilli set her beer on the counter and turned to Badge. "Call Erik. Do it now." Erik was guarding Holly and the girls. Holly and Lilli were the only old ladies. Show was the only Horde who had young kids.

Badge did as she asked. "No answer."

"You calling his burner?" No answer on a burner meant trouble.

"Yeah, of course."

Her heart racing, Lilli nodded and looked hard at young Badger. "Okay, bud. Listen. You know that's bad. In light of what we just dealt with, you know that's real bad. You and I are gonna load up and head over there. You follow my lead, okay?"

"Lilli, I can't. I can't let you get hurt."

"Bud, Erik's guarding Show's family, and he's not picking up his burner. Who's in town? Any Horde stay back?"

"They didn't tell me."

Well, that was fucking stupid. These guys really were out of their depth. "We don't have a choice here, Badge. Show has three daughters. If somebody was here with a shotgun, then there might be somebody there with a shotgun. And Holly's not me."

"I gotta call Isaac now. I gotta."

Lilli agreed. They needed to know who was in town. "Good idea, bud. But I'll do it." Her phone was in her bag, which was still outside on the ground. She ran out and grabbed it, pulling her phone free and dialing Isaac. No answer. Hoping that wasn't the bad sign she was afraid it could be, she left a message, trying to be clear but not freak him out so much she got him hurt. "Isaac, we've had some excitement here. We're going over to check on Holly and the kids. Could use some backup—wondering if you left anybody back on patrol. Call soon as you can." She closed the phone and gave her bodyguard a somber look. "We're on our own, Badge."

Badger looked like he needed to put his head down—pale and bug-eyed. "Oh, man. I don't know what to do."

Putting her hand on his bony shoulder, Lilli kept her voice calm. "I'm telling you what to do, Badge. We're going over there, and we'll deal with what we find. Just like we did here. Okay?"

The kid swallowed, his Adam's apple bobbing. "Okay. Okay."

Before they left the house, they stopped at the gun cabinet and loaded up.

~oOo~

This time, Lilli wasn't giving up surprise. She had Badger stop about half a mile from the house. They both armed themselves, then ran the last distance, Badger following Lilli's lead.

If there was trouble here, then they were likely too late. By the time Lilli had dealt with her own shit and worked the problem through, hours had passed. The shadows were long and thin in the waning light as they worked their way to Show's house.

Lilli heard screaming—no, wailing—coming from the house. She took a single beat to listen and get a sense of the location of the sound. Front, near the door. Probably the living room. Signaling for Badge to follow her, Lilli eased up onto the porch and flattened herself against the wall next to a large picture window, covered with sheer curtains. Peering around the side of the window, she got a view of the room, obscured by the gauzy fabric but clear enough to comprehend.

She saw Show's two youngest, Rose and Iris, eleven and eight years old, sitting next to each other on the floor under the side window. They were bound but not gagged, and it was their cries Lilli heard— was still hearing. Face down on the floor in front of them was their mother. She was not gagged, either, but she was silent.

She was being raped. In front of her daughters.

Lilli spun and tried the door. It opened readily, and, knowing the shot she needed to take, she dropped to her knees as she crossed the threshold into the room, aiming and taking the shot she had, catching the putrid son of a bitch in the ear. He flew off of Holly and skidded across the floor, dead before his body stopped moving.

The instant she was free, Holly, naked from the waist down, crawled to her screaming girls, drawing them into her arms.

As Lilli rose to her feet, Badger fired the rifle he was carrying, and she dropped flat. The girls screamed again, and Lilli rolled to her back, aiming as she did. Badger was standing at the front door, looking catatonic. Following his frozen stare, she saw another backwoods asshole sliding down the hallway wall, leaving a smear of blood as he dropped. He was still alive, blood already beginning to bubble out of his mouth. Badge had hit his lung. Lillie turned and looked at the Prospect. "You want me to finish him?"

Badger shook his head slowly, aimed the rifle, and put another round in the guy's forehead.

"Good man." Lilli turned to Holly. "How many, Holly? Are there more?"

Still crying hard, Holly shook her head, clutching her girls. But only two. Show and Holly had *three* daughters. Daisy, the oldest, fifteen years old, wasn't here. With the faint hope that she simply had not been home when all this went down, Lilli asked, "Holly, where's Daisy?"

At that, Holly lost her mind, and her little ones went with her. Their wails trebled in intensity. "Dammit, Holly, please. Where is she?"

"They—they—they took her. They took her first." Holly tried to get up, but Iris and Rose held on tight. She waved down the hall, toward their kitchen. Lilli was surprised that she wasn't trying harder to get to Daisy, but people did surprising things in trauma. She held her gun in both hands, at the ready, and turned to head down the hall. She saw Badger in the dining room, squatting at a pair of denim legs and heavily-booted feet. Erik, she assumed.

"Badge?"

He looked up, stricken, and shook his head. Goddammit. She nodded and headed down the hallway to the kitchen at the back of the house.

Daisy was on the floor, naked, bruised and bloody. She was lying with her limbs spread, and Lilli was sure she was unconscious at least, but when the floor creaked under Lilli's step, Daisy opened her eyes with a hoarse gasp and pulled into a ball.

There was a big table in the kitchen, covered with a cotton tablecloth with brightly-colored fall leaves all over it. Lilli pulled the cloth off the table and covered Daisy with it. She tried to press the cloth between her legs, but Daisy was too tense. Lilli did the best she could, as gently as she could. "It's okay, honey. It's over now. You want your mom?"

128

She wasn't crying. She was barely breathing. She was curled into that ball, her eyes open and staring. She didn't acknowledge Lilli's question. The pool of blood under her was bad, and she was waxy pale.

"I'll get your mom, honey. I'll get your mom." Lilli made sure she was covered completely, and then she went to get Holly.

Just as she got to the end of the hall, two Harleys roared into view—Dan and C.J. They must have been on patrol in town—which meant that Isaac had gotten her message, which meant that he was okay. Even in the midst of all this, Lilli knew relief. Badge was out the door first, heading out to meet them. Turning to Holly, Lilli said, her voice sharp, "Daisy needs you *now*," then followed Badge, stopping on the porch. She understood that she needed to hang back a little and not get in Horde business, especially not with these two, neither of whom liked her much. She'd let Badger deliver the news. But when C.J. hauled off and socked Badger in the mouth, knocking him to the ground, she jumped off the porch and ran toward them.

"What the hell are you doing?" She went straight up and got in C.J.'s face. He was no taller than she was.

He didn't answer her question. Instead, he grabbed her hard around her biceps and asked, "What the fuck are you doing here, bitch? You were told to go home. *He* was told to keep you there. What kind of trouble did you start here? I oughta break your goddamn jaw for you." And then he cocked his fist back.

Badger was still on the ground. As he said, "Ceej, wait. It was bad inside. Lilli stopped it," Lilli—thinking only that she was fucking sick and tired of men trying to force women to their will, and damn sure this fat old son of a bitch's fist wasn't coming anywhere near her—broke his hold, dropped, spun, and took his legs out from under him. He landed hard on his back with a grunt.

Badger had regained his feet in the meantime. Now, he looked at Lilli. "Oh, fuck. Oh, fuck. Lilli, you hit a patch. Oh, fuck."

"No, Badge. I didn't." She stood over C.J. "But I will. Right now, I don't give a shit what you wear on your back. Holly and Daisy are really hurt. Iris and Rose are traumatized at least. Erik is dead. And there are two bodies of tweaker assholes in there. There's another at our place. So holster your dick and be of use."

C.J. glared at her as he struggled stiffly to his feet. Dan, though, took her elbow in his hand. Lilli spun hard, ready to fight him, too, if she had to, but he stepped back, his hands up. "Easy, Lilli. Really hurt how?"

Dan was the club medic. "In the kind of way they're not going to want a man anywhere near them. Daisy's really bleeding. They need a hospital. Now."

"Oh, fuck. Oh, Jesus fucking Christ. Okay. Ceej, call Tash."

Lilli asked, "Who's Tash?"

"She's a doctor at County General. Gotta make sure she'll meet us there. Let's move. Lilli, I'm gonna need your help."

CHAPTER ELEVEN

Isaac, Show, and Len barreled through the double doors of the emergency wing at County General. Heedless of any obstacle, Show tore up to the intake desk. Isaac and Len stayed right with him, and Isaac scanned the waiting area for familiar faces. Before he found any, he saw a security guard—beefy, but no match in size for Show or Isaac—coming quickly up to them, his hand on the butt of his gun. Knowing how three bikers in kuttes rushing the nurses must look, Isaac moved to stand between Show, who was shouting now at a tiny blonde nurse in pink scrub pants and a floral top, and the guard. Isaac put his hands up, indicating they meant no trouble. Len went up to stand beside Show and calm things down.

Show's deep voice grated through clenched teeth as he answered the nurse's question. "Holly and Daisy Ryan. Where the *fuck* are they? And Iris and Rose?" He slammed his fist on the surface of the high desk. Isaac turned around and laid his hand on his friend's thick, inked arm.

The nurse—even in this moment, Isaac's lizard brain noted that she was a pretty little thing—flinched at Show's anger, but said only, "Are you family? I need ID."

He pulled his wallet out of his jeans and opened it to his Missouri driver's license. "Husband. Father." The wallet shook in Show's hand, and the chain rattled on the surface of the desk. The nurse nodded and pulled a neon pink hospital bracelet from a small box on her lower part of the desk. As she started writing Show's name—

Robert Ryan—and Holly's on the bracelet in Sharpie, Isaac turned and scanned the room again. He saw Dan and Badger and returned their nod. But no Lilli. His stomach rolled.

Show let the nurse put the pink bracelet on his wrist, and then she led him back into the trauma rooms. The guard stopped Isaac and Len from following. Giving Show's shoulder a hard squeeze, Isaac nodded at him, then turned with Len and went over to Dan and Badger.

The St. Louis run had been quick and dirty. They couldn't hit Ellis directly, not yet, but they could hit his henchmen, the guys who'd been doing the dirty work on the ground in Signal Bend. Isaac had met with his friend Kenyon Berry, head of the Underdawgs, a rival crew of the Northside Knights and an ally to the Horde. Kenyon had been reluctant to bring his crew too deeply into the Horde's war with Ellis, but on St. Louis turf he openly offered the Underdawgs for backup. And more, Kenyon had given the Horde the target: a stash house—an old office building, really—on the city's derelict northern edge. Two guards, showing Northsider colors. Isaac and Show had killed the guards, and then Victor had fired the building.

They'd all silenced their phones during the job. When they'd cleared the St. Louis metro area, they pulled off for a quick debrief, and Isaac had checked his phone. He'd had a message from Lilli. He'd called Dan the second he heard it, and then tried Lilli, but had gotten her voice mail. Show had stared at him, his eyes fiery with fear and rage, as he'd pieced together what was going on from Isaac's call with Dan. When he was off the phone, Isaac had confirmed what Show had surmised. Then they'd flown toward home.

Isaac had taken Lilli's second call from the road, telling him what had happened and where they were headed. He'd pulled the Horde off the road again, broken the news to Show, and had given out orders that sent Bart, Havoc, and Victor into town while Isaac, Show, and Len detoured to the hospital.

"Where the fuck is Lilli?" Isaac hadn't yet come to a full stop when he turned the question on Dan.

"She's okay, boss. She took Iris and Rose to the cafeteria."

Huffing a heavy sigh of relief, Isaac nodded and pulled Dan into a deep corner. Len and Badge came with them. "What the hell happened? Details. I need details."

Dan shook his head and pulled Badger forward. "Badge has the story. Ceej and I came in on the credits."

Isaac listened intently as Badger told the whole story. Badge had a way with narrative, and as he listened, Isaac began to understand what Ellis had done. He'd taken the most dangerous men in Signal Bend out of the equation, and then he'd attacked their most vulnerable spots—the families of the club leaders. He'd used his own cannon fodder to do it, too. Nobody important to his mission. Those three dead bodies Bart, Vic, and Hav were disposing of? Isaac wouldn't be at all surprised if no one in Ellis's organization even knew more than a first name. If that. They'd probably wrought that chaos for the price of a teenth.

They'd wondered at the quiet at the stash house they'd destroyed. Now, Isaac wondered if those Northsiders hadn't been cannon fodder themselves. Had Ellis willingly given them and the location to decoy the Horde?

133

And why had that been the address Kenyon had given them? There was a wrinkle in the line somewhere. Somebody knew too much.

That was more than Isaac could think about right now. Right now, he needed to see his old lady. He gave Badge a sharp pat on the shoulder. "Good man, Badge. You did good."

Badge rubbed his shoulder and said, "I'm sorry I couldn't keep Lilli at your house."

He laughed at that. Even *he* couldn't keep Lilli where he wanted her. Badge didn't have a prayer. "S'okay, kid. Show's whole family would probably be dead if you hadn't gotten there. I fucked up not telling you Dan and Ceej were in town."

Badge got a little pale at the mention of C.J.'s name. "Oh, man. C.J."

"Fuck. What? He whole?"

Dan put his hand on Badger's shoulder and took over. "Yeah, boss. He and Lilli had a…thing. He's pissed. You could have some trouble over it."

Isaac was more weary than he could say. He sighed. "Just fuckin' tell me."

Dan sighed, too. "Ceej was pissed to see her in the middle of the shit at Show's. He came at her pretty hard. She put him on the ground."

"*What* do you mean, 'he came at her pretty hard'?"

"Usual Ceej smack. Threatened to break her jaw for her. Pulled his fist back like he meant it. You know his bit."

134

"And then she took his legs out. Like she did with you in the ring!" Badge was grinning around his split lip, but he wiped it off when Len slapped him on the back of the head.

All Isaac could think of was what he would have done to C.J. if he'd actually made contact with Lilli. He didn't fucking care how much of the old bastard's threat was impotent bloviating. He nodded. "Fine. Maybe he wants to take it up with me in the ring. Happy to oblige him." He turned to Len. "You call me the second you see Show or there's word about what's going on back there. I'm going after Lilli and the girls."

~oOo~

He found Lilli sitting with the girls. They had cake, ice cream, and sodas. Under normal conditions, Holly's head would explode to see the sugar her girls were being fed. But they were quiet and seemed calm. Rose, a shy, fragile girl, had her head down, swirling a plastic spoon through melting vanilla ice cream. But Iris looked up and smiled when she saw him coming up to their table. Lilli had her back to him, but she turned around to see what Iris was grinning at. Seeing him, she stood. "You're okay. Oh, thank God, you're okay," she whispered. She'd talked to him—she'd known he was okay. But he understood. He hadn't believed it, either, until he'd seen her with his own eyes.

He pulled her into his arms, and at the touch of her body, the iron hold he'd had on calm crumbled away. Motherfucking Christ! Somebody had been in their house, had pointed a gun at her. He'd

135

sent her off with fucking *Badger* with barely a second thought. And God, Show! Holly and Daisy! And these two little ones, forced to see it all.

He clutched her tighter and tighter, feeling like he needed her closer no matter how close he got her. He pressed his face into the curve of her neck and held on, his throat swelling with grief, with fear, with love. And guilt. Fuck, the guilt was going to swallow him whole, from the inside out.

He felt her hands in his hair, lacing above his braid and holding him as tightly as he held her. "Jesus, baby, I'm so sorry. I'm so fucking sorry." She didn't reply; she only held him closer.

His burner went off, and he released his hold on her and pulled the phone out of his pocket. Len. As soon as Isaac had the phone to his ear, Len said, "Gotta get back up here now, boss. Think you should bring the girls."

"Yeah." He snapped the phone shut and looked at Lilli. "Something's up upstairs. We all need to go up."

When they got back to the ER waiting area a few minutes later, Dan, Len, and Badger were still standing pretty much where he'd left them. But now a doctor was standing with them. Tall, slim, and pale, her bright ginger hair rolled into some kind of Grace Kelly-looking style. She wore green scrubs under a white coat. Tasha. The only other woman who'd ever spent a night in Isaac's bed.

Len nodded as they approached the group, and Tasha turned fully to face him, her amber eyes flaring slightly. Their breakup was...fuck, fifteen years old, but it had been explosive, and things were dicey even now when they were in the same room together. Tash's father, long dead now, had been Horde, of Isaac's father's generation, and she had stayed a friend of the club, even after his death, even after their breakup, easing their way when they needed real medical attention, keeping things as quiet as she could.

"Isaac." Tasha looked at Lilli as soon as she'd said his name.

"Tash. What's up?"

"Show asked me to talk to you. He wants you all with him and Holly. Holly is being released, but Daisy's been rushed into surgery. They need the girls with them."

"What happened?" Lilli asked the question. Tash gave her a quick glance again and directed her answer to Isaac. He could feel Lilli putting the interpersonal equation together. That, though, was a discussion for another time.

"There's a lot of damage. We thought we had all the bleeds, but she crashed again. Isaac, it doesn't look good."

"Why aren't you with her?"

"I'm an ER doctor, not a surgeon. She's with who she needs to be with. Come on, I'll take you to Show."

~oOo~

When they got to the surgery waiting room, Show and Holly were alone. It was late—only emergency surgeries happened so late in the

137

evening. Holly looked awful, bruised and pale, her long blonde hair plastered to her head. She was a naturally curvy woman, and she'd grown soft and rounder in motherhood, but she looked emaciated and tiny sitting as she was, wan and weak, next to her big old man, in the stark, high-ceilinged room. She was sitting next to Show, but they weren't touching. When Iris and Rose came into the room, each one holding Lilli's hands, Show stood and then dropped to his knees, his arms outstretched. The girls ran to him, and he pulled them in tight, his face screwed up in a mask of violent pain. Holly sat where she was, her arms crossed, looking like she'd checked out and left her body behind.

Isaac knew that something had gone wrong with Holly's body after Iris, and that she and Show had stopped having sex because the pain was too much. He didn't know more than that; it wasn't something men talked about, not even men close as brothers. But he couldn't imagine how much worse what had happened to her was because of that.

He went up to her, but she didn't acknowledge him at all. He didn't know whether he should touch her, or what he should do to tell her how sorry he was, that it was his fault, not Show's, that she should lay her hate and pain on him. He started to reach out, just to put his hand on her shoulder, but Lilli pulled him back. When he turned to her, she only shook her head and pulled him to sit with her a few chairs away. He hooked his arm across her shoulders and brought her to his chest. He felt an overwhelming need to feel her body, as if he couldn't believe she was safe if he wasn't actually touching her. She settled in, her hand snaking under his kutte to rest on his belly.

His cock swelled. He didn't understand why. He couldn't think of a worse time for it. But he felt the need for her acutely. Forcing

138

himself to ignore it, even as his pulse picked up its familiar staccato beat of arousal, he rested his head on Lilli's and waited.

Tasha had gone through the doors to the surgical wing after she'd led them to the waiting area. About two hours later, she came back through, this time accompanied by a male doctor in scrubs and a surgical cap. Tasha caught his eye as they walked to Show and Holly.

"Oh, fuck, no. Oh, no."

Lilli sat up. She apparently hadn't seen the doctors come in, because she sat up straighter, seeing them now, and then turned to Isaac. "What? What is it?"

Isaac didn't answer. He watched as Tasha put her hand on Show's shoulder. She said something, and Show nodded and lifted Rose and Iris off his knees. Tasha took their hands and turned around, looking like she wasn't sure what to do next. Lilli stood and collected the girls, bringing them back to Isaac. When her eyes met his, Isaac knew that she understood, too.

Tasha went back to Show and squatted at his side. The other doctor looked around uncomfortably and then sat in a chair almost facing Show and Holly. Isaac couldn't hear, but he didn't need to. He wasn't surprised when Show dropped his face into his hands. Holly only nodded, her face blank.

After a few minutes, the foursome stood. Show came over, his face wet with tears. Without saying anything to Lilli or Isaac, he squatted in front of his little girls. "Jesus wants Daisy to live with him in heaven, girlies. She's sleeping now, resting up for the trip, but I want you to come back with Mom and me and say goodbye."

Iris put her head on her father's shoulder. "No scary men in heaven."

Now Show looked at Isaac, and their eyes filled with tears. "That's right, baby flower. No scary men in heaven. Come on, now. Don't want to keep Jesus waiting, right?"

When Show stood and took his daughters' hands, Isaac stood too. He didn't know why. He didn't know what he should do. But it seemed wrong to sit. Lilli rose with him. Len, Dan, and Badge followed. They stood silently. Isaac held his friend's eyes until Show nodded and then turned around. Leading his girls, he followed the doctors and his wife through the doors to say goodbye to their first child.

Who had been raped to death.

Isaac stood and stared at the silver doors through which his friend had passed. Rage swirled with guilt and grief and filled him up, whirling to a poisonous foam in his heart and head. When he was full to bursting, he spun around with a roar, grabbed up the chair he'd been sitting in, and threw it across and out of the room. It slammed into the hallway wall and landed with a crash on the floor, sliding several feet down the hallway.

Lilli put her hand on his arm, and he shook her off. He stalked after the chair, picked it up, and threw it again. A nurse came through the doors, saw what was going on, and then went back through. Probably to call security, but he just didn't give a fuck. He had to put this anger somewhere. He stalked up and down the hallway, hoping a guard would confront him. That would help. He could use a good fight right now. He needed to hit, he needed to hurt. He needed to get it OUT. He slammed his fist into the wall, taking a gouge out of the plaster with his rings. Not enough. He did it again, and this time felt the skin break on his knuckles. Good. He did it again. And again.

140

And then Lilli was on him, holding his arm. She put her other hand on the wall, over the bloody patch, and he pulled up at the last second, before he drove his fist into her hand. Fuck! He glared at her, jerking free, but she grabbed him again. She didn't say a word, just held on and stared at him. But fuck! He needed.

She had his kutte in both fists. She broke eye contact with him to look around, and then she was dragging him a few feet down the hall to a door. She tried it. When it opened, she pulled him into the dark space and closed them in.

They stood in the dark, the only sound Isaac's labored breathing, and then light came on above their heads, as Lilli found the switch. Linen closet. Why the fuck had she brought him in here?

"What the fuck, Lilli?"

She still said nothing. But she reached over his shoulder and grabbed his braid, yanking his head down to hers. She kissed him violently, her free hand pushing under his shirt to rake at his bare skin. She grabbed his belt and worked it open, then yanked open the fly of his jeans. Her touch left electric traces over his skin, and he groaned. He got it—*she* got it. His beautiful, amazing woman, redirecting him. He put his hands around her waist and shoved her against a wall of shelves filled with blankets. He worked her jeans open and pushed them down off her hips. She toed off a boot and pulled one leg free of her jeans, then wrapped her arms around his neck.

"Give it to me, Isaac. It's okay. You know I can take it."

His heart ached for Show and for Holly. But he needed this. He needed Lilli. He needed. He needed. He grabbed her thighs and lifted

141

her up, hooking her legs around his hips as he sank deep into her. Sweet Jesus, the feeling of her hot pussy enveloping his bare cock.

She gasped and then said, "Hold up, love. Condom."

No. No. Jesus Christ, no. He *needed*. "No, baby, please. Make a baby with me. Fuck, make a baby with me. I need it. I need you. I need a baby with you. A family. A chance. Please. Lilli, please."

He didn't even know what he was saying. It was insane to want to get her pregnant now, he knew it was. Show had just lost his baby. Violence—*club* violence—had taken her, taken her horribly. How could he ever want to bring a child into the world they now lived in? It made no sense.

But he did. Now, more than ever. It was important. It was *crucial*.

They stared at each other, Isaac feeling like he was one slender thread from losing his mind completely and for good. He tried to read her look, but all he could see was intensity. He tried to send his plea through his eyes. He'd never begged for anything the way he was begging for this.

And then she nodded.

Relief washed over him with such gusto that his vision blurred. When it cleared, he leaned in and kissed her, plunging his tongue into her mouth, tasting her, savoring her. She tightened the grip of her legs around his hips, and he moved. He didn't try to make it last. They were in a fucking linen closet in the hospital, and Show was saying goodbye to his daughter. What was happening here was as wrong as it was right. It was neither. It was necessary.

He slammed into her, driving himself to desperate release, holding her close, not sure if she was finding any pleasure in their coupling. But then he felt her muscles spasming around his cock, skin to skin, and he heard the familiar sharpness in her exhales. "Oh, yeah, baby. Yeah. Come with me. Baby, come with me," he rasped.

Her forehead on his shoulder, she nodded again, and he picked up his pace, pushing one hand between them to tweak at her clit. Then her body tensed, and he felt her teeth bearing down on his kutte. He thrust a few more times and then came inside her, free inside her, biting down on his own lip until he tasted blood.

When it was over, he dropped his head to her shoulder and sobbed.

CHAPTER TWELVE

Her arms and legs wrapped tightly around him, Lilli held Isaac as he wept. He was still hard inside her. Bare inside her. She'd let him come inside her. Intentionally. Because he wanted to make her pregnant—when they fucked in a hospital linen closet, while, down the hall, Show and Holly said goodbye to their dead daughter. Her head wanted to spin, but she held that tight, too. She was in battle mode, dealing with what was before her, letting her higher mind do the higher thinking without taking her attention away from the immediate.

They were going to need to talk about the idea of a baby again—soon—when they could talk calmly. It wasn't a decision they could make like this. She'd let him because he'd needed her to let him. But they needed to talk it through calmly before they committed to a decision of such magnitude.

Isaac was quieting. He took a deep breath and lifted his head from her shoulder. His face was wet with tears and sweat, and Lilli uncoiled an arm from his neck and brushed her hand over his cheek, wiping his grief away. "You okay, love?"

He laughed quietly. "No. But I'm with you, so I will be. I love you so much, Lilli. So much."

"And I love you." Pressing her lips to his scarred cheek, she murmured, "We should get back out there. Show's gonna need you."

144

He nodded, then lifted her and pulled out. She dropped her legs, and they put their clothes back to rights. When they were ready, Isaac pulled her into his arms and held her for another few seconds. Then he opened the door, and they went back out into the hall.

No sign of Show yet. Dan, Len, and Badger were sitting quietly in a corner of the waiting room, which was still empty but for them. Len made eye contact with Lilli as she and Isaac came into the room. He nodded, and in that gesture she read understanding. She took Isaac's hand, and they sat next to his brothers. They sat vigil for Show and his family.

Show, Holly, Rose, and Iris came through the double doors about half an hour later. Show look ravaged. He opened the door, and Iris and Rose went through, looking sad and something like confused. Holly came through, her face a stony mask, but then Show put his hand on her back as she passed him, and she flinched as if he'd hit her. He pulled his hand away. Even from across the hall and across the waiting room, Lilli could see how pain tore at him.

The broken family walked into the waiting area, and Lilli and the Horde stood. Holly froze in the middle of the room, staring at Isaac, and something on her face seemed to slip. Show was standing right behind her, his height and breadth dwarfing her. It always did—he was a full foot taller than his old lady, and though she wasn't thin, his mass was considerably greater—but she seemed much smaller in this moment, her body bruised and brutalized, her heart broken.

Then, with her two youngest, now her only, daughters at her side, Holly turned around, pulled back one shaky arm, and slapped Show across the face so hard the force turned her whole body. Then she did it again. And again. Show closed his eyes and stood for it, his head turning with the impact and then coming back to center to take it again.

The girls looked shocked and terrified, and Lilli started to go to them, thinking to pull them away, but just as she moved, Isaac's hand was on her arm and he went forward instead. But when he got there and took hold of Rose and Iris's hands, Holly wheeled on him. Her stoicism entirely shattered now, she was in a frenzy of rage.

She screamed at Isaac and yanked hard on Rose and Iris's other hands. "GET YOUR HANDS OFF MY GIRLS. GET YOUR FILTHY, MURDERING HANDS OFF MY CHILDREN!" The girls began to wail. She pulled them to the far side of the waiting room and sat them down. Then she turned back to Show, who had not moved. Isaac was standing next to him now; Holly stepped between them, her back to Isaac, and looked up at Show. He tipped his head down to let her look him in the eye. When she spoke, her voice was low and steady.

"You keep away from us. You keep away. I'm taking them and going as far away as I can. You keep away."

Still Show didn't move. Holly turned back to Rose and Iris and took their hands, pulling them up from their seats and heading toward the elevators, and still Show stood, rigid, in the middle of the waiting room.

Lilli went after Holly and put her hand on her shoulder as she was pressing the elevator button. Holly flinched and looked back. "Get out, Lilli. Get out now. There's nothing but death and ruin here."

Ignoring that statement for more immediate and practical concerns, Lilli asked, "How are you getting back, Holly? You need a ride back to town. Badger's got the van."

Holly laughed. "I'm not going anywhere with any of them. I'll call somebody." The elevator opened, and Holly dragged her weeping daughters in with her and pressed the button. When the door closed, Lilli turned and went back to Isaac and Show. Show still had not moved. Isaac now had his arm over Show's shoulders. Len, Dan, and Badger were standing nearby, looking somber and uncomfortable.

Isaac shook his friend a little. "Come on, man. Let's sit down." Letting Isaac lead him, Show finally moved. They sat together. Show stared at the floor between his feet.

Len turned to Badger. "Go get coffee for everybody or somethin', man. Get lost." Badge nodded and turned to do as he was bid.

Knowing that she, too, was an intruder in this moment, Lilli put her hand on Isaac's shoulder. He looked up and gave her a ghost of a smile. "I'm going to help him with the coffee." She bent down and kissed his cheek, then followed Badger.

~oOo~

The night was edging into dawn when they made a somber caravan back to Signal Bend: Isaac and Show riding side by side, Lilli riding bitch with her man; Len and Dan riding behind; Badger picking up the rear in the Horde van. They all pulled into the clubhouse lot. Show dismounted and strode immediately into the clubhouse without comment or pause; Isaac and Lilli, and the others, followed him. The rest of the Horde were there, most of them at the bar; all stood when Showdown came in. When he continued through the clubhouse, headed straight toward the dorm, Isaac called out, "Show. Hold up, man."

Show stopped. He didn't turn around. He stood in the middle of the clubhouse as he'd stood in the middle of the hospital waiting room. Unmoving. Immovable. Isaac walked around him and faced him. Lilli went to the bar, giving them space, and watched. She and Isaac had barely talked all night, had said almost nothing at all to each other since they'd come out of the linen closet.

As tall and massive as Show was, Isaac was bigger. He laid his hand over his friend's slumped shoulder. "Don't go off by yourself, brother. Not tonight. I don't want you alone."

Show lifted his head. Lilli was behind him, but she knew he was looking Isaac in the eyes, and she could almost feel his expression of livid grief. "Too late." The words were softly spoken, but clear. Show sidestepped Isaac and continued on to the dorm. Isaac turned and watched him go.

Then Lilli went to him and circled her arms around his waist. He looked down at her, his green eyes dark and bleak. Pressing his lips to her forehead, he held there for a long moment, then said, "Let's go home, Sport." She laid her head on his chest and nodded.

His arm around her shoulder, he walked them first to Len, who was standing at the bar. "I'm taking her home. Keep on eye on him. Call me."

Len nodded. To the whole room, Isaac said, "Get some rest, people. The Keep at noon." Then he turned and led Lilli back out into the new dawn.

~oOo~

They were inside the house before Lilli realized that Isaac hadn't been in it since the morning before. He hadn't seen the aftermath of the intended attack on her. Now, she wondered if there was still a body in the shed, some fresh horror for them to have to contend with.

Isaac clearly hadn't forgotten. He stood in the front hall as if he were scenting the story. Focused on Show's tragedy, they had not yet spoken at any kind of length about what had happened in their home, but he knew that she'd been attacked and had killed the man. She figured he'd gotten the story from Badger, anyway. She and Badger had cleaned all traces of that violence from the house, but she had not yet set the ransacked bedroom to rights.

She put her hand on his back. "Isaac?"

He turned and took her hand, pulling her forward. "Tell me, Lilli. Tell me it all."

Just then, they heard a tiny mewl, and Pip, alone and lonely, came into the living room from the kitchen. Crying the whole way, he came up and climbed onto Lilli's boot, latching his claws into her jeans to begin his trek up her leg. Slipping her hand from Isaac's grip, she bent down and gathered the tiny orphan in her arms. "Hey, guy. It's okay." He settled under her chin and commenced purring loudly.

Sad as he was, Isaac grinned. "He sure loves you."

Lilli shrugged. She figured she wasn't much more than a familiar port in a night of scary storms for the little guy, but she felt better holding him.

"Come on, Sport. Let's talk." His hand on her elbow, he guided her into the living room, and they sat together on the couch. With Pip purring on her shoulder, Lilli told him the story of her day. As she spoke, she found her eyes drifting again and again to the spot where the body had lain. She didn't know why, exactly. She wasn't sorry she'd killed him. She felt the death; she took responsibility for it, as her father had taught her. But she knew she'd made the right call, done the right thing. It wasn't the first time she'd killed a man, either. Several tours in Afghanistan meant that she had taken enemy lives. And yet this death unsettled her.

Isaac sat with his hand on her knee and listened. By the time she was finished, he was gripping her so hard his hand and her leg were shaking. It hurt, but she didn't mind the pain.

"I don't know if the body's still in the shed. The cats are buried under the big elm by the barn. Oh—I should go out and bring the horses in—they've been in the pasture all day!" She was suddenly worried and guilty. She wasn't used to thinking about animals to take care of. She had no idea how bad it was not to have brought the horses in, and it was early daylight now. Dammit.

He took her hand, bringing it to his lips. "They're in the barn, Sport. Bart and Vic took care of the asshole in the shed, and they brought the horses in and got them set up for the night. That's handled."

Lilli blew out a sigh of relief. "There was just too fucking much today."

"I'm so sorry, Lilli. God, I don't know where to put this filth I feel. I let you down. Show. Holly—God, Daisy. Erik. The whole thing was a goddamn trap, and I fell right into it and took everybody down." He laid his head on the back of the couch. "We aren't enough. I'm not enough. We can't win this."

Lilli sat and watched him as he stared at the ceiling, still gripping her knee in the vise of his big hand. She said nothing; he needed to work through his doubt on his own.

And after a few minutes, he did. He sat up and stared into her eyes, the varied greens of his irises flashing fire. "I don't fucking care. What he did? He doesn't get away with that shit. I don't know how, and I don't care. I will end that motherfucker, or I will die trying. Maybe I'll have to do it myself. I won't force anyone to stand with me. But I am taking Lawrence Ellis down."

"You won't have to do it alone, love. I'm with you." She put her hand over his.

But he shook his head. Finally releasing his grip on her knee, he turned his hand and wrapped it gently around hers. "No, Sport. Not if you're pregnant. Absolutely not."

Well, they needed to talk about that, too. "Then maybe I shouldn't be."

Isaac reacted immediately and harshly. He dropped her hand and wrapped his fists around her upper arms. Pip stirred and jumped out of Lilli's hold. "Don't take it back, Lilli. Jesus Christ, don't take it back."

He was much calmer than he had been in the hospital, but he was not calm. The day and night—the week, the past few months, all the time they'd known each other—had been too fraught with death and danger for him to be calm. But she'd let him come inside her, and unless she wanted to make the decision herself, they needed to discuss it, calmly, soon. Now. So she pulled free from his hold and took his hands in hers. She spoke evenly. "Isaac. I'm not taking it back. But it's not a decision we should have made in that moment. We need to talk about it sanely, not desperately. Tell me why it's so important to you that I get pregnant now, with everything going on."

He stared down at their hands, and for a very long time, he said nothing. Lilli had expected a long spiel. She knew he'd been thinking about this, and wanting it, before today. When he looked up, his eye were calm. Sad, but calm.

"I love you, Lilli. Like I didn't know I could love. Fuck, I feel spun by it. When you were in the hospital and I didn't know if you were gonna wake up, I saw the life I wanted. I sat there at the side of your bed, waiting for you to wake up, and I saw it all. I saw the man I wanted to be, the life I wanted to have. All of it was you. I saw you pregnant. I saw you holding our baby, me holding our baby. I saw a family. Seeing all that, it gave me hope. It made me know you would be okay. Because what I saw was so clear, it had to be real.

"I'm not an idiot, Sport. I know this seems like a crazy-ass time to be talking about making a baby. I know. But to me, it's not. It's the right time *because* it's so bad out there. I don't want to live my life with you like I'm afraid I'm gonna lose it all. I want to live for a future with you. A future where all this shit is behind us. It's hope, Lilli. It's hope. And damn, you're gonna be an amazing mother."

Lilli was moved by his words. She was persuaded, even. She understood. Except for the last thing he'd said, which struck at the core of her own fear. "We don't know that, Isaac. I've never even thought about being a mother. I've hardly been around any mothers. My own mother was insane. Literally. And I'm not a nurturer. I'm a fucking soldier, Isaac. I wouldn't have any idea what I'd be doing, and I don't want to fuck anybody up."

Isaac laughed. "You really don't see it, do you? Baby, you got a nurturing streak a mile wide."

He was talking about the cats. He always brought up the fact that she liked the cats, like that somehow meant she'd be a good mom. As if baby felines and baby humans were analogous. She huffed her frustration. "Dammit, Isaac. Because I wanted to bring the kittens in from the cold does not mean I know how to teach a tiny person to be a grownup person."

"No. I'm not talking about the cats, or the horses, but yeah, Sport. That's you taking care of others, and it counts. I'm talking about the way you are with *people*. You read them, read their moods, what they need, and you take care. The way you were tonight with Show—and Holly. The way you knew to take the girls away from the trauma at the hospital. The way you were with me."

"I left Daisy bleeding on the floor of that kitchen, because she flinched away from me when I packed a cloth against…where she was bleeding. I left her there and went into the other room and yelled at Holly to take care of her."

153

Isaac's eyes had closed at Lilli's mention of Daisy. He opened them and looked at her. "Well, I wasn't there. But it sounds like maybe this is another way to think of it: a badly hurt and traumatized girl was afraid of you, a near stranger, so you sent her mother to help her."

Lilli could feel her resistance ebbing. All that was left was the real core of her fear. "Isaac. My mother was crazy. Bipolar, I'm sure. She killed herself and left me to find her body. Bipolar is genetic."

He pulled her close, and she let him, feeling suddenly exhausted and vulnerable. "Oh, baby. Don't let that be the thing that stops us. You're fine. I'm fine. Who knows what kind of genetic jumble of us our kids will get. But if there's a problem, we'll deal. If your mom was bipolar, she didn't have help, right? That wouldn't be the case for our kids. Lilli, this is all about fear. But you're brave as fuck. You don't let fear get in your way. Don't let it get in ours. If you don't want a family, that's a different conversation. But if you're afraid, fuck fear. Let's take what we want."

He kissed her head. "Besides, maybe I already knocked you up."

If that was true, it wasn't too late to do something about it. But the thought that she might have the tiniest start to Isaac's baby already inside her didn't scare her the way it should. In fact, it made a warm, calm place in the center of this cold, bleak day. He was right. It was crazy, but it was right. It was hope.

She turned and brought her leg over his lap, straddling him. "Okay. Let's make a baby, then."

He smiled, and for a moment, the pain of the day was gone from his face. He was simply happy, and his love for her was palpable. She felt his hands grip her ass and hold her firmly to him, and then he stood, his eyes locked on hers. She wrapped her legs around him and held on as he walked her out of the living room, down the hall, and into their bedroom.

He stopped inside the door. The room was a disaster—drawers pulled out and upended; the closet emptied, its contents on the floor; their bed stripped, the linens scattered.

"Jesus. This is our fucking bedroom. I want to kill the motherfucker who did this."

Lilli kissed his cheek. "Already taken care of, love. He's dead. And this is just mess. He didn't ruin anything. He didn't take anything. There wasn't anything in here to take, and we were here before he could do more. It's just mess. Don't worry about it now. We'll lie on the mattress tonight. Won't be the first time we fucked on a bare mattress." Their very first time had been on a bare mattress in Lilli's little rental house.

Isaac walked to the bed and lay down with her, propping himself over her on his hands. She released her legs from around his hips but kept her hands linked on the back of his neck. His braid lay over her fingers. "How are you so damn calm, Sport?"

She knew exactly why she was calm. She'd had time he hadn't yet had. "What happened here today is old news to me. I had my breakdown earlier. Burying the kittens and Havi, when I thought that was the worst of it, and it was over? That's when I lost it. I hate that somebody was in our house, and I hate what he did, but he's dead now. And we're together. Today—or, yesterday—was horrific, and there's more bad shit coming. But right now, I'm with you, and we're okay, and that makes me calm." She unlaced her fingers and looped one hand around his braid, sliding down to the band that held it together. She pulled that free. Isaac's hair was long, thick, and dark, and she loved it loose, especially when they were intimate. The feel of his hair and hers like silk against her skin made her shiver.

When it was loose, draping around them and brushing her face, she began to unbutton his black shirt. His bare chest, covered with just the right amount of dark hair, his Mjölnir pendant swinging from its leather strap near his throat, was another favorite feature. In fact, everything was a favorite feature. She could not have conjured a more perfect man for her. She was throbbing and wet. "If we're making a baby, then I want to feel you naked inside me. I want to really feel it, not like at the hospital. I want to savor you."

He pushed away from her and knelt between her legs, shrugging his shirt off his shoulders and tossing it to the floor. Then he shoved his hands into the waistband of her jeans and yanked open her button fly, his movements so forceful her hips came off the bed a little. Lilli moaned, her underwear fully soaked now. She loved it like this, when he used his power to move her body. As he pulled her jeans and underwear off her hips and down her legs, she pulled her t-shirt over her head and then undid her bra. She was still wearing her boots; he stood at the side of the bed and pulled them off, then rid her of her pants.

He rid himself of his own boots and jeans, his eyes never leaving her naked body. She felt his gaze like a caress, and she arched up toward him.

"Jesus fuck, baby. You're perfect. God, you're perfect." The low rumble of his deep voice rolled over her like his eyes had, a nearly physical sensation. But she needed the touch of his body. As she raised her arms to beckon him, the thought crept into her head that

Show was grieving in a dorm room right now, that it was disrespectful to be wanting Isaac the way she was. As Isaac got back onto the bare mattress, on their bed surrounded by the chaos the intruder had left behind as a legacy, Lilli set that thought aside. Somehow, what had happened made their love more important, made their coupling necessary.

This was what Isaac had meant. Hope. What they had was new. Their life together was still the future. Together, they were hope.

Isaac settled on top of her and drew her breast into his mouth. She gasped at the electric rush of sensation. Her eyes closed, she focused on what she felt. His hair lying over her chest and arm. His beard on her breast. His mouth around her nipple, drawing pleasure through her in a steady beat. His big, rough hands, gripping her hip and shoulder. The coarse brush of the hair of his legs, chest, and arms against her smooth skin. The hot silk of his breath. The hard, heavy weight of his strong body. The rigid length of his cock on her leg.

Her need for him was absolute. Sliding her fingers into his hair, she pulled his head up. His green eyes sparked at her. "Fuck me, Isaac. I need to feel you fucking me. I need it hard."

He said nothing; his rapt expression did not change. He simply shifted upward, the hand that had gripped her hip moving between them, and then he shoved inside her, his eyes still intent on hers. She cried out at the hot, thick, deep feel of his beautiful, bare cock inside her. God, she never wanted to use a condom again. This felt like being *part* of him, like he was alive inside her. He shifted again, drawing her legs up in his arms, bringing them to her chest, opening her wide. Then he drove into her, heavy and hard, every grunting thrust on the slender edge of pain. Right where she liked it. Oh, God, it was good. The position had her pinned, though, and she needed to touch him. She could only reach his arms, so she grabbed hold of his forearms, above the leather cuffs he still wore, and closed her eyes, releasing herself to the pleasure.

"Oh, fuck, Isaac. Oh, yes. Yesyesyes. Oh, God. Don't stop, don't stop, don't stop." It had to be the exhaustion and emotional overload of the day, because she didn't think she'd ever gotten to orgasm so quickly. But it was there, and it was excruciating in its intensity. Before she had a chance to come down from it, before she had even completed, he pulled rapidly out of her and flipped her to her stomach, then dragged her up to her knees. Then he was inside her again, his hands clawing into her hips, yanking her back on him as he surged into her, and she went right back up, screaming every time his body slammed into hers. She was going to have an aneurysm or something; she'd been coming forever, spinning at her peak. Their sex was often rough; they both preferred it that way. But there was a desperate, fiery blade to this fuck that was new.

Isaac was still grunting ferociously with every thrust, and she could feel his sweat at every point their bodies touched. It dripped down onto her from the ends of his hair and beard. And yet he had not come. Bare as he was inside her, as hard as he was making her come, he had not. Then, as she thought she'd need to stop him, just so she could catch a breath, he growled, "Fuck, baby!," and pushed her flat to the bed, lying on her, still thrusting, deep and steady, his head on hers. He let go of her hips then and slid a hand between her and the mattress, pressing it to her belly, spreading his fingers wide. The pressure of his hand there, his weight on her, as he thrust his big cock into her, brought her over again.

"Jesus, Isaac. Fuck!" She gritted the words out; she couldn't take much more. Three orgasms, one right on the next, each one more intense than the last. Her head was killing her and her pussy ached.

Finally, with a heartrending roar, he slammed even harder into her and then froze, his body locked into place. She could feel his release, the hot wet of it filling her, his cock throbbing and swelling. He collapsed all at once on top of her.

Their bodies were so wet that he actually slid off her. He laughed a little at that, the breath of it tickling her ear, and then he pulled out and turned to his side, turning her to face him as he did. He smiled sadly, his breathing, like hers, still loud and heavy. "That was somethin' else, Sport. You okay?"

She nodded. "Yeah, I think so. You?"

He answered in the way he had every time she'd asked over the past couple of days. "No. But I will be. I've got you." He brushed his hand over her belly. "I've got us."

CHAPTER THIRTEEN

Isaac woke with a kitten sleeping on his shoulder, curled into a tight, black ball. Lilli was sleeping on her back, tucked snugly to his chest. His hand rested on her belly. God, he wanted his baby in there. He wanted them to have made their child in that damn hospital closet. In the middle of all the horror. He didn't even know why, but the want was like a physical pain.

He was still rocked by the way that loving Lilli had changed him. The need to make a family with her rode him hard, a constant presence in his head. Before he'd loved her, he'd had no thought to have even a woman, much less a family. He'd made the decision young to fly solo, and he'd never felt the slightest tremor in that choice in all those years. Not until Lilli entered his life and shook it to dust.

Tasha had been the last—the only other—woman with whom he'd been serious. No, that wasn't true. He hadn't really been serious with her. He'd thought he'd been serious. He'd been exclusive with her. Until the end, anyway. But Show was right; he'd been an asshole to her. They were together for a couple of years, but he never offered her his ink. He never called her his old lady. She hadn't been. She had wanted it—she'd been all in, and he'd known it, he'd exploited it—but she hadn't been his old lady. He hadn't loved her like that. Maybe, thinking about it now, knowing love like he felt for Lilli, maybe he hadn't loved Tasha at all.

She had loved him, though. When she got impatient and started pressing him for the things she wanted—the ink, the commitment, things he didn't want to give her—rather than be a man about it and end it clean, he'd started fucking around with the club girls. Not being discreet about it at all, wanting to get caught. Tasha was a club daughter, so it didn't take her long to catch him. Their end had happened in the middle of the Hall: public, loud, and nearly violent.

Because Tash was club, and the older members thought of her as a daughter, he'd taken heat for the way he'd hurt her to end it. Even though she was a woman, and he was a patch, they'd ridden him hard. And he'd deserved it. It had pissed him off at the time, but he'd deserved it. He thought that sentiment, the way the club had offered her its shoulder and him its fist, was the reason she was still a friend of the club. And that had come in handy a few times once she'd finished med school. It had certainly come in handy yesterday.

The late-morning sun was streaming brightly into the bedroom—Isaac noticed for the first time that the drapes had been pulled down, rod and all. Jesus, that piece of shit tweaker had had a field day in here, for no reason but destruction. He felt yesterday's anger and bloodlust curl around his heart like a fist. The kitten—this one, the only one now, was Pip, he thought—must have caught his vibe, because he jumped off Isaac's shoulder and landed on Lilli before he leapt off the bed completely.

She stirred and stretched. When her eyes blinked open, he pushed his rage back and smiled down at her, bringing his hand to her face. She was so fucking beautiful. They had only slept a few hours, but she'd slept quietly and looked rested. "Morning, Sport."

"Hey." She smiled, and he traced his thumb over the lush swell of her lower lip. "What time is it?"

He looked over his shoulder at the clock on his nightstand. "Almost eleven. Gotta get moving. I want you to come with me to the clubhouse. I don't want you alone."

She shook her head. "No, love. I need to get the house back together, and I have work of my own to do. A deadline. And I don't want to leave Pip alone again."

The rage came up again and moved through his blood. Not wanting to turn it on her, he closed his eyes and took a slow breath. When he spoke, he managed calm, but it was a struggle. "I. Don't. Want. You. Alone. What the hell, Lilli? What else needs to happen before you'll get how fucked up everything is? And you could be pregnant *right now*. I won't let you be alone. Absolutely not."

She shoved him away from her and sat up. "I get how bad things are, Isaac. I was there. But if this is how you're going to be, then I don't want to be pregnant. You know that I can take care of myself. Fuck, I'm more experienced than you are. I won't be hostage to your macho bullshit. I'll go to the pharmacy today and put an end to it."

Without even thinking about it, he had a fistful of her hair, snarled at her nape. "Don't you fucking do it."

She was perfectly still, her grey eyes frosty. "Let go of me right now, love. You'll only hurt me in anger one time. You won't get another chance."

What was he doing? He needed to get control of himself. As frustrated and furious as he was with her, he didn't want to hurt her. God, he didn't. He let her go. "Fuck!" Turning to sit up against the headboard, he took a few more calming breaths and said, "Baby, you can't threaten that shit. Don't hold that over me. I need to protect

162

you. I can't do what I have to do if I'm worried about you. I know you're strong. I know what you can do. But I can't lose you."

They didn't have time to fight this out. He had to be at the clubhouse in an hour. But he needed her with him. He needed her safe. "Can't you work from the clubhouse? You've got that secure satellite connection."

She huffed—as pissed as he was, probably. She was just naturally calmer. "You know I can't work in a public place, Isaac. Look. I know you're worried. I understand. But I can be as safe here as there. We have weapons everywhere here, and I'm on alert now. I'll keep my Sig on me. I'm staying put."

"Lilli—"

With a flare of her eyes and a firm shake of her head, she cut him off. He was going to lose this fight, and he was going to spend the day—and every day—worried sick about her. Goddammit.

But then she gave him something. "How about this—if you don't need him otherwise, bring Badge over. I could use his help, and he and I know each other a little now. We went through something together. If we need to again, we understand how we work. He's a good kid."

She was humoring him, he knew. But it was enough. He relaxed and smiled. "Thank you, Sport. Yeah, that works."

He pulled her close, and she came willingly. Negotiating with her to keep her safe during this crap with Ellis was going to drive him mad.

When he got to the clubhouse, everyone was waiting for him. Except Show. Isaac went to Len, sitting at the bar. "How's he doing?"

Len shook his head. "Not good, brother. He won't talk. He wouldn't answer the door, so about an hour ago, I dug up the master key and barged in on him. He was just sitting on the side of the bed. Still wearing his kutte, his beanie. Don't think he moved all night."

"Alright. Get everybody in the Keep. I'm going back to talk to him, but we need to let him sit this shit out." Bart came in from the side hallway. Isaac hoped that meant he'd been working, maybe in contact with Rick, the master hacker Lilli had set him up with. "You got anything for us, Bartholomew?"

The youngest Horde nodded. "Think so, boss. Like to talk before the Keep, though."

Isaac liked everything on the table. He wasn't one for secrets, not from people he trusted. But there was a kink in their line somewhere, so maybe he needed to be a little more careful with his trust right now. "Yeah." To the room at large, he said, "Chill for a spell, people." He gestured to Bart to send him back toward the office, and he followed.

When they were in the office, Isaac shut and locked the door. He sat at his desk; Bart sat in the chair at its side. "Okay. What you got?"

Bart looked nervous and unhappy, and that put Isaac's already jangling nerves to the test. "What, kid? Spill it."

"I was thinking that what happened yesterday was too...coincidental. Attacks on the only club old ladies, in their houses, at the same time that almost the whole club is on a payback run? It's like the fire at the Keller place was a trap. I mean, that doesn't make sense, we know why Ellis would burn that down, and not just to get to Holly and Lilli. But what happened yesterday still feels like it was part of a larger plan, the whole thing, the past few days, all of a piece. And the place we hit in St. Louis seemed ready for us. Like they knew that's what we'd hit. Not one of their homes, like they hit Will, but that stash house."

Isaac knew where Bart was going. He'd gotten there himself. But he wanted the kid to say it all, and say it straight. "Make your point, Bart."

Bart swallowed hard, like what he had to say got stuck in his throat. "Somebody knew. They knew when we'd be too far away to protect the women. They knew where we'd hit. Somebody knows too much about us. Shit, it's like they knew no one would know Dan and C.J. were in town on patrol. We have a rat. Or a plant."

Isaac nodded. Agreed. "Big difference between a rat and a plant, though. Rat's one of us. Plant's somebody new we let get too close. Which do you think it is?" He'd been thinking about this, too. The Horde were a small, tightknit group. Smaller now, since Wyatt had turned. That had been a bitter betrayal, but understandable—Lilli had been gunning for his younger brother. Isaac couldn't see the angle for the remaining Horde to flip. So a plant was more likely. Somebody newish, who spent a lot of time around the club, enough time to overhear or be told the kind of detail that made the past few days possible.

Bart said what he was thinking. "Plant. I'm thinking a woman. We've had some fresh pussy in here lately. The regulars have been hanging back since this Ellis shit started. So one of those, or…" He let his sentence die out. When Isaac realized what would have finished that sentence, he stood, his hands clenched into fists and shaking.

"Don't you fuckin' say it, asshole."

Bart, brawny but much smaller than Isaac, and younger, too, looked terrified. But he said it anyway. "Boss, I know. But we gotta look at all the possibilities, so we can clear them off the table. Lilli's new. Her trail is still short and walled off. She knows *everything*. And she didn't get hurt yesterday. She came too late to help Holly and the girls. We gotta look at her. Are you *sure*?"

"I'm sure. I'm fuckin' sure. You bring that up again, you raise that doubt to *anybody*, and I will rip your heart clear from your chest and drink from it. Catch me?" Bart nodded, his eyes wide. "Have another idea, asshole." Isaac sat back down.

"Okay. I do. Vic's been tapping a new girl pretty regular. Marissa. I'd call her his favorite, last month or so, and she hangs back, waiting for him. Pretty thing—tiny. I ran her, and she's not our usual club girl. She's college, even. Went to Illinois—U of I. She's working at the Walmart now, but she comes from big Chicago money. Her dad is a heavy hitter in the Chicago Merc. She's not the first rich college girl to lose access to daddy's money and end up in a shit job, or the first one to like getting fucked rough by a biker, but they're rare, and rare is worth a look right now, especially since she's got Chicago ties. Rick and I are working the dad's deets."

Vic wasn't a looker. Balding, heavyset, with a long, red, unkempt beard that had a tendency to house parts of his most recent meal. Not the kind of guy to bring home to a Daddy who moved on the Chicago commodities scene. Which might well be the sole point. But he had a tendency to be rough with the girls. If a girl like this Marissa was pushing up on a guy like Vic, that warranted some attention. He was a talkative drunk, and that might be motivation to withstand the discomfort of bending over for him. "You had low-hanging fruit like her, and you thought you'd start your suspicions with Lilli? Asshole."

Bart was standing firm, and Isaac had to respect it. "Gotta see the whole table, right, boss? All I'm saying is it needed to be seen, so it could be discounted."

It was a fair point, but Isaac wouldn't admit it. "Bring Marissa up at the table. Don't say anything to Vic until then. Get every fucking thing you can on her and her dad. Her dad's gotta be the link to Ellis. I need to talk to Show before we sit."

"Wait, Isaac. One more thing. I'm waiting to get confirmation on it from Rick, but if we're right, I think I know how to get to Ellis." Bart laid out his idea, and Isaac felt the first glimmer of real hope. It was brutal, nasty business, but it might tip the scales finally in their favor.

"Good job, Bartholomew. That's good. Bring it to the table." Isaac stood again, clapped Bart sharply on the back, and left him in the office with his laptop.

Isaac went down the side hallway, into the eerily quiet Hall, where the rest of the Horde were sitting, drinking, and waiting. He scanned the room for this Marissa whom Bart had mentioned. There were a

167

couple of girls in the Hall at the moment who were new since he'd been with Lilli. He no longer paid much attention to the club pussy, so he didn't know either girl's name. Isaac thought of all women as small, but one of the new girls was so small she was child-size. Long, straight, pale blonde hair. Decent rack, but no hips and a skinny ass. Lots of freckles. Vic could break such a little thing in two. The other new girl looked a bit more used, had some meat on her. More like a typical club fuck. Isaac guessed Blonde and Freckled was their college girl. He didn't care how young and tiny she was. If she'd given up info that got Daisy Ryan killed, he'd tear her apart with his own hands. Unless Show wanted to do it.

He turned down the dorm hallway and headed to the room Show preferred. He didn't even bother knocking. Trying the knob and finding it unlocked, Isaac opened the door and found Show sitting just as Len had described: side of the bed, shoulders slumped, staring at the floor, kutte and beanie still on. He walked in and sat down next to his friend. "Show, man. Talk to me. Tell me what I can do."

Without moving, Show answered, "There's nothing. No fix for this."

Isaac was at a loss. He wanted to support Show, help him, but he was inadequate to the task. Lilli would probably know. She had a powerful kind of empathy. He wished again that she'd come to the clubhouse with him.

All he could do was put his hand on his brother's back. His voice low, he said, "I'm so fucking sorry, Show."

Then Show's back began to shake. He hadn't moved, was still staring down at the rug between his feet, but the shaking grew, and then he was sobbing, tears falling onto the rug. Isaac had nothing he

168

could offer but his shoulder, so he pulled Show's head down and held him while he wept for the loss of his daughter and his family.

After only a minute or two, Show reined in his emotions and sat back up. With a vicious swipe at his eyes, he dried his tears. Then he sat staring again.

After several seconds, Isaac said, "I gotta get to the Keep, brother. Bart has intel, maybe a lead on how yesterday went down. We might have a plant in the clubhouse. And we have to plan our next move. You stay put. You're out of this. You have more important things."

Now, for the first time, Show turned and looked Isaac in the eye. "No, I don't. I have this. It's all I have. And I am going to end anyone that had a hand in killing my girl. Anyone."

Isaac nodded. "Okay. Then let's go."

~oOo~

The rest of the Horde were surprised when Show followed Isaac into the Hall. They came up in turn and gave him a hug and said a word. He took it stoically, but Isaac could see that it was causing him pain. There was no comfort to be had. He scanned the room again and lit on the little blonde. Catching Bart's eye, he nodded toward her and raised his eyebrows, asking. Bart nodded. Marissa. He wondered if Show meant it, if he could kill such a little chick. Show, tough and big as he was, was at his heart a gentle, chivalrous soul. If he couldn't do it, Isaac could. If she'd put those sick, tweaked-out sons of bitches in Show's house, then he could kill her bloody without a twitch. Maybe sic Len on her first, give her a taste of what Daisy got.

Daisy. Skinny, bookish Daisy. Long legs, braces, thick glasses over blue eyes. Hair the color of brown sugar, like her dad's, but she kept hers cropped short. Had a big crush on Isaac. Charmed, he'd gently encouraged her, giving her a wink or a smile just for her. She'd started playing chess with her dad. Isaac had challenged her to a game awhile back, teasing her that her dad was letting her off easy, but she'd blushed crimson and declined.

Damn. Sweet Daisy. The first of the flower children. The girls' names had been Holly's idea, a connection to her own name. When they found out Iris would be their third girl and Holly had told Show what she wanted to name her, Show had confided to Isaac that he thought the girls' names were silly. But he gave Holly what she wanted. In most things. He'd worked hard to make his old lady and his little garden of girls happy.

As far as Isaac knew, the only thing Show had ever refused Holly was the Horde. She'd hated it and wanted him to give it up. He would not. And now it was all he had.

Isaac put his hand on Show's shoulder. "Come on. Time to talk."

At the table, they made arrangements for Erik's memorial. His people were in Joplin, so they'd escort his body there and have a party in his memory at the clubhouse. He was only a prospect, and a brand new one at that, but he'd died in the service of the club, and that did not go unacknowledged. Then the talk turned to the attacks on the old ladies, and the somber mood of the room turned sharp and black. Isaac gave Badger's and Lilli's descriptions, which had aligned perfectly. Of course they had. Dan and Ceej told what they saw. Showdown sat silently, his hands knotted into heavy fists on the table, his knuckles white.

Then Isaac looked around the room, his glance holding on Vic. Vic was pure club, no doubt about it. He could be counted on to do what was asked, without question. He wasn't mean. In fact, he was fucking jovial. But he was rough, and he had an inventive streak. It made him a very good enforcer and their go-to interrogator. But he was loose. He drank hard, he fucked hard, he worked hard—all the more since he'd come back from Iraq. They'd had to clean up after him more than once, greasing the palms of angry tavern owners and bruised, sometimes bleeding women.

His real flaw, however, was that he talked a blue streak, especially when he drank. He would never intentionally share a secret, but he was not a bright guy. Get him drunk, put a willing, wet pussy on his lap, and he'd eventually answer any question she asked. In normal times, it wasn't a big deal. The club girls were known, and they knew to shut the fuck up, and the club business was small potatoes, comparatively. But these were not normal times.

Not paying attention to the new girls hanging around was yet another of Isaac's misses. He needed to wise the fuck up and stop leading this club as if it were the same club it had been for years—mainly quiet, running the town, only part-time outlaws. They were in the thick of the shit now. He needed to lead like it.

As of now, Bart was going to need to start running checks on every fucking person who showed up even twice in this clubhouse. Too little, too late, but at least they could stop it from happening again.

He'd thought all that in a pause of a couple of seconds. Now he turned his eyes from Victor and focused on Bart. "We obviously have a leak. What happened was too well timed to be coincidental. Yesterday's attacks had to be Ellis, and he knew we'd be gone. He knew Lilli and Show's girls would be vulnerable. He knew we'd be in St. Louis. And he knew where we'd hit. Whole fucking thing was a gambit, and we left him a huge opening. We think we know the leak. Bart?"

Bart began explaining about Marissa. While he spoke, Isaac could feel Show's tension increasing. He looked over; Show was staring at Victor, and it was clear that, even though Bart had not yet suggested that Victor was the source of information if Marissa was the plant, Show had put the pieces together. It was also clear that Show had decided whom to kill first.

Isaac turned to Victor, who was also watching Show. He, too, had put the pieces together, and he could read Show's intent as clearly as Isaac had. He spoke up, interrupting Bart. "Show, man. No. Not from me, she didn't. No *way* I'd give up your girls. No *way* I'd say anything to get them hurt. I know it. Not me."

Show stood, towering over the table. "You fucking loudmouth piece of shit. You never fucking shut up. Jesus, was it fuck talk? Did you tell her when the murdering raping meth fucks could get to my girls while your dick was buried in her ass?"

Everyone at the table had come to their feet while Show gritted out his words. Len and Isaac had their eyes on Show, but Isaac did a quick scan around the table, and the rest of the Horde were looking murder on Vic. This was bad. Isaac needed to get control of it. He put his hand on Show's arm. Show yanked away, but Isaac grabbed him. "Easy, Show. You want vengeance, and you'll get it. But let's get it right."

172

Show moved his blazing gaze from Victor to Isaac. Isaac held until, finally, Show nodded. Breathing out his relief, Isaac turned to the table. "Sit down. Let Bart finish. He has a plan."

Once the table was seated and calm again, Bart went on. Victor and Show were still waging silent war, but Isaac felt reasonably sure Show would hold. Bart got Show's full attention when he explained what he knew about Marissa's father. And then he laid out the plan.

"Martin Halyard is a bigwig Chicago financier. I traced his connections and client list, and I came up with LGE Ventures. It was buried behind dummy companies, but it was there. LGE is Lawrence Gaylord Ellis. It's the link. Bright as the sun, if you know where to look. I'm working with Rick Terrance, the megahacker Lilli put me with. He's so much more badass than me it ain't even funny. Seriously, you should kick my ass out and bring him in. He can break into the fucking Merc—the Chicago Mercantile Exchange. It's like the stock market. From there, we can get anything we need. But here's the thing. This Halyard guy is up to his ears in Ellis finances. One way or another, even though a shit ton of it is buried behind walls and dummies, Halyard is swimming in Ellis money. It's fucking beautiful, how well protected Ellis is. But we're in. And we have Halyard's only child not twenty feet away from us. I don't think daddy disowned her. I think she's daddy's pride and joy. I think she's here on his word. And I think we can flip him if we use her." Finished, Bart sat back with a heavy sigh.

Isaac looked around the table. "Anybody got a problem leaning on that new little blonde bitch?" Horde heads shook as he scanned the table. No one had a problem, no. Victor looked livid, and Isaac thought, assuming they didn't take his patch over his big mouth, that little freckled Marissa would have a tougher go with Vic than with anyone else, save Show.

Isaac met Show's eyes last. His grieving brother stared, his eyes steely. "I want her head. Mail it to daddy in a box."

CHAPTER FOURTEEN

Lilli went into the feed store, with Badger, who had been her closest companion over the past week and a half, trailing behind. She had a list Isaac had made for her of different grains, supplements, and other supplies they'd need for the horses. Looked like Gertie, Flash, and Ebony were with them to stay. Her next errand was a trip to Signal Bend Realty to sign the papers—she was about to spend half a million dollars on the Keller property. Her father's death money.

She knew it was the right call, the right thing to do, but a dull kind of anxiety burbled in her gut. Even in the rightness, there was something wrong about spending her father's money to buy the Keller place. She should not own it. Will Keller should own it. He should be living on it with his wife and kids. Even though she knew she was helping to save the town and in that way preserving Will's legacy to at least a nominal extent, and even though she knew her father would be proud of her choice to buy the property, she felt an ill wind rising up around this purchase.

Maybe it was simply that she knew that doing so, interrupting Ellis's plans to buy the land himself, plans in the service of which he'd exerted a great deal of energy and expense, would shift his attention to her. But Lilli wasn't one who backed down from a fight, and her life had been on the line many times before, so she wasn't sure why this fight had her more anxious than any other.

Except that now she had Isaac and a future she cared about.

The feed store drew patronage from a wide radius and was fairly busy, one of the few businesses in town that had remained steadily healthy. There was a line at the counter where Isaac had told her she'd need to order the bulk feed, so instead of dealing with that, she wandered around the stock area. She found the supplements Isaac had listed—sheesh, even those came in huge buckets—and sent Badger over for a pallet cart, since they apparently would be loading up here. Good thing she'd taken Isaac up on his suggestion that they take his truck today.

She got the various supplements, the grooming supplies, new feed buckets. Waiting for the feed line to dwindle more, she wandered over to the tack section and examined the saddles and bridles. The saddles were gorgeous. All of them tooled and shaped, some with beautiful stitching on the seat, a couple with silver trim. And wow. Not cheap.

The bridles surprised her. There were a lot of different kinds, and the heavy metal parts, which she assumed were the parts that went into the horse's mouth, were all different. Some were one solid piece, others were pieces that were linked in different ways, one kind didn't seem to have a mouth piece at all. In addition to the complete bridles, There was a whole section just of the metal parts, and another of the leather harness parts. Just looking at the bridles told Lilli that there was a world of shit she didn't know about horses.

Badger was leaning on the pallet cart, watching her, an awfully damn condescending smirk on his face—which he wiped off as soon as he saw her looking at him. "Too late, bud. I saw that. Okay, so teach me, since you know so much."

There was a confidence in his laugh that said he knew plenty, born and raised in the country, and he certainly could teach his President's city girl about horse tack. He went to the section of metal parts. "These are bits. Which one you want depends a lot on which one a horse was broke to. Sometimes you change a bit out if you're not getting the response from the horse you want. And sometimes you change out a harsher bit for a gentler one once the horse is in hand. Depends on the trainer. A horse that's broke right shouldn't need a bit change, though, unless something else is going on."

He picked up a solid metal piece, shaped something like an "H," with an arch in the center. "This is a curb bit with a port mouthpiece. Pretty standard, especially for the kind of riding we do around here." Putting that one back on the display, Badger picked up one with two linked pieces, a ring on either side. "This is a jointed snaffle. The snaffle means it only has the two rings attached to the mouthpiece, instead of the four connections—purchase and shank—that the curb has. A mouthpiece like this moves in the horse's mouth. More pressure, could pinch. People tend to use something like this on a horse that needs a firmer hand, but I think that's just bad training." He continued, picking up each kind of bit, explaining it, and setting it down. The last one he picked up was big, the metal of the bit dark. The mouthpiece was made of twisted, jointed metal pieces and looked positively medieval. "Double twisted wire. This one is fucked up. In the wrong rider's hands, it'll tear hell out of a horse's mouth. Far as I'm concerned, any rider who'd use it is the wrong rider."

Lilli was impressed. Not only did young Badger know a lot, but he was confident and opinionated about it. He tended to be shy and easily intimidated around her and around the Horde, but now he was holding a master class on horse tack. He moved to the leather parts—the headstalls, she learned—and explained the halter, split ear, and Western styles, among others. The one that didn't have a bit was a hackamore.

Jesus. All that for just the bridle. She was afraid to ask about the saddles. Maybe another day. But she wanted to learn to ride, and they didn't have any of this stuff. So she asked, "Well, okay. That's a lot. What should I get for, say, Gertie?"

Badger shook his head. "Don't know. Don't know Gertie well enough. Isaac would, though. You should bring him to buy this kind of stuff."

Lilli looked over her shoulder and saw that the line had petered out. "Okay. Good idea. Let's take care of the feed and hay, and get out of here." Badge nodded and took control of the pallet cart, back in Prospect mode.

~oOo~

As Badger and one of the kids working—someone Badge was friendly with—were loading up the truck, Lilli saw Show pull into the lot in his pickup. He ran the feed store, but so soon after what had happened, and with the Horde stuff so heavy right now, Lilli thought it strange to see him coming in to work like a regular Joe.

She hadn't seen much of him since Daisy had died. She hadn't seen that much of Isaac, either, frankly. The Ellis business was taking up a lot of his time. He'd been cagey about what was going on, and she didn't pry. She was curious—it affected her, too—but her military training and natural reserve kept her mouth shut. He knew he could talk to her when and if he needed. That he wasn't, she assumed, meant that he didn't want her to know. Whatever the reason for that, she trusted him.

She knew that Show was just as deep in the club work as Isaac, and when she learned what Holly had done, she understood his need to stay busy. Within three days of the attack, Holly, Rose, and Iris were gone. Utterly. She'd packed up everything she could in her old Suburban and moved back to her hometown, in Arkansas. She'd arranged for Daisy to be sent with them, to bury her in her family's plot. She hadn't even given Show the chance to be present at his daughter's funeral.

Lilli understood Holly's desperate, furious need to get clear of Signal Bend. She understood her need to get her daughters far from here. What they'd all gone through was horrific, and there was no guarantee, until Ellis was stopped, that it wouldn't happen again. But Lilli did not understand the focused heat of her fury at Show. Holly hated the Horde, but Show had been Horde when she met him. She had married and had children with him knowing he was Horde. She had appreciated the status Show's position gave her in town. Lilli knew it wasn't her place to know what went on between that married couple, but it did seem to her that Show was being punished harshly and unduly.

She supposed he was Holly's clearest target for what must have been unbearable grief and rage. It was a naturally human thing to do, to blame the person easiest to blame. When the desperate anger was too much to withstand, most people found a way to send it outward. But as Lilli stood there and watched him shut the truck door and turn, she saw a broken man. A man who'd lost his daughter. And who'd then lost his entire family. A man hunched over under the weight of guilt and grief, turning his own anger and desperation inward.

179

He saw her and raised a hand, a corner of his mouth lifting in an almost-smile. Lilli raised her hand in return, then looked quickly over at Badge, just as he was slamming the gate on the pickup. "Hey, Badge. You think you can kill an hour or so without me?"

"No way, Lilli. You know Isaac will use my intestines for sausage casing if I leave you."

She laughed. "Nice imagery. No, I want to talk to Show, see if I can get him over to Marie's for lunch. So I'll be in better hands. No offense, of course."

The kid who'd helped Badger with the feed sacks piped up. "I got lunch in ten, Justin. I'm heading to No Place to pick up pizza for everybody. You can come with if you want."

For a second, Badger looked torn. Then he nodded. "Call me, though, if you need something. Back here in an hour."

It was an order, not a request. Lilli smirked, and he blushed. "Don't get bossy, bud. I'll kick your ass, and you know it. But yeah, I'll meet you at the truck in an hour." She turned and trotted after Show, who'd just gone through the door into the shop.

"Show. Wait up."

He stopped, still holding the door, and turned. "Hey, Lilli." Her heart hurt to hear the defeat in his voice. He stepped back into the lot, and she stepped up and hugged him. He stood like a stone at first, and then he sort of melted into her, his arms coming around her.

She leaned back and looked up at him. "Come have lunch with me?"

He shook his head. "I'm just in to get paychecks out. Gotta get back to the clubhouse."

"Show. Come to Marie's with me. Just an hour. Half an hour, even. Come on. Buy me some fried chicken. I just sent Badger off to get pizza with some random kid in a Trace Adkins t-shirt, so I'm in need of bodyguarding."

At that, he smiled and shook his head. "Billy is the Adkins fan. And you're gonna get Badge missing important body parts if Isaac catches him playing fast and loose with his job."

"But I'm with you now."

His smiled disappeared. "That won't keep you safe."

She could have kicked herself for running over that territory. Rather than apologize and make more of it, though, she simply ignored the self-loathing in his comment. Hooking her arm around his, she said, "Come on, Show. Take me to lunch."

He stared down at her, then nodded and walked with her back to his truck.

~oOo~

There was a decent lunch crowd, and the hum of conversation stopped cold when Show and Lilli went into the diner. Show nodded at Marie, behind the counter, and then walked to the last open booth. The people they passed—most of whom Lilli now knew—nodded soberly at Show as he went by. She appreciated the quiet way these people had of showing respect. Just a nod, then they left Show to himself. There was a lot to be said for country stoicism. They might gossip like fishwives later, but they kept their mouths shut now, and that was good.

Marie was right behind them, coffeepot in hand, when they sat. She poured, they ordered, and then, when she left, Show gave Lilli a look. "Why am I here, Lilli?"

She didn't know quite what to say; she wasn't entirely sure why he was there. She'd seen him looking so sad and broken, and she'd wanted to take him to lunch. "You looked like a guy who needed a minute away from your life, I guess."

He scoffed. "No getting away from this life."

"No, I suppose not. But I'm a pretty good listener, if you have something you need to talk about."

He shook his head, and for a while they sat there in silence. Lilli stirred creamer and sugar into her coffee, watching the white liquid swirl and disappear. Marie brought their meals. Lilli picked a little at her chicken. Then Show said. "I was going to take her for her learner's permit today."

She heard him and understood. Setting her fork down, she looked at him but said nothing. She waited to see if he had more he wanted to say.

"I keep thinking about that. I was quizzing her on the road rules, helping her get ready. I knew she'd pass. She's—was—such a smart thing. Holly and I had a big fight about it. She didn't want her on the

road yet. One of the few fights I ever pushed hard enough to win."
He laughed harshly and looked out the front window. "I was going
to take her up to that frozen custard place in Worden after. Just her
and me." Still looking out the window, he sighed. "I'm a shitty
father to say it, I know, but she's—was—my favorite. Most like me.
Rosie and Iris, they're all about dolls and dress-up. Rosie cries over
every little thing, and all Iris can talk about is these cartoon
princesses. I don't really get 'em. I love 'em, but I don't get 'em.
Daze liked what I liked. I knew how to talk to her. And she got me."

His head sagged, hovering over his plate. Lilli put her hand over his
fist, where it was coiled on the table. He looked up, his expression
angry. "That what you want to hear?"

She pulled her hand back. "No, Show. I don't mean to pry. If you
don't want to talk, that's cool. I just wanted you to know you can. If
you want to step away from the club shit and talk to somebody, I'm
here. I'm sorry if I'm prying, really."

"Naw. I'm sorry. It's okay. Not a share-my-feelings guy. Don't even
know how. But you're right, I guess. I'm coming out of my skin.
Fuck, I miss Daze." He laughed sadly. "You know, I don't even miss
Holly. Last few years, our shit was hard. I want to die over what I let
happen to her, but I don't miss her. I miss my girls, but not my wife.
I'm no kind of man."

"That's bullshit, Show." He raised his eyebrows at that. "It is. I
know you need to beat yourself up. I get it. But falling out of love
doesn't make you anything but human." She sighed and put her hand
on his again. "Arkansas isn't so far away. You can still see Rose and
Iris."

"No." He shook his head and turned back to the window. "Sent the papers back today. Signed what she sent me. Divorced. Child support, but no custody, no visitation."

Holly had wasted not one second. "Jesus, Show. She cut you out?"

He continued to stare out the window. "Yeah. She threatened to rat if I didn't. Left me the choice to give her what she wanted or keep her from talking some other way." He turned suddenly, his eyes wider, as if he'd shocked himself. "Lilli, fuck. That's a confidence. The Horde can't know that. Not Isaac or anybody. They'll go for her for the threat alone."

Lilli knew how to keep a secret. Even from Isaac, if necessary, and this was. "Okay. Mouth shut. But Show, I'm so sorry."

"Yeah." He pushed his plate of uneaten food away and pulled his wallet out, its chain rattling against the Formica table. "I gotta get back, Lilli."

When Show parked his truck at the feed store, he got out and came around as Lilli was climbing down. He grabbed her arm and pulled her into a quick, hard hug. Then, without saying a word, he let her go and went inside.

Lilli stood at the side of his truck and watched him, feeling low and helpless. Then she heard Badge laughing. She followed the sound, and found him, Billy, and a couple of other young guys grouped around a picnic table at the side of the store, two large pizzas from No Place spread over the top. When Badge saw her, he finished the slice in his hand, wiped his hands on his jeans, waved a goodbye to his friends, and trotted over to take her and her horse supplies home.

~oOo~

When she heard Isaac's Harley roaring up to the garage, Lilli had Gertie tied off in the middle of the barn and was brushing her while Badger installed the new feed buckets in the stalls. Flash and Ebbie were grazing in the paddock. They needed more room to run, but Lilli didn't yet have confidence she'd be able to get them to come back to her if she turned them out in the big pasture. Isaac called them in with a loud whistle, his thumb and forefinger in the corners of his mouth. Lilli couldn't whistle at all.

Isaac came into the barn door, pulling his shades off and hooking them in the pocket of his kutte. "Hey, baby. Looks like you were busy today." He put a gloved hand on Gertie's nose and hooked a finger through Lilli's belt loop, drawing her close for a kiss.

Lilli's day had been stressful—the heartbreaking talk with Show; signing off on the property purchase, which meant dealing with Mac Evans and his unsettling way of looking at her; and one last impulse call she'd made that had stirred a lot of old sadness up. She'd needed Isaac. She hadn't realized how much until his mouth was on hers. She dropped the brush and turned into him, wrapping her arms around him and opening her mouth to take his tongue. Gertie nickered and nibbled at her arm.

Isaac kissed her back, hard and deep, and then pulled away to look down into her eyes. "You okay, Sport?"

She nodded. "Missed you." He pulled her closer, and her body throbbed and grew wet.

As if he'd caught the scent of her arousal, his eyes flared and, without moving his gaze from her, he called out, "Badge! Hit the road. LaVonne is waiting for you in the Hall."

From the corner of her vision, Lilli could see Badge's head pop up over the front wall of Ebbie's stall. "LaVonne? Really? I—um—need to finish installing this, though."

Isaac grinned down at Lilli, then turned to Badge. "I got it. You go on. Don't keep her waiting, and don't make her sorry. You make her sorry, you make me sorry. Then I make you sorry. Catch me?"

Lilli looked over to see Badge's grinning, moony face. LaVonne was apparently a big deal. Badge came through the stall door so quickly Gertie started a little and then huffed at him, irritated. "Thanks, boss! Nobody'll be sorry, I promise. See you tomorrow, Lilli!" And he was gone.

They watched him go, then turned back to each other. "Sounds like LaVonne is a helluva reward."

Isaac winked. "She can, as we say, suck the chrome off a tailpipe."

"And you know this personally?" She knew the answer; she just wanted him to squirm a little.

But he didn't. He shrugged, still grinning. "I have a past. You jealous?"

"Nah. But I might have to do some sucking myself, make sure you appreciate me."

186

He set her back and untied Gertie. "That's no way to make a baby. So first, I'm gonna fuck you screaming right here in this barn. Later, you can suck whatever you want." He led Gertie into the paddock. Lilli used those couple of minutes wisely, and when he came back, she was naked. It was pretty damn chilly on this late-autumn evening, but she knew he'd warm her up right quick.

He stopped dead inside the paddock door. "Jesus Christ, woman. I love you."

~oOo~

Much later that night, after a brilliant barn fuck—if she wasn't already pregnant it damn sure wasn't for lack of trying—chores, dinner, and another multifaceted round in their bed, Lilli lay on Isaac's chest, running her fingers through the happy trail of hair down the muscled ridges of his belly. Isaac kissed the top of her head. "Thank you for what you did for Will's wife and for the town. For us. I know it was hard."

"I know it's the right thing. I'm glad we have the horses. We'll have to figure out what to do with the property, but not till all this crap is settled down. As long as Ellis is gunning for it, we should let it sit."

"I'll keep you safe, Sport. I won't let him hurt you. I swear it."

She sighed. She didn't want to fight him, but he knew as well as she did that a vow like that was pointless. If Ellis wanted to get to her— and he would—then he would get to her. She had to be ready to fight back. And hope that they were able to get to him first.

Deciding that he needed to let her know he wanted her safe more than she needed to remind him yet again that he couldn't keep her safe, she changed the subject. "I did something today that feels kind of scary."

He shifted under her, shrugging his shoulder so that she'd lift her head and meet his eyes. "You okay?," he asked.

"Yeah. Not scary like that. I called my dad's lawyer back after all the real estate stuff was done and asked him to clear out my storage locker and ship everything here. It's mostly books, and a few boxes of heirlooms from my Nonnie and my dad."

Isaac grinned widely. "Lilli, that's great. That's awesome. Why is it scary?"

She wasn't sure how to explain it, but it had been eating at her vaguely all evening. "I don't know. I think maybe it's because it means I'm really settled. I mean—I don't mean that I don't want to be here with you. I do, so much. And I know I've been struggling because I wasn't feeling like I had a place here. I do now, and that's why I wanted my stuff. But...it's weird. My whole past is in those boxes, and I haven't seen any of that for more than a decade. All this time, my most permanent address has been that storage locker. It feels weird to give it up. And it feels weird that it feels weird." She laughed. "It's all very weird."

He hugged her close, tucking her head under his chin. "I get it, Sport. I do. It's a big change. But it tells me only good things. In some ways, to me, it's even bigger than you being ready for a baby. You're moving in. Now you're moving in."

They were quiet for long minutes after that. Lilli started to doze, snug in Isaac's arms. Then his voice rumbled up against her ear. "I want to give you my ink."

She understood what that meant. It didn't surprise her; they were already planning to be married. She'd figured it would probably be something that happened at around the same time. But she knew that, to a man like Isaac, ink was the bigger deal. That was the lifetime commitment. She wondered if Holly had Show's ink.

"Take my ink, baby. Don't make me wait for that. Take it now. Please."

When she realized that there wasn't even a decision to be made, something deep inside her calmed, and she knew that she was already settled, truly home. "I will."

He rolled, laying her under him, and kissed her deeply. When she felt his cock lengthen and harden again on her thigh, she knew the night was not yet over.

CHAPTER FIFTEEN

Isaac sat up against the headboard and watched Lilli sleep. The morning was getting ripe—almost ten o'clock. She almost never slept this late, so she obviously needed the rest. He hated to wake her, but it was getting late, and he would need to get moving soon. More than waking her, he hated to leave without letting her know.

She'd had a rough night, waking three separate times in the clutches of her nightmare. He wished he knew a way to keep her safe from her dreaming. But he didn't know a way to keep her safe from anything.

Ellis had yet to make another move. Liza Keller had bought them some time by demanding of Ellis's associates—and, surprisingly, getting—time to bury her husband before she dealt with his offer. By the time she had, the sale to Lilli had been inked. Now, they had Liza and her family fully under the protection of the Scorpions in Florida, and, in Signal Bend, they were doing what they could to suppress the information about the sale. But that was borrowed time. When Ellis found out who the new owner was, he'd come for Lilli. The Horde needed to get to him first.

They'd been working Marissa Halyard for almost two weeks. They'd started easy. Victor had held off a vote for his patch by feeding her fake intel. It was his idea, and it was a risk, since they'd had no idea if he could pass off the fake stuff as real, but she'd bitten. They had confirmation now that she was the leak, and the intel they'd fed her had cleared a good path for Bart and Rick right to her father's door.

190

Now it was time to use her in a different way. Make her daddy sweat, get him to open Ellis's door so they could walk through it.

It was a helluva thing for Isaac to wake up, curled close with his woman, his first thought love and concern for her, and his second thought the realization that he would spend the day torturing a twenty-three-year-old girl. His life was chaos.

He slid back down and turned to his side, brushing his hand over the silky, firm skin of her waist and hip. He traced his fingers over the sentence inked in Italian script up her side, from her hip to her ribs: *L'amor che muove il sole e l'altre stelle.* The love that moves the sun and the other stars. Dante. The last line of *The Divine Comedy*. A memorial to her father. And the kind of love Isaac felt for her.

Her first tattoo was a butterfly on the back of her left shoulder. Intricate, black and grey, the kind of tattoo a young woman got before she'd figured herself out. He traced its delicate lines, and she brushed at his hand in her sleep, sighing deeply, but she still slept.

Finally, he ran his fingers lightly over the back of her neck and down between her shoulder blades, where her new ink was healing well. The very next day after she'd agreed to take his ink, he'd called Tony, the Horde's guy, and had taken her to his little shop in Millview. He'd already known exactly what he wanted it to be: Mjölnir, with his name worked into the pattern. His mark. Where he could see it, touch it. No matter where they were. She was his.

"Hey." She said it on a breath, then rolled to her back, her body sliding against his as he held her. "Morning."

He brushed her hair from her eyes. "Morning, Sport. Rough night."

She made a face but said nothing; she didn't like to talk about the dreams at all. After a few seconds, she asked, "Time is it?"

"'Bout ten. I gotta get movin', but I wanted to spend a little time with you first. Could be a late one tonight." He kissed her, and she opened her mouth and drew his tongue in. Groaning as his cock swelled, he pulled back. "Don't have that kinda time, baby. Unless you want to shower with me." He loved showering with her, but getting her to agree to get in there with him was tough—she had a weird privacy thing—so he grinned when she nodded. "Good girl. I'll get it started."

He got the water very hot, the way she liked it, and stepped in. She came into the bathroom a minute or so later and slid the curtain back, standing there gloriously naked and beautiful. She looked tired, though, still. But she was smiling, and she looped her arms around his neck as he pulled her close with one arm. He held his swollen cock in the other hand and pushed it against her folds, making her gasp and flex.

There wasn't a lot of time, but he didn't want to rush this, either. Relishing the hot slide of her wet body on his, so pliant and delicious, he slid his cock between her legs, letting her thighs hold him snugly, sensuously. Then he bent his head to take a beautiful, rosy nipple between his teeth. He suckled her hard, the way she liked. Her hands curling into his hair, she moaned his name.

And then she went completely limp in his arms. Surprised, he nearly dropped her, then nearly dropped her again when she remained limp and her slick body slid through his embrace.

"Lilli! Baby!" She was out cold.

Holding her tightly, he swept her legs up and carried her out of the bathroom, both of them dripping wet and the shower still running. When he got back to their bed, he laid her down and pulled the comforter over her. She was pale. Had she been before? Had he missed that?

She was breathing, but her pulse was pretty fast, and he was alarmed. Sitting on the bed at her side, he held her hand. "Baby, come on." He was going to have to get her to the hospital. Out here, 911 was a joke in an actual emergency.

He ran to turn the shower off, then jumped, still wet, into his jeans. A thought was occurring to him, but he was no less scared. She was still out, and that couldn't be good. He was grabbing his shirt off the floor when she came to. He dove to his knees at the side of the bed.

"Oh, thank God, baby." Her eyes fluttered shut again, and he shook her gently. "Hey. Stay with me. What's going on?"

She blinked and took a deep breath. "Not feeling so well, I guess. I'm okay, though."

"Scared the shit outta me, Sport. Gettin' to be a habit with you." He ran his fingers through her wet hair. "You sure you're okay?"

"Yeah. Just got lightheaded. I'm better. Tired, but better. Might sleep some more."

None of this was like her. He asked the question that had occurred to him. "Lilli, when's your period due?"

He saw her understand. Since they were trying—very enthusiastically—to knock her up, they probably should both have been looking for signs, but everything was so busy and nuts that he, for one, hadn't even thought to watch the calendar. But he'd just done a quick count, and they'd been going at it unprotected for more than two weeks, so...

"Couple days. It's too early for me to have any symptoms, though, right? Even if I am?"

He grinned. "You're asking the wrong dude, Sport. I got no idea about any of this. I'm gonna have Badge get you a test, though, before he gets here."

She sat up fast, then—too fast. She put her hand to her head, worrying him again. "Lilli?"

"No fucking way is Badger going to pick up a pregnancy test for me. I have errands to run today. I'll pick one up then. When he's not looking. Nobody needs to know. Okay?" She pushed lightly at him. "I thought you had to get going."

He really did, but he didn't want to leave her. He wanted to be with her when she took the test. He wanted to make sure she was okay. And Badger wasn't there yet, anyway. But, fuck, he really did need to go.

"You sure you're gonna be okay, baby?"

She rolled her eyes. Her color was better, and she was feeling well enough now to get pissed off. "I'm fine. I'm going to sleep more, and then I'm going to have my day. I'll have Badge around if I need help. So get out. Go do your thing."

"Bed's wet. You're wet. C'mon. I'll help you with that before I go."

She started to protest, but then she gave up and nodded. He helped her up and followed her to the bathroom. Once there, she flipped him off and closed the door in his face. Grinning stupidly, feeling a bizarre and nearly debilitating mélange of hope, happiness, concern, and blinding fear, he stripped the wet bedding and remade the bed. Lilli came out of the bathroom, her wet hair braided down her back. He helped her into one of his t-shirts and guided her back to their now-dry bed. That she let him fuss as much as she did told him how crappy she really felt.

"Hey. Wait to take the test until I'm home, okay? I want to be here." Her eyes closed, she nodded.

The kitchen door squealed, and Badger called out, "I'm here, boss!" Isaac bent down and kissed her forehead. "Badge's here. I gotta go, baby. Call me if you need *anything*. Okay?"

Her only answer was a quiet moan as she drifted back into sleep.

~oOo~

Vic's little friend Marissa was already bound when Isaac got to the clubhouse. It was his custom to be last in—he fucking hated waiting for people. Show was sitting at the bar with Bart when he got there. Dom was putting away clean barware. The Hall was otherwise empty. That wasn't so unusual in the late morning, when people were off at their work, but there was a heaviness in the air that was different. Isaac knew what it was—the work of the Horde today was dark business.

Show and Bart stood when he came in. As Isaac approached, Show said, "We're good to go. Ceej and Dan are leading patrol. Vic, Len, and Havoc are in there with her."

Isaac looked at Bart. "You set up?"

Bart nodded. "Yeah. I'm in her Skype, got the signal protected. We should have a good window to transmit what we want without anyone making record of it. Can't keep Halyard from recording if he wants, but otherwise we should be clear."

They planned to Skype Marissa's session with the Horde to her father. Isaac wanted him to see their faces, but he wanted to avoid the chance that someone could snag the feed and record it. Video evidence of what they were about to do could take them all down, send them inside for a long time. Until recently, the Horde had been a small-time club. They were careful with the meth, and otherwise they'd barely been outlaws. Only C.J. had done serious time—an eight-year stretch back in the day. Isaac didn't relish the thought of landing the whole club in Marion. So he hoped Bart's protections were solid. Because this day was going to be fucked up.

A cyclone filled his head. He'd left Lilli sick, maybe pregnant, and thoughts of her clamored even more loudly than usual for the lead. But those thoughts were in direct conflict with his plans for the day—the torture of a young woman while her father watched. Dark shit. She deserved it, and her father deserved it. They'd gotten Daisy killed horribly, and her mother brutalized. Yet Isaac questioned what the Night Horde had become if they'd reached a place where what they were about to do was the right course. He didn't know how he was going to live with this day on his conscience.

Through force of will, he pushed those thoughts to the back of his brain and let them squabble there. To the fore, he pulled resolve. This was their play; they'd all agreed. Times were desperate, and Marissa and her father could be the key that would open a path to success for them. Success meant saving Signal Bend. And saving Lilli, who, Isaac knew, would be Ellis's next target.

He looked at Show, who had pulled himself together fairly well over the past two weeks, focusing his energy on the job and on his need for revenge. "You ready for this, brother?"

Show nodded, and the three of them headed down the hallway to the Room. Bart went through the double doors and hanging plastic dock strips, but Show pulled Isaac back.

Isaac turned and raised his eyebrows, questioning Show's hesitation. His eyes intent and his voice low, Show gritted, "She dies, Isaac. She doesn't go home to daddy. Don't give a fuck what he gives us or what you promise him. Her life for Daisy's. Don't take that from me."

Isaac heard a desperate bite to his friend's tone, and he put his hand on his shoulder. That kind of bloodlust wasn't part of Show's makeup. He looked like a badass motherfucker, and he was tough as anyone, but he wasn't brutal. He was thoughtful. He was honorable. He treated women with a gentle respect. Or he had, before his teenage daughter had been raped to death. "I told you, brother. It's your call. When it comes to it, it's your call."

Show nodded with evident relief, and Isaac guided him into the Room.

197

Little freckled Marissa was a blubbering mess. Vic had fucked her hard one last time and then dragged her naked ass into the Room. Now she was bound to one of the metal chairs. She was gagged, too, but she was still making a fair amount of wet, whimpery noise. They hadn't done anything to her yet, other than the humiliation of being naked and bound to a chair, circled by a bunch of angry bikers. But she wasn't stupid. She knew exactly why she was there, and her fear was so heavy it stank.

Isaac pulled a stool up and sat down in front of her. Her eyes were huge and wet, mascara smeared across them like a mask. She had a fair number of bruises and bite marks, especially on and around her tits. Vic's reputation as an animal was well earned. She'd worked hard for the intel she'd gotten out of him. He wondered if she still thought it was worth it. She wouldn't by the time they were done.

Victor's culpability in this disaster had not yet been addressed. Show wanted his patch, but Isaac had talked him down. They couldn't afford to lose another member, not now. Vic had been happy to have the chance to buy back some good grace by feeding this skinny little bitch rigged information, but Isaac knew that if they were still standing when this crisis passed, Vic's patch would probably be up for a vote. He was sure Vic knew it, too. That made him extra loyal and careful now, and Isaac intended to put that to good use.

"I'm gonna talk to you a little, honey. I can see you know enough to be scared, and that's smart. That college education didn't go to waste, then. You should be scared. We know what you've been doing. Taking advantage of poor, stupid Vic like that. That's some bad shit, little Marissa. You know what happened because of you?" He stopped and gave her the chance to respond with a nod or a shake of her head, but she simply stared, her chest heaving, snot running from her nose.

He looked at Len. Normally, Vic would be his go-to for this work, but Vic had done all he was going to do to her. He liked it too much, and Isaac didn't want him enjoying himself now. Len could go equally hard, but he was cold-blooded about it. He didn't get off on it. He worked, he didn't play. Len came around now with a long, slender metal cocktail pick. That was all it was—a cocktail pick. Isaac stood so that Len could take the stool.

His mouth set grimly, Len lifted Marissa's fingers with a gentle grip. As if he were studying them to determine where to start, he massaged each one. Marissa tried to talk, to beg, through the terry cloth of the towel with which she was gagged. Len selected her index finger and slid the pick between her nail and its bed. She went rigid, and she screamed—one continuous, muffled note that took on a higher pitch when Len pulled the pick back out.

When she was quiet again, Len stood and Isaac sat. "Okay, honey. I asked you a question. Just nod or shake. You answer it, and then I'll let you know how the rest of the day plays out. Do you know what happened because of you?"

She nodded, her head bobbing emphatically. Isaac wasn't surprised that she'd known, but to have her confirm it—she'd *known*. She'd known what the intel she was getting could do, how it could hurt, and she'd kept right on taking what Vic gave her and sending it along to the people who would use it. He had no appetite for what they were doing now, but he had no sympathy for this girl, either. She was no innocent.

Weeping, she tried to talk again, but her words were obscured by the towel. Isaac had no need yet for her words. She had nothing he needed to hear. Her father, though, might.

199

"You don't need to talk right now, sweetheart. Just do what I say. That's the way to play this. Things'll go better for you that way." He looked over at Show, who was regarding him steadily. He'd meant it when he'd said it was Show's call. He would probably have to make promises today, but the only one he knew he'd keep was the one he'd made to Showdown. What happened to Marissa Halyard would be up to the man she'd hurt most. It was the least Isaac could do.

It was all he could do.

He nodded at Bart, who brought another stool over and set a laptop on it. Isaac looked back at the shaking, weepy girl, feeling no sympathy for her, yet feeling the weight of what they were doing nonetheless. "Here's what's next, Marissa. We're calling your daddy. Using your Skype account, so I bet he picks up. We're gonna let him get a load of you. And then we're gonna talk to him. You're gonna do whatever we say. If it comes to it, you're gonna say what we tell you to say. That's how you keep hope alive that you walk out of here. Catch me?"

Again, she nodded emphatically. Her sobs and tears had abated for the moment.

"Good girl. Okay, let's do this."

Isaac stepped out of the way, and Bart placed the call. The face of an obviously wealthy man—with thinning but elegantly groomed white hair, a ruddy golfer's tan, and an expensive and perfectly pressed striped dress shirt—filled the screen. Behind him, a wall of windows overlooked downtown Chicago, Lake Michigan glittering off in the distance.

His expression was warm and devoted at first; then he really saw the state his daughter was in. "What—Marissa? Oh, sweetheart. What—who? Jesus! Who's there?"

Without moving in front of the camera, Isaac said, "Calling back in one minute. Make sure you're completely private and won't be disturbed when we do." Bart killed the connection.

Looking down at Bart, who was squatting next to the laptop, Isaac asked, "You're sure you'll be able to tell if he's alone or tracing the call?" Bart nodded, and that was good enough for Isaac. He didn't need the technical description that he was sure Bart would love to give him. Not the time to let the kid's geek loose.

Bart placed the call again, and this time, when Halyard came onto the screen, he looked aptly horrified. He'd put his daughter in the middle of the lion's den, served her right up like a pig on a spit, and Isaac knew he'd believed her to be safe. Rich people. Thought they were above everything.

"Marissa, sweetheart. I'm so sorry." Her father's voice was rough with regret, and Marissa whined and began to cry again.

Isaac sat down on the stool between the screen and Marissa. "Okay, Martin. This is our endgame. You play right, on my side, and Marissa's hurting as bad as she's gonna. You miss your play, and you watch her hurt more. You disconnect at any time, and she dies hard. You know what went down here a couple of weeks ago. You had your hand in that. So did she. So you can imagine what's owed now. Think about that, and make your move."

Martin's face warped into a snarl. "You're an animal."

Isaac sighed. "No. Actually, I'm pretty civilized. Can't say that about everybody in this room, though. First mistake, Martin. Not looking good for your little miss here." Ignoring the sick weight in his gut, he stood and nodded at Len, who grabbed Vic. They walked to the far side of the room, picked up a metal table, and carried it back. Then Len unbound Marissa from the chair. She fought, screaming around the gag and kicking, but, with Havoc's help, Len muscled her to the table and bound her to it, her arms over her head and her legs spread. He looked back at Isaac, who nodded again, and Len removed her gag.

"Please don't. Please. Please!" Her words collapsed back into sobs. She was tiny, naked, and shaking, and Isaac felt the first stirrings of sympathy for her. He looked over at Show, who was staring at the far wall, his jaw twitching rhythmically. Isaac didn't know how to read that. He sat back down and faced Halyard. "You see how this is going, Martin?"

"*What is it you want?*" Halyard slammed his fist down, and his image on the screen shook. Marissa had fallen into a steady, moaning whine.

"You know what we want. Lawrence Ellis. Enough to take him down. You're his money guy. You give us what we need."

"I *can't*. You have this naïve idea that you have a chance. You don't. You can't beat him. He's beyond your reach. You're all idiots for trying to fight him. This isn't David and Goliath. It's Tom Thumb and Gargantua. Pack up and get out before he really comes for you. You think he's hurt you? You have no idea what he can do to people in his way. I do. I know. Nothing you can do is as bad. I *can't* help you."

He wasn't saying anything that Isaac hadn't already confronted in his own head. All the Horde knew that their chances were so slim they might as well be nil. But they were not men who lay down. They fought for what was theirs. And now, Martin Halyard had forced Isaac's hand. With a sigh and a sad shake of his head, he stood again and nodded once at Len, who immediately walked to the end of the table, opening his belt as he went.

"Hold up. No." That was Show, who stepped up to the table. "It's me. This is me."

Jesus Christ. No. Isaac couldn't let him do it. Len, Havoc—those guys could do the dark work and come out the other side intact. They could compartmentalize. Vic, well, he didn't need to compartmentalize. He was a sick fuck and enjoyed it. But Show would come to regret this. He'd never recover from the loss of his girl if he laid the abuse of this one on top of it. He held up his hand, stopping Show, then spun back to the laptop and squatted down. "Last chance, Martin. Give us Ellis. Now. Won't ask again." Christ! Halyard *had* to give them something. Could a father let this happen to his child?

Marissa screamed, "Daddy, *please*! Oh *please*!"

Halyard was sobbing as hard as his daughter was. "I can't. Oh, God. Oh, Marissa. Sweetheart, I love you. I'm so sorry." He stared at the camera, his anguished eyes meeting Isaac's. "Please. I will do whatever I can. I will give you money, help you start someplace fresh. All of you. But I can't give you what you're asking for. *I can't*."

"Isaac." Show's voice was low and sharp, a warning.

"I'm sorry, too, Martin. Really am. But this is our home." He stood and turned to face the vista of the room: Marissa Halyard, bound to a table, weeping quietly. Len, belt still unbuckled, standing behind it, his face a blank. Havoc, looking serious and alert. Bart, sad and nauseated. Even Vic, hanging back near the tools, looked ill.

Show stood at the end of the table, staring down at the trembling girl. Isaac addressed him quietly. "Show. Brother, think. Think first. I told you it's your call. But I want you to think. Don't want to lose you, man. I need you strong. I need you with me."

Show didn't answer. He stood, staring silently down at Marissa. The room froze, waiting for him to move. Long, tense seconds passed, and then Show said to Marissa, "Her name was Daisy. Say it."

She looked at him, her brow furrowed. "Wh-what?"

Show kicked the table, hard, and she screamed. "SAY IT," he shouted over her.

"D-Daisy. Her name was Daisy."

"She was fifteen. Say it."

"She was fif-fifteen." A lilt of fragile hope entered Marissa's voice.

Then Show stared again. From the laptop behind Isaac, Halyard whispered, "Please."

Show turned his stare to Isaac and held for a few seconds. "Do what you want with her." He turned on his heel and left the Room.

Isaac watched him go, then turned back to his brothers. Marissa was quiet, finally, maybe relaxing a little, thinking the danger was

204

passing. From behind him, Halyard said, his voice quavering, "Isaac? Mr. Lunden?" Isaac ignored him.

For the first time, Havoc spoke up. "He said to do what we want. I want to give him justice." Isaac looked at Len, then Bart. Both nodded, Len readily, Bart reluctantly.

Vic, still farther back from the rest, said, low, "Head in a box, man. That's what he said."

Everything was sideways. How had they ended up in a place where they were torturing women, ready to rape them, deciding to kill them? How the holy fuck had it happened?

Ellis. It came down to that one elusive son of a bitch. Isaac wanted *his* head in a box.

He nodded at Havoc, who turned and headed toward the tools. But then Vic charged forward, his arms over his head. "You vicious *cunt!*," he bellowed and brought an axe down on Marissa's neck, cleaving her head neatly from her body. She didn't even have time to scream.

Her father did, however. He screamed until Bart slammed the laptop closed.

~oOo~

Isaac left Len and Havoc putting a beating on Vic for acting out of turn. Isaac thought Show might be right—if they got clear of this shit, Vic's patch should go to a vote. Maybe more. But for now, they needed the warm body. As soon as he was clear of the double doors, Isaac slumped against the hallway wall and closed his eyes. He did not recognize himself. Or his brothers. Or his club. They'd become something he didn't understand. And that was his fault. He'd led them down this path.

But there was no way back, not until Ellis had been dealt with. Or until he'd won, when it wouldn't matter anymore.

He went out into the Hall and sent Dom back to help Bart clean up the mess. The Room had been the repair bay back when the clubhouse was Signal Bend Construction. Walls and ceiling of concrete, drains in the floor, it was an ideal space for wetwork now. A bleach rinse, a trip into the woods for a fire and a burial, and Marissa Halyard no longer would exist in any identifiable way. Except on Isaac's conscience.

Show was at the bar, a bottle of Jack in front of him. No glass. He didn't acknowledge Isaac coming into the room. Isaac pulled his burner out to call Lilli. His hand shook as he opened the phone.

She answered on the first ring. "Hey. You caught me putting groceries in the truck. Can I call you back in about five minutes?" She sounded significantly stronger than she'd been when he left her in the morning, and he felt a measure of relief, even amidst the stress of the day.

"No, Sport. Take a break, because I need to talk now. Where are you?"

In the pause that followed, Isaac knew her brain was pulling out the real information in the few words he'd said. "At the Walmart. Groceries. And, you know, other things. What's wrong?"

Other things. Christ, he'd fucking forgotten the pregnancy test. "Maybe trouble. We're locking down. You know what that means?"

No pause this time. "Yeah. What do I need to do?" It lightened his heart a little more that she began problem-solving immediately, casting aside any other questions.

"You carrying? Badge?" He knew they were; since the attacks, he was militant about that. Even he thought he was obnoxiously fixated on it. But he still wanted to hear her confirm it.

He didn't miss the aggravation in her voice when she answered, "Of course."

"Go back in, get enough basic food for about forty-fifty people for a few days. Coffee, booze, and beer we got, but not much else. Then get your beautiful ass here. Don't go back home."

"Isaac, the animals."

"I'll cover that, and I'll make sure to get you some clothes. But I don't want you back there. Lilli, don't fight me. We're in deep here."

"Okay. Be safe." He heard the military carriage in her tone. She was on the job. His warrior woman.

"You too, Sport. Jesus. You, too. I love you."

He closed his phone and turned to Show. "She's dead, brother. Her father watched. You really want her head sent his way?"

Staring straight ahead, Show said, "No. It's done. Now what?"

"Now we hope Bart and Rick give us something more. We did that for nothing. It didn't get us any stronger in the fight. Maybe upped the risk."

"Not for nothing. That was justice."

Isaac wasn't going to argue the point. "Okay. I need you now. We gotta pull everybody with ties to us in, let the rest of the town know to batten down. You up for that?"

Show took another swig from the bottle and then put the cap back on. "Let's do it, boss."

CHAPTER SIXTEEN

Badger and Lilli pulled into the lot about three hours later. Badge had to honk and wait for the gate to open, and then, as soon as they were through, the hangarounds at the gate ran to close it again. Lilli looked in the passenger door mirror and watched as they looped a chain and closed a big padlock. By the time Badger had parked, Isaac was at her door. He opened it and pulled her out of the car into his arms. Feeling the tension vibrating in his arms, she let him hold her, wrapping her arms around his neck.

"That was too long, baby. Too long." He'd called her three times, checking in, so he'd known she was okay. But this was a thing with him—he had to see her to believe she was safe.

"You gave me a lot to do. I'm here now."

He took her face into his hands and kissed her. "Come inside. The others will get the stuff." He took her hand, then stopped. "Do you have the thing?"

She smiled and patted her messenger bag. Next to her Sig were two boxes of pregnancy test kits, two tests in each.

Life was very strange these days.

~oOo~

Lilli spent the afternoon making sleeping arrangements for the patches, hangarounds, club girls, and family members. Every room except Isaac's office and the Room was full with cots and sleeping bags, and every couch and remotely comfortable chair was made up for sleeping. She hardly knew most of the people, but they knew her, and it turned out that, by virtue of being Isaac's old lady, she was in charge. She didn't mind; she was good in charge. But she was surprised how readily she was accepted in the role. Apparently, the clubhouse was hers to run.

She wasn't sure how she felt about that. She hadn't yet spent enough time around the clubhouse to get to know anyone but the members, but she'd spent enough time to understand that running the clubhouse under normal conditions meant keeping the food stores up and, most likely, managing the girls, who currently more or less managed themselves. A sort of pack hierarchy had developed, she'd noticed. It seemed to work well enough, and she saw no reason to disrupt it. She wasn't keen on becoming what amounted to a madam for free whores.

She gave herself a little mental slap for the severe judgment in her thought. She had no problem at all with women using their bodies in any way they chose. And she was certainly no prude. But she didn't much like the dynamic among the women. She hated to see women tearing each other down, especially over the slim pickings of men who saw them as little more than an assortment of warm, wet, willing holes.

The Horde were in and out in groups throughout the afternoon and evening. Lilli focused on getting dinner out, and she was pleasantly surprised to find that the women were eager to help with that, expecting her to run the meal, doing what she asked without complaint. By the time the meal was ready, with serving dishes arrayed across the bar, all the Horde were in for the night. Show, Isaac, and Len were last in, their faces grim. When Isaac saw her, though, his face softened, and he winked. She grinned back at him and opened her arms as he came up to her and brought her close.

His lips soft and sexy against her ear, he murmured, "How you feelin', Sport?"

She was feeling good, all things considered. Her weakness and wooziness in the morning had shocked the hell out of her and laid her low, and she'd slept until the afternoon. Then, though, she'd felt fine, had no problem running the errands, and being busy here at the clubhouse had been energizing. She liked to be in charge. She liked a problem to solve. Whatever had happened to force the lockdown must have been bad—worse even than they'd yet dealt with—but keeping busy had given her focus. She'd hardly thought of those test kits in her bag.

"I'm good. Glad you're back."

He turned and surveyed the eats and the eaters. Big tubs of baked mostaccioli and trays of garlic bread. She hadn't bothered with a vegetable—cooking for Isaac had taught her that these guys were deeply suspicious of vegetables, as a rule.

"Wow. You rocked it. I told you to get basic food, though. What's all this?"

She laughed. "Basic food."

He laughed, too. "I meant hot dogs and burgers, Sport." She shrugged. She was Italian. Baked pasta was basic food.

"Well, then, you'll be eating better than you expected, locked down here with me. There are big sheets of chocolate cake, too."

She ate with Isaac, feeling satisfied with the way things were organized. It had apparently been a while since there had been a lockdown, and longer than that, it seemed, since an old lady had taken charge. As serious as things were, there was an air of…not celebration, not that, but…family. There was comfort in this group.

The Horde went into a meeting after dinner, and the women cleaned up. By the time the meeting was over, Lilli was exhausted. The few people with children—a few nieces and nephews of members—had taken them back to bed in the dorm, and the Horde were grabbing women. Len looked like he was collecting a set.

Isaac was talking to Show, standing just outside the Keep doors. Lilli caught his eye and nodded down the side hallway. She was going to bed.

She went into his office and closed the door, then just stood there and absorbed the relative quiet for a minute. It had been awhile since she'd been in such a crush of people for such an extended period of time. She was out of practice.

Pip crawled out from under the desk and sat on her feet. She picked him up and gave him a little snuggle, but he wanted to explore, and he squirmed until she set him back down. By the time she and Badger had gotten to the clubhouse with supplies, Pip was already ensconced in Isaac's office, with food, water, and a litter pan. And one of her duffels was about half full with clothes and toiletries for her and Isaac. He'd done well.

The door opened behind her, and Isaac walked in. Lilli stayed where she was, waiting, and he came to her and wrapped his arms around her waist, nosing her ponytail out of the way to press a kiss to her new ink. In the few days since it had mostly healed, he'd taken to touching and kissing it often. It was sweet.

He pulled the band from her hair. "Need to pee, Sport?"

She chuckled. She'd forgotten again. "I could probably squeeze out a drop or two. But it might be better to wait a couple days, see if I even miss my period. I don't know if it'll be accurate this early."

"Can't wait. I gotta know. If it comes up no, then we'll see if you're late." He kissed her neck. "Come on, baby. Pee on a stick for me."

Turning in his arms, she grabbed his kutte and pulled him against her. "Wow. You're quite the romantic." She let him go and stepped around him, grabbing her bag from the floor next to his desk. "Back in a few. Don't go anywhere."

"I'll be right here." The sofa in his office folded out into a bed; Lilli had made it up earlier in the day. Now Isaac sat on the end and grinned up at her. "Right here."

She went down the hall to the one bathroom. Luckily, it was empty, and she ducked in. Never having needed to take a test like this before, she read the instructions (which amounted to "pee on a stick and wait") and took the test. She really did have to pee, so that wasn't a problem.

True to his word, Isaac was sitting right where she'd left him, leaning back on his elbows. When she came in, he sat up. "Well?"

She handed him the stick.

He looked down at the result window. "Jesus Christ. Sport, Jesus Christ!" When he turned his face back up to hers, it was blank with shock. She expected something different. She wasn't sure what, but different.

"That's what you wanted, right?"

He shook his head as if to rearrange it and grinned. "Yeah—yes!" Setting aside the stick, he grabbed her thighs and pulled her between his legs. "It's what I want. You, me, a baby. It's all I want." He rested the side of his head on her belly and held her tightly. Charmed and touched, she threaded her fingers into his hair, and they held each other like that.

Lilli had been terrified when the second stripe appeared in the window—vivid pink, no denying the result. Second, third, fourth thoughts had crowded into her head immediately. They were being crazy, making the decision they'd made. The fight they were in was dangerous, as dangerous as any war. Isaac could die. She could die. And now they were responsible for another fragile life. They were crazy.

But standing here between his legs, enclosed in his huge, strong arms, her doubts dissipated. She was afraid—of what they faced now, of what kind of mother she'd be, of whether life in Signal Bend would ever be easy—but fear was part of life. She wasn't fearless. Fearlessness looked a lot like stupidity. But Isaac was right; she didn't let fear get in her way.

"I love you, Isaac."

He turned his face up to hers. "I love you, baby." He smiled. "Baby." Then he opened her jeans and pulled her underwear clear so he could press his face against the bare skin of her belly. "Baby."

There was something powerfully sensual in what he'd done, and the muscles between Lilli's legs spasmed hard. She was wet almost instantly, and she flexed against him with a little moan, her fingers curling into his hair. When he looked up at her again, the light in his eyes had changed.

He pushed his hands under her jeans and underwear and slid them down her thighs. He leaned in and kissed her just above her clit, and she moaned his name.

Gently, he slid his finger into her folds. "Ah, Sport. You're so wet for me."

Impatient to be naked, Lilli toed off her boots and worked her jeans, underwear, and socks off. Then, she yanked off her top and bra and stood before him, feeling strangely strong in her nudity.

She watched Isaac watch his hands as they moved over her hips, up her sides, to her breasts, cupping them gently. Oh—they were even more sensitive, suddenly, and when his thumbs passed over her nipples, she cried out and bent backwards. Damn.

He met her eyes with a grin, then stood up, his long, broad body, still fully clad in all his leather and denim, brushing hers all the way. That made her moan, too. She wanted to get him as naked as she was, and she pushed her hands under his kutte, over his shoulders.

He let it slide down his arms and caught it, then leaned over to hang it on the back of his desk chair.

She went for the buttons of his shirt next, but he grabbed her hands to stop her. "Don't get impatient, Sport. I want to go slow. I want to love you easy. Let me take care." He moved his hands to cradle her face and kissed her, his mouth and beard soft on her lips. "I had a helluva day, baby. I need to be gentle now. Let me love you."

She nodded and looped her arms over his shoulder, pulling the band from his braid. With a rumble deep in his chest, he swept her into his arms and carried her to the side of the folded-out bed, laying her gently down. He stood and stripped, his eyes locked with hers. His body was pure power, dense and ridged with muscle, but he came down to the bed softly and lay at her side.

Lilli felt nervous and tried to understand why. Suddenly, things were different between them. Even deeper, more permanent. With that second pink strip on the test stick, they'd become inextricably entwined. There was a new intensity in Isaac's green eyes and in the gentle touch of his rough, calloused hands. Propped on his elbow, staring down at her, he skimmed his hand over her arm, her side, her leg, bringing it to rest on her belly.

"You are going to be an amazing mother, Sport. This kid is one lucky little shit." He bent down and kissed her.

She wasn't ready yet to think about what kind of mother she'd be. She had plenty of fears and worries on that score. She'd need some time to learn and process, so she could do it right. She had about nine months to figure things out, apparently. To stop him talking more, she pulled his chest down onto hers and kissed him hard, plunging her tongue into his mouth. He came back at her likewise, but then he pulled up. "Easy, baby. We're going easy tonight."

He caressed her softly until she thought she'd go mad. Every time she tried to take him in hand and change the tempo, he held her off. The slow, soft slide of his skin and lips on her was splendid torture, and her whole body began to shake with need. Then he drew a nipple into his mouth and finally slid his fingers inside her, and she arched off the bed with a harsh, desperate cry. Jesus, she needed to come.

"Isaac, please. Fucking Christ, you're killing me."

He released her breast and grinned up at her. "Nah, I don't think so."

"I want you to be fucking me."

"Not gonna fuck you tonight, Sport." Before she could worry that he meant to tease her and leave her in need, he rolled between her legs, and she felt the steely pressure of his cock at her core. As he slid in—and holy God, it felt so good to feel him filling her—he whispered, "I'm goin' slow. So slow. Be still, baby. Let me do it."

He did. His hair shielding her from the sight of anything but his face, he loomed over her and moved deliberately. She could feel all of him in her, like a caress. Propped on his elbows, he moved, the hair on his chest caressing her nipples, making them hard, hypersensitive buds of pleasure. She felt the pressure of his body on her clit, rubbing as he thrust into her. She felt everything. She stopped trying to accelerate things and relaxed into the overwhelming sensory assault. Her climax came on slowly, and even that was newly intense, as though she were watching it emerge from fog, every thrust, every slide of skin on skin, just slightly more powerful than the one before.

His breathing was becoming labored, and sweat had coated his body, but he kept up his slow, methodical pace until she whispered, "Oh, fuck! Oh, fuck!" Exerting a last force of will, she stayed still and let her release just have her, completely let go. She came quietly, for her, making only a series of tortured moans, but the experience was among the most intense she'd ever had—and not just orgasmic. It caught her somewhere deep inside, someplace so private it seemed unknown even to her.

He came as she did, also quietly, groaning into her shoulder as his body turned briefly to iron. As he relaxed, emotion overwhelmed Lilli, and she began to cry.

He shifted off her immediately and came up on his elbow, panting. "Baby, what's wrong?" She felt his hand on her face.

Nothing. Nothing was wrong. Or everything. She had no idea. She was caught up in a swell of emotion so deep and fierce she couldn't begin to comprehend it. She couldn't even breathe. She shook her head and tucked tightly to his chest, the sobs shaking her, body and soul.

Isaac held her close and kissed her head. "Lilli. Baby, what did I do? Did I hurt you?" His hand went to her belly. "Fuck, I'm sorry."

Knowing she had to get control of herself and quit freaking them both out, she screwed up her will and took a deep breath, shutting down the tears. When she could, she said, "No, I'm okay. I don't...I don't know what that was. But I'm okay."

He set her back enough to look hard into her eyes. "Yeah?"

"Yeah. Sorry." She sniffled.

He laughed. "You're just never gonna stop scaring the shit out of me, are you?"

With a sheepish grin, she shrugged. "Keeping things interesting?"

"Definitely. You're giving me grey hair." He turned, leaning against the back of the sofa, and pulled her close. She nestled in, laying her head on his shoulder and her hand on his chest.

Emotion ebbed into fatigue, and, with the soothing rhythm of Isaac's fingers combing through her hair, Lilli began to doze. She was drifting deeper when he spoke, his voice making a deep echo in his chest, against her ear. "I want to marry you before the little squirt shows up."

Becoming fully alert again, she tipped her head up. "I kind of have an idea about that already."

She'd surprised him, she could tell. "Yeah?"

She sat up. She needed to really see him to have this conversation. "I told you that I sent for the stuff in my storage locker. Oh—that's supposed to be here this week, so I don't know what to do about it if it comes while we're here."

"I'll go over with Dom and Badge. Don't sweat that. What's your idea, Sport?"

"There's one more thing in storage. I wasn't sure how to handle it, but I think now I know. My dad's car. A '68 Barracuda. God, he loved that thing like a son. It was too rare and identifiable for me to drive it under an alias, but"—and here was something else she'd decided since they'd been working on getting pregnant but hadn't said anything about yet—"I'm going to end my contract work. The stuff here in town is getting too intense, and I don't want to risk crossing my lines. So, anyway, I can get my dad's car back and—"

Isaac interrupted her. "Hold up, Sport. You're quitting your job? You really okay with that?"

It had been an easy decision to make, honestly. The cloak-and-dagger shit wore hard fast, and knowing too much about how things worked—or didn't—wore even harder, even faster. "Yeah. I mean, I don't see myself taking up knitting or rug-braiding, but I'll find something to do. Something that will help the town, maybe."

His smile was wide and happy, but then it faltered a little. "Will they just let you quit?"

She laughed. "It's not indentured servitude, Isaac. I'm not a prisoner. They'll have me sign a bunch of forms that say I'll spend the rest of my days in Leavenworth if I talk about what I did, and then I'm out. Simple as that."

Linking fingers and pulling her hand up for a kiss, he said, "Well, I think that's fantastic. But get back to the main story. You have your dad's badass cage. You want it here. What does that have to do with us gettin' hitched?"

"How about, soon as this thing with Ellis is over, we fly out to California, pick up the 'Cuda, and get married in Reno on the way home?" The more Lilli had considered the idea, the more she'd liked it. She could—would—be Lilli Accardo on that day.

But Isaac looked doubtful. "That's a three-day ride. Three days in a cage? I don't know if I can deal. You know how I get, cooped up like that."

"Three days in a *fast* cage. My head in your lap."

At that, he grinned. "Fair point. I'm in."

~oOo~

"We need anything else?"

"Toilet paper. At least a couple of the big bulk packs. And, I don't know. Like a couple of kids' games or jigsaw puzzles, maybe?" Badger snorted at that, and Lilli was immediately aggravated. Hell, she'd already been aggravated. Now she was pissed. "What? We're going on five days, and there's nothing for the kids to do except play those video game things they all have."

"Jigsaw puzzles, though? Geez, that's like a grandma's idea of fun. They're fine. All they want to do is play those video game things— Nintendo DSs, by the way." His grin was decidedly, slappably, condescending, but she forbore.

She wanted the errands to be over. She felt like shit. Apparently, passing out and being sick in the morning was a real thing, and she had it like gangbusters. She'd already bent twice over a toilet in the store's restroom. Being cooped up in the clubhouse for days wasn't helping. And then, this morning, they were out of almost everything, and she couldn't even wait until she felt better to head to the store. Isaac had left early with most of the Horde. Feeling ill and petulant, she hadn't called to tell him she and Badger were going out. The only reason she had Badge with her was that he'd caught her on her way and asked what it was she had against him, trying to get him killed so often.

So here she was, in the Walmart Megacenter or whatever they called it, getting teased by a skinny, pimply kid because she'd thought buying jigsaw puzzles would keep the six kids trapped in the lockdown happy.

"Fine. Fuck you. Get the toilet paper, and let's just go." She leaned on her shopping cart as another woozy wave came over her. Being pregnant sucked ass.

"You need to sit down again?" Badger sounded deeply worried. Probably less about her actual well being and more about what Isaac would do to him if she passed out in the middle of Walmart and conked her head.

"I'm fine, asshole. Get the stuff. I want to get out of here." It was almost an hour drive back to the clubhouse. Why she was in such a rush to get back to that increasingly foul-smelling prison, she had no idea, except that she wanted to lie down. On the increasingly medieval fold-out sofa. At least she could get Pip cuddles.

Twenty minutes later, she walked their empty carts to a parking lot corral while Badger secured their purchases in the back of Isaac's truck. On her way back, she was swept up in a wave of déjà vu, brought on as she remembered Isaac doing the same thing in Springfield, weeks ago now, on the day that Will Keller was killed.

Out of the periphery of her vision, she saw the blacked-out van driving toward Isaac's truck. It took a couple of beats for her to understand her sense of foreboding and suspicion, and by then two things were true: the van had pulled in alongside their truck, and she had made it as far as the tailgate.

She reached for her bag, where her Sig was. But her bag was on the passenger seat, where'd she'd left it as she decided at the last minute to help Badger out with the carts.

Badger was squatting inside the truck bed, tightening down a tie. The side door of the van slid open, just as Lilli called out, "Badge! Get down!"

Instead of down, he popped up, searching for her. There was a low but clear and sickeningly familiar "pop," and Badge went down, shot by a silenced handgun.

The shooter came out of the van—a well-built black man with short dreads. With no other choice, Lilli turned and ran, intending to use the cars in the lot for cover. Without her bag, she had no phone, no weapon, nothing. All she could use was the open, public space. But before she could get to the next car, she was on the ground, her right shoulder singing with pain.

Almost at once, the world went sideways and spun, warping and wending. Sound seemed stretched. She watched feet running up to her, and then she was being picked up. The pain in her shoulder was wrong, somehow. All of this was wrong.

Her last thought as a shimmery black curtain came down on her consciousness was, "They fucking tranq'd—"

CHAPTER SEVENTEEN

Isaac rode toward Signal Bend with Show at his flank, and Len, Bart and Havoc rolling behind. They'd met Kenyon Berry at a secure location, off the grid. St. Louis was too hot for the Horde right now, but he'd needed to talk to Kenyon.

Kenyon was dealing with his own shit. The Horde's payback on the Northsiders and Ellis, the day of the attacks on Show's family and Lilli, had gone far too quietly. They'd been expected, and Kenyon had been the one to give Isaac the address of the stash house they'd fired. It had shaken Isaac hard to think that Kenyon had set him up. He hadn't. Kenyon had a kink in his own line, one much worse than the Horde's little college princess. Kenyon's right hand, Marcus Grant, had given him that address. Marcus had flipped for Ellis.

He'd been dealt with, permanently, but the Underdawgs were in disarray. Marcus had flipped others, and now Kenyon trusted no one in his organization. Isaac had met a weary, watchful man at that off-the-grid location. Kenyon had come alone, unprotected, because he'd felt safer alone than out in the country with any of his crew.

Ellis had now gained one huge victory: he'd broken the Underdawgs, the only competition in the St. Louis metro area for his own lackeys, the Northside Knights. With that win, he'd quashed the Horde's most powerful ally, put the Signal Bend meth business on life support, and made St. Louis a fucking deadly place for a man wearing the Flaming Mane patch.

They were losing. Their every gambit failed. Torturing and killing Marissa Halyard had served only to make Ellis take them more seriously as a threat instead of a nuisance. Lilli's idea to use hackers had been their best shot. Rick and Bart had managed to hack in close, but they'd been tagged and kicked before they could accomplish anything. They had information, lots of information, but they couldn't use any of it. They'd almost gotten all the way to his money. They knew where he lived. They knew his family, his habits. But he and his family were all protected as if every one of them were the fucking President of the United States. Isaac had briefly considered suggesting a sniper assassination, but Lilli was the only one they had with anything like that kind of skill, and no fucking way was that going to happen.

Everything they'd learned reinforced what Isaac had been told right off the bat and repeatedly since: Ellis was untouchable. He was too powerful, too connected, too careful. They could not beat him. Now, Isaac believed it.

The question weighing on him now was how he'd break it to the town. All his speechifying and rah-rah bullshit, telling them how they were the ones who'd stayed, so they were the ones who were strong—it was nothing but vapor. Now he had to tell them the hard truth: pack up and go, or make what peace with Ellis they could. They could not fight.

Isaac would not fight. Five days ago, he would have Bravehearted the fucker, ready to fight to the last man, exhorting these poor folk to stand with him. But Lilli was pregnant. It changed everything. He had to get his family out of this fucking mess. He couldn't fight a futile war and face a certain death knowing that their child had taken root inside her. He wouldn't.

225

Tonight, with their nearest and dearest packed into the rooms around them, the Horde would sit around their table, and Isaac would argue for conceding the fight. His read of his brothers was that the vote would be split but would go his way. Tomorrow, he'd tell the town. He was sure that soon thereafter, Signal Bend would be a ghost town, and the Night Horde MC a memory.

His heart was lead in his chest.

His burner went off in his pocket, and, without pulling up his bike, he reached for it and answered.

It was Dan. He, C.J., and Vic were on duty in town. "Boss, we got trouble." Isaac heard gunfire in the background, and pulled his bike into the first gravel drive. The rest of the riders followed suit.

"What's up, brother?"

"It's like the fucking O.K. Corral or some shit, Isaac. Five, maybe six SUVs rolled down Main Street and started shooting. People started shooting back, and they pulled up and puked out a lot of guys from those trucks. Now, man, I ain't jokin'. We got a Wild West situation." There was a burst of automatic gunfire. "Except with much bigger guns."

"Fuck! We whole?"

"For now, I think. Don't know if anybody got hurt in the shops, but the club's accounted for so far. We need help."

"We're comin', brother. Hold on."

He closed the phone and told Show, Len, Bart, and Havoc what was going on. Len asked, "What about the Scorps? Ain't we getting backup from them?"

"Not due until late tonight. I'll call Tug and get his ETA. Fuck. Get movin'. I'll catch up. I'll call Dom, too—stop at the clubhouse and load up. We can't fight this with what we're carrying." Len, Bart and Havoc fired up their bikes again, and Isaac shouted, "WATCH YOUR BACK!" Havoc waved, and they peeled out.

Show sat, straddling his bike. Isaac glared at him. "Get outta here, Show. I'm right behind you after I talk to Tug and Dom."

Show stood pat. "Not leaving you alone. Make your calls."

Isaac didn't have time to argue. First, he called the clubhouse and talked to Dom, whom he'd left in charge when he'd sent the Horde out in the morning. After he told him to get guns ready for the four of them to grab, and to lock down hard and pull everyone back from the Hall, the only large space with windows, he ended that call and contacted Tug, the leader of the crew of five the Scorpions were sending from their nearest charter in Alabama. They were still four hours out, even if they pushed it.

~oOo~

On their way through the clubhouse gate, Isaac and Show passed Len, Bart, and Havoc heading back out. Dom was waiting for them, a crate of guns on the ground at his feet. As they loaded up, Isaac asked, "Where's my old lady?"

227

"She and Badger went for supplies. Couple hours ago."

Good. She was clear of this mess, then. He was pissed she hadn't told him she was going, but he was glad she was away. "Call Badge, tell him to keep her away until he hears from me or Show."

"Will do." Dom picked up the empty crate and went back into the clubhouse.

Isaac turned to Show. "You ready, brother?"

"Nothing to lose." Show fired up his bike. Isaac did as well, and they rode out toward the center of town, the gates of their compound closing behind them.

Dan was right. It was a scene straight out of the nineteenth century, except the technology was different. As they approached the main drag of Main Street shops, Isaac saw that most of the windows had been shot out. There were cars parked at forty-five-degree angles in front of the shops. Not many; it was a weekday, traffic was always light, and most of the shops were closed up this week, anyway, so they were mostly the cars of the shopkeepers. But several had taken heavy damage. Six vans and SUVs, all black and blacked out, were parked as if randomly sown down the middle of the street. These guys—Isaac had to assume they were Northsiders on a job for Ellis—hadn't come in to do a drive-by. They were here to kill townspeople. Isaac had no idea if they'd yet succeeded.

Three men came around the nearest black SUV and started shooting; Isaac and Show veered off the street into an alley and dismounted as quickly as they could. Both had AKs strapped to their backs, holsters under each arm, and knives tied to their legs. They had hunting rifles, too. Country weapons, with which they were most comfortable.

Full-out war had come to Signal Bend.

They ran up to the building and flattened themselves against the wall. Just as Isaac turned to Show to tell him they needed to move forward, the back door of the shop on the other side of the wall opened, and Diane Lindel, the shop owner, leaned out, a double-barreled shotgun in her hands. "In here!," she whisper-shouted, and Isaac and Show ducked in.

Once in the dim, crowded back room, Isaac looked back at Diane. She was a solid woman, maybe fifty years old, with short, iron-grey hair. A sensible, no-bullshit kind of woman. "What's the story, Diane?"

She answered right away, looking up into Isaac's eyes. More than a foot shorter than he, she carried herself like she was perfectly confident in her ability to kick even his ass if it came to it. "Dan and C.J. are holed up across the street in the ice cream shop. Seven people of use with them. We're in phone contact—everyone on this side of the street grouped here. He said you were coming, told us to sit tight. You told us to be armed and ready, and we all are. There's a few more guns in my back room and plenty of ammo." She cast a skeptical eye at the AKs Isaac and Show were sporting. "Not for those, but for the rest, we got ammo. You tell us what you want us to do, Ike. We're together on this."

"Who's 'we'?"

With a brusque nod, Diane led them through the back room into her shop—one of the several businesses selling used knickknacks and household goods on Main Street. Sitting in a line along the counter and back wall were ten people, seven of them armed. Three looked like they had been innocent, out-of-town shoppers, now caught up in Signal Bend's drama. They were obviously terrified and confused.

But the seven were townspeople, and they did not look defeated. They looked angry, resolute. And they were waiting for him to lead them.

Ten people in Diane's shop who would fight, including Isaac and Show. Nine people in the ice cream shop, including Dan and Ceej. Where were Len, Bart, and Havoc?

Addressing the whole room, Isaac asked, "Anybody seen Len? And how many are out there?"

Martin Fosse, the mayor, stood up. "Those SUVs were full. Six of them, rolling into town like some kind of military caravan. I'd say thirty in all. And I think those trucks are armored or something. Not taking damage like the other cars out there. I saw three other Horde riding in—didn't see who, but they went around the other side. I think they must be across the street somewhere."

Thirty? The Northsiders were big, but not that big. They had help. Of course they did. Ellis's resources were apparently limitless, and he'd taken his time planning this attack.

Show, who'd gone up to the blown-out front window and surveyed the situation, came back now and said, "Quiet out there now, but I see maybe two dozen men at cover. What about outside town? Any word of trouble?"

Fosse shook his head. "This looks like their stand right here." The mayor looked at Isaac. "This is bad, Ike."

No shit. Isaac's head was pounding. It was more than he had any idea how to deal with. He pulled his phone and dialed Len. It took three tries to get the call through.

When it finally did, his SAA picked up immediately and answered in a whisper, "Boss! You whole?"

"Yeah. You?"

"Bart took fire, clipped his shoulder and took his bike out. We got him in cover. Hav and me are in the alley, south side of Main."

"We're right across the street, in the Treasure House. Dan and Ceej are up at the ice cream shop. Can you get to them?"

Len was quiet, and Isaac knew he was planning the move. "Think so. Gotta get Bart movin' with us, but it's quiet now, so we'll go."

"Careful, brother. We got maybe thirty bad guys walking around with big fucking guns. Call me when you're there."

"Yep."

Isaac ended that call and dialed Dan. That call went through on the first try. When he answered, Isaac first asked, "Vic with you?"

"No. Ain't been able to raise him for half an hour. He was going down the row, sending people up here. Went alone. He's down, gotta be."

Fuck. Two brothers down, at least wounded, maybe worse. Jesus fucking Christ. "Dammit. Okay. I hear you've got nine people over there, seven ready to fight?"

"Yeah. Nine fighters, including me and Ceej."

"Look out for Len and Havoc, coming in from the back. They're in the alley. They got Bart—he's hit."

"Fuck."

"Yeah." Then Isaac said, "Put Ceej on." C.J. and Victor had military training. He needed their insight.

"Yeah," C.J.'s voice was gruff and strained.

"Ceej. Brother, we need military-grade ideas here. What's the play?"

And he had one. Isaac listened as C.J. detailed a decent plan. When he ended the call, he pulled Show aside and explained it to him. Then they brought it to the people arrayed on the floor, their hunting rifles and shotguns in hand. Except for the poor customers tucked into a corner, to a one, with grim determination, they agreed.

The plan required more patience than the Northsiders outside had, and automatic gunfire again began spraying the buildings, coming into the broken windows and destroying stock. Bits of china and glass rained down and flew around, catching glints of sunlight before landing on the roughhewn floor.

Hopefully, though, people were safe enough for now. Isaac pushed Diane, Martin, and the rest back into a far corner, and then he and Show crabbed their way to the front of the store. Isaac saw Dan and C.J. up front across the street, too. Rather than use his AK, Isaac pulled his Remington rifle around and sighted it. He wanted accuracy. Patience and accuracy. Better to think of this as a hunt than a war.

He got his crosshairs on the top of one head, just showing over the hood of a Land Rover. He took a breath and fired. Through the sight, he saw the bullet shear the top of that guy's head clean off and caught a glimpse of pink brain before the body dropped.

Show saw what he was doing and did the same. Sitting at the front window, using the sill as cover and support, they began sighting on bad guys. They got three kills and a wounding before they had to bail, as several AKs were aimed directly at Diane's destroyed storefront. But that was four bad guys they didn't need to fight again.

Dan and Ceej were shooting, too, until they took a hail of AK fire as well.

After that shower of bullets ended, Isaac heard what they were waiting for. The earthshaking rumble of heavy farm equipment on a paved road. The reinforcements had arrived. Massive tractors rolled down Main Street, a man with a gun standing on every one. Don Keyes led the pack, driving his biggest dozer, his brother Dave braced behind him with a rifle in each hand.

His phone in his hand, the line to Dan open, Isaac called out, "Now!" and armed townspeople came through doors, or stepped over the broken glass of display windows, and entered Main Street, shooting all the way. The Northsiders were surrounded, and the heavy machinery, especially Keyes' dozer, was turning their own vehicles into weapons against them. Their AKs were flashy, and scary, but hard to control. Finding cover where they could, a town full of lifelong hunters took the Northsiders down with Remington rifles and Mossberg shotguns.

When the air was quiet again, twenty-six men showing Northsider colors were dead or wounded on the street. Six of Signal Bend's population were wounded, including Bart, with his shoulder wound, and Vic, shot in the chest and in bad shape. And the town had lost five, including Diane Lindel. She was a widow, with a teenage son, Evan.

And Dan, who got caught early, in the first barrage of bullets as the tractor cavalry had arrived. He'd never made it out of the ice cream shop.

There was no such thing as being remote enough to keep what had happened off law's radar, and there was no way to cover it up, either. Too much bloodshed and destruction. But there were five civilian witnesses to Signal Bend's self-defense, so Isaac wasn't unduly worried. He had no control over that fallout, and he had more important things to worry about. He wanted Dan's body out of its pool of blood. And he needed to talk to Lilli. He sat down in the ice cream shop next to his brother's body and pulled out his phone to call his old lady. He noticed that he had a voice mail and a text—they must have come through while he was on the line with Dan.

He checked the text first. From Dom. *No answer from Badger*.

He checked the voice mail, also from Dom. "Isaac, call coming in over the police band. Shooting in the Walmart parking lot, young male injured. They're describing your truck, boss."

His heartbeat shrieking in his ears, he called Lilli. The line picked up on the second ring.

234

A smooth male voice answered Lilli's phone. "Isaac Lunden?"

Isaac knew who'd spoken, and his blood turned to painful ice. He'd never heard the voice before, and there were times he'd felt nearly sure that there was no actual man behind it, times he'd wondered if his nemesis was nothing more than a legend. But he was real. Isaac was going to rip this son of a bitch into tiny pieces with his bare hands. He swallowed and forced his voice to be steady. "Ellis."

"Indeed. Well deduced."

"If you hurt her, you will die hard and bloody."

"Yes, well. I think you ought to be careful about the kind of threats you make, considering what I have of yours."

Isaac closed his eyes. Bile rose in his throat, and his hand shook, but he kept his voice even. "What do you want?"

"Oh, nothing from you. I'm done with you. What I want, I want from her."

The line went dead.

Isaac redialed, but it went straight to voice mail. Ellis had turned Lilli's phone off.

Ellis had Lilli. Ellis had Lilli.

Ellis had Lilli.

CHAPTER EIGHTEEN

When consciousness found Lilli, before she'd made sense of what had happened or where she was, she rolled to her knees and vomited. When she was done she sat back, feeling shaky, sore and confused, and made her brain work.

She ran her hand through her hair and learned that she had apparently puked before; it was caked in her hair. Leaning against a wall, she looked around, taking stock of her surroundings and herself.

The room was bright and bare. Concrete floor covered in peeling green paint. Grey cinderblock walls. High ceiling—fifteen, maybe twenty feet—with three long, fluorescent light fixtures suspended from it. A steel, windowless door in one corner, the same green as the floor.

The room was completely empty except for a plain metal desk against one wall.

Her own physical state was less than top-notch. A jackhammering pain filled her head, and her right shoulder felt about three sizes too big. The pain had all but immobilized her right side—her dominant side. And she was violently nauseated. Bringing that point forcefully home, her gorge rose again and she rolled back to her knees. This time, though, she only dry heaved.

She was dressed but barefoot. Her jacket was missing as well as her boots. Her bag, too—no, she hadn't had that; she'd left it in the truck. The truck—with that thought, the rest of the memory clarified. This was Ellis. She'd been tranq'd. Badger had been shot—tranq'd, too? Was he here, too? She didn't know. She had no idea how long she'd been out, or where she was, or who was with her.

Her head was clearing despite the intense pain, and she was beginning to think well again. She examined her surroundings more closely, looking for vulnerabilities. There was a camera high in one corner, a red light glowing. Somebody was watching her. In another corner, an old grey speaker, like the intercom speakers she remembered in her grade school classrooms.

The room was utterly bare, not even a bucket to piss—or puke—in. But there was the metal desk. Lilli struggled to her feet, leaning against the cool cinderblock wall until the world stopped swinging, and walked to the desk.

There was a document placed neatly, squarely in the center, a cheap plastic ballpoint pen lying on the paper. Lilli moved the pen and picked up the document. A sales contract, for the Keller place. The purchase price was listed as $520,000. Ellis had actually listed himself—not a dummy or proxy, but himself—as buyer. There was his signature, big and bold, signed with a fountain pen.

Lilli palmed the flimsy plastic pen, sliding it into the sleeve of her sweater, then turned to the camera and ripped the contract into pieces.

~oOo~

She'd been sitting against the wall again for at least an hour, and no one had come in to deal with the neat stack of paper shreds she'd left on the desk, or to torment her, interrogate her, offer her water—which she could really have used—nothing. She sat and waited and thought.

Ellis wanted the Keller property. Well, that was hardly news. But why didn't he just kill her, then? All he'd have had to do was shoot her dead in the Walmart parking lot, and within a matter of a few weeks, the property could be his, probably with no more fight from anyone. She had no heirs, no family. She and Isaac were not married. She had no will. Once she was dead, there would be nothing to stop Ellis from buying the property, for a good deal less money than he was offering on that contract she'd torn up.

He was a smart man, so he had to know. So why was she still alive?

Because it was personal now. That had to be it. Ellis was pissed off that Signal Bend, the Horde, she herself had caused him so much trouble over the past few months. Success was no longer enough. He'd fallen into the trap of the powerful man. He could not tolerate the idea that anyone, particularly someone whom he thought worthy of nothing more than neglectful contempt, might get in his way. He no longer simply wanted to win. Now he wanted to beat his foes. Break them. He wanted to force her to sign, make her give up.

That was a vulnerability. Maybe she could use it.

The door burst open, and three armed men came into the room, dressed in black paramilitary gear and carrying M16s—an awful lot of firepower for one unarmed woman. The one in the lead, tall and broad, with a blond ponytail, charged toward her and leveled his weapon at her head. "Stand up!," he barked.

She did. Behind him, one of the other men cleared the torn paper off the desk and put a new contract down.

Blond ponytail waved his 16 at her. "Strip. Now."

Fuck. Fuck. It came as no surprise, but it still sucked. This was how it worked. Humiliation and sexual abuse were Chapter One of the handbook on torturing female subjects. She didn't humiliate easily, however. The worst part was that it would take the pen from her. Her only weapon. She'd hoped they wouldn't notice; clearly the effects of the tranquilizer had been muddying her thinking.

The question now was whether to do as he said or make them strip her. Doing as he said might suggest that her will was weaker than it was. Refusing would show fight, which would probably get her hurt more. She took off her clothes.

When she was clad in only her bra and underwear, she stopped and made a show of folding her jeans, sweater, and camisole, testing to see how far they'd take it. The pen was still in the sleeve of her sweater. She felt a pang to lose it.

Ponytail waved the 16 at her again. "Not done, sweetcheeks. All the way."

When she was naked, without taking his eyes or weapon off her, Ponytail kicked the pile of her clothes toward one of the other guys, who was shorter and shaved, with copper skin and matching eyes. "Check for the pen," said Ponytail. Yep. Hadn't pulled anything over on these assholes.

Copper found the pen and walked over to set it on top of the new contract. Then the three men backed out and left her alone in the room.

She stood where she was, waiting to see if they were really done with her for now. After a few minutes, she went over to the desk. The new contract offered $400,000. Ellis's elegant signature still had a touch of the shiny sharpness of fresh ink.

He was here, in the building with her.

She set the pen aside—nowhere to try to hide it now—and picked up the contract. Facing the camera, she tore it to shreds.

Immediately, she heard a heavy, metallic chunk. A breeze kicked up from the ceiling, and the temperature in the room began to drop.

~oOo~

Lilli tried as long as she could not to let the cold get to her. But the temperature had dropped maybe thirty degrees in the past hour, and now she was curled into a tense, shivering knot in a corner of the room. She was freezing cold, desperately thirsty, and the pain in her head was so bad, she had to force back the irrational need to run away from it. The tension and shivering from the cold was doing that pain no favors at all. Her right shoulder felt like a hot ember had been embedded in it, but that gave her no warmth. The only thing she had going for her was a lack of hunger. She was too nauseated to be hungry.

She kept her mind off all that by trying to work the problem. She didn't know if Isaac was in trouble himself, but if he was capable of knowing, then by now he knew she was in trouble, and if he was capable of doing something about it, she knew he was trying. But that might be the point. Maybe she was bait.

Maybe, but probably not. She wasn't bait. She was a target. If Ellis was after Isaac, too, then he was playing that on a different field.

So, okay. Rescue was unlikely. If she was getting out of this, she was doing it on her own. She had no idea where she was or what kind of building she was in. The same three men had come in twice; they were obviously in direct charge of her. Ponytail seemed to be the squad leader. Ellis was on the premises, somewhere.

Her only resource was herself. What use she could be to herself, in her current condition, was certainly a variable. A lot depended, too, on what Ellis knew about her. He'd had time, so she assumed he knew her real name. If he knew that, then he knew she had a military background—that might account for the way her guards were armed. He had the same information that Bart had been able to trace.

If he had more than that, Lilli didn't think it was much more. Her past was very well protected, and getting through the walls around it was extremely risky. Ellis wasn't reckless enough for that—and he'd only recently begun to take her seriously as a threat.

So the most he probably thought he knew about her was that she was a former military pilot, highly decorated, who had choked under pressure and gotten a whole squad of soldiers killed.

Not the truth, but not even the U.S. Army knew the truth about what Ray Hobson had done. And the story the Army did have about her was still buried pretty deep.

But say he had that much. Maybe Lilli could use that misperception in her favor. He thought her breakable. It very likely reinforced his standing perception of women. That was why the nakedness. He thought—most men thought—that women were fundamentally weak and insecure. He thought stripping her would make her feel vulnerable. But she felt no more insecure naked than she had in a sweater and jeans. Colder, but no less secure. She'd feel more secure in armor, of course.

As a woman in the military, Lilli had learned to use men's preconceptions and expectations against them. They thought of her as a piece of ass? She used that angle to get what she wanted. They thought she was weak and emotional? She used that to get their guard down. She had yet to encounter a man, civilian or military, who feared and respected her for what she could do until he'd seen it for himself.

It didn't bother her at all. She liked the room it gave her. And she loved the stupid expressions on men's faces when they got a load of her. She needed to find the room Ellis had given her. If indeed he had.

She had only been so vulnerable and weak one other time, and she had not been able to save herself from Hobson. She had needed Isaac to save her. But she had not broken.

She knew she wouldn't break now, but did she have enough left to fight?

~oOo~

She had almost mastered her shivering when a voice materialized out of thin air. Or, more accurately, out of that old intercom speaker high on the wall.

Miss Accardo. I respect that your will is strong. But truly, this unpleasantness must end. I am a businessman. A philanthropist. An important member of my community. The events of the past several weeks are...well, they are sordid and sad, and not at all the civilized way to conduct a business transaction. We can put an end to this, you and I. You have no ties to that desiccated old backwater of a town. There is no need for you to give up so much in its name. Especially now. Signal Bend has fallen. Your friends with the motorcycles are dead. All of them. There is nothing left for you to fight for...except the life inside you. The last piece of its father. Sign the contract, my dear. Take what you can and move on with your life.

Lilli heard him but refused to believe. Isaac wasn't dead. No. No.

She gave herself a stern mental shake, refusing to entertain that thought. Even if he was dead, it changed nothing, except to harden Lilli's resolve. If Isaac was dead, she would not grieve until she'd taken Ellis out. She didn't know how he knew she was pregnant, but that changed nothing, either. She would not break. She turned to the camera in the ceiling and raised her middle finger.

Again, Ellis's voice filled the room. *I am truly sorry that you have chosen stubbornness over reason. Things are about to become extremely unpleasant for you, my dear.*

~oOo~

By her estimation, about ten minutes, and another ten degrees, passed before the door crashed open again, and her three guards were back in the room. This time, Ponytail's 16 was on his back, and the other two had their weapons trained on her. Saying not a word, Ponytail crossed the room, grabbed her by the hair, and dragged her to the desk, pushing her, face down, onto it.

She'd known this was coming. She'd known. This was how it went. She'd known. Her goal was to live as long as she could and not break. No matter what they did, she would not break. Ellis would have to take that property over her dead body. She turned her mind away, to Isaac. He was alive. He had to be.

She would not break.

~oOo~

Lilli lay on the floor. It wasn't cold in the room any longer. Or if it was, she'd stopped being able to tell. She had no idea how much time had passed. Maybe days by now.

It had seemed endless, what they'd done.

She was bruised and bleeding. Cramping. She hurt so fucking bad. She didn't think she was pregnant now. She didn't know how she could be.

When they'd gotten inventive, she'd fought, and they'd beaten her. One eye was swollen shut, and her nose was broken. Blood was caked on her face.

The door crashed open. Oh, God. They'd just left. They couldn't be back for more. Please, they weren't back for more.

She struggled to focus. Ponytail came into the room, his sidekicks right behind him. He was wearing a bandage over his left eye. He put another motherfucking contract on the desk, and they backed out and closed the door.

She lay on the floor for a few more minutes, building her resolve back up. Then she struggled to her feet. No—not to her feet. She couldn't get there. So she crawled to the desk, every inch an agony, and pulled the contract down. Now the offer was $200,000.

She faced the camera and tore it up.

~oOo~

She'd fallen into a dazed semi-consciousness, too hurt to really sleep, when the door crashed open again. When they put their hands on her, at first she didn't even open her eyes. But they put her on her feet and bound her hands. They led her out of the room, still naked and bleeding, sandwiched between two guards, Ponytail at her side. She brought herself as quickly as she could to full alertness. If she was moving, then there was opportunity. They'd bound her hands in front—that was a mistake. She hoped she could exploit it. She had to keep her eyes open and her wits sharp. She ignored her pain and focused.

They led her into an elevator and pushed "4"—the highest number. When the doors opened, they walked out into a different world—the sleek architecture and décor of an executive suite.

It appeared to be empty, and the sky outside the wall of windows they passed was black. Full night. At a minimum, six hours had passed since she'd been taken. She caught a glimpse of the Arch glowing at medium distance—they were in St. Louis, just west of downtown. Only a couple of hours from Signal Bend. For the first time, Lilli really confronted the idea that Ellis had told her the truth, that Isaac might be dead.

They stopped her in front of two burled wood doors. Ponytail knocked and then opened both doors and pulled her through. A chief executive's office, with high-end Danish furniture, gleaming modern accessories, and abstract artwork on the walls. Lilli saw a Rothko. Probably not a print.

In front of an expansive teak desk was an unassuming, armless chair, chrome and red vinyl. The kind one might find in the waiting area at the local tire store. A white painter's tarp was spread under it. Ponytail shoved her onto the chair and then stood back. It took all the will Lilli had not to scream at the pain of sitting down.

Lilli heard a toilet flush, and then a door at the side of the room opened, and a small man, maybe five-five, trimly built and richly dressed, with a thick head of sandy hair going to light grey, stepped out of a bathroom, wiping his hands on a thick, gold towel. He turned and hung the towel neatly on its rod and then came into the room.

He waved impatiently at her and looked at Ponytail. "Please, Derek. There's no need to be inhumane. There's bedding in the closet in my assistant's office. Bring her a blanket."

When Derek was back and had draped a soft blanket over her shoulders, Lawrence Ellis sat down at his desk and smiled sweetly at Lilli. "Miss Accardo. It's time we put an end to this."

CHAPTER NINETEEN

Show leapt through the front window of the ice cream shop, his handgun drawn. "Isaac, what?!"

He'd been drawn by Isaac's bellow. Now, Isaac shouted, "Ellis has Lilli. Fuck, Show! He's got her!"

"What? How? You sure?"

"He answered her fucking phone!" Without thinking, knowing only that he had to save her, Isaac ran by Showdown and leapt through the window and onto the sidewalk. Before he could head off to his bike at a full run, Show's hand was around his arm, pulling him back.

"Isaac, stop! Think! Where is she? Do you know?"

He didn't know. He had no idea. Not as far as Chicago, certainly, but that was all he knew. He looked at Show, feeling desperate and terrified and without a clue what he could do to save her. "I don't know. God, Show! I don't know!" A thought occurred to him. "Where's Bart?"

"In the candy shop. He got hit, remember? Evelyn Sweet is sewing him up."

Isaac turned and ran down the sidewalk, headed for Sweet's. He could hear Show running behind him. He jumped over debris and bodies, and he barely noticed. He didn't care about anything but finding Lilli.

Bart was sitting on a red vinyl stool at the soda counter, as Evelyn wrapped his shoulder in gauze. Isaac tore up to him and grabbed his good arm. Bart still winced at the movement. "Bart—Ellis has Lilli. He answered her phone and then turned it off. Can you trace it? Even if it's off?"

He had Bart's full attention. "Yeah—long as the battery's in it, I can trace. But I need my gear. My bike's down, and I can't ride like this, anyway."

Evelyn handed Bart her keys. "Check out the Silverado. I had it parked in back—maybe they didn't get to it."

Bart kissed her cheek. "Thanks, Evie." To Isaac and Show, he said, "I'll meet you at the clubhouse?"

Isaac nodded and ran out the door and across the street to his bike.

~oOo~

While Bart worked, Isaac paced. The clubhouse was still crowded with people and their belongings, so he went into the Room for some fucking peace, trying as he paced to make his head work. He had to think.

But he couldn't. Ellis had Lilli. The thought took over everything.

249

Show came in and blocked his way. "Boss, stop. We need to work this. I talked to the Sheriff. He's holding the Staties and Feds back long as he can, but that won't be long. The story is we're chasing some of the attackers, and that's why we're off the scene. It's just me, Len, and Hav, but we're with you."

Show put his hands on both of Isaac's shoulders, and Isaac knew he had bad news. His heart was going to come clear through his chest. "I got some news on what happened, and I need you to maintain. Tyler told me that Badge is gonna be okay, but he's still out, and there's no sign of Lilli. Witnesses on the scene saw a blacked out van pull up next to the truck, shoot Badge where he stood in the bed, and shoot Lilli as she ran. They carried her off with them."

They'd shot her. Oh, fuck. They'd shot her. "God, Show—I can't...I can't..."

Show put his arm around his shoulders. "I know, Isaac. Maintain. We'll find her, but we need you steady and clear."

Bart came in, holding his bad arm to his side. He looked peaked, but focused. "I got her. Office building in St. Louis. One of Ellis's fronts. Keeps an office there. Her phone is there. Don't know if that's where she is, but that's the best place I think we can start."

Isaac pulled his burner out. "I'm calling Tug. The Scorpions should be in the St. Louis area by now—maybe even through it. That's five more bodies." He called, got Tug to pull up at a park just west of the city and wait for them.

When he was off the call, he looked at the men he had left. Dan was dead. Vic and Bart were wounded. C.J. was with their fallen brother.

The healthy Horde were four men. No army at all. But he met each of his brother's eyes in turn and then said, "Let's load up and ride."

Then he headed into the Hall. As he passed the bar, he stopped. There was a stack of Kevlar vests at the end. He turned to Show, who was coming up right behind him.

"What's this?"

"Courtesy of Sheriff Tyler. One each for the four of us."

Isaac nodded and handed them out. Good to know they still had a few friends.

~oOo~

As they rode toward St. Louis, Havoc and Dom pulling up the rear in the club van, Isaac tried to shove away the despair pressing down on the edges of his thoughts. Hours. He hadn't seen her for hours. Ellis had had her for *hours*. If he'd kept her alive, that is. Maybe he'd just killed her.

No, he hadn't—if he had, why carry her off, then? He'd taken her alive for a reason. Maybe she was still alive for a reason, then. But *hours*. She'd been at his mercy for *hours*. He began to imagine what could be happening to her if she was still alive, and he had to shut that off. Those thoughts would undo him.

One thing he knew to be true. Before he would allow himself to rest, either Ellis would be dead, or he would be. Isaac's hands tightened around his bike's controls as he gave himself over to the image of ending that bastard's life.

Strategy. Forcing himself to set aside despair and vengeance for now, Isaac turned his thoughts to strategy. He needed a way in. The address Bart had given them was an office building on a block full of office buildings. It was late, and the St. Louis business district rolled up its sidewalks by seven o'clock every evening and all weekend long, but that didn't mean they could go in guns ablaze. And how would the Horde find her before they were made?

The answer was, they wouldn't. They'd be made shortly after they got in. Len could pick a lock, but they weren't burglars. They weren't spies. They weren't subtle. They'd have to bust their way in, take out the guards they could, and announce themselves, intentionally or not, within minutes of breaching the building. Assuming they could overpower the guards—Isaac had no doubt that there would be plenty of guards around this fucker; he'd seen that already in the intel Bart and Rick had gotten—they'd have to spread out and comb through the building to find her.

Ellis would have plenty of time to kill her, if he hadn't already.

Lilli was strong and capable, a skilled fighter in her own right. She could defend herself against pretty steep odds. Unless she couldn't. They'd shot her; that much he knew. Isaac had no idea whether they'd hurt her more, or, if they had, how badly. He had no idea if she was in any condition to fight for herself.

They pulled into Lone Elk Park and, leaving Havoc and Dom to wait on the road, skirted the closed gate and headed to the meeting place, where Tug and four of his Scorpion brethren were waiting. Together, they were an army of nine. It had to be enough.

252

They made their greetings, and Isaac began explaining the plan, such as it was. Before he'd finished his third sentence, his burner went off. Bart.

"Yeah, brother."

There was a spark of excitement in Bart's voice. "Boss, I been moving in on the security of that building. It's high-end, but not custom. The exterior locks are electronic, with manual backup. I can get in, give you some room. If Len can pick the manual lock, I can disable the rest. I need, like, an hour."

Isaac felt a tiny bud of hope open in his gut. "Good man. But we'll be there in thirty. We need it then."

Bart didn't answer right away. Then, he said, "Alright. Hit me when you're there."

Isaac closed the phone and looked around at the men arrayed before him. He briefed them on Bart's call and continued explaining the plan—which wasn't much different, just quieter, now, and with a slightly better chance of success.

When he was done, Tug stepped up. Tug was older, with a face that had lived every one of his years. He had long, grey hair, around which he wore a faded red bandana as a headband. The scorpion tattooed on his throat was scarred and faded. Like all the Scorpions, he was a legitimate outlaw, up to his elbows in heavy shit as a matter of course. "It's a solid plan, Isaac. Needs one adjustment." He opened his saddlebags and pulled a silencer out. "We got a few extra rigs, should work with what you're carrying. If we can do this quiet and get the fuck out, then we're all better off."

They loaded up and headed off into the city.

~oOo~

Not wanting to announce their presence with the roar of their Harleys, they parked a couple of blocks away and all piled into the Horde van with Dom and Havoc. Dom at the wheel, they drove into the alley behind the building and pulled up. As everyone sat hunched together in the van, Isaac called Bart. He put the call on speaker, so he wouldn't have to take time to brief the crew after.

Bart answered immediately, and Isaac said, "We're here, man. Tell me somethin' good."

Bart's voice was sharp with agitation, but there was something else in it, something shaken. "I'm in, boss. Okay. There's cameras everywhere. I caught some footage of empty space, and when we're ready, I can loop it, send it to the monitors. It'll give you time, so you just have to deal with the guards you come across. There are a dozen on patrol. I also rerouted the signal from the security company and the emergency alerts, so cops, fire, won't get contacted by the system. When we're go, I can unlock the electronic locks, and the Len can pick the manual backup. It's a standard commercial lock, should be no sweat."

Isaac looked over at Len, who nodded.

Bart wasn't done. "Isaac. I...I think I know where she is. And...I know a lot of what's happened. It's bad, but she's still alive. At least she was fifteen minutes ago."

"Bad how?" The phone creaked, protesting the ferocity of his grip.

"Real bad. There's, like, a cell in the basement. They kept her there for hours. They...she's hurt. But they took her out about fifteen minutes ago, and she walked out on her own power. They took her to the fourth floor—the top—and I lost sight of her when they went into a blind room. Far as I can tell it's the only blind room in the building, other than storage closets. Even the bathrooms are monitored."

"What did they do to her?" Fury pulsed behind his eyes, warping his vision.

"There's no time. And I just sped through the footage. Just...she's gonna need help. Boss, she's naked."

With a roar, Isaac punched the wall of the van, shattering the phone in his hand.

Show put his hand on Isaac's shoulder and pulled his own burner out, calling Bart back.

~oOo~

They got in through a side door into a stairwell when Bart alerted them that the stairwell and adjacent hallway were clear. Then, when Bart said the basement was unoccupied, the Scorpions took the first and second floors. Hav and Len took the third. Show and Isaac climbed to the top floor. Where Lilli was. They stood outside the stairwell door, waiting for backup. Isaac didn't know how long he could wait. Not long.

They knew three men had taken Lilli into the blind room on this floor. They had no idea how many men were in there with her; Bart hadn't had time to comb through enough footage. But Isaac knew there was at least one more: Ellis.

The Horde and Scorpions were all armed with two handguns, an automatic rifle, and a knife. They had spare mags for everything. And they had surprise. It had to be enough.

From below them, gunfire exploded, and Len burst into the stairwell. He yelled up, "We're made! Go!"

Without the slightest hesitation, Isaac and Show slammed through the stairwell door onto the fourth-floor executive suite.

CHAPTER TWENTY

She'd been sitting in this office for at least fifteen minutes. Ellis had offered her a drink—she'd refused, not trusting anything he'd give her—and settled the blanket more fully over her shoulders, keeping her warm and covering her better. Then, in true supervillain fashion, he'd launched into a monologue, giving her the full history of his fight with Signal Bend, including a lot of details she hadn't known, things he'd clearly expected to shock her. He'd been disappointed in that regard. He seemed sincerely regretful about the way things had gone down—the "whole sad affair," as he called it. Not that she gave a fuck about his regrets.

Now Ellis stood in front of her, holding out yet another fucking contract. On the line for the purchase price, this time he'd written $1,000,000. He shook it a little, expecting Lilli to take it in her bound hands. She only stared at him.

He sighed, and even that sound was genteel in some indistinct way. Setting the contract behind him on the desk, he said, "Miss Accardo, truly, I have no appetite for the things that have gone on here today. In fact, I find everything about my dealings with the people of Signal Bend to be...beneath me. My enterprises run smoothly. Cleanly. I take great pride in that."

"You sell drugs." It was the first time she'd spoken since she'd woken up in the basement room. Her voice sounded rough and strange. Thirst and a broken nose, she supposed.

257

Ellis grinned, an unsettling rictus across the lower part of his face. His teeth were brilliantly white and perfectly straight. "Yes, well. A small part of a diverse array of ventures. And your long-haired man sells them, as well, so I wouldn't say you have much room for disapprobation, would you?"

Sells. He'd used the present tense. Isaac was still alive.

Her plan had been to present herself as weaker than she was, to use their preconceptions about women and wait for them to relax and give her room. But she couldn't do it. Maybe it was because she was too sick and hurt to think clearly, but she couldn't do it. It was the smart play, probably the only thing that might still get her out of here both alive and unbroken, but she felt a rage almost beyond her control, and she could not let this man have even the temporary, false satisfaction of having thought he'd broken her.

When she didn't respond to his gibe, he continued. "As I was saying, this is not how I like to do business. But I have spent too much time now, too much of my attention, on this little problem, and I would have it resolved. So I present you with my final offer. The choices are simple: sign, and walk away with a million dollars—a tidy profit for a few weeks of ownership—or continue to refuse, and I allow Derek to kill you in any way he sees fit. The offer expires in thirty seconds."

In the time she'd been in this room, she'd tried hard to see every possible option, to notice any slip in their focus. Her bag was on the desk—that probably accounted for how Ellis guessed she was pregnant, or that she had been, since the unused pregnancy tests were still in there. She wondered if her gun was still there. The only other thing truly weapon-like, besides the weapons her guards carried, was an elaborate gold letter opener on the desk. Three against one—four against one if Ellis had any kind of a sack—meant that the letter opener wasn't much of a weapon at all. She doubted she'd have time to dig through her bag, even if her gun was there. She needed to disarm one of these guys.

Her hands were still bound, resting passively now in her lap, but they had not bound her feet, and they had not bound her to the chair. Ponytail—Derek, a truly sick bastard—stood in front of her, a bit to her left. She couldn't see the other two. They were behind her; presumably at the door. *Presumably* was a very dangerous word in a situation like this. But, hell, she was going to die anyway. At this point, being able to take Derek down with her was the best result she could hope for. And she had some hope for that: as Ellis talked, Derek had grown bored, and his M16 had sagged—not much, only a couple of inches, but it gave her maybe one second. Maybe two if she was really, really lucky.

Lucky wasn't really a word that applied to her today.

But then, as those last thirty seconds ticked away, she got lucky. The sound of gunfire on a floor below them, and then a door slammed, much closer. Ellis looked up; so did Derek, training his one good eye on the door.

Hold...hold...wait

Ellis nodded over her head. "Alan, Cameron—go."

She heard the door open. *One more beat.*

She waited that one beat, then kicked out with both feet, hard as she could, catching Derek in his left knee. The impact hyperextended it, bending it backwards at a sharp angle. He screamed and dropped to the floor. She stood as he was trying to raise his gun, and stomped him in the crotch. He screamed again.

Ellis was yelling for the other two guards, but she couldn't worry about that. She'd abandoned the goal of getting out of here alive, and the thought that the commotion giving her this chance meant possible rescue hadn't gained purchase yet in her head. Her only goal was doing all the damage she could before she died. Derek was still incapacitated, and she went for his 16, but it was strapped across his shoulder, and she couldn't get it from him.

He had a sidearm, though, holstered at his hip. She pulled it free with her bound hands and turned to Ellis, cocking as she turned. He was behind his desk, upright, clutching it as if the expensive wood had some kind of mystical protective properties.

He started to speak—to plead with her or to yell again for help, she did not know—and she shot him in his open mouth. Before he dropped, she shot him again, this time in the forehead. Brain tissue splattered on the silk draperies, and he collapsed to the floor.

Derek had quieted and was moving in a way that got her antennae twitching, and she looked down to see him raising another handgun, aiming it at her. The shoulder strap on the 16 must have been getting in his way, too, where he lay on the floor. She shot his hand, and his gun flew across the room and fired where it landed. The bullet whizzed past her ear, moving her hair, and struck the wall several feet to her side. Realizing how close she'd come to basically killing herself, she began to laugh.

"You shot my hand, bitch!" Derek was not the sharpest knife in the drawer, but he had an astute grasp of the obvious. That thought got her laughing even harder. Tears had started to stream from her eyes, even the swollen one, when she set the gun down and picked up the fancy gold letter opener from Ellis' fancy teak desk. It was sharp. Turning it inward, she sliced open the tie that bound her hands.

Derek was still mewling on the floor, holding his mangled hand. What a little bitch—so wrapped up in his pain, he'd stopped paying attention to her. Coming down with her knee on his crotch, making him squeal again, she straddled him, unhooked the strap from the 16 and, grimacing as she put her hands on it, set it out of his reach. Then she began stabbing him. She'd dispatched Ellis quickly. Derek, she wanted to suffer. The others, too, if she got the chance. He was wearing a Kevlar vest, so she stabbed him in his face and throat, starting with his good eye. He put up virtually no fight, merely mewling for awhile and then going silent. She stabbed and stabbed, starting methodically, but soon losing herself in the vengeance, even after there was no one there to wreak it on.

She felt hands on her shoulders, and she yelled wordlessly—a battle cry—and turned, striking out with the letter opener. She struck true, and the hands released her. But then one wrapped around her wrist, immobilizing the hand that held her weapon, so she tried to yank and overbalance whichever fucker had her.

"Lilli! Baby, stop! It's okay. Stop, baby, stop. It's me."

Isaac? She hesitated, tried to get her bearings. The room was full of men, and she jumped to her feet, ready to keep fighting. But hands pulled her close. Familiar hands, coarse and gentle. Isaac. All at once, her legs could no longer hold her up. He held her as she collapsed, and he went to the floor with her.

"Oh, fuck, baby. Oh, fuck."

"Isaac? Isaac, I…" She didn't know what words would follow. There were no words. She was in Isaac's arms. Then the blanket was on her again. He was alive. She was alive. Was it over?

As if he were answering the question she hadn't asked aloud, Isaac pressed his lips to her forehead. "It's over, baby," he whispered. "We're gonna get you to the hospital, and you're gonna be okay. It's over."

No. Not the hospital. No cold rooms, no strangers. No. No.

"Home. I want to go home. Please, I want to go home. Take me home."

As the adrenaline waned, pain and exhaustion took its place, and when the world began to blur and go grey, she let it. The last thing she heard was Isaac's rich, deep, soothing voice.

"Okay, baby. I got you. Let's go home."

~oOo~

She woke in the van, in Isaac's lap, his arms holding her tight to his chest. She was still wrapped in the blanket. He smiled down at her, but his eyes shone oddly in the flashes of streetlights and headlights. Her first thought was that he hated being in a cage.

"Where's your bike?"

He laughed a little. "Don't you worry, Sport. I got it covered. Sleep. We'll be home soon."

She slept.

~oOo~

She was in her own bed, the bed she shared with Isaac, when she woke again. She began to weep with relief, but the pain everywhere was too much, it hurt too much to cry, and she choked off her tears. Her head still didn't seem to be working quite right. All her thoughts were slow now.

She was alone, but she could hear Isaac's voice. At first she thought she was blind or something, but then she realized that she was seeing. He simply wasn't in the room with her. The door was open, and she could hear him talking. To a woman. There was a woman in the house. Who?

She tried to sit up, but couldn't. She tried to speak, but only croaked. It was as if she'd used up everything she had in Ellis's office.

Then Isaac was standing in the doorway, smiling. "Hey, Sport." He walked to the bed and sat down carefully at her side. "I have somebody here—a doctor—to take a look at you, okay? I know you didn't want the hospital, but you're hurt bad, baby. Can my friend Tasha take a look?"

Tasha...the name was familiar, but she had no idea why. Isaac reached out and brushed her hair back. She flinched hard, surprised by the gesture. He pulled back, leaving his hand hovering in midair. His forearm was wrapped in a heavy gauze bandage.

"Easy, Lilli. It's just me." He let his arm drop. "Can I bring Tasha in?"

She knew the pain she was feeling was too much not to need medical help. She knew a doctor would hurt her more—it was what they did—but she nodded. Maybe at least she'd get some painkillers out of it.

Isaac nodded and called out, "Okay, Tash."

Tash—she should be able to remember. She was good at names and faces. A tall, fair redhead walked in, and Lilli got it. This was the doctor who'd helped Show and Holly. There was something between her and Isaac. Lilli had never asked—it hadn't seemed important in the midst of everything, and then she'd forgotten. It still wasn't important.

"Hi, Lilli. I'm Tasha. I'm a doctor. We met once before—I don't know if you remember." Lilli nodded. "Good. That's good. Isaac asked me to examine you. Is that okay?"

Lilli nodded again.

~oOo~

Yes, it hurt. A lot. But now it was almost over. Her nose was set, and she had stitches in her face and elsewhere. Tasha had asked Isaac to

264

leave the room for the last, longest part of it, but Lilli hadn't wanted him to go. She felt anxious about him being away from her, so he sat with her and held her hand. She squeezed hard as Tasha did her thing, trying to put her pain in her hand. Isaac's body shook next to her. The look on his face, when he wasn't looking at her, was dark and violent.

Other than to ask Lilli to move in certain ways, or to tell her if something hurt, Tasha said very little during the examination. When she was done, she pulled off her gloves and gave Lilli's raised knee a gentle pat. She looked shaken.

"I'm so sorry you went through this, Lilli. God, really sorry."

Lilli said nothing. Nothing to say.

"Okay. There's a lot of damage, but it will heal, if you take it easy. The sutures I put in will dissolve on their own." She sat at the end of the bed. "Lilli, Isaac told me that you found out you were pregnant a few days ago." She paused, and Lilli stared. She'd come to terms with the reality that she'd lost the baby. But Isaac's grip on her hand tightened.

After a silent beat, Tasha continued. "There was a lot of blood, I know. But your cervix is still closed. The damage doesn't appear to go that far, and the blood wasn't uterine. In a couple of weeks, if there hasn't been more bleeding, we can do an ultrasound and make sure. But I think there's a good chance you're still pregnant."

CHAPTER TWENTY-ONE

Isaac woke when the bed shifted as Lilli got up. Lying still, he watched in the dim moonlight as she left the room. She was walking better, less gingerly, now, a week after her encounter with Ellis. He hated to be alone in their bed, but he let her go.

He should let her go. She should leave him. They'd barely been together six months, and in that time she'd been horribly hurt and almost killed *twice*—both times a direct result of her association with him.

What Ellis's men had done to her—if he let himself think too long about it, his blood eddied to a poisonous froth in his heart and head. He was out of people to kill, but he felt the need no less. After Tasha had first examined her, she'd given Lilli an injection of morphine. When Lilli had fallen into an opiate sleep, Tasha had pulled him into the living room and explained in detail what Lilli's injuries suggested. He'd called Bart immediately afterward and forced him to say what was on the video feed. Then he'd left Tasha with Lilli, had gone outside and, with no other outlet for his frenzied rage, chopped about a cord of wood.

The guards he and Show had killed had gotten off far too easy with bullets to the head. Even the guard he'd found Lilli destroying with a fucking letter opener had gotten off too easy.

Forever burned into his brain like a brand was the image confronting him when he'd entered Ellis' office. His beautiful woman—naked, bruised, bleeding, her hair caked, her face hugely swollen—straddling a guard, holding that letter opener in both hands and driving it into the guard's face and neck. Into his eyes, his mouth. She'd been making guttural, bestial sounds, and she'd been splattered gorily with blood.

Without thinking, he'd run to her and grabbed her. She'd turned on him, and there had been no sign of recognition in her face as she'd stabbed him. That moment, when she'd turned those feral, unknowing eyes on him, had chilled him. But then she'd seen him, and she'd come back to him.

In the first couple of days, when she'd stayed in bed, she hadn't wanted him to be away from her at all. She'd slept a medicated sleep most of the time, but she'd gotten panicky if she woke and he wasn't with her. He'd spent those days lying on the bed at her side, watching her sleep, leaving only when Show brought business that would not wait to be discussed, or to prepare her meals.

He wasn't any kind of a cook, but that didn't matter. Their fridge and freezer were chock full of ready-to-heat casseroles, soups, and stews. They had loaves of fresh bread, baskets of fruit and vegetables, cakes, pies, cobblers. He could start a restaurant in their kitchen from all the homemade meals the women of Signal Bend had brought. Thanksgiving had happened since Lilli had been taken, but they hadn't missed it. The town had brought it to them.

They were heroes. The Horde, Isaac, and Lilli. Heroes. And not just in Signal Bend. He wanted to talk to Lilli about it, but she wouldn't. Any mention of what had happened caused her to shut down hard and immediately. Even a week later, she had no idea what had transpired since she'd killed Ellis. He and the Horde had held off the outside world, making a quiet bubble for Lilli to recover in peace.

And she was recovering. She was stronger, healing. Her face, though still discolored, was back to its normal shape. She'd have a scar through one eyebrow, and her nose had taken on the slightest bump across the bridge, but she was healing well. Tasha had told him she was healing well everywhere. And she had not bled any more. She was still sick in the mornings. They had another week to wait before an ultrasound could tell them anything, but Isaac felt hope that their baby was still growing inside her.

But she was so damn quiet. He understood—or, God, he understood as well as he could—but he was scared and lonely. Even as she clung to his hand, unwilling to have him out of her sight, he could feel her closing up inside. In the past few days, as she'd gained strength and had been able to move around with less pain, he'd noticed her stiffening if he touched her anywhere but her hand. As if she had to prepare herself for his touch. It made him ache.

Knowing in his head that she would be right to leave him did nothing to settle the fear in his heart that she might. He couldn't let her go.

After the first few days, Lilli stopped the Percocet, but still she hadn't dreamt, at least not violently. Isaac thought that was a small blessing. But she didn't sleep through, waking in the early morning and leaving the bed. This was the fourth night it had happened. He'd let her go every time, and had found her sleeping on the sofa she hated a few hours later. As if she'd come out to get away from him.

This time, he couldn't spend the last hours of the night sitting in the dark. He felt like he was letting her down somehow by letting her go off in the middle of the night. At least, it should be him sleeping on the couch. He got out of bed and headed to the living room.

She wasn't there. Or in the kitchen, or upstairs in her office, or anywhere in the house. His heart had a hair trigger these days, anyway, and it began to race erratically now. God. Where was she?

Her boots were missing from the front hall. So was her jacket. It was below freezing outside, but she must have gone out there. Isaac pulled on his boots and jacket and went onto the porch.

Everything was quiet. He didn't see her anywhere, nor any sign she'd been out here recently. But then he saw the barn door open, a faint yellow glow. She was with the horses?

She was. As he got to the open doorway, Isaac found Lilli standing with Gert, forehead to forehead. He stayed back for a few minutes, watching. Neither she nor the horse moved. It was a picture of a melancholy peace.

"Lilli." He spoke loudly enough for her to hear him halfway through the barn, but he didn't shout. Nevertheless, she jumped as if he had. Gertie threw her head up and turned an indignant glare on him. He walked in.

He hated to see her react to him like that. "Sorry, Sport. Didn't mean to scare you. I didn't know where you'd gone." He'd reached Gertie's stall. When he put his hand on Lilli's lower back, he felt her body go rigid. Just for a moment. Then she swallowed, blinked, and relaxed. He hated it. He knew what she'd gone through, and he knew that it had only been a week, but he had to say something. He could give her all the time she needed, but he couldn't give her silence.

"It's cold out here. Come inside and talk with me."

Without turning to look at him, she shook her head. All week, she'd never initiated a conversation, and rarely did more than answer questions he'd asked.

"Lilli. Baby, please. We don't have to talk about that, if you don't want to. I want to talk about us. I feel like I'm losing you. Let me back in."

At that, she looked up at him. First they just stared into each other's eyes. Then she reached out and put her hand on his side. Other than needing his help to get around at first, or the way she'd stayed curled against his body the first day, this was the first time she'd touched more than his hand all week. He stood still, resisting the powerful urge to pull her into his arms.

Then she slid her own arm around his waist. The other arm followed. She rested her head on his chest. He let himself put his arms around her, gently. She tensed a little, but then he felt her really relax against him.

"You're not losing me. I love you. But I just need some time. I'm not ready to talk. About any of it."

That scared him, but he wouldn't push harder. "Okay. All the time you want. But let me stay close." He kissed her head. "Come inside with me, baby. Please."

"Okay." She took his hand, and they walked back toward the house together.

~oOo~

A couple of weeks later, things were a little better. Christmas was around the corner, and Lilli had turned her attention to planning a party for the town at the clubhouse on Christmas Eve. Having something to accomplish seemed to be doing her a lot of good. And the town deserved a celebration, while they were in the midst of the cleanup and still reeling from Ellis's attack. They had survived. They had won.

Lilli hadn't lost the baby. Though the confirmation that she was still pregnant had not seemed to have made a marked difference in her still-quiet demeanor, for Isaac the news had lightened his spirits considerably. They were still intact, still bound together. And there was hope now for a good future. A safe future.

They had survived. All three of them. They had won.

He went upstairs and knocked on her office door. She no longer did secret work for the government, but this room was hers, and she had a need for privacy.

"Come in," she called. He went in to find her reading, curled up in the leather armchair he'd built—the first new piece of furniture he'd finished for the house. Her face had almost healed, and she was curled up in a big sweater and jeans that had gotten a bit baggy over the past few weeks. She looked fresh and lovely, even though the bruises and cuts weren't entirely gone.

There were stacks of books everywhere and boxes more that hadn't been opened yet. The contents of her storage locker had arrived. In the kitchen, there was a pretty amazing set of Italian dishes and crockery, too, from her grandmother. And drooping over a stack of boxes in the corner of this room was a decaying, black and white spotted, stuffed dog.

He walked over and kissed the top of her head. She leaned into it, and he sighed his relief. She was warming to his touch again. It would be some time yet before they could again be intimate together, until she'd healed completely—if she was even ready then—but she no longer stiffened when his skin touched hers, and that was enough.

"I gotta get going pretty soon." He'd called the Horde in to discuss what appeared to be the end of the Ellis problem. In the few weeks since Lilli had been taken, a lot had changed. "But before I go, I want to talk to you about something. Got a minute for me?"

She set her book aside. "Sure. What's up?"

He got down on his knees in front of her chair and took her hands in his. "I want to marry you, Sport. Now. We're clear of the shit, and the baby's okay. I want to do what you said—fly out to California and get your dad's 'Cuda, then stop in Reno and get married. I want to go tomorrow."

The incredulity had grown in her eyes as he'd talked, and now she said, "Isaac...," making it clear in the way she drew out the syllables that she thought he'd lost his mind.

But he hadn't. This was right. There was no good reason in the world that they couldn't elope right now. "Come on, baby. Let's put it all behind us, get to our future. Come on. Come away with me."

"Isaac, it's December. If it's snowing, we'll never get through the mountains without chains, and I'm not putting chains on my dad's car."

"If it's snowing, we'll go south and get hitched in Vegas."

"It's almost Christmas. I'm planning that big-ass party."

"You're good at giving orders. Delegate. The guys will help. And there's a whole mess of women who'd be all for gettin' involved. We'll make sure we're back in time. Come on, Sport. It's my Christmas wish. All I want is a wife."

"You're insane."

He laughed. "Where you're concerned, that is not news."

She sighed, but she was smiling a small, sweet smile. "Okay. Then get your ass out of here, because I have a lot to do today if we're running off in the morning."

Grinning so widely his cheeks ached, he raised up on his knees and kissed her. She kissed him back and, without thinking about it, thinking only of his relief and happiness, he deepened the kiss, cradling her face in his hands and pushing his tongue into his mouth.

She stiffened and pulled back.

"I'm sorry, baby." Pushing his disappointment away, he kissed her forehead. "Sorry."

"No—it's okay. I just…"

"I know. It's okay. We're okay." Picking up her hands again and kissing them both. "Get busy, Sport. I have to get to the clubhouse. I'll be back in a few hours."

Isaac stood and headed to the door. Before he stepped through, he turned back and said, "All the reservations are taken care of. You just take care of what you need to do. The trip is done."

She smirked at him. "And if I'd said no?"

He winked and headed downstairs. He'd had to believe she'd say yes.

~oOo~

The Horde were heroes. Fucking heroes. *Folk* heroes, even. Isaac was amazed. The gunfight down Main Street had drawn the attention of the media as well as state and federal law. News crews had descended on the town in the hours and days afterward. "The Shootout in Signal Bend"—that was what people were calling it. Like it had starred John Wayne and Clint Eastwood. Dan had hit the nose when he'd said it was like the Wild West.

Dan.

They'd buried him and the others in the town cemetery. MCs from all over the country—even those with which the Horde had no relationship—had sent representatives. The funeral at St. John's, and the wake in the clubhouse after, had been covered by several major news organizations and maybe a dozen bloggers.

They were heroes because by the end of that day, the two major gangs in St. Louis—the Underdawgs and the Northside Knights— were decimated. The Horde had nothing to do with the demise of the

Underdawgs, their friends, but the general populace was no less pleased they were gone, and no less happy to credit the Horde with it.

Lawrence Ellis had been simultaneously exposed as one of the most powerful drug kingpins in the country and eliminated. Bart and Rick had—anonymous and heavily shielded—blasted out to all those news organizations, and the FBI, the information they'd hacked from Ellis. That included the footage Bart had pulled down from that office building in St. Louis. Most of it. He'd destroyed the worst parts of what had happened to Lilli.

The day before, Isaac had taken a call from a Hollywood producer, wanting to 'option' the story. Whatever that fucking meant. *Hollywood.* The guy had spoken some kind of hipster lingo that had aggravated the *fuck* out of Isaac, who'd told him to shove his 'option.' But then the guy had said that the story was out there and would get told. The Horde and the town could profit from it, or somebody else could. As he'd talked, Isaac had realized that Signal Bend needed to control the story, not just profit from it. So Isaac, grudgingly, told this 'Stan' guy that he'd get back to him. He'd take it to the table.

Meth was dead to Signal Bend. The focus on the town, and the demise of the Underdawgs, their primary buyer, had killed it as a viable economic plan. At first, Isaac had lamented to Lilli the irony of all this hero worship, which had saved them from the specter of prosecution—there was no appetite at any level for putting away the guys that had accomplished in a day what law enforcement had been trying for years to get done, and the Feds had a real interest in keeping Lilli's past controlled—being the thing that killed the town after all.

But Lilli had said, "Use it." In the first conversation in which she'd fully participated since she was taken, she'd described ways that the town's newfound notoriety—no, popularity—might be useful. It wouldn't bring the family farms back, but it could draw people to Main Street, and bring life to the shops, to Marie's and the other little cafes. More growth could feed off that. They'd had themselves a modern-day shootout, and the town had banded together and fought off the bad guys.

And now Hollywood was calling.

Isaac sat at the head of the table and laid out the story. Though the Horde had met at table a few times over the past few weeks, those meetings had been focused on specifics, dealing with the fallout of that day—understanding the potential legal risks to the Horde and its allies, organizing the cleanup and repairs, planning Dan's memorial, updates on Vic and Badger's conditions (both were pulling through and would recover). They'd put Vic on a year's probation, his patch in the balance if he fucked up even once. This was the first meeting in which they were looking forward.

"We gotta get out of the meth business. We got nobody to buy what we'd be selling. The void in St. Louis will fill, but we don't know by who, and we got no relationships with any of the likely players. It's too hot. We got a pass—and that's a fuckin' miracle—because we took the Northsiders and Ellis down. We need to use this chance to get on the right side. Dandy and Becker are on board. Even the Sheriff is ready to be out. These last few months have killed greed."

He was gratified to see the heads around the table nodding. He'd known they'd be in—no one had any appetite to continue the way they'd been going—but it still felt good to know for sure. He looked at Show, who'd lost so much to this business. His VP was staring at his hands where they gripped the edge of the table. He was working his way back, Isaac knew, but it was a slow go. No telling whether Show would ever be the same. Isaac hoped so. They were a team. If Isaac was good at the head of the table, it was only because Show was at his side.

He had a sense that the table was unified, but a sense was not enough. "All those in favor of ending the meth trade in Signal Bend. Aye." He went around the table: Show. Bart. C.J., with Vic's proxy. Havoc. Len. It was a small table these days, but it was unified. They were out of meth.

Isaac nodded. "Carries. I've called the cookers all in, and I want us all in the meeting. That's three kitchens down. All those people not making or spending money. We're gonna need to give them a way to earn. We can put them to work on the rebuild, but that's a short term deal, and the insurance money isn't a get-rich scheme."

Bart leaned in. He was still in a sling, but nearly back to top form. "I got some help for that. We can do a Kickstarter, get funding for the rebuild that way. Ties in with the idea of using the shootout as a public draw."

C.J. asked, "What the fuck is a kickstarter?"

Bart laughed. "It's a website for crowdfunding. Basically, you start an account, describe a project you need money for, and then ask people to give you money. You give them some kind of swag for certain levels of donation—twenty bucks, fifty, a hundred—like we could get coffee mugs made or t-shirts, whatever, and—"

"Fuckin' charity? *T-shirts*?" C.J. snarled and crossed his arms. "That's bullshit. What's twenty bucks gonna do for us, anyway? Asshole."

Unfazed, Bart grinned at the oldest member. "Dude. People make fucking millions for their projects. *Movies* have been funded this way. We're rebuilding a town. Everybody thinks we did some kind of public service—think about it as getting paid by the public for it. Considering the publicity, I bet we get enough to make a nest egg for the town."

C.J. scowled at Bart. "Call me *dude* again, asshole, and I'll feed you your teeth. Charity's charity."

"Okay, guys. Ceej is on record. I say we vote. All in favor of Bart doing this Kickstarter thing. Hands." Isaac raised his hand and looked around the table. Every hand but C.J.'s was up.

"Carries. Bart, do your thing. Now—do we talk to Hollywood or not? I expect the town to follow our lead. Hands for this, too." Again, every hand but C.J.'s—Signal Bend was going Hollywood.

"One more piece of business." Isaac felt oddly nervous about announcing the next part. He cleared his throat. "Show's in charge for the next few days. I'll be reachable, but I'm taking my lady and making an honest woman out of her. She's baking my kid in her oven."

Show turned sharply at that last bit of news. Isaac hadn't said anything to anyone about Lilli being pregnant. Len slapped his back. Havoc applauded. Bart was grinning like an idiot. C.J. sat expressionless. Isaac was getting damn tired of the old man's attitude, but he ignored him and took the congratulations of his other brothers with a broad smile. Meeting Show's eyes, he saw a somber kind of hope.

And then Show reached out and grasped his arm. "That's a good woman. Don't fuck it up."

With a laugh, Isaac nodded and turned back to the table. "We leave in the morning—flying to California to pick up her dad's '68 Barracuda and then driving back. Stopping in Nevada to do the deed. Right now she's working out instructions for the Christmas party. I know it sucks worse than a gunfight, but I need a volunteer to handle the party plans while we're gone." The table was silent, the men shifting awkwardly in their seats. "Come on, brothers. It's just telling a bunch of chicks what to do. You're all great at that."

Len sighed. "Are there flowers and shit?"

Isaac laughed. "This is Lilli. The party is here. No flowers. Probably a Christmas tree."

"Fuck. Fine, I'll do it."

"My man!" Isaac slapped his SAA on the back. "Okay. Let's talk to the cookers." He gaveled the meeting to an end.

~oOo~

"Come on, Sport. You're making us late for our own wedding."

279

"Chill, love. There's a reason I don't dress like this. It's a pain in the ass."

Isaac stood outside the bathroom door. He didn't know what her fuss was about. They were heading down to the wedding chapel in the hotel for a ten-minute wedding. He was dressed the way he always dressed—except that, yes, he'd made sure his kutte and boots were extra clean, and, sure, maybe he'd taken a couple of extra minutes with his hair, leaving a lot of it loose, the way she liked.

The day before, they'd landed in Sacramento and picked up a rental car for the ride to Stockton. They'd collected the 'Cuda—which was indeed a magnificent car—then returned the rental and headed for Reno. They'd gotten lucky; though there was heavy snow cover in Tahoe, the roads were clear. Lilli had insisted on driving all the way to Reno, much to Isaac's chagrin. He did not ride bitch. Not when a woman was behind the wheel. But she'd pointed out that, first, it was her car, and second, she hadn't been able to drive it for years. So he'd acquiesced.

She drove like fucking Danica Patrick. Jesus. He'd actually been nervous, speeding over winding mountain roads, weaving around slower traffic—which was everyone. He'd been damn glad to see the hotel. But she was letting him drive the rest of the way. He had an image to uphold, so they'd be making it home in record time, even with a honeymoon night here in the hotel tonight.

Assuming they got married today. The chapel had a strict "fifteen minute" policy, only waiting fifteen minutes past the scheduled appointment before they moved on to the next wedding. They were in that grace period now.

Finally, the knob turned, and Isaac stepped back as Lilli came out of the bathroom.

Holy fuck. She was...holy fuck...wearing a short little white lace dress, with sleeves that were almost long, showing a *lot* of leg. And the most astonishing pair of sky-high heels he'd ever seen. Red suede. Jesus. He'd never seen her wear heels before. Or a dress, for that matter. Lilli had great legs and a *stupendous* ass. The outfit was definitely working for her. He shifted his swollen cock, trying to find a place for it in his jeans.

She saw him and grinned, then looked sheepish and awkward. She was still a week or more away from being physically ready for sex, and who knew how long before her head was ready. He didn't care. She was beautiful, fierce, strong, brilliant. And she was his. He took her face in his hands and kissed her softly. "I love you, Lillian Accardo. You are mine. And you look fucking amazing. I don't know where or when you got that outfit, but I'm glad you did." He stepped away from her, to the table at the side of the room. "And hey. Those shoes go with this." He handed her a single, long-stemmed, red rose, which he'd had delivered to the room while she primped. Corny, maybe. But the smile on her face told him it was right.

She took his hand. "Come on, love. Let's go get official."

~oOo~

That night, their wedding night, for the first time since Ellis had taken Lilli, they slept naked together. Isaac savored the feel of her warm, soft body at ease in the curl of his own. They slept with his hand on her belly and her hand over his, their ringed fingers linked.

It was enough. It was everything.

CHAPTER TWENTY-TWO

Party planning was not something with which Lilli had any real experience. She'd been raised in a family which had mostly kept to itself, without extended relations on the same continent, and after college she'd gone into the Army. Any party planning she'd been part of in the past had involved kegs and pizza.

But Signal Bend deserved a real Christmas. The town had been under siege for weeks—months, really. Years, if the economic disaster in the midst of which they'd been struggling was taken into account. And now Main Street was all but shut down. Everyone but Lilli had been stunned at the damage all those bullets had done. It wasn't just windows that needed to be replaced. The buildings with wood exteriors, the plaster and drywall interiors, the stock—all of it was a mess. And Don Keyes' dozer had pushed three vehicles straight through the entire front of Fosse's Finds.

There was a lot to be done. The town morale was rising, and people were happy to do the repairs, but something told Lilli that they needed some kind of event to mark to end of trouble and the beginning of hope.

She knew she needed it. She needed to keep her mind busy. She'd quit her job, and she needed something to fill her head. When she was idle, she felt like she was losing control of it. She'd said nothing to Isaac. He knew she wasn't quite right, but he thought it was temporary. He didn't know she was worried that what had happened in St. Louis had broken her, after all, that maybe it had unlocked the crazy her mother had left behind in her.

And she was pregnant. God. What if she really was broken? What if she was destined to be the kind of mother her own mother had been?

Staying busy kept those thoughts away. Planning this huge party gave her focus, made her feel like Isaac was right, and the crazy was just a normal, temporary part of recovery from trauma. When the party was over, she was going to have to figure out what the fuck she was going to do with her life, though. Because being Isaac's old lady was not a sustainable profession. That felt like a one-way ticket to crazytown.

She'd had to jump through hoops to quit her job, but she'd managed it. Honestly, they were glad to be rid of her; the Signal Bend story had drawn far too much attention for comfort. They'd changed her faked history, fleshed out parts, redirected others, making it, ironically, able to withstand a bit more scrutiny, since there would no longer be anyone standing at the gate, as it were. And she'd signed all the requisite forms promising to keep her mouth shut. And then 'delivery men' had come to the house to take her hardware and debrief her. Her physical condition, with scars and bruises still evident, had been a source of much discussion, and that in itself, the detail they required, had been traumatic, but they'd gone away satisfied that their secrets were safe.

She was truly a civilian, for the first time since high school. She was still Lilli Carson, since that was how people knew her here, where she'd put down her stake, but she was just a regular person now.

No—she wasn't Lilli Carson. She was Lilli Lunden now. She was glad for it. She was happy to be Isaac's wife and to be carrying their child, but she was terrified, and nothing felt entirely real. A lot of her attention was spent trying to keep all that turmoil under wraps, trying to show Isaac that things were okay. That *she* was okay. She was hoping that would eventually be true.

He was being incredibly patient with her—overprotective, yes, but she didn't mind that so much at the moment. He hadn't pushed her at all about the physical stuff. Tasha had told her to wait at least a month, better six weeks, before they tried anything, but it had been just more than a month now, and Lilli was nowhere near ready. It had taken her weeks to get comfortable being touched in any kind of intimate way—a passionate kiss, or, hell, even Isaac's hand on her back, any touch that had once been sensual between them, had made her stiffen and remember. She'd had to work hard to get to a point where she could just feel *Isaac.* It wasn't that she didn't want him. She wanted him desperately. But she hadn't yet figured out a way to close off the memories from that day in Ellis's cell, and any intimate touch set them careening through her head.

Goddammit; she was stronger than that. She'd shoved bad memories aside her whole fucking life. She'd always believed—*known*—that life could go to shit in a heartbeat, no matter how hard anyone tried to be snug and safe, and that the only thing to do was not to get caught up in the shit. Do one's best. Be true to one's truth. Love as fully as one can. Understand that anything else is chaos and try to navigate around it. That meant setting aside the bad shit and not letting it take over. But this time, she couldn't find the strength or focus to clear it away.

Maybe part of it was that she still felt wrong, inside. It wasn't pain, exactly. The pain had been bad, but she knew she was healing well. But she felt different. It was as though Ponytail and his sidekicks had left something behind, or had somehow made her different inside. She hadn't been able to make it any clearer to herself, and she certainly had not said anything to anyone else. She was sure it was all in her head, but that actually made it worse. It meant she really was crazy.

Like her nagging conviction that she was no longer pregnant. She knew she was. She'd had several more tests, including an ultrasound. She was sick in the mornings. Her breasts hurt. She had all the symptoms. And still she felt wrong—another thing she hadn't told Isaac. He was already fully involved in making ready for a baby, opening up the room upstairs that had been his sister's, clearing it out, preparing to remodel it, and ordering wood to build nursery furniture. He'd put all of his anger and grief over what Ellis had done to them and the town into his hope for their family. She tried to take energy from him and quiet her irrational fears. But when she put her hand on her utterly flat, firm belly, she felt empty.

Focusing on the party gave her something else to think about, and then she felt mostly normal. She'd felt good while they were away, picking up the 'Cuda and getting married. She'd had fun and had been able to relax a little, like she'd left her worries and fears at the Signal Bend border. She and Isaac had been focused on each other, and the days had passed swiftly. It was in Reno that she'd finally been able to seek out his touch, to be comfortable skin to skin with him, and even sleep with him behind her, without having to psych herself up like a fucking drill sergeant. But the trip had been a short one, and they'd come back to their life, where the worries and fears awaited her.

Now, she was standing in the middle of the Hall, managing Dom and the new Prospect, Omen (his given name was Damien, and Lilli had been in the clubhouse when Bart and Havoc, thinking themselves quite brilliant, had laid the name on him), while they put up the massive real Christmas tree. It was Christmas Eve, the party was later that evening, and the decorations, including the tree, were

286

supposed to have gone up while she and Isaac were away, but they'd gotten home the day before to learn that Len had not been able not bring himself to deal with the decorations, not even enough to convey to one of the club girls, or a town woman, what Lilli wanted. He'd managed food and everything else, but the thought of evergreen garlands, red velvet bows, and colored lights had apparently been more than his macho, inked heart could take.

She'd seen the trailer he called home. She understood. His barn, where he bred and raised his horses, was a thing of gleaming, efficient beauty, but his house was a trash bin with a roof. Decorating was far beyond his abilities. So she'd given him a punch in the ribs and taken back over. The Hall was going to look fucking festive if she had to string Len's intestines around the room and hang mistletoe from his severed fingers.

Which she'd said to him. In so many words. He'd grinned, kissed her cheek, and made himself scarce, muttering something about hormones.

And she'd felt a pang of loss. Which was crazy. *She was pregnant.* Why couldn't she believe it?

When the tree was up, she and a couple of club girls put up the decorations, while Dom and Omen moved on to stringing the lights and garland. C.J. and Havoc sat at the bar pelting them with peanuts, while Badger—still on restricted activity but recovering well from a bullet to the back—stacked clean barware under the bar. She'd tried to get the peanut-throwing to stop, but they'd ignored her. So she'd have somebody sweep once they got their middle school mania out of their system.

287

She stepped back to take a look at the tree as Candy, one of the perkier girls, stood on tiptoes at the top of the ladder to put the glittery, flaming horse, which somebody had made for the Horde at some point, on the top of the tree. Candy, at the top of the ladder in her teeny little skirt, had all the guys' attention.

All but one.

"Me, Sport." Lilli felt Isaac's hands come around her waist and rest on her belly. He'd taken to announcing himself when he came up on her from behind, because she leapt out of her damn skin if she wasn't expecting to be touched. She could relax into his body now, but not unawares. Maybe never again unawares. But knowing he was there, she was fine, and she leaned back against him as he nuzzled her neck. "You two doing okay?"

Her and the baby, he meant. God, he was so sweet and attentive, so much in love with the idea of this baby. So much in love with her. She wanted so much for it to be real, for it to be right. The thought that something was wrong scared her more than maybe anything ever had.

No. Stop. Jesus, what was wrong with her head? Why couldn't she just relax and be happy? With a breath for strength, she smiled and tipped her head to his. "We're good. About done here, I think. I want to lie down for a while before tonight. If you think I can leave the cavemen unattended for an hour or two without them destroying all this hard work."

Isaac turned her in his arms. "They'll behave. Want some company?" He kissed her, and she hooked her arms around his back.

"Sure." It was good to be able to enjoy being close to him again, even if that was all they had. She hoped she'd be able to do more before he was no longer able to be patient with her.

He grinned and took her hand. On their way past the bar, Isaac dropped a heavy hand on Havoc's shoulder. "Don't fuck up the party shit, boys, or you're getting ass-kickings for Christmas. We'll be in my office. Emergencies only."

~oOo~

Lilli didn't dream when she napped, so she woke after almost two hours feeling rested, her head on Isaac's chest. There was something strangely cozy about napping on the sofa bed in his office, hearing the vague sounds of the clubhouse around them.

"You awake?" Isaac's deep voice rumbled in his chest.

She stretched. "Yeah. That was nice."

He chuckled. "Yeah, it was." Her left hand was on his belly, and he picked it up, playing with the rings he'd given her. In the few days they'd been married, he'd already taken up the habit of playing with her rings.

They'd gotten lucky with their rings. Neither of them had had heirloom rings to give each other—their parents' marriages had been tragic in one way or another—and they'd not had a lot of time to think about rings before they'd arrived in Reno. But Nevada was a state that catered to the unprepared bride and groom, especially in the larger cities, so there were four jewelry stores within a block of their hotel—including one inside the hotel. They'd separated, and within two hours of arriving in Reno and realizing they needed rings, they had made perfect choices for each other.

Even though they'd never been officially "engaged," it had been important to Isaac that she have two rings, and that they make a statement—a declaration, even. Lilli had been worried that he'd saddle her with some kind of blingy atrocity, but he'd picked a perfect set. He'd chosen for her a large but simple amethyst solitaire in a platinum setting, square cut and bounded by small, pavé diamonds. The bands of the solitaire and of the matching wedding band were also set by pavé diamonds. Amethyst was her birthstone, and she loved the nontraditional choice. She liked to see the rings on her finger, and so did he.

Lilli had gone to all four shops before she found the right ring for him: a wide, heavy band of hammered platinum. His hands were huge, so she'd had to ask them to set it aside so she could bring him in and make sure they had one sized well. Miraculously, they did. It looked perfect on his finger. His wedding ring had displaced a heavy silver ring with a runic "H," like a signet. He'd moved that to his right ring finger and no longer wore the horse head ring he'd worn there. That horse head could put some hurt down in a fight, so Lilli had been surprised to see him choose the signet over it. He'd told her he was hoping to live a life in which being able to take a guy's eye out with a punch wasn't something he really had to plan for anymore.

That would be nice. A quiet life. Lilli thought she'd like to try that.

Isaac lifted her hand to his lips. "You ready to get your party on, Sport?"

Curling her fingers around his, she pulled his hand to her lips, too. "Yep. Let's make merry."

~oOo~

The party didn't exactly go off without a hitch, but it was a success nevertheless. Badger's friend, Billy, was in a country band that was just getting started, and the Signal Bend Christmas party was their first paying gig. There had been a lot of hitches getting them finally playing, but they weren't so bad, once they started. Lilli hated country music, but the crowd got to dancing almost right away.

The food turned out well. The club girls wandered around as servers, something they were used to, and C.J. played a particularly rough-looking Santa, handing out gifts to the kids. People were laughing and dancing, and having a good time. Lilli felt proud.

About ten o'clock or so, when the families had almost all left, and Billy and the Kids (Lilli had rolled her eyes when she'd heard that name) were packing up, the mood changed, and the holiday party began to take on the features of a regular drunken orgy at the clubhouse. Lilli headed to the kitchen to check on the cleanup and stay out of the way.

Isaac found her there and took her hand. "Leave the girls to do all this, Sport. They're not going anywhere anytime soon." He winked at Gwen, who was turning on the dishwasher. "But you are. Time to go home. I want to be alone with my wife."

"Isaac." She hesitated, pulling back a bit on her hand, hoping he didn't mean he wanted sex for Christmas.

He met her eyes when he felt her pull and smiled a little, shaking his head, reassuring her. "It's okay."

Hating that she needed that reassurance, hating herself for not being able to put her shit behind her, she smiled and said, "Okay. Gotta get my bag, then let's go."

~oOo~

The dreams were so much worse now. The first couple of days, when she'd been taking the painkillers, she'd been able to sleep without dreaming, but she'd gotten off the Percocet as fast as she could, because of the baby, trying to make the right choices despite her head's crazy ideas about the pregnancy. Before, the dreams had been bad, and had driven her to tense wakefulness, but, even after Hobson, she'd been able to push them away almost instantly and go back to sleep.

Now, she almost never woke up alarmed, because she wasn't able to wake up in the middle of the dreams. They played themselves out to their bitter, brutal ends, and she would come awake slowly, beset by phantom pain and a cloying sense of death and doom. Unable to shake it or face sleeping again, she'd get up and sit in the dark living room, or, sometimes, walk out to see the horses. Isaac let her go, or he didn't wake, and she was glad. The heavy blackness she was feeling was not something she could share.

In the early hours of Christmas morning, Lilli came awake, the brittle pain and fear of the nightmare still acute in her body. Isaac's heavy leg was hooked over hers, and she lay still for a moment, trying to find that strength she'd once had to shove the dreams away. It was Christmas. Isaac hated to be alone in bed. She should stay.

She couldn't. She eased her leg from under his and got up. Pip, who'd been sleeping on a bottom corner of the bed, stretched and went to curl in the middle of her pillow. Wearing one of his t-shirts over a pair of boy-cut underwear, she left the room. She thought she'd go into the living room and just sit, but when she got there, she turned and went upstairs instead. She put her hand on the knob of the door into her office, but, again, she turned, and instead went into the room across the hall, the room Isaac was turning into a nursery.

The room had been locked up and neglected since his sister, Martha, had left home at sixteen, when Isaac was twelve. He'd be forty in March, so "stale and dusty" hadn't begun to describe what they'd found in here. Isaac had stripped decomposing wallpaper from the walls and hauled an old, narrow wrought-iron bed out to the shed. He'd stripped the paint from the floors and had pulled the built-in shelves, weak from dry rot, down from the walls. Currently, the room was in the clutches of chaos—stacks of decaying boards from the shelves Isaac had pulled down right before they'd left for their trip, used buckets of paper stripper, a ladder, piles of rags—all the disarray that came from renovation. Stacked against one wall were the supplies for the improvements—wood for new shelves and a window seat, stain for the newly bare floors, paint for the stripped walls.

It was wrong. All wrong. It was…a bad omen, or bad luck, or just plain bad news. Bad. There was no baby. She'd lost the baby in that fucking cold room, when those bastards had—that thought would not fit into words, what they'd done. But she hadn't fought, not enough. She'd let them do it, and they'd taken everything. She'd thought she was being smart, not fighting, trying to live. But she hadn't been smart. She'd been weak. She'd let them.

She'd given up. There was no baby, not anymore. Her hand on her damnably flat belly, she felt sure it was true. She was supposed to be more than eight weeks now, almost ten, mostly through the first trimester—shouldn't something be different, if there was still somebody in there?

With a jolt, Lilli was overcome by a violent compulsion. No fixing this room up. It was wrong. It made a mockery of everything to make a room for a baby that was just a hope. She started gathering up the new boards, thinking she'd carry them outside to the fire pit and burn them away. She bobbled and dropped a board, giving herself a fucker of a splinter in the process, but she ignored that and picked up the errant piece of wood.

As she stepped out into the hallway, Isaac came up the stairs, taking them two and three at a time, his Beretta in his hand. He pulled up short at the landing, face to face with Lilli and her burden.

Decocking his handgun and tucking it into the back of his jeans—all he was wearing—he said, "Jesus fuck, Sport. What the hell are you doing?" Lilli could hear relief, concern, and more than a hint of irritation in his voice.

She found herself unable to put on her sanity face. He'd caught her naked in her turmoil, and she blurted out, "This room is wrong. I'm not pregnant. This room is wrong." The words confused even her as she heard them leave her lips.

"*What?*" He leapt at her, ripping the load of boards from her arms, throwing them to the floor with a crash, and yanking her t-shirt up to her waist. Confusion wrinkled his brow as he took in her unharmed, unbloody, unswollen state. "Baby, are you hurt? Come on—I'll get you to the hospital. It's okay."

"No!" She pulled back hard, feeling frantic, and overbalanced, landing on her ass in the middle of the dim hallway. And then she was crying. Fuck, she was sobbing. She was so tired. She couldn't find the strength to hide all this from him.

He dropped to his knees and tried to pull her close, but she fought him off and wrapped her arms around her legs, turning her body into a protective ball.

"Baby, I don't understand. Why do you think you're not pregnant? If you're hurting, let me take you to the hospital. God, baby, please."

"No! It's too late. I lost it...*then*. I let them take it. I let them." She dropped her head to her knees and just bawled. She had no control over her head at all.

"Lilli, what—what do you"—he paused, and then she felt his body against hers as he sat down at her side, his arms coming around the shell she'd made of herself. "Oh, baby. No. We *know* that's not true. We saw that little blurry blob thing, remember? It was little, but they said it for sure was a baby. Fuck. Lilli, no. Those sons of bitches didn't take anything from you, from us. Our kid's as strong as its mom. And you beat them. Baby, you *beat* them."

Still sobbing, she could only shake her head. Isaac moved in front of her and grabbed her head in his hands to stop her. He made her face him. "Yes, you did. You won. We won. And you fought to keep you and the squirt alive. You won, baby."

"It can't be true. I'm empty. I feel empty. Isaac, what they—they…" She swallowed, and her throat clicked dryly. She hadn't even been able to think the whole thought of the thing she was about to say. She didn't know why she was saying it now, but the words were coming. "The *gun*, Isaac. The fucking *gun*. It can't be true after that."

His brows drew together in a violent grimace, and when he spoke, she heard a catch of tears in his voice. "I know, baby. I'm so sorry. I'm so sorry." His hands still cradling her head, he dropped his own head to her knees. "So fucking sorry."

He knew? She hadn't been able to talk about any of it. She couldn't believe she was talking about any of it now. How did he—?

Bart. That damn camera. Oh, sweet Jesus. Did they all know?

Instead of freaking her out even more, that thought—that little bit of problem solving, deducing how it was that Isaac knew specifics about what had happened to her when she hadn't been able to even think those thoughts—called back a sliver of her sense. She took a breath, and calm filled her.

"I can't keep control of all the shit. It's taking over in my head." Her voice was quiet and steady. "I'm losing my mind, Isaac."

He sat back, his hands moving to her legs, wrapping around her calves. "No, baby. You're not. It's just that you keep trying to do it on your own. You need to talk to me. You lock me out, and then you're all alone in there, and I'm all alone out here. We don't need

296

to be alone anymore." He lifted her left hand and kissed her ring. "Please talk to me."

His face was wet with his tears. She loved him more than anything. So she tried.

CHAPTER TWENTY-THREE

"We're getting a real good look today. Do you want to know?" The technician turned from the screen and smiled at them both.

"Yes. Please." Lilli didn't hesitate. Isaac heard the thin thread of anxiety in her voice that he'd become accustomed to over the past few months. He'd been rocked on Christmas morning to discover how scared, how *scarred*, his warrior woman was. He'd known she wasn't all right—he could feel it like a low-voltage current under everything she said and did, especially when she thought he wasn't watching—but he'd had no idea how high the voltage was in her head.

Fuck. He'd thought her dreams had been better, not worse. And he'd had no idea she couldn't believe there was still a baby, or that she thought she was becoming sick like her mother had been. He felt like a goddamn asshole for not picking up on any of that. He'd been so wrapped up in his own guilt for what had happened to her, thinking that her distance was distrust of him, that he'd never considered that she might be tearing herself apart.

But God, it made perfect sense, once she'd finally let him in and told him. They'd sat on the faded runner in the upstairs hall for hours on Christmas morning, and he'd learned that his wife had been drowning in a mental hell. After what she'd been through, what they'd done to her, how *could* she believe that everything was okay? They'd torn her up. She'd confronted death—hers and the baby's—and come to terms with it, sure neither could survive. And the world

298

she'd come back to was materially changed, in large part because she *had* survived—more than that, she had prevailed. No wonder it felt unreal.

Jesus, she sucked at communicating. She was great at fighting, and at intuiting. She was even great at talking. She knew just what to say to help him, and just when he needed it. But her shit, the things that scared her or made her feel weak—no. She shoved it to the side until it spilled over onto everything else. It had taken him too long, but on Christmas morning, he'd come to understand that he'd always need to manage that, be vigilant about drawing her out. If he pushed right, he could get her to talk. Help her, the way she helped him. But this was all new to him, too.

Every little milestone—hearing the baby's heartbeat for the first time, a few days after Christmas; the day her jeans stopped closing; the day she finally felt a flutter of movement inside her—improved her handhold on belief. After hearing the heartbeat, she'd let him go back to working on the room, but she wouldn't come up to see, and she wouldn't give him any input about the decisions he was making. The day she'd felt movement was the first day she'd stepped back over the threshold. Still, though, she hadn't participated.

Tasha had suggested he buy a device that would let her hear the heartbeat at home, whenever she wanted, once she got a little farther along. She listened to that fucker several times a day, her hand on the growing mound of her belly. It had helped, become like a talisman, keeping her grounded. But still she resisted making any plans—at least not for the baby. She'd hurled herself into plans for the town and for her work, but couldn't yet think about their family. That had to change. He was beginning to feel like *he* was the one who had it wrong.

He hoped it would be today. This scan, when they could both see they were looking at an actual child inside her, a child with a strong, steady heart, squirming and sucking its little fingers as they watched—this had to be the proof she needed to believe. His own heart was about to break his ribs. His child. His *child. Please, Sport. There. Right there. We're okay.*

She wanted to know the sex. Good. They hadn't even talked about it, but he did, too. No surprises. She needed to know everything she could know.

The technician raised her eyebrows. "You're sure?"

"Yes!" Maybe that was a little too much like a yell, but Isaac was on edge, and Lilli had already answered the fucking question.

The technician—she'd said her name, but Isaac didn't give a fuck—flinched a little at the sharpness of his tone, but she recovered her smile quickly. "Okay." She moved the scanner on Lilli's round little belly, like half of a basketball. With her other hand, she moved a cursor on the screen. "That's a perfect shot, see? Bottom, legs, umbilical cord. And right here…nothing. We have us a baby girl."

A girl. Holy fuck. A little girl. The technician typed something, and it came up over the image. Isaac didn't know what she'd typed. He was barely seeing anything in front of him. No more 'it.' *She.* His daughter.

"Really? Are you sure?" He turned and focused at the sound of Lilli's voice.

"She obviously wanted you to know. Sometimes babies get shy, and it's hard to tell, but she put her little garden right out there for us to see." What's-her-name laughed. "Better watch out for this one, Daddy."

Isaac thought this bitch could do with a punch in the jaw. She'd just called his little girl a slut. He glared, and maybe growled a little. Again the technician flinched, and this time her smile faded entirely. She hit a couple more keys, and a copy of the image on the screen came out of the machine. She handed it to Lilli, at the same time handing her tissues with which to wipe up. She pushed the machine to the side and left the room.

The words on the picture read, *Baby Girl Lunden.*

Lilli wiped her belly and then sat up. She looked as dazed as Isaac felt.

"Sport? How you doing?"

Her eyes met his, and Isaac searched their beautiful grey depths for an indication of how she felt. His chest felt full with happiness and worry. "Lilli?"

"She was sucking her thumb." A whisper. She'd used the feminine pronouns, though—that had to be a good sign.

Isaac nodded. "I saw."

"My dad's name was Johnny. In Italian, that's G-I-A-N-N-I."

He knew that. Not following her train of thought, but not wanting to get in her way, he nodded again. "Yeah."

"She's Gia. I want to call her Gia. For my dad."

That feeling in his chest—it had to be his heart exploding. "Baby, that's beautiful. Really beautiful. Gia Accardo Lunden? What do you think?"

Lilli—his beautiful wife, his scarred warrior woman—nodded and began to weep. Isaac stood and folded her into his arms, tucking her close to his chest, under his chin. "Baby, baby. It's okay. Right? We're okay?" He felt her nod against his heart.

~oOo~

Approaching the rise to Will Keller's place about a week later, the sun low on an early spring evening, Isaac felt a pang of nostalgia. Time was, cresting this rise meant a spectacular view of the Keller's big, bright white farmhouse and long, burnished red barn; the fields, the woods, the animals grazing sedately; the wide, glittering sweep of the quartz gravel drive. Then Ellis had burnt it all down, and for awhile there was nothing but charred earth where that expanse of natural folk art had stood for more than a century. Every visit during those dark days had chipped away pieces of Isaac's love for this place, this town.

But that had been months ago, and the town had not been idle. As they'd come together to keep the town on its feet during the hard years, and they'd come together to fight off Ellis and his hired thugs, so had they come together to undo the damage he'd done—as much as they could. Bart's idea for the Kickstarter had brought in some serious cash. Main Street, nearly destroyed in that shootout, was rebuilt and nearly ready for its Grand Reopening. It looked better than it had in years—bright paint, gleaming windows, new wooden walkways. They'd freshened up the little grassy block that was their town park. All that was left now were some interior finishes on the shops and stocking new inventory. And then people to buy it.

And there was this: Keller Acres. Lilli's grand plan. Isaac crested the rise and grinned. He pulled up and sat at the top, astride his bike, taking in the new vista. The valley was teeming with people. The fields were being sown. Fences were being rebuilt. And in the middle of it all, where the Keller house had stood proudly, a big, beautiful white clapboard house, not much different from the one that had been lost, but with a wide, wrap-around porch, was being installed on its new foundation.

'Installed,' because it was a modular building, delivered in pre-built chunks. Once Lilli had gotten it in her head what she wanted to do—and it was a great idea—she hadn't wanted to take the time to have a house built on site. So she'd found a modular model and, when she was satisfied that she wasn't erecting some half-assed excuse for a building, she'd put everything in motion. That had only been a few weeks ago. Now, workers were about done with the installation.

Lilli had built the Keller Acres Bed and Breakfast. Her idea was to use the public interest in Signal Bend to make it a destination. As remote as it was from the highway, she thought people would be more likely to come if they had a place to stay and make a weekend of it. The Keller place, so picturesque, was the perfect location.

She'd offered the farmland to the Brown brothers and Steve Bohler—all of whom had starting cooking after losing their own family farms. Now, with the meth business closed, they were going back to their roots, splitting the acreage here. Lilli was asking only for a small percentage of their profits from their yield in return.

303

She'd sat down with Show and run some figures, estimating enough of a percentage to break even.

The next phase of the plan was a horse barn, where Will's barn had stood. She wanted to fill it with rescue horses, for guests to ride. There were good riding trails in the adjacent woods. She was making arrangements with a rescue organization for the horses, but the barn had to happen first, and she'd been thwarted on that score, unhappy with any of the modular versions she'd found. She had a clear idea what the barn should look like.

Isaac knew a solution, but he hadn't told her yet. He had it in his head that he would surprise her. He'd better get to it, though, before she figured out her own solution. She didn't know shit about running a hotel or taking care of horses, or building barns, or any of the things she'd undertaken, but she'd researched endlessly, reading online, and hounding Show and Vic, and Don Keyes, who owned the farm implement shop. She was fucking brilliant, and Isaac figured by the time the place opened in the summer, she'd be a pro.

He could see her standing down there on the lawn, talking to a guy in a hardhat. When she turned and walked away, the guy crossed his arms over his chest and cocked his head. Isaac knew that stance. Bastard was checking out his woman's ass. Lilli's ass was so perfect it was like…poetry. Since her belly had started to grow, she'd also put on a hint of extra curve in her hips, improving on perfection. It was a sight to bring a man to his knees. But only *he* got to get a look like that. He stopped his woolgathering and got his bike moving, roaring down the drive. He was gratified to see that hardhat bastard jump at the roar of Isaac's engine and turn back to work.

That night, after supper and chores, the usual activities of a quiet country night, Isaac and Lilli sat in the living room, on the same, ancient couch, and watched *To Have and Have Not*, Lilli's favorite movie. When he'd sat, he'd pulled her onto his lap, and she'd settled in, her legs stretched across the cushions and her head tucked against his neck. He had his arms around her, a hand tucked into her yoga pants and resting on her belly. Sometimes, when she asked, he thought he could feel something, but he hadn't felt anything strong enough to be sure. Maybe wishful thinking. But he loved the sweet swell of her belly anyway.

Sometimes it was hard to be this close to her. No—it was always hard to be this close to her. As long as he'd known her, her very proximity had been an aphrodisiac. Her smell, her sound, everything about her got to him deep. At a cellular level. They hadn't had sex since the morning she'd been taken—months ago. She was carrying his child and more sexy to him in that state than ever before. But she wasn't ready, and he'd sooner cut his dick off than push her. He had only so much mastery over his body, though. Tonight, watching Bacall tell Bogey how to whistle, with Lilli so warm and calm in his lap, her hair loose over his arm, her fingers twirling absently in his hair where it lay against his neck, her gorgeous ass resting on his crotch, Isaac thought he'd lose his mind. He fought off the erection as long as he could, knowing she'd get up as soon as she felt him. He thought of anything and everything but her and his need. He tried, at least. But she surrounded him. He felt immersed in her. Immersed in her.

And that thought did him in. His cock shot painfully to fullness, and he eased his hold on her, taking his hand out of her pants so she could get up as quickly as she needed to.

But she didn't get up. He knew when she felt him, because she stiffened and shifted, and he expected her to slide off his lap to sit next to him. Instead, though, she tipped her head on his shoulder and pressed her lips to his neck, her hand spreading out over his jaw. He groaned.

"Lilli, baby—I'm having a little trouble right now. I need a minute."

She didn't answer or move. Then he felt her tongue on his neck. He jerked back and took her face in his hands.

"Not cool, Sport."

Her eyes were wide and serious, regarding him steadily. "Isaac. I want…to try."

That quickly, his pulse was thundering in his ears. But she had to be sure. He had to be sure she was sure. He didn't know how he'd cope if they lost ground because they'd gone this way before she was ready. "You sure? Don't do it for me. I'm okay."

She smiled. God, he loved her. "I'm not. I miss you."

"Fuck, baby, I miss you so much." The words came out in a rush, and he wanted them back as soon as they were gone, but he hadn't freaked her out. Her smile grew, and she scooted off his lap to stand in front of him, holding out her hand. The rings he'd given her sparkled in the light of the television.

"Slow, though. Okay? Sweet?"

He took her hand and brought it to his lips. "So slow. So sweet. Only what you want. Only as much as you want. Talk to me, though, okay? Don't try to deal."

"Okay. Come on." She pulled on his hand, and he stood, letting her lead him into their bedroom.

When they got to the bedroom, he pulled her back and took her into his arms. At first, he held her, finding some calm and focus in the quiet touch. His heart was fucking hammering against his ribs. It was excitement, yes—definitely—but it was anxiety, too. The thought that this could traumatize her, or even actually hurt her, weighed heavily. But there was also the thought that they could have back that part of them—or have something similar but new.

Their couplings had often been intense, even adversarial, in the past. It had been what they'd both preferred, Lilli most of all. What would happen tonight wouldn't be anything like that. In fact, Isaac couldn't imagine ever being rough with her again, even if she wanted him to. He couldn't imagine her wanting it, either. Not after everything.

Tonight, to every extent that she'd let him, he would love her. Worship her. Make her feel safe and loved and desired. Make her remember what had been good. Make her really want it. Give her the pleasure she'd lost. His throat thickened at the thought, and he set her back a little so he could look down into her eyes. She smiled up at him, but he could see her nervousness. Leaning down to brush his lips over her mouth, letting his beard graze back and forth over the silk of her lips, he whispered, "You tell me what you need. You tell me, Lilli. Promise."

She nodded, coming up on her tiptoes and looping her arms around his neck, but he pulled back and shook his head. He needed to hear the words.

"Promise. Say it."

"I promise. I'll tell you. I need you to take me to bed."

Grinning, he swept her up into his arms and carried her across the room. He laid her down in the middle of their bed and stretched out next to her, propped on his elbow. For so many months, even kisses had been rare—lately, he thought, more because she didn't want to get him stirred up than because she didn't enjoy the kissing itself. He wanted to make up for some lost time, and he wanted to take this very, very slowly. So, his hand on her rounded belly, over her pants, he bent down and kissed her, sucking on her full lower lip, brushing his beard over her chin and cheeks, until she moaned and pushed her tongue into his mouth.

Then he moved his hand to her face—Christ, he was shaking—and held her close, kissing her more deeply, letting his tongue explore her mouth, remember it. Her arms came up on his back, hooking over his shoulders. She felt so good in his arms, being in this moment with him.

They kissed like that for long minutes. Isaac felt almost afraid to do more—already they were closer than they'd been in all the time since that day. When Lilli's hand left him and pushed between them, he had a moment of perfect despair, thinking that she was done, they'd gone too far. But she reached for the hem of her t-shirt and pulled it up over her head, tossing it to the floor next to the bed. Her bra followed it. Then she went for the buttons on his shirt.

He'd seen her body during these months. She'd only been shy about that the first couple of weeks, and then she'd dressed and undressed in front of him as before. Since Reno, they often slept nude together. At first, after the shyness had passed, she still been reluctant, not wanting to be unfair to him, but he'd told her—and it was true—that he'd rather be able to see and touch her than not, even if it was all they could do. He'd needed that closeness so he could feel that she was with him.

So he'd seen her body, touched it, but now—this was worlds away from that. When his buttons were open, and she pushed his shirt off his shoulders, he tossed it to the floor on the other side, and then he wrapped his arms around her and pulled her tightly to him. He needed to feel her bare chest against his, her breasts—growing recently, her nipples darkening—on his skin. He felt her nipples harden, and he groaned. Laying her back down, he put his hand on her shoulder, his eyes intent on hers, and stroked a long, gentle path down her arm and back up, then over her shoulder to the ridge of her collarbone, then down. He paused with the heel of his hand resting at the point where her breast began to swell.

"Tell me, baby."

She took a breath and let it out. Isaac heard the shake in it, but she nodded. "Yes. Please."

He moved his hand down, over her taut nipple, to cup her breast in his palm. He brushed his thumb over her nipple, just lightly, and rejoiced inside when she arched up a little, and her eyes fluttered closed.

Still teasing gently at her nipple, he leaned in and pressed his mouth to her neck, sucking at the pulse point there. Her pulse skittered against his tongue, but her hands clung to him, and he kept going, drawing his tongue down the same path over her chest that his hand had taken. When he got to her breast, he stopped and looked up. Her eyes were closed. She looked a little tense.

"Lilli? Tell me."

She opened her eyes and smiled a tiny smile, one corner lifting. "Yes."

He bent to her breast, brushing the sensitive skin with his beard, his lips, his tongue before drawing her nipple into his mouth. His own pulse was fast and erratic, pounding behind his eyes. To have her again! She gasped then and hummed the air out, her hands coming to weave into his hair and hold his head. He could feel her relaxing, her body moving in a way he found familiar, a way that meant arousal. Continuing his ministrations at her breast, he moved his hand to her side, drawing slowly down to her hip, into her pants, over her delectable ass, down to the outside of her thigh. Her legs were relaxed and slightly spread, but as he moved his hand over the top of her thigh and slid upward, he felt the tension coming on her. He could feel himself tensing, too. He released her breast and looked up. Her eyes were closed again.

"Tell me."

This time, she swallowed and didn't open her eyes. She nodded.

"Lilli. Look at me. Tell me. Don't deal. Tell me."

She opened her eyes. There was a challenge in them that made him wary, but she said, "Yes."

"Be fair, baby. Don't bottle it up. No good for you or me. Right?"

"Right. I want you to keep going." Her voice was steady.

Nodding, he sat up and grabbed the waistband of her pants, pulling them off her hips and down her legs, casting them aside. Then, still in his jeans, he stretched out again and bent back down to suck harder at her breast, flicking his tongue over the bud of her nipple, drawing her attention there. He moved his hand upward on her thigh—slowly, giving her time to stop him at any point. She didn't.

Not until he reached her hot, soft, utterly dry folds. And she virtually leapt from his arms, scooting high up on the bed and curling into her protective ball, as tight as her belly would let her, crying, "No! No! Nononononono!"

Fuck. Oh, fuck.

He sat up, feeling his very soul fill with cement. "It's okay, Lilli. I'm not—I won't—it's okay. We're done. I'm not gonna hurt you. We don't need this." He didn't know if any of those words were helpful. He didn't know what to say or do. He only knew he'd shrivel up if she pulled back into herself, away from him, again. He thought of Show and Holly, and how their marriage had dwindled to a dry husk after they'd lost their physical connection. No matter what, no matter if Lilli could never enjoy sex again, Isaac wanted her with him, really with him. He couldn't let her shrink away from him.

She wasn't crying. She was simply coiled up in that cocoon, her head on her knees. He didn't know if he should leave her alone, or bring her closer, or just sit there and wait. Since sitting there and waiting was the default, that was what he did. When he couldn't stand the silence any longer, he murmured, "I love you, Lilli. Lilli *Lunden*. This doesn't matter. We don't need it. I could live the rest of my life without this. I only need you. You and Gia." It was the first time he'd used their daughter's name like that, as if he were referring to a person in the world.

She looked up. "No. *I* need it. I can't stay crazy, Isaac. I need to break their hold on me. It's making me weak. Like that day is shackled around my neck. It chafes at everything and holds me back. Those men live in my head. They torment me. Every fucking day and night. We have to keep going. We're having sex tonight. I don't care if it hurts. I don't care if it terrifies me. I don't care if it makes me puke or scream or cry. This is over. Now. I want my head back. I want my body back. I will not let the crazy have me."

Isaac felt sick. "Lilli. Do you hear what you're asking me to do? I...can't. I can't cause you pain. I can't. Jesus, baby. I won't *be able* to do what you want me to do." That was true—his cock had thoroughly deflated as she'd spoken.

There was a hard gleam in her eyes. He knew the look and what it meant about where her head was. She called it "battle mode." His idea of making slow, sweet, healing love to his old lady was shot all to hell.

"Use your mouth then. Eat me out. Or your hand. I don't care. No—I do care. I want your cock. Those fucking deviant pieces of shit—they don't get to be the last dicks inside me. No motherfucking way." Her voice had taken on the sharp edge of command, and he knew she was either getting her way or they were fighting. There was no other possible outcome when she got like this.

But he couldn't give her what she was demanding. He could not hurt her, or traumatize her. He couldn't. He would do anything for her. Anything but knowingly cause her pain. "No."

She lashed out so fast, he was holding his jaw almost before he knew she'd punched him. It fucking hurt, but he knew what she was about, and, flexing his jaw a little, he said only, "Ow. No, baby."

She punched him again. He saw this one coming and moved with it, taking the edge off, but she'd hit the same damn spot. "Ow."

She hit him again. He wondered how long his patience would hold up—hell, he wondered how long his jaw would hold up. But he wasn't going to fight back. He'd leave before he came at her, even if that was what she wanted. Their first time back together was not going to be any kind of a battle.

"You're gonna hurt your hand, Sport. Because I'm not fighting you. No."

Like a fucking hellcat, she launched at him then, driving him down to the mattress and lying on top of him, biting and scratching and hitting. Worried more about the baby squished between them than himself, he finally reacted, grabbing her wrists and rolling over with her. He sat astride her legs, holding her arms above her head with one hand.

She was struggling mightily against his hold, and he used his free hand to push down on her chest, between her breasts. "Enough, Lilli. There's got to be another way. I want to help you. But I won't hurt you. I won't do it."

"Fuck, Isaac! Please! I need *you*. I need to feel *you*. Remember *you*. Get them out of my head! I'm asking you to fucking save me!"

She was breaking his heart. "Don't ask me to hurt you. I don't want that to be your memory of us. I can wait, baby. We can talk—"

313

He cut off, forgetting entirely whatever it was he'd planned to say. As he'd spoken, he'd been stroking her with his free hand, trying to calm her. His hand was now frozen on her belly, as, against his palm, he felt a series of little taps, almost rhythmic but not quite, like somebody was knocking on the other side of her belly. "Jesus, is that—do you—?"

"Yeah. You feel that?" Lilli, too, was suddenly calm, derailed by this moment.

"Yeah!" Grinning, he pressed down a little harder on her belly, and the taps stopped—and then there was another, stronger than the others, as if his little girl had just turned away in a huff. He laughed. "I don't think she wants Mom and Pop to fight."

"Pop? That's what you're going with?"

Shifting to lie at her side, his head on her chest, just above her belly, he said, "Sure. Why not?"

"I bet you a hundred bucks she calls you Daddy."

He looked up at her to see her grinning. That moment with their girl had cleared all the shit they'd just been in the middle of away, like it was nothing. "What makes you so sure?"

"I don't know. I like the thought of it. Seems right. Daddy's girl."

He kissed her belly, lingering at the place he'd felt their little girl. Gia. Who would call him Daddy, or Pop, or anything she wanted. Who would not pass a single second of her life without knowing love.

314

Lilli moaned quietly and flexed her hips. "Isaac. Please. Use your mouth. Make me wet. Let me remember. I want you back. I want me back. Please."

He shifted between her legs and slid his arms under her thighs. From that position, ready to give her what she wanted even if it burnt his soul to ashes to do it, he looked up over the length of her torso, the rise of her belly. Her eyes were closed. "Lilli. Look at me. Don't close your eyes. You want me back? You want to remember me? Then see me. Watch. Do not close your eyes. You hear me? Stay with me. Watch."

She nodded. "Yeah, okay."

Awash in trepidation, his cock sound asleep, he leaned in and kissed the inside of her thigh, brushing his beard along the smooth, taut skin. She smelled so amazing to him. Even dry, just the natural state of her scent was an elixir. But she was tense. As he kissed a line to her center, he paused at the joint of her hip and looked up. He met her eyes. He smiled a little—reassuringly, he hoped—and nuzzled into her folds. Smooth and dry, and her body went rigid. He looked up again. Still staring intently between her legs, she nodded.

"Lilli—"

"Do it. *Please.*"

He leaned in again, this time drawing his tongue through her folds. In his hands, her ass clenched hard. But her smell and taste filled his head, more muted now, without her wet, but still so fucking perfect. He'd missed her so much, needed her so much. He hadn't let himself feel the full extent of what *he* had lost, because he didn't fucking matter in this equation, but now, with his face pressed against her hot, beautiful pussy, he felt everything he'd missed. His throat was tight with the loss, and he pressed closer to her, sucking her clit into his mouth, needing her taste and touch for himself. He licked and sucked like a starving man, his cock now tempered steel in his jeans, his pulse throbbing through it.

She was tense for a long time, only his own saliva making her wet at all. He didn't know if this was helping her. He wasn't even sure anymore if it was helping him. He shifted, bringing her closer and hooking his arms around her hips so he could lay his hands on her belly. He spread his fingers wide, covering her swell completely, not wanting to miss it if Gia moved again.

When he did that, encompassed her belly in his hands, she gasped and went wet. The taste filled his mouth. Shocked, he pulled back and looked at her face, where he found her eyes still watching him.

"Baby? Okay?"

She laughed. "Yeah—yeah. It's good. Make me come. Oh, shit, Isaac. I think I can come."

Wasting not a millisecond, he dove back in and sucked her into his mouth. When she arched and moaned, pressing harder to him, he brought one hand around and gently, carefully, slid a finger inside her. She froze at that but didn't stop him. He slid another finger in, moving slowly, only caressing, until her hips began to move in a rhythm he'd come to know very well. Her fingers came to his head and tangled in his hair, holding him close, and he sucked and pumped until she arched off the bed, moaning.

Panting and tense, Isaac stayed still, his mouth on her, his fingers inside her, on a knife's edge of his own climax, until she relaxed onto the bed again. Her body began to shake hard—she was sobbing. Motherfuck. He pulled away as fast as he could, coming up on the bed to lie at her side and take her into his arms. "Did that hurt? I'm sorry."

"No," she gasped. "No. Relief. These are relief. That was good. Good." Taking a breath and sighing it out, she stopped crying. "Now I want your cock. Be inside. Come inside. You. I need you."

Drowning in his own need and encouraged by her orgasm, he didn't need more invitation than that. He stood and stripped off his jeans, then returned to lean over her. "This is gonna be fast, Sport. I'm so fucking close right now it's embarrassing." He rolled so she could straddle him. No way he was going to be on top, pancaking their kid, and no way was he coming from behind. Maybe never again.

She straddled him, and he could feel that, still, she was nervous about this. He could feel her anxiety in the banded muscles of her inner thighs. But she slid down onto his rod, so hot and silky wet, the way she should be, the way that was right. She slid slowly down until she was settled on his hips.

And then she came right back up, fast. That had almost been enough for him; he'd almost blown his wad. This was ridiculous. But she'd come up with a pained, "Ooh," and now he grabbed her hips. "What's wrong, Sport?"

"Too deep. Too much. That hurts. I don't—maybe they did something? Changed something?" If they did, if those sons of bitches had made it so he was too big for her, he'd find some fucking relations of theirs to kill. To be so close and not—GODDAMMIT!

No. Wait. Think.

317

He did. As she was getting off him, looking stressed, he held on. "Wait, baby. I have an idea. Unless you want to stop."

"No. I don't want to stop. But that's gonna hurt too much."

He sat up, wrapping his arms around her waist. "Then I won't go so deep. Here. How about this?" Holding her close, her knees still on either side of his hips, he swung his legs over to the side of the bed. Sitting up like that, his feet on the floor, he lifted her thighs a little. "Wrap your legs behind me." She did.

He reached between them and grabbed his cock, which was absurdly hard and weeping with need. "Hop on, Sport." She eased back onto his cock, settling in with her legs around his hips and her arms around his neck. He leaned forward a little, which had the effect of holding her a couple of inches off his base. "That okay?"

It was fucking *great* for him. And she nodded, wearing a smug little smile that he adored. "Good. That's so good. Let's sit tight for a minute, okay? I need to get hold of myself."

In response, she began to rock. Jesus. Her breasts moving on his chest. Her belly—Jesus. He didn't have this kind of control. "Baby, I can't"—he could barely get the words out.

"I don't want you to try. Let go. I want to make you come. I feel you here. Inside me. You. And it's good. I want you to come."

Already in the throes of it, he nodded and let himself go. With his head tucked tightly on her shoulder, he came so hard he saw stars.

They'd had sex. He was inside her now, her naked body wrapped around his. They were together again. That had been the best sex of his whole goddamn life.

When he could, he lifted his head from her shoulder and brushed her hair away from her face. "You okay, baby?"

She smiled. "Yeah. I think I am."

"We okay?"

Before she could answer, the baby kicked again, hitting Isaac in his belly. They both jumped and laughed, and Lilli said, "I think we will be."

CHAPTER TWENTY-FOUR

Lilli leaned back in her chair and glared at her laptop. Her calendar was open on the screen, showing her appointments for the day. What a load of crap. When she'd had the brilliant idea to turn the Keller place into a B&B, she'd been driven by a series of compulsions—to honor Isaac's friend and make his death meaningful, to help the town, and to help herself get clear of the hurricane in her head. She'd come at the project like a woman possessed.

Now, the house was built, the fields were sown, the fences were up. All that remained of the build was the barn, but Isaac was handling that, and she was trying to let him. He knew what she wanted. She had six horses, five goats, and a burro coming from the rescue ranch, once the barn was finished. Four of the horses were broken—or, no, it was 'broke.' They were 'broke' to ride. Either way, it was an awful term, but it meant that they could be saddled so guests could take trail rides through the woods. Badger, now officially her livestock manager, was going to get the other two horses under saddle (that term she liked a lot better) once they were on site.

One of the horses was trained to pull a cart, and Lilli had this tiny idea that someday she might have a cart and a sleigh for Edgar to pull. She envisioned hayrides in the fall and sleigh rides in the winter, complete with bells. She apparently had been assimilated completely into the country lifestyle, but she wanted the Currier and Ives version, not the David Lynch they'd been living.

All that was great, and she'd enjoyed planning and learning and organizing all of it. But she was absolutely buried under bureaucratic bullshit and paperwork. The hotel permits and insurance forms were the worst, by far. At seven months pregnant, Lilli was about out of patience dealing with incompetent, officious asshats. Show had been telling her she needed to hire a manager with experience, but her mission here was to help Signal Bend, not hire people from outside, and no one in town had the kind of experience she needed.

He'd kept pushing, and she eventually understood that she'd found her own limit. She couldn't teach herself to be a hotel manager in a few months. She had too much going on—more than that, she fucking hated it, and she was not exactly doing a great job at getting bureaucrats on her side. Usually, she was good at finding an in with people, getting them to do what she wanted.

Not now, not for this. She'd yelled at a lot of people at whom it had been counterproductive to yell. They'd already had to push back the opening because she was being particular about the barn. She didn't want to have to push it back indefinitely because every paper pusher in Jefferson City had it out for her and her bad attitude.

This had to work. She was sinking her father's money into the project at a rate that was beginning to freak her out. Everything was beautiful. The barn, when it happened, would be beautiful. But it had to work as a business, too, and Lilli had discovered her limits.

So she'd contacted headhunters in St. Louis, Kansas City, and Tulsa, and she'd spent the past two days interviewing candidates for a hotel manager position. Within the first couple of interviews, she'd realized that the publicity Signal Bend had recently garnered was a big draw, and the first people she'd spoken with had been looky-loos more than anything. They had the credentials, but they were much more interested in being a part of the story than in running her bed and breakfast. So, no. She revised her questions specifically to weed those people out. She wanted someone who could see himself or herself settling in Signal Bend, even after CNN stopped doing stories about it. Even after Hollywood went away.

If, in fact, Hollywood ever actually showed up. The town was in negotiations to sell the option to the story, but whether that would turn into anything remained to be seen. If it did, and if they filmed any part of it in town, that would be a huge boon to Signal Bend's resurgence. But if it didn't, Lilli wanted stability. With the right people and the right plan, Signal Bend could stay on its feet as a cute little place to spend a quiet weekend and do some shopping.

They were out of the meth trade, and they needed to stay out. If they could get the town to earn a straight dollar, then Lilli and Isaac could raise their daughter in safety. No more attacks, no more kidnappings, no more torture, no more death. Just a life. Quiet and full.

She heard the roar of a Harley and pushed away from her desk, hoisting herself out of her chair. Her belly wasn't colossally huge, but her center of gravity had certainly shifted. She didn't mind. She'd spent the first half of this pregnancy in a horrid mental dungeon and had only been able to really enjoy what was happening inside her for the past couple of months. Now, with Gia doing acrobatics routinely, Lilli felt fully connected. She would almost be sad for her daughter to be born, when she'd have to share her with the world.

She came out of the office, past the little front desk, with its antique bell she'd found on eBay, through the lobby/parlor area, and out the door. The hotel was ready to go. She needed someone to get the

322

permits arranged. Three more interviews this afternoon, after lunch. Lilli sighed.

Badger had pulled up the gravel drive on his new Dyna. Well, not new. The club had given him Erik's bike as sort of an award, or a token of appreciation, for taking a bullet when Ellis's men took Lilli. Erik had given his life in the Ellis affair. It had been a very hard year for Horde Prospects—another Prospect, Rover, had died on duty before the Ellis business had kicked into full swing.

Badge dismounted and set his helmet on the handlebars. He was looking pretty good. He'd been shot in the back, but since he'd recovered and had started helping out here, he'd been putting on some muscle. He was still a skinny shit, but he had some definition in his arms, some broadening in his shoulders. Hope for him yet.

She stepped off the porch, making sure not to waddle. There would be no waddling in this pregnancy. "Hey, buddy. How's everybody doing?" He'd been up at the rescue ranch, checking on their adoptees. Lilli had already adopted the animals and was paying for their upkeep until the barn went up and passed the gajillion inspections it needed to pass.

"They're good. Gypsy—Lilli, she's the shit. Damn, that's a fine horse. Got some spirit." He grinned sheepishly. "I was thinking she'd make a great lead horse." Gypsy was a big, black Tennessee Walking Horse.

Lilli laughed. "Meaning you want her, right?" He blushed. "Hey, bud. That's your call. You're the livestock manager. You want Gypsy for your ride, that's fine with me." His grin spread across his whole face then. He was cute. Someday, another year or two removed from his adolescent battle with acne, some time spent

323

hauling fifty-pound feed sacks and giant hay bales, he might even make it to hot.

"Hey—I was headed to the kitchen for some lunch. There's meatball sandwiches and macaroni salad. Want to join me, update me on the rest of the furbabies?"

"Sounds great." They turned and headed back into the house. Lilli resisted the urge to pop him a good one when he took hold of her elbow and helped her up the porch steps.

~oOo~

After lunch, Badge, good boy that he was, helped her clean up, and then they headed back out to the lobby. Lilli was not looking forward to the afternoon interviews. Only one candidate so far had seemed remotely worthwhile, and that one, a woman maybe ten years older than Lilli, had seemed a lot less interested once Lilli had explained that the bikers everywhere were a permanent feature. Signal Bend was a biker town. Lilli was a biker old lady. They were around. And they weren't politically correct.

The candidates who were there for the bikers—they were trouble of a whole different sort, and Lilli was not interested in them.

Badger was in the lead as they came through the swinging kitchen door. He stopped short, and Lilli, her head already deep again in work thoughts, ran right into his backside, belly first. Gia gave an irritated little kick and rolled at the impact.

Lilli was irritated, too. "Dude. What?"

Badger jumped. "Sorry, Lilli. Um..." He trailed off, looking embarrassed, then turned back to the lobby, continuing to stand in her way like a lump. Lilli looked around his shoulder. Oh. There was a woman in the lobby. Lilli checked the clock behind the front desk. It was fifteen minutes before her next interview, but she'd wager that this was the candidate, sitting on one of the new sofas.

"Badge. Can you get out of the doorway, please?"

He jumped again. "Oh! Sorry. I'll...um...I'll...yeah."

"Show and Isaac are in back, working on the gazebo. You were going to talk to Show about the feed order, right?"

"Right—yeah, okay." Finally, he moved, turning to head out the side door.

Lilli came through into the lobby. As she approached, the woman stood. She was tall—at least as tall as Lilli—five-nine or five-ten. Maybe a little taller. In the heels she was wearing, substantially taller. And she was gorgeous. No wonder Badge's brain had shut down. Rich, red, shoulder-length hair (had to be colored—nature didn't come that perfect), clear, pretty, intelligent face, and good God, a Marilyn Monroe body. Boobs and curves that were practically aggressive. Lilli, tall and extremely fit, confident in her looks—but seven months pregnant—had a disorienting moment of insecurity. For a half-second, she felt dumpy.

The woman wasn't dressed especially provocatively. She was wearing a very nice, well-fitting suit, a forest green damask with a pencil skirt. Simple navy shell under it, navy peep-toe pumps. Nice.

Not Lilli's taste, but more stylish, she thought, than the basic navy blue uniform look she'd already seen repeatedly during these interviews. It fit her very well, so that the conservative nature of the clothes did nothing at all to camouflage the va-va-voom underneath.

Lilli's first impression was no way. A woman built like this was a very bad fit for the job. She'd never survive the Horde's attention, and Lilli was fully aware how little control she'd be able to keep over her Neanderthal family. The last thing she wanted to deal with was a fucking sexual harassment suit.

But she couldn't just turn her around and march her right out, so she flipped through her mental files and pulled the name of her next candidate up. Holding out her hand with a smile, she said, "Shannon?"

Shannon smiled back and took Lilli's hand. Her grip was confident. "Yes. I know I'm early—sorry about that. I guess I didn't estimate the travel time from Tulsa so well. But better early than late, right?"

"Right. No problem. You're not that early, anyway. You want to go ahead and get started, then?" Lilli indicated the door to the office. Shannon nodded, and they went back.

~oOo~

Well, shit. Shannon was perfect. She had the credentials, the experience. Her references, if they stood up, were great. She was smart. She had a dry wit, and she'd used it. Lilli appreciated the risk—showing one's sense of humor in a job interview struck Lilli as

326

something that could backfire. Not that she had a lot of job interview experience herself. Shannon asked good questions about the plans for the place. And hallelujah, she had contacts with the state.

They'd been talking for almost an hour. At some point, the interview had stopped being a question and answer session and had become a conversation. So Lilli brought up the problem of the Horde.

"One thing about this place. It's deep country. You know, you drove it—we're a ways from almost anything that resembles civilization. So we get a little insulated. I mean, I'm new here myself, not quite a year, so I'm still getting used to a lot of it. But this is a biker town."

Shannon smiled. "Hard not to know that. Signal Bend was in the news a lot recently."

Lilli nodded. "Yeah, true. But my point is—these guys are amazing. This town is something really special. But things here aren't like things anywhere else. We're sort of caught in a time warp. People around here think of things like political correctness as "newfangled." They still talk about "that women's lib garbage.""

"Ah. You know, I was raised in Karville. You know where that is?" Lilli didn't, so she shook her head. "Deep in the Missouri Bootheel. I know country folk. I get what you're not saying, and I know how to handle a redneck. Lots of experience." Shannon leaned back and crossed one leg over the other.

As well as this interview was going, and as great as Shannon seemed to be, Lilli was on alert. "I have to be straight, Shannon. Your resume is great. You're clearly smart and on the ball. My antennae are up, though, because this seems like a strange fit for you. You're leaving a second-in-command position at a luxury hotel in a city. For

327

an eight-room B&B in the boonies. I have to ask how that's a good career move. If this is a fangirl thing, hoping to be around if a movie gets made here, then no."

Shannon was quiet for a few moments, and Lilli got the impression that she was forming her answer. When she spoke, her blue eyes were serious. "My references are strong—and they include my current boss. My resume speaks for itself. As for why I'm looking for this kind of move, I'm going to have to ask you to believe me when I say that it has nothing to do with my professional life or my abilities to manage a facility like this. And I am not a fangirl. I'm not into actors *or* bikers. If there's a movie, and it films here, that would be exciting for the business, but not something I'd be looking forward to on a personal level. My reasons for wanting to leave Tulsa are personal. I'd like you to respect that."

In Lilli's estimation, that was a perfect answer—to the point, establishing a clear, respectful boundary. She hoped Shannon was serious when she said she could handle the guys, because the job was hers if she wanted it. She'd check her references before offering her the job, but Lilli's search was over. She smiled. "Fair enough. I've got everything I need. If you don't have any more questions, would you like a tour?"

~oOo~

Shannon wasn't wearing the right shoes to hike over the property, so Lilli gave her a tour of the main house, showing the rooms, each uniquely decorated, with its own powder room; four full bathrooms

328

shared among the eight guest rooms; the kitchen, with its professional setup; the dining room, with service for up to fifty; the lobby/parlor; and the office, with the manager's apartment behind it. Then they went out onto the porch, and Lilli described the workings of the farmland, where the barn would soon be and the animals it would house, and the woods with its trails and spring-fed creek. They walked around the porch to the back yard, of which Lilli was perhaps most proud: the garden. She'd done—or was doing; it was spring, so things still needed some filling out—an English garden behind the house, with riots of blooming plants. There were six main sections, each with a theme and a feature of its own—a gazing ball, a fountain, a kissing bench, things like that. In the very center stood a gorgeous gazebo, which Isaac had designed and crafted. Or it would be standing in the center, once Isaac and Show got it up.

They were working on it now, both of them shirtless and sweating in the May afternoon sun. Show was still wearing his black beanie, of course. In almost a year, Lilli had never seen the top of his head. Isaac swore he wasn't bald up there, but Lilli didn't believe him.

They looked damn good, though, the giants of the Horde, broad of back and rippled of muscle. Show had more ink than Isaac—fully covering his arms and shoulders, and a rampant black horse with a fiery mane and tail dominating his back. But as far as Lilli was concerned, Isaac was the real specimen, perfect in every conceivable way. She paused in the middle of describing the garden, caught up for a second in ogling her man. When Isaac turned and saw her, he grinned widely and waved her over.

She looked at Shannon, who seemed to be doing her own staring. Yeah. Not into bikers, she'd said—except when they looked like this. Lilli felt a little territorial. "That's my husband, Isaac. Come on, I'll introduce you." She went down the steps, expecting Shannon to follow. There were stepping stones lining the paths, so even in heels, she could probably navigate fine.

Isaac folded Lilli up in his sweaty arms as soon as he could reach her. "Hey, Sport. How're my girls?" He rubbed her belly.

"We're good. I wanted to introduce you to Shannon Bannerman. She's interviewing for the manager gig." Isaac raised his eyebrows, and she knew why. She hadn't introduced him to any other applicant, and he was around most of the time. She wasn't sure why she'd brought Shannon down here, except that she'd seen her staring and wanted to mark her claim on Isaac. Which was absurdly immature. But here they were.

She turned to Shannon then and realized that it wasn't Isaac she'd been eyeing. It was Show—massive, ink-covered, long-haired, long-bearded, beanie-wearing Showdown. Oh, poor Shannon. Show was doing a lot better since he'd gotten through the hell that had been the Christmas season, his first without his family. But his heart was locked up tight. His body, too. Since she'd embraced the role of the President's old lady, she'd gotten to know the club girls some and was privy to their gossip. She knew that Show, even after his divorce, was not availing himself of their offerings at all. He was all business, all club, still living in the clubhouse, letting his own property go to rot. He wanted no kind of contact with women. Except Lilli, but that was a different thing altogether.

Shannon took the hand that Isaac offered and smiled. Isaac cocked his head toward Show and said, "That's Showdown. Show, Shannon."

Show nodded without looking and began hammering a nail into a board. Shannon looked confused at first, but recovered quickly and said to Isaac, "This is gorgeous. Craftsman style—nice choice."

Isaac grinned—he was a sucker for someone who knew anything about the stuff he did. "Yeah. Don't like the foofaraw of most gazebos. The curlicues and like."

"I get you. Good lines to this. Suits the view, too, with the rows of crops and the fence line."

Isaac looked over at Lilli and winked. She nodded. Yeah, the job was filled.

~oOo~

A barn raising. That had been Isaac's big idea. Now, feeling like she was standing in the middle of a Rodgers and Hammerstein musical, Lilli was surrounded by almost literally the entire town. The men were putting up the barn, and the women were standing at long tables, feeding the troops. Baked beans, fried chicken, sausages, corn bread, potato salad, bean salad, pies. Kids ran all over—playing volleyball and tag and whatever. Geez. It was like they went out of their way to be quaint.

Today was the raising. The rest of the long weekend was interior finish and painting. And this picnic, every day until the barn was done. When Isaac told her his plan, she'd scoffed. She loved the design, but the idea of a barn-raising seemed silly and unnecessary.

They could afford to have the thing built. The money faucet was running too fast, yes, but they didn't need to go begging.

He'd pointed out that the town would love it—that it would serve as a celebration, the last piece of the reborn Signal Bend, and everybody would be involved. And he'd been right. Lilli had never seen a happier group of people working their asses off.

Shannon, the newly hired manager of the Keller Acres Bed and Breakfast, was here, too. Lilli had wasted no time checking her references—and Isaac had had Bart do some investigating, too—and Shannon had wasted no time accepting the job. Within a week of being hired, she was living on the premises. And today, two days after moving in, she was working the town, meeting everyone. The women were a bit guarded with her, but friendly enough. As Lilli herself knew well, it took a lot longer for the women to accept a new resident. Shannon would have to prove that she wasn't on the prowl for their married men (not that there was a big pile of hotties in the batch) before she'd get some room from the women.

The women were going to be jealous, and some were going to be catty about it. Shannon was the kind of woman that made an old-fashioned country wife feel insecure. Shit, she'd made Lilli feel insecure for a minute. But she was neither flaunting herself nor kowtowing to the smaller minds. She was dressed appropriately for the "women's work," in jeans, low boots, and a loose, black peasant top, her fiery red hair pushed off her face with a pretty scarf. People were just going to have to get used to the fact that she was pretty and had a body built for sin.

Almost every man on the premises had looked his fill, but Shannon didn't seem to pay any of them particular mind. Her attention had its focus already. And that man had looked in her direction but not seen her at all. She'd noticed his lack of notice, that was obvious. Lilli wondered whether she should say something to dissuade her, but there was nothing she could say without telling a story which wasn't hers to tell. Signal Bend's newest resident would have to figure things out for herself.

As the sun was dropping behind the tree line, the barn was up. The men packed up their tools, and the older boys cleaned up after them. The women got going with round three of the food: dinner. Lilli, exhausted and her back aching, absented herself and went to sit on the porch swing at the main house. It was a lovely view—the long shadows of the spring sunset, the bright new barn, the whole town milling about, laughing, talking, eating, drinking. The smell of spring foliage and freshly sawn wood. And her man, his braid loose and disheveled, his bare chest wet and streaked with sawdust, walking toward her, pulling a black shirt on over his shoulders.

As he climbed the porch steps, he asked, "You okay, Sport?"

"I'm good. Happy. Back hurts a little."

He sat next to her on the swing and put his hand on her belly. "She givin' you trouble?"

"Uh-uh. She's been pretty quiet today."

He raised his eyebrows—the baby was usually very active. Lilli wasn't worried—she felt right. But he didn't know that. "Should we be worried about that?"

As if to answer the question for herself, the baby rolled hard, and a little elbow or heel made a sharp mound as it pushed from one side of Lilli's belly to the other. Isaac laughed and gave her a pat. "Okay, I guess that's a no."

Lilli was tired. She was happy, but she was about to drop, and her back was singing. The picnic was turning into a party, and the thought of several more hours here tonight and then back at it all again tomorrow made her want to weep. "Would it be bad if we went home right now? I mean, since they're building our barn, it would be bad to leave first, right?"

He kissed the top of her head and held her close. "One: you hired a manager, who lives here. I'll bet she's not going anywhere tonight. Leave her in charge. Two: you're baking my kid, so if you want to go home, I'm fuckin' taking you home. Three: when we get home, I'll rub that oil on your belly and back."

She laughed. "You trying to get lucky, biker man?" They had reclaimed their sex life in the past couple of months. It was different, and there were things she'd once loved that she didn't think she'd want to do ever again, but what they had now was wonderful. It might even be better than what they'd had before. More significant.

He gave her a wide-eyed, innocent look. "Not me, baby. You say you're tired and your back hurts, I'm not making a move. I mean, that oil gets you all relaxed and feelin' good, and you start thinkin' you need a little somethin', I'm happy to let you use me. You know."

"Well, that's very generous, love. Okay, take me home. Oil me up."

CHAPTER TWENTY-FIVE

Isaac was on edge every second that he was away from Lilli. He was on edge every second he was with her, too. She was beyond irritable, and he was getting barked at or ignored pretty much nonstop. But at least when he was with her, he was there, ready to help her. Her due date had passed. Nearly a week now, and no obvious sign yet that their daughter was getting restless. Yesterday, at her appointment, her doctor had scheduled an induction for the following Monday. Lilli didn't even want pain meds during the labor and had tried to make Isaac promise not to let her have any. He'd refused that ridiculous demand. When she wanted drugs, she was getting fucking drugs. But the idea of her labor *starting* with drugs had her even more stressed out and depressed. Nothing he said or did seemed to make her feel better.

He'd had Horde business he had to take care of—finalizing the movie option deal—but before the ink was dry, he was on his bike and heading home. He'd called before he left, but she hadn't answered. He hoped she was sleeping; she napped often these days. But he always got anxious when she didn't pick up. He thought he might never be calm about that again.

He trotted across the yard and into the house—and saw his nine-plus months' pregnant wife at the top of the stairs, trying to wrangle down the solid maple cradle he'd made. He ran up the stairs and took hold of it.

"Jesus fucking Christ, woman! What the *fuck* are you doing?"

She stared down at him, flushed and panting. Her hair was loose, hanging in her face. She was wearing nothing but one of his t-shirts. He could see up and know that she was wearing absolutely nothing but his shirt. She'd given up underwear awhile back, when her belly got too big for anything but what she called "granny drawers." In the last week or so, except to go to the doctor, she hadn't really bothered with clothes at all.

"I want it in the bedroom. Why did we put the nursery upstairs? That was fucking stupid. She needs to be close to us. I can't believe we were so stupid. We need to redo everything."

Okay. Lilli had lost her mind. As soon as he thought it, it chilled him. He'd almost said it out loud. But he hadn't, and that was good. These last couple of weeks, her worries about her mother's mental illness being visited on her, or on Gia, had resurfaced. She'd been dealing with it better than before, talking to him about it, working through the anxiety. But the last thing he needed to say out loud was that she was being crazy. Even if she was.

He needed to be calm.

He pulled gently on the cradle, taking the bulk of the weight from her hands. She wouldn't let it go, however. "Okay. Lilli, listen to me. I think it's a great idea to bring the cradle into our bedroom. You shouldn't be carrying it, but I will take it down right now, because you're right. When she's first home, she should be with us. But when she's ready for the crib, we have the video monitor, so we can see her. It'll be okay that she's upstairs. We talked about all this, remember?"

It had taken forever to get her involved with the nursery, but once she was, they had together made a beautiful refuge for their girl—

336

and for them. With the town rebuild, and the B&B, and the orders
he'd already taken before the Ellis shit blew up, he hadn't had time
to build anything more than the cradle, but he'd picked up some nice
unfinished maple pieces and had coated them with a ruddy stain. The
room was all in cream, with faint touches of pink and green. Lilli's
choices. It was worthy of a magazine. He'd be damned if they were
undoing it.

"You're talking to me like you think I'm crazy. Maybe you're right.
But I'm not stupid. So fuck you." She yanked hard on the cradle—
and her water broke in a rush, splashing and flooding over the
hardwood stairs.

She looked down at the wet, dripping staircase. "Oh, shit."

His pulse instantly in overdrive, Isaac went into action. "Lilli, let go
of the cradle. Now." She did. He hefted it in his arms and went
backwards down the stairs, praying he didn't miss a step and break
his damn leg. As soon as he hit the hall floor, he turned and set the
cradle down, just inside the dining room. Then he ran back up the
stairs and took hold of his old lady. "You know what we need to
do?"

She nodded. "First, I need to get clothes on. Then I need to call the
doctor. Then we need to go." About halfway down the stairs she
gasped and stopped.

"Sport?"

"I get what they meant by feeling pressure. Kinda hurts."

Pressure? Should it be pressure already? They'd gone to some
childbirth classes—and he was never going to live that shit down in

337

the Keep—and he tried to remember about the stages. He didn't know. Fuck it—whatever, they needed to get moving. "I'll call the doctor. You get dressed. We need to go."

"I made a mess, though."

"Don't worry about it. I'll call Badger." He met her eyes, and they both laughed. Poor Badge. "Come on, Sport. Let's get our girl."

~oOo~

Isaac had expected yelling. Screaming. Or something. But Lilli was almost completely silent. She had his hand—well, three fingers—in an impressively badass grip, to the point that he'd needed to take his rings off, but she made no more noise than the sound of her labored breath. He'd stopped trying to talk to her, because she only scowled at him when he did. Things had been grinding on and on for hours, but now everything was happening really fast, he thought. Her water had broken almost twenty hours ago, and they'd been trapped in a kind of a loop for most of that time, left alone for long stretches. But now the room was full, and people in scrubs were moving around, changing the bed, setting things up. She was ready to push.

She pushed a lot. She was pale and soaking wet, but still silent. Isaac did some calculating in his head, and he thought it had been half the day since she'd said anything but the shortest possible answer to a question a nurse or doctor asked. Her focus on her task was complete.

"Okay, Lilli. I think we've got one, maybe two more pushes. We ready?" Lilli nodded and sat back up. She really liked this doctor. Isaac liked her, too, normally. He was very glad it was a woman's hand up his wife and not a man's. He wasn't sure he could be okay with that, and he knew Lilli couldn't. But he was mightily tired of the way she said "we," when it was obviously Lilli doing all the work.

She pushed again. Her face had gone red with every push; this time it didn't. Her grip on his hand had been bone-breaking, but not this time. The push over, Lilli dropped back to the bed, and the room was filled with a full-bodied wail. Isaac, who'd been focused intently on his wife, turned at the sound and saw his girl—squishy, covered in bloody goo, and screaming her fool head off.

Perfection.

He turned back to Lilli. "Holy fuck, Sport. Look what you made!"

Her eyes closed, she smiled. And then her smile faded, and her hand drooped around his fingers. He grinned and lifted her hand to his lips. "You fall asleep, Sport?" Jesus, she was pale. "Lilli?" He looked at the doctor. "She okay?" They were muttering down there between her legs.

Dr. Andrews looked up, her eyes serious over her mask. "Why don't you go check on your daughter, Isaac. Lilli and I have some work to do."

Fuck that bullshit talk. He looked over Lilli's shrunken belly. Fuck, the blood. "What's wrong?"

A nurse came up to Lilli's side and put an oxygen mask over her face, then injected two syringes into her IV. Dr. Andrews said, "She's bleeding. We're taking care of it. Go see your little girl and let us work."

He couldn't leave Lilli. "No, I have to—I can't—"

"You're in our WAY, Isaac. Trying to save her here." Andrews' voice was sharp and direct, and in her tone, Isaac understood that he was losing Lilli. He felt a hand on his arm, and he jerked away, twisting around. It was a little nurse, trying to lead him to the corner, where they were doing whatever they did with babies. He couldn't leave Lilli. But he couldn't be in the way of the people trying to save her.

"Come on, dad. Come see your miracle. Let them take care of mom. That's the best thing you can do for her. Love on your daughter and let them work."

He let the nurse lead him over. His daughter. Lilli's daughter. Gia. What a ride they'd been on, the three of them.

She wasn't so gooey anymore, and she'd stopped screaming, but her face was still squished up. The nurse put a little plastic band around her tiny ankle and then held one out to him. On autopilot, he lifted his arm, and she put the I.D. band on him. She smiled and patted his hand. "Seven pounds, eleven ounces. Twenty-two inches long. She's tall!" He nodded, staring.

Dr. Andrews raised her voice a little, and Isaac spun around. They were still working busily, and Lilli was still unconscious, as pale as the white hospital linens. Andrews was standing up between her legs, pressing into her belly. A nurse ran out of the room, and the nurse in the corner with him put her hand on his arm. "Here, dad. Why don't you cut the cord, and we can get her wrapped up." She handed him a kind of scissors, and he took them and cut where she said, not really understanding what he'd done.

The door opened again, and the nurse was back, with an IV bag full of blood. Oh, Jesus, oh, Jesus. He stood at the bassinet or whatever it was and watched them hook up a transfusion for Lilli. The floor under her legs was pooled with blood. So much blood.

He couldn't lose her. They'd survived so much. She had survived so fucking much.

"Dad. Here's your girl." He turned, and the nurse presented him a pink bundle, wrapped up like a burrito. He took her, letting the nurse shape his hold so he had her right.

Her eyes were closed. She looked mad. But she was perfect. She had her mother's mouth, with that extra fullness in her lower lip.

"You have a name yet?"

Isaac looked at the nurse, his head gone blank. She smiled and raised her brows. She was kind, and she was trying to keep him distracted, he knew. Oh, name. "Gia."

"Oh, that's so pretty. I've never heard that name before."

"It's Italian. Lilli's Italian."

"Well, I love it."

"Isaac." Dr. Andrews walked over, her scrubs bloody. "We need to talk."

341

He looked over at Lilli—still. So fucking still and pale. No. Fucking no. No way. Uh-uh.

"No. *No.*"

"She lost a lot of blood. It's called postpartum hemorrhage. We got the bleeding stopped, but if it happens again, the prognosis isn't good. We need to move her up to the ICU until we can get her stable. Baby can't be in the ICU. You're going to need some help here, I think. Can't be with both at the same time, not until Lilli stabilizes."

"She's okay?" All he heard was that she wasn't dead. He'd thought he'd lost her.

"No, she's not. But she has a chance. We're going to take her up now. Why don't you stay with the baby now, and I'll have somebody fetch you when we have Lilli settled upstairs. Okay?"

~oOo~

Isaac sat at her bedside and watched. Again he was sitting at her bedside in the fucking Intensive Care Unit. They'd been together just more than a year, and he'd nearly lost her time and time again. He was incapable of keeping her safe.

He'd stayed with Gia until a nurse told him he could go up, and then he'd set his daughter in a bassinet in a big nursery and left her without a second thought. He had to be with Lilli. She would kick his ass sideways when she woke up, but he didn't give a shit. And now he sat and stared at her still form.

"Brother, I'm here."

He turned and saw Showdown standing in the doorway. He hadn't known who else to call. Show was his best friend, his advisor, his confidant. But he was a broken, grieving man, just beginning to find a way to have a life again. Isaac had no business asking what he'd asked, but he had no other choice, no one else he trusted.

"Thanks, Show. I know—"

"No, Isaac. It's good. I'm here. She in the nursery?"

"Yeah. I signed something so you can go in. Her name's Gia. Lilli won't want her lying alone in that plastic thing."

"Okay, brother. I got her. I know girls." He grinned sadly.

"I love you, man."

"Yeah. Me too." He nodded at Lilli. "You get her well. Girl needs her mom."

~oOo~

It was another three hours before Lilli woke, but she did wake. She was weak and disoriented, but she was awake. Isaac leapt out of the chair and kissed her cold forehead.

"Lilli. Fuck me, baby. My heart can't take this shit."

She wrinkled her brow at him, looking confused, and for a second, Isaac felt more panic. Andrews had been up to talk to him, to explain some concerns about the effects of the blood loss. He was familiar. Last summer, she'd lain in this same ICU, nearly dead from blood loss. So he knew: organ failure, brain damage, stroke. But she'd gotten the transfusion quickly, this time. Not like last summer.

"Isaac? Is she okay?"

He laughed, relief flooding his muscles and making him weak. He shifted and sat on the edge of her bed, her hand clutched in his. "She's perfect, Sport. She's so beautiful. You did an amazing thing. God, I love you."

She smiled and relaxed. "Where is she?"

"She's down in the nursery. They won't let her up here."

At that—as he suspected—she was instantly upset, trying and failing to sit up. "She's alone? You left her alone?" The heart monitor alarm went off.

"Lay back, baby. It's okay. She's not alone. Show's with her. I'm sticking with you, and until you can kick my ass, you're gonna have to live with it."

A nurse came in and pushed him aside, taking her vitals. "Good to see you awake, Mrs. Lunden. But you need to rest and take it easy." She turned a disapproving look on Isaac. "People should be helping you stay calm."

"I need my baby. I'll be calm with my baby."

344

"No babies up here, honey. You don't want her to get sick, now, do you?" The nurse patted her hand. "You rest." With another displeased look at Isaac, she left.

"I want Gia." Her words were losing their sharpness as she began to drift off.

He kissed her on her lips, softly. "Then get better, Sport."

"'Kay. Love you." She was out.

Isaac spent the night watching the monitors.

~oOo~

Until he put the car seat in the back of the Barracuda, it had not occurred to Isaac—or apparently to Lilli—that they needed a different kind of car. A classic 'Cuda did not have the kind of back seat that was conducive to car seat installation. Getting it secured back there required flexibility Isaac had not known he possessed. His truck had no back seat at all. The government had taken the Camaro back—not that that would have been any better. They were a family now. They needed a family car.

But for the moment, he was working a car seat full of his daughter into the back of the 'Cuda. And she was screaming, which was apparently something she really enjoyed doing. Once he got her secured in there, he helped Lilli—who wanted to sit in the back seat, too. Weird. But, okay. He'd play chauffeur. Whatever. He just wanted to get his family away from this fucking hospital and home in one piece. What a long week it had been.

Gia screamed almost the whole way home. He watched in the rearview to see how Lilli was holding up, but every time he looked back, he saw her smiling down at their girl. When Gia took an occasional breath, he thought he could hear Lilli humming quietly.

Gia finally dropped off to sleep about five minutes from the house. They pulled down the drive—and *shit*. Bikes every fucking place. He was bringing his weak wife and his crabby daughter home to a Horde party? He had some necks to wring.

"Goddammit. I'll get rid of them. Sorry, Sport." He met her eyes in the rearview.

She was still smiling. "No, it's okay. They want to see her. They've been patient."

He'd kept everybody but Show away from the hospital, wanting to keep Lilli calm and let her rest. Other than phone photos, nobody else had seen his baby girl yet.

"She's gonna wake up and start screaming."

Lilli laughed. "She's going to do that anyway, as soon as we take the seat out. Let her scream in her uncles' ears for awhile."

But she didn't. She seemed to like the commotion, getting passed around from paw to paw. She was quiet and awake for a couple of hours, her longest stretch of good humor in her week of life, and she had the Horde utterly charmed. Good. He was going to enlist those assholes as babysitters so he and Lilli could get some sleep someday.

~oOo~

That night, after they had their house to themselves again, Isaac and Lilli lay together in their bed, their daughter asleep between them. Isaac lightly brushed a finger through the dark hair on her little head, and she sighed.

"What do you think, Sport? How'd we do?"

"She's amazing. I've never felt like I feel now."

"How's that?"

"I don't know. Full, I guess. Like my heart grew, or something. Happy." She leaned down and kissed Gia's petal-soft cheek. "I'm going to want more of these. We might need to add on to the house."

He understood. Not even Gia's penchant for screaming could dampen his joy in his family. But they couldn't have more. "Lilli, the doctor said…"

"I know what she said. She didn't say it *would* happen again. She said there was a greater risk." She looked into his eyes. "We'll talk. It's not like I want to do it right this second. Right now, I just want to bask."

He let it drop, but they would talk again. Because he was through risking her. But she was right—now was a time to bask in what they had. "We came through it didn't we? We came through it all."

She grinned. "We did. I love you so much, Isaac."

Leaning over their sleeping newborn child, Isaac took his old lady's face in his hand. "I love you, Sport. You are everything to me. You and Gia—all that matters."

Gia woke then and began to fuss. Lilli, topless, shifted on the bed and offered her breast, and Gia latched on with a tiny whimper. Isaac pressed a kiss to the back of his little girl's sweet-smelling head and relaxed on his pillow, his arm protectively over his wife and child.

He looked over Lilli's shoulder out the window, into the dark sky of this summer night. The stars were a brilliant, glimmering multitude, filling the vast space. In the country, where the ambient light of civilization was low, a clear night was always ablaze with cold, bright light. Isaac had spent so much of the past year with his head down, focused on the filth around him, that he'd forgotten the beauty of his world. Lying here now, cocooned with his little family, that infinite expanse a background to his contentment, hard-earned, Isaac felt…significant.

He had fought for what mattered. The town had fought. Lilli had fought harder than anyone. They had sacrificed and bled, but they had not given up. Against seemingly infinite odds, they had persevered. And they had won.

THE END

The Signal Bend Series continues with

INTO THE STORM

Susan Fanetti is a Midwestern native transplanted to Northern California, where she lives with her husband, youngest son, and assorted cats.

Susan's blog: www.susanfanetti.com

Susan's Facebook author page:
https://www.facebook.com/authorsusanfanetti

'Susan's FANetties' reader group:
https://www.facebook.com/groups/871235502925756/

Twitter: @sfanetti

Made in the USA
Monee, IL
01 April 2021